**Lehman's Terms**

by

Leonard McClane

Cover Design by **Mark Flaherty**
**(www.meandalan.cc)**



[2nd Edition]

**Reviews for "Lehman's Terms"**

*"If Shane Black wrote a Geordie private eye thriller for Ross Noble this would be it!"*
**Emily John**

*"An unconventional action thriller; purposefully meandering (in a good way) but when it kicks into gear its impossible to put down! It's dark, funny AND actually quite moving!"*
**Sarah Mitchell**

*"I, and hopefully a wider audience, found [McClane] quite enjoyable as a guide into the world of the P.I."*
**Thomas Ludlow**

*"An exciting, investigative, thrill-ride where lots of stuff gets smashed the f**k up!"*
**Rob Leatt**

*"If you like 80s action movies, s**t soft rock, comedic ramblings about pop culture (specifically the ending of The Fugitive) and an irreverent new spin on old private eye tropes, THIS is the book for you! This is DEFINITELY the book for you!"*
**James Grant**

*"*****... by the time you get to the shocking reveal it is impossible to put down!"*
**Helen Grover**

*"It's assured in its style and sets that out from the start. I blasted through it for one reason: It's f**king good!"*
**Mark Flaherty**

In memory of my Grandma:
who didn't live long enough to see her biggest wish come true!

For 'Peaches McClane'
…. who chose me!

And

For my boys…
who taught me how to live!

## [Prologue]

## or

## "Giving the reader what they want…"

First things first, movies and TV lie so badly. I'm telling you this right now from immediate first-hand experience okay? You can't jump off a skyscraper tied to a fire hose and survive. I know this because I just jumped from a balcony onto an escalator that was two storeys down at best and it genuinely fucked my shit right up. Also, this is a really important one that I know has been said before but I just want to reiterate it – you don't walk away from explosions all cool and collected without flinching. You just don't. That was one cliché I always took as truth and thought it looked really awesome and then I was face first with an explosion earlier on and it put me right on my arse end and, well, I'm fairly certain it melted every filling in my mouth too.

And taking a bullet? Honestly, that's such a crazy, crazy, continuing lie. You see it all the time in action films. They take a hit and don't even flinch. Nicolas Cage took a bullet wound to the arm in Con Air and he didn't even break his stride, twenty minutes later he was hanging off the back of a fire truck going down the Las Vegas strip at 80mph. Now let's flash cut to the reality – a bullet to the shoulder has… I'm just going to be straight up and frankly honest here… it's made me do a little bit of poo in my pants. It hurt *that* bad.

I could go on. I could go on about the clichés and lies pertaining to dirty cops and private investigators and… No, wait. Let me get this one out as well: What is it with this thing about private investigators always having that glass office door with their names stencilled on it? And the lone female who always walks through it with "trouble in her eyes and ice in her heart" and all that bullshit? That really pisses me off, that one. Every single private dick tale has that going on within the first couple of chapters. Eurgh.

Anyway, listen, studies of the average book-reader indicate they all want a strong dynamic opening that captivates your attention from the get go so… I'm bringing you straight in at the bit with all the raging fire and bullet holes. Because that's pretty exciting and intriguing, right? I mean everyone likes a bit of fire and bullet holes! Except fireman and gunshot victims, I guess?

In fact, let's lean into the clichés for a second:

… So there's me, all bloodied and beaten. My ribs are broken. Pretty much every bone in my face definitely feels like it is. I'm being held up and walked out by this young slip of a twentysomething girl called Holly as 2,200,000 square foot of what was once the North East's premium indoor shopping district burns behind us. She's being careful not to touch the bullet hole just below my shoulder. Which is considerate but would totally be more gratefully received if she hadn't been the one that put the fucking bullet in my fucking shoulder in the fucking first place but… we'll come back to this one!

We're limping out of there as quickly as possible – limping to the police waiting for us at the doors, limping through the fire officers bustling past us to go deal with the flames and straight into the path of a line of armed response officers.

I've already thrown away my firearm. I use the term 'my' loosely by the way but it's been chucked nonetheless. There's still an expression on a couple of these gunned up meatheads' faces that suggests they're going to shoot me anyway. Gun or no gun.

You know these type of guys; they got their dicks hard watching John Woo movies and straight-to-DVD shoot 'em ups about military 'brahs' taking down bad guys so they joined the police and waited out their probation then they filled in the application form for an armed response position, passed the interview panel, sat the tests, spoke with the psychologists, done their time on the range and got told they got the job holding the gun and looking tough. They probably went out and bought an extra thick paracord bracelet to celebrate – maybe they even bought a second one in a khaki colour for when they're on their days off. Then… and really only then… did they realise that they joined an armed response team in Newcastle Upon Tyne where generally the only thing a person is armed with round here is their wit and an attitude. So they spend most of their days training for their 'moment' then going home feeling dejected and they put on John Woo movies and straight-to-DVD shoot 'em ups about military 'brahs' taking down bad guys to water down the hurt, wishing that one day it could be them firing guns whilst diving in slow motion or whatever.

And then tonight their 'moment' arrived. They got the call of shots fired – yes, actual shots fired – at the Metrocentre. They've rushed to the scene, got here too late and are now pointing guns and expressing looks that say "There better be SOMEONE that needs shooting! I put on my best ballistic vest… SOMEONE is getting shot tonight!"

I limp. Holly hoists. "You're not going to pass out are you?" she asks nervously.

"You mean from the blood loss? The blood loss from the bullet hole?" I shoot back, pardon the pun.

"I said I was sorry – but in fairness I also saved your life!" she offers before being interrupted by a distressed looking plain clothes detective pushing through everyone and coming to an abrupt halt in front of us which in turn causes Holly and I to stagger to a stop too.

"Jesus Christ!" gasps DI Andrews, looking me up and down. "Are you…"

He thankfully stops himself because I hate the guy enough already without him accentuating that by asking me if I'm okay as I bleed to death in front of him.

Andrews is my mortal nemesis in the best comic book styling of the two best friends who were pulled apart and re-forged as protagonist and antagonist for the purposes of conflict. You know, like in Disney's The Fox and The Hound? Except we're not going to end this thing sitting on the Widow Tweed's porch for a good old singalong!

Andrews hasn't written a goddamn book has he? And Andrews isn't the one telling you this story is he? So no matter what he tries to make out or tries to say, he's the bloody antagonist here!

"We found the body back at your office!" he says.

"The recording? Did you..." I started to speak but the pain in my face bristled and then sent sharp shocks to my brain so intense they weakened my legs. I leant in hard against Holly, forcing her to stumble and DI Andrews to step forward and take hold of us both.

"I watched it..." he replied before faltering and holding his hand to his head and freezing. He searched for words and then continued. "... Jesus, Jake! This is bad. This is bad, right?"

"You tell me Andrew?" I said, knowing he hated it when I called him Andrew because that's "not [his] name" apparently and I'm "only calling [him] that to be a dick"! And he's right on both accounts. Andrew isn't his name, it's Andy. And I am a dick.

I am.

I shouldn't really be confirming this to you at what is meant to be the 'captivating' stage but I am. Most people who meet me or interact with me find me incredibly irritating and "disagreeable" (I'm hearing that last one a lot lately).

I mean I'm not as much of a dick as whoever thought calling someone 'Andy Andrews' was remotely acceptable but... well... forget that. We'll get to that later too.

I took a step forward and lifted DI Andrews' chin so he met my eyes. I wanted him to see something deep inside that I can't really put into words but I knew would come with decades of knowing each other. I took a deep breath as best I could through my swollen face, braced myself for how much this was going to hurt and then went for it. "Remember I told you a long time ago that a line was drawn and that we both needed to make a choice regarding what side of that line we stand on? Remember that?"

"You've never let me forget it, have you?" he answered.

"It's not too late to step back over. It's not." I said. "It should have been put out there for everyone to see and stopped a long time ago. You know that deep down, don't you? But it's going out there now for everyone to see. Tonight. Everyone is going to know the truth finally. And you have to decide right now where you want to stand... You can be the one who takes people down or one of many that are taken down?"

Silence followed. Painful silence. I just landed a pitch perfect 'hero' monologue and in return I'm met with the sort of silence that comes when the fourteen year old spotty-faced Dr Who loving perpetual victim in the school yard just walked up to the best looking girl who happens to be his bully's girlfriend and asked her if she'd like to go on a date.

A burning Christmas tree on the second floor gave way and fell to the ground directly behind us, creating an almighty crash that unsettled everyone. DI Andrews and a couple of waiting paramedics jumped forward and started to lead us out.

"What are you asking me for?" DI Andrews finally whispered in my ear as we walk. "I don't understand where it is you're asking me to stand right now."

... Then let's pull out from there, okay?

Think of this like 'end credits of a *good* Die Hard movie' imagery or the final shot of an 1980s Peter Hyams film – we're pulling out and surveying all the emergency service vehicles and smoke and fire as the camera tracks the hero being helped into an ambulance and an 'old standards' version of a Christmas Carol is sang over the top of what you're seeing before giving way to Beethoven's 'Ode To Joy'.

And I've got you, right?

Tell me I've got you?

You're like Page 10 or something in and I've given you burning buildings, bullets, flaming Christmas trees, intriguing conflict and the like. If I've done my job right you're sat wondering why Holly shot me, who's dead body is in my office and what the hell is on that memory card that I keep referring to as a 'tape' – because everyone still does that in this day and age even though no one has recorded on tape since 1997 or something!

Most importantly of all obviously you're probably wondering just who exactly I am and what this is all about. Or... you know... you're not? Because the blurb on the back of this book gave away far too much of the plot? They do that far too often now don't they?

Don't you hate it when they do that?

I've pandered and I've given you the exciting and intriguing introduction like they suggested. I mean, seriously, if I had my way I'd have just come straight in with starting at the beginning before realising that the beginning wasn't the day I walked into that solicitor's office. The beginning was probably hours earlier when I was begging for that junkie's life... Wait, I'm going off topic here. I'll probably do that a lot. I am not the narrator of this whole sorry saga that you deserve. I accept that.

But I'm all you're getting unfortunately.

I'm not really sure where the beginning is on this. Is this whole Stephie Jay thing I'm going to tell you about even *really* the beginning? Did this all really begin when my police career ended? I don't know.

I don't know why I'm doing this.

I'm not a non-linear fan.

I hate all that flashback shite.

Remember that awful movie with Hugh Jackman and John Travolta in the terrible wig (like that's a strong definitive indicator anymore, huh??) about computer hacking that none of us really wanted to watch but we were all more perverted misogynistic pigs back then than we are now so we watched it anyway because we heard Halle Berry showed her boobs? That movie pissed me off for many things but it really pissed me off by opening with that whole explosion done in bullet-time and Travolta talking to the camera about misdirection or something and then it went back to detail how we got to the point of the cool explosion. Only two hours later you realise they never ever had anything better than the explosion you watched at the very beginning and you've just wasted your time.

I don't want to be that guy.

I don't want to be the bloke who gives you explosions and intrigue then tells you to sit tight and hands you a shit sandwich a few hours later.

The whole flashback thing is such lazy bullshit anyway, don't you think?

'Here's a big shoot-out and the hero's taken a hit to the chest and he's bleeding out. Is he going to live? Is he going to die?' We fade to black and then next think you know it's a month earlier or something and the hero is off doing some innocuous bullshit that has nothing to do with anything but it's there to lead you in on what type of 'character' he is.

Honestly, that really annoys me enormously…

## [1]

## or

## "Two weeks and four days earlier..."

The air was like a wall of ice. It had been for a week or so now. We'd been promised that the arse-aching cold was just the 'pre-show' for big blizzards and a "wondrous and long overdue White Christmas". But I couldn't see that happening. Snow would be good. Big, knee-deep, thick mounds of snow that would cover up the dirt and debris of city streets falling to bits as its infrastructures cratered around them. But I didn't think we'd see a drop.

Now... you're all like "Hold up! We're jumping from the intriguing 'end of what could be a cool action sequence' prologue to discussions about the weather?" And to you I say "Listen, just be patient okay? I've got to 'set scenes' and act like I'm one of those professional storytellers like Dennis LeHane or Stephen King so... I don't know... just shut up and come with me on this. I'm trying my best."

It was two am and however cold you think cold is you're still not close. If there were homeless people out now in this hour then they'd be frozen to the pavement like gargoyles until Summer.

My leg's bad at the best of times but it's always worse in the cold. I'm a thirty-seven year old man with the body of a eighty-year old retired sweatshop worker. Cartilage and muscle damage in the right leg. My back's riddled in constant pain and my hips and knees are drenched with arthritis.

I didn't want to get out of the car. For one it was cold as hell out there but more importantly the radio station was playing Chicago's "Will You Still Love Me?" which is a *great* song that has a proper 'build' to it in its final stretch that most modern ballads just don't have anymore. Hell, I don't even think there's such a thing as 'ballads' in music anymore is there?

I pushed staying in the car for as long as I possibly could then gave up the proverbial fight and climbed out, marching away with the doors locking behind me as much as someone like me can march. It generally hurts to move these days but if I don't move I don't earn. It's as simple as that. Years of taking kickings and not doing yoga or whatever have started to take their toll maybe two decades or so earlier than I'd probably have hoped. I scrunched my body up, pushed on and swung left through one of the many old alleyways the city has running like veins through its streets up in the West End, landing almost immediately in front of what used to be Cooper's Gym, the once fabled training ground for some of the best boxers the North East has ever produced.

Now? Now, like pretty much everything else in Newcastle it's all but an abandoned husk. People can't afford to pay their monthly subs to keep using it. The council have no more grants or funds to keep injecting into it. The greats of boxing who owe their sporting careers to it have conveniently forgotten it exists. It stands now as just one of many little 'pockets' within the city that Bobby Maitland has claimed as an "emergency meeting point" for him and his lads.

Bobby Maitland – or Robert Maitland, if we're reading his name directly off his birth certificate – is "the last of the old guard" as gangsters go. You know those bars and clubs you go to and blow what little money you have left from the job you're barely holding on to? He owns those bars and clubs. If he doesn't own them he's certainly the guy putting the security on all their doors. And by putting the security on all the doors of all those bars he puts the influx of drugs that are dealt, bought and consumed directly into them. If there's drugs being dealt or drugs being taken in a single bar or club in Newcastle and they've not come from one of Bobby's people then you're in trouble. If you get in hock to Bobby's people with regards to your drug intake? Yup, you're in trouble. And if you get in hock to Bobby and his people *then* screw them over? Jesus Christ, you can just open up any copy of the dictionary and flick to the word 'trouble' and it will say "See 'Fucked'!" and then you'll flick to 'fucked' and there'll just be a photograph of you there in lieu of any actual definition.

So fucked in fact that your last chance saloon and appointed saviour will manifest itself solely in the form of a local private investigator, barely holding his own shit together. A private investigator so desperate for money that he's dragging his arse out on a bitterly cold night at two in the morning to try and negotiate for your sorry excuse of a life… That's me, by the way. I'm that aforementioned private investigator. My name is Jake Lehman.

I probably could've introduced myself from the outset, I guess. I'm terrible at introductions… This isn't going too well is it? I'm not doing a good job at all. It's like I've thrown you in with a bit of an intoxicating tease via the whole burning shopping centre, hero-striding prologue and then I'm just rewinding back, dropping in random blurts of "I'm a broken up whinging blowhard!" and "I'm thirty-seven, by the way!" and "Oh, I'm Jake Lehman and I'm a private investigator!" It's not very good at all is it? I'm sorry. Look, let me just get this out the way and I'll try and tighten things back up with a proper introduction alright? We good? We're good! Cool. Anyway…

Standing at the rusted, bent, decrepit gate for the dilapidated Cooper's Gym was my old friend, Jimmy Brody. I went to school with Jimmy and he was on the road to boxing greatness from the age of fourteen right the way into his early twenties. Until one day he just stepped off the road. No one knows why. One day we're talking about Jimmy Brody seriously as the next champion of the world. Then maybe three or four days later we're talking about him like he's some utter degenerate as decrepit and dilapidated as the building he stands in front of right now, a guy who threw it all away to become just another drunken arse hanging around Newcastle, looking for any bit of work that will put change in his pocket.

Jimmy occasionally turns up at my door asking if I've "got anything" for him. No matter how many times I tell him I've barely got anything for myself, he comes back every other week chancing his luck once more. Occasionally, very occasionally, I'll have the odd bit of process serving (which, for those who don't know, is hand-delivering court orders and legal documents generally to scumbags, wastrels and shitheads) where I can tell in my gut that it's going to be trouble so I throw Jimmy a few quid to come with me and stand in a foreboding manner that suggests to the person I'm holding the papers out to that it would be very unwise of them to, shall we say, not be nice to me.

Tonight, or more accurately this morning, Jimmy's getting thirty quid from me to simply show up to where Bobby and his lads are and sort of make an 'introduction'. I put introduction in inverted commas like that because it's the best way in written form to get across that it's not really an 'introduction', if you know what I mean? If you don't know what I mean, let me be more clear: Bobby's met me quite a few times throughout the course of me doing my thing as a PI and him doing his thing as drug-peddling, ruthless, violent son of a bitch. Therefore this isn't an introduction in the conventional sense. The problem is he doesn't like me. At all.

I'm not particularly likeable so he's not totally out of order, but I have some relatively tolerable qualities. Not to Bobby though. He can't stand me. It's something to do with the fact that I talk a lot, I'm irritating and… oh yeah… he knows that I think he's a drug-peddling, ruthless, violent son of a bitch. Mind you, there's also the fact that Bobby was terrible for paying his bills and settling with suppliers at any of the numerous businesses he had ownership of. He was awful before the country went off a cliff on a suicide dive and he was even worse after it when everyone started getting desperate for money. And if you don't pay your bills you tend to get hit with Statutory Demands. And if you get hit with them it is generally private investigators who are the ones serving debtors with them. So, yeah, I guess you can say Bobby is no fan of me based off our previous encounters with one another. Hence Jimmy's here to get Bobby to listen to me for five minutes and not stove my head in.

Jimmy was hunched up against the brick wall on which the hinges of the gate were barely staying affixed to. He was breathing big cold air clouds that left his mouth in one bulbous mass, got about five centimetres from his face and thought "Stuff this!" before rewinding back into the orifice from which they came. He pulled his hands from the pockets of his scuffed and torn jacket then banged them together in one dull clap.

"You're late!" mutters Jimmy.

I wasn't. But whatever energy it takes to argue with a punchy ex-boxer in sub-zero conditions at two in the morning outside of a broken up building that already smelt of piss before I'd stepped within ten feet of it, I didn't have it. That complete absence of energy led me to apologise and keep walking through the gate past where he stood, ushering him with me as I went because the last thing I wanted to do was get stood talking in the cold longer than I needed to so I just went with "How you keeping Jim? Is he in there?"

"Man, you look like crap!" smirked Jimmy.

"Really?" I smiled back. "I thought I was holding it together pretty well, all things considered?"

"Nah, you definitely look like crap!"

I shook my head laughing and doubled-down with my question. "Is he in there or not, Jim?"

"They're all in there, mate" replies Jimmy. "It's not looking good for your man though, I've got to say! Maybe you want me to go in first and sort Bobby out then call you in? Would that be better?"

I shook my head. Jimmy shrugged indifferently enough that it suggested his offer wasn't that genuine anyway. He pulled the door open to what was once Coopers Gym. It was what remained of an actual door plus one of those huge wrought iron security panels nailed to it that council's stick over doors and windows of abandoned properties. With the strain Jimmy put into moving it just enough for us to get through, I was kind of thankful that he'd agreed to come tonight. Not just because he was my best hope for Bobby Maitland not kicking my teeth in but also because judging from the weight of the door, I'd never have got it open on my own in order to put my teeth and Bobby's foot in the same room as one another. Though maybe that's a good thing?

We ventured through into the main floor space where the gym itself used to be. Me more cautiously than Jimmy, because I didn't know what I was walking into in more ways than one and the complete absence of lighting wasn't helping. After a few seconds of stumbling off to my right, we came upon an area lit by battery powered floor standing lights in each corner of the room and what the lights illuminated did not look good.

It didn't look good at all.

Standing in the centre of the room was Bobby Maitland, his head ricocheting back and forth between the guy being pushed onto his knees to Bobby's right and the beaten and bloodied man hanging from the rafters by a chain around his hands to his left.

Bobby looked good though. He looked 'put together'. He looked like he'd got up and coordinated an outfit and then had it ironed and what not. He did not look like he'd got a phone call at quarter to one in the morning, saying he had an appointment to go mess someone's shit up then hang them from the rafters. Nor did he look like he's finished that phone call, jumped out of bed and threw the first things on that was in the washing pile at the top of the stairs because he didn't want to disturb the wife and kids by going rooting through drawers. I, on the other hand, most definitely look like I took that call.

Bobby was in his late fifties. He'd been around. His face for all its expensive treatments and leathering from five holidays a year at a Spanish villa he paid for in cash, told a story of having seen some shit. It was also a face that had endured owning an unofficial controlling stake in an entire city that had had its ups and downs but was now so far down it had lost sight of the next potential up. He had a scarf done up nice and tight against his neck, clearly to keep out the cold.

The tag on one end of the scarf was purposefully and perfectly positioned to be on show, most probably to let the people he was about to beat to a pulp know that his scarf cost more than they earned in their whole sorry excuse for a life.

If the scarf didn't get the message across then his watch definitely would. He was wearing a Breitling Chronomat 44 bracelet watch, the two-coloured model. It retails at £10,000.00. I notice these things, you see. It's kind of built into my mechanisms now. A way in which I read people.

Bobby started to pace back and forth between the two men, his warmly wrapped neck clearly having got tired from bouncing back and forth on its own like he was watching a tennis match. He was clearly agitated and levelling up for the kill.

Holding the man on his knees to Bobby's right was Ryan O'Flaherty. Ryan was Bobby's 'Tom Hagen from The Godfather'. His "consigliere". His fixer. If you pissed Bobby off you would come to learn what Ryan's knuckles smelt like. I had somehow miraculously managed to escape such a pummelling by Ryan at Bobby's instruction and I don't have a clue how.

Ryan spotted us first. He locked eyes with his boss and tipped his head in our direction. Bobby looked up at Jimmy, clocked me standing next to him and visibly grimaced a little bit. He pointed to a spot to our left whilst picking up an old, cobwebbed piece of metal that could have once been a dumbbell bar and handing it to Ryan. Anyone else would have been even slightly perturbed that two guys have just wandered in on you in a derelict building with one man bloodied and strapped to the rafters and another on all fours at your feet. Not Bobby. He just barked "You two stand there and shut up for the minute… I'll get to you." Then went straight back to what he was doing.

I scrunched my eyes into the four conjoining beams of light coming from the floor lamps and took a good look at the man's face as he started to shake under Ryan's grip. He wasn't my guy. My guy was definitely the one hanging from the rafters with his mouth taped shut and eyes that screamed an upspoken horror indicating he knew what was coming to him. Bobby turned away from us and crouched to get into the eye line of the man now cowering on all fours, pointing back at the man hanging from the rafters.

"This filth? I expected this from filth like that because he's a fuckin junkie and this is what junkie's do!" spat Bobby at the man on the floor. "But what he did he did because you were so incompetent you allowed it. You gave a junkie enough leeway to run up £5k on my tabs? Five thousand pounds? He robbed my pub to pay me back my money? That's on you…"

Every word Bobby spoke was louder than the last. Every word pushed more congealed white matter to form at the corners of his mouth. He was working to escalate his own sense of agitation. And then the words got quiet.

"… So here's what I'm going to do to HIM - I'm going to have Ry' here drive this rusty barbell right through his junkie gut then you're going to keep attaching twenty kilogram plates from over there to each end until you split his difference and the barbell hits the floor, you get what I'm saying? And whatever spills out of him you're going to drown in because Ry' is going to hold your head down in it!"

That was so horrifyingly specific in had to be true. You don't think something like that up and not go through with it. That's the sort of sick shit you think up because you'd love to see it brought to life. I looked around the room and saw that everything that Bobby needed to fulfil what he'd just threatened was actually there.

Bobby gave a clean and very obvious wink to Ryan who, without missing a beat, swung that hunk of metal off the man's head opening the side of it above his ear with a clean swish of his arm, making an empty clunk as it made contact with the skull bone. Blood didn't spray up. It just flopped out onto the floor between the man's hands like someone had smashed a water balloon filled with blood off the ground. The man went to fall forward as his arms gave out from underneath. He was held in position solely from the grip Ryan still had around the scruff of the man's shirt collar. You could read a great deal into the fact that Bobby is the sort of guy who had no problem whatsoever in busting a human head open in front of you, without nary an attempt to contextualise or justify doing so.

I looked to Jimmy. He caught my eye. I mouthed "Now!" at him. Jimmy looked back at me with the sort of empty eyes that made me realise that the cogs weren't working behind the scenes in Jimmy's head. I went to repeat what I had just mouthed only for Bobby to interrupt our moment with a loud, scowl-soaked bellow of "What do you two want?"

What do we want? Well, Jimmy wants what I want because if I get what I want then Jimmy gets the thirty quid he was promised plus an extra twenty as a bonus. I didn't have the twenty on me though. What on earth makes you think I'm in a position to be walking around in the dead of night with fifty quid on me? I barely pulled together the thirty in the first place.

This is a little bit of a white lie, by the way.

My inside pocket right now is stuffed with two thousand pounds in cash. But it's most certainly not mine to spend.

Jimmy doesn't need to know this right now though.

I'm digressing.

You're making me digress. I'm sorry.

Anyway, what do I want?

I want the guy hanging from the rafter.

That guy hanging from the rafter is Richard Willis. You can shorten Richard. You can adapt Willis to Willy. All roads lead back to 'dick' and Richard Willis is a humungous dick, trust me. He's the twenty-four year old offspring of lovely, middle-class parents who were so careful as parents to never bring negativity into raising their one and only son that they forgot to ever say no to him. Richard Willis was what happens when you never hear no. Since getting expelled from university, he's expanded his drug addiction into one that has turned his parents' home into an empty shell as he routinely stripped it of valuables to sell to feed his habit. Coke was of course Richard's drug of choice. Sniffed, licked or cooked, he didn't care how it got into his system. Just as long as it was always there. Always. The minute the 'vibe' dulled, he needed to top it up. And that made him any drug dealer's best friend.

The man on all fours in front of Richard with a new ninth hole in his head was Alfie Vern, Richard's drug dealer and one of Bobby's many foot soldiers. Alfie bled Richard dry of every penny he had, every valuable he could pawn and every relative he could rob. Then once he'd done that, he stupidly handed him a line of credit – a hundred here, a few more hundred there. It added up. It all added up. It soon added up to three thousand in fact. With a bit of interest applied and a couple of weeks with his head buried in the sand, Richard soon had a debt to Alfie that sat somewhere just south of five thousand pounds. But the debt to Alfie was a debt to Bobby and Bobby was not happy.

This debt was not, however, what made Bobby unhappy. The debt displeased Bobby greatly, don't get me wrong. But the fact that Richard tried to clear it by robbing a pub in the centre of Newcastle at the close of business on one of its busiest weekends at the start of 'Office Christmas Party Season'? A pub that, unknowing to Richard, belonged to one Robert 'Bobby' Maitland?

Well that vexed Bobby considerably.

It vexed him that someone would have the audacity and the guile to do it. But the pub got damaged in the process and people got hurt because let's be honest, Richard is an incompetent and desperate junkie so health and safety was probably not at the forefront of his thinking at the time he smashed his way in there with a machete and a plastic gun with the red end coloured in black.

And that vexed him the most because someone doing that to one of his places and to some of his people ran the risk of making Bobby look weak.

And tonight, right now, in the hallowed walls of what used to be the glorious Cooper's Gym, Bobby was out to prove that he was most definitely not weak.

Which is what put me in his path.

You see, my clients were Mr and Mrs Willis, Richard's still inexplicably devout parents. They paid me to find their son who'd disappeared down another one of his junkie rabbit holes and not resurfaced like he usually did. I found him but by the point I had he was already in way over his head and in Bobby's clutches. With their permission and Jimmy's help, I was here to try and negotiate a deal for the life of Richard Willis.

"This is Jake, Bobby…" began Jimmy.

My eyes scrunched and burrowed into the side of Jimmy's head. 'Don't introduce me like the guy's never met me before Jim,' I thought. 'I've ran up against him hundreds of times. Come at Bobby all strong and assertive. You know? Earn the fuckin thirty quid, son!'

"I know this prick, what do you's want?" came Bobby's predictable reply.

"Jake wants five minutes of your time?"

Bobby looked me up and down like I'm a piece of shit. I wouldn't argue back with him if that's the label he wanted to tag me with either. I've not washed since the previous night. I'm wearing clothes that were in the washing pile at the top of the stairs because I didn't want to disturb the wife and kids by going rooting through drawers at quarter to one at night when Jimmy's call came through. I can't remember the last time I ate a vegetable and, unlike Bobby clearly, I've never moisturised.

"He's got three!" Bobby said.

You've got to know when to negotiate, when to drive a harder bargain and when to frankly just shut the fuck up.

This was one of the 'shut the fuck up' moments.

I moved forward half a step, immediately regretted doing so because it felt like I'd suddenly either shown a proactive interest in wanting to get involved in the head-busting or I was wanting to 'come at' Bobby himself. No, the step forward wasn't wise. So I stepped back. Essentially committing the most half-baked 'Hokey Cokey' ever performed in an abandoned boxing gym in the back end of Newcastle's West End. At 2am on a freezing December morning.

"Hi Bobby..." I nervously began. "... I've been asked to come tonight and make you a cash offer to spare the life of that guy right there!" I slowly and cautiously raised my hand in the direction to which Richard hung. "Richard's parents love him very much and they've been made fully aware of what he has done and they believe he should be held completely accountable. With the police. They also don't believe you should be left high and dry and that they'd like to do their best to reimburse you for what Richard has..."

"Shut up!" spat Bobby. "God, your voice just grates on me. I don't care whether that was three minutes or not. Your time is up. I don't do 'police'. I don't do lawful accountability or whatever you're selling. What I do is straight up, blunt force reaction to an action. Tell this shitbag's parents they raised a thieving junkie and I'll send them his ashes."

Here's the thing that I've tended to find in my time as a private investigator that popular culture doesn't really push hard enough as being an important prerequisite for the job – most of it is all just bluffing, bullshitting and cajoling in service of the single goal: namely achieving the objective you've been set by your client.

You need a copy of a document but you've not gone through the proper channels regarding Freedom of Information and what not? Take a trip down to the place where the document is stored and start flirting, laying out sob-stories, whatever it takes. You need someone to tell you something but they're holding out? Construct an entirely false rapport with them based completely around the idea that you're on their side and possibly the only thing standing between them and something bad coming their way. Eighty percent of the things I say to people in execution of my role is utter bullshit that I hope I'm not going to get called out on. The other twenty percent of the time? I surprise myself when I hear something truthful and genuine.

I came up with a stupid name for it a long time ago and it has stuck too hard now to get rid of. I call it 'the chuff'. 'Chuffing' people to uncover the leads and secure the facts.

Now, watch me deliver a precarious and highly dangerous 'chuff' that could end up with me getting split in half by a barbell full of weights at Bobby's hands.

"I hear what you're saying Bobby. I totally do. This junkie deserves to die. We've not always seen eye to eye, you and me, but I absolutely respect you as a businessman and what you do for this city."

"Don't you fuckin bullshit me you brown-nosed piece of..."

"I'm not bullshitting you, Bobby. I swear." I hurriedly offered back. "I'm here to make you an offer on behalf of Richard's parents but most importantly I'm here to keep you completely clean what with the whole police thing blowing up right now…"

That's chuff number one. Total lie dressed up as a seedling.

"What police thing?" replied Bobby, taking the seedling and giving it sunlight.

"Well, the thing is the police are involved because Richard was spotted getting picked up and someone called them." I said, looking directly at Ryan as I did and in the process landing chuff number two. This was another total lie and it was a precarious chancer of a lie too because not only did no one to my knowledge actually see it but I had no certainty that Ryan was the one that grabbed Richard in the first place.

"… That tied in with Richard's parents' missing person report," I continued. "It all got me so worried that I dragged my arse out of bed, met quickly with Richard's parents to discuss recompense to you and got Jimmy here to bring me straight to you so that this drug-addled shitbag's body doesn't turn up in bits tomorrow and the police come knocking at your door because he was last seen being dragged away by one of your guys!"

Lie. Lie. Lies. More lies. Chuff. Chuff. And…

Bobby's head slowly turned with an expression of silent fury and landed with a hard stop upon his right-hand man Ryan.

The look said to me that there was indeed some truth to Ryan being the man that grabbed Richard off the streets.

The hard ballsy punt had landed me a hole-in-one.

The sunlit seedling had been fed fertiliser and it was now growing exponentially.

The truth of the matter was that I had no clue and certainly no evidence that ascertained Richard had been picked off the streets by Ryan or anyone else representing Bobby. What led me here tonight was a presumption off the back of good, old-fashioned, tried and tested detective footwork – specifically speaking, after being hired by Richard's parents to find him once he'd disappeared following another drug binge, I hit up all the usual homeless hostels, haunts and crack-dens that I'd uncovered and come to take note of in my time as a police officer and a private investigator. I hit a dead end at all of them bar one stinking hell-hole of a crash pad for junkies. There, for as little as ten quid, an absolute mess of a human stopped repeatedly punching his toes with a needle in the hope of getting some sort of actionable vein now his arms were shot to high heaven, and chose to tell all:

*"You know that woman that got put in the coma? You know? The one that was in the news the other week because the armed robber threw her head first into the cellar at the pub he was turning over? Remember that? Well Richie was that fuckin robber, dude! So considering who owns the pub, I'd say start looking in the sewers because dead or alive that's where you'll probably find him hiding out from the revenge coming his way, man!"*

And with that information, I was off and running – one quick phone call to my old friend Jimmy firmed things up pretty tightly. Jimmy and Bobby are close. Not as close as they used to be but there was still a connection. Back in the day when Jimmy was at his peak, Bobby looked after him because Bobby saw championship potential and a huge future cash cow in Jimmy going pro. He paid Jimmy a wage to train, made sure his fridge was always well stocked with the right foods and supplements and got him the best training gear. All that sort of shit. Then one day Jimmy was back down to being a nobody with dreams of being a somebody, just like the rest of us. Bobby still watched out for him here and there. He just didn't throw him the financial assists like Jimmy used to get way back when.

Off the back of my enquiry, Jimmy did some digging and bobbing around, and sure enough he came up from with an 'apple' in his mouth – namely that Bobby had Richard in his so-called custody and once the other staff members who'd endured the bar robbery positively identified him, Richard was going to be murdered. The debt was irrelevant, ultimately. The dealer Bobby had struggling around on the floor under Ryan's grip was going to be held accountable for that. No, Richard was going to be murdered because he disrespected Bobby's place of business and seriously harmed one of his honest, hardworking, innocent members of staff – a single mother working minimum wage to provide for her two kids at home. Two kids who were currently facing the prospect of the rest of their childhood in care homes if their mother didn't pull through, apparently.

So, with that big info-dump of back story out of the way, let's do this huh? Ladies and Gentlemen, we're going in for the Def-Con 4 of chuffs, cross your arms across your chests, close your legs and… 3… 2… 1… here we go:

"The police are out there now, combing the streets looking for someone that fits your guy's description, Bobby." I said, pointing definitively at Ryan. "How easily can he be tied to you? How sure can you be that your DNA or clothing fibres aren't going to be on Richard's body in the cold light of day? Bobby, seriously, this city is dying on its arse now. It can't afford to have you taken off the street because of a murder charge."

Bobby was starting to silently seethe. I could see it in the air. It was heating this building all on its own.

I continued. I was building in confidence and I was going to keep going until Bobby shut me down. "Richard's parents are disgusted by what he did at your pub and how that woman behind the bar got hurt. They are. I swear. They think Richard needs to be taken to the police so he can hand himself in and go to prison for what he did. They very much believe that. And they also, whilst not agreeing with your business practices as such, at least respect that you ultimately do run a business and you shouldn't be out of pocket for their son's actions."

Bobby slowly moved away from grimacing at Ryan in a way that made it look like he was preparing to pounce and bite his face off any second. He lifted his head back and cocked his nose to the air in my general direction.

"They're going to pay his debt?" asked Bobby, curiously.

"They're not rich people, Bobby." I offered. "They don't have the kind of money accessible that their son has ran up. They're on pensions and have little in the way of savings. The whole fall-out from the collapse of the economy is hitting them just like it's hitting all of us. But they've pulled everything they've got."

This is what we'll call a semi-chuff. Mainly because I didn't feel it was necessary to start explaining that the two grand I was about to offer was after my fees had been considered and actually the final figure I told them to make without leaving themselves truly crippled.

"How much?"

I reached slowly into my inside pocket and pulled out the battered and torn padded envelope, held together with a big run of parcel string because I couldn't find any elastic bands.

"It's two grand." I held out the envelope.

Bobby scoffed. "That's less than half. Go fuck yourself and when you've finished go fuck them too."

"I understand." I countered, nodding as I spoke. "To you this will be insulting. To them it's everything and there's a chasm between you guys on this. But maybe you can consider this – it's not that bad when the alternative is killing him, clawing back zero pounds and having a whole world of police shit land on your door. This way, you can have confidence you've scared him within an inch of your life, he's getting thrown into prison possibly for the rest of his days and you've shown you're not weak enough in any way to be taken advantage of because everyone is going to know it was you that grabbed him, you that kicked the shit out of him and you who then threw his arse to the coppers. You've kept yourself clean with the police. And you're not completely out of pocket. What do you reckon? Would you reconsider?"

Chuff. Chuff. Chuff. Chuff.... And now we hold.

No talking.

No nervous filling in the silence.

No extension or recalibration of the offer. The offer is on the table. It's built on semi-fictitious and chance-taking piffle that we don't want close scrutiny drawn to.

We hold.

We hold in spite of the sweat inexplicably accruing around my hairline even though it's colder than a psychopath's heart in this building right now.

We hold regardless of the puppy-like mutterings of "Bobby, I swear I thought I grabbed him clean!" and "Honestly, I don't think the police give two shits!" that were emitting from Ryan.

We hold in the face of whatever sense of doubt that's building as we quietly question whether Bobby is buying what we're selling, causing our chest to ache from the heavy yet rapid banging of our heart.

We *hold.*

Less than ten minutes later, I was gunning it as quickly as my ropey legs would carry me back through those windy alleyways and dirty side streets. Thick coats of ice hung on every inch of the ground, causing me to slide out of my gait and nearly slip off my feet with every corner I took. Behind me - walking with more certainty and an enviable sense of balance and composure given the ground beneath him and the extra man he dragged alongside him – stomped a silent Jimmy and a staggering mess of the unfortunate excuse for a human that was Richard.

We got to my car. I opened the passenger door, pulled a roll of bin liners from the glove compartment and snatched off one. I yanked it so it opened up into a larger form and lay it down on the passenger seat in one fluid motion. The bin liner wasn't going to do jack-shit about the stench of piss and crusted shit that seemed to omit from Richard. But it would certainly keep the car seat from having to interact with whatever grime was hanging off every inch of his clothing.

"You!" I barked, pointing at Richard. "Get in. Sit on that. Don't touch anything."

Richard did exactly that and I slammed the door behind him, pulling bank notes from my jeans pocket as it banged shut. I handed them in a crumbled heap to Jimmy.

"There's thirty there," I said. "Can I get the other twenty to you later in the week? I'm good, I swear. I just don't have it on me."

"We're good, Jake! I'll catch you in the week!" he replied.

"Thanks for tonight, Jim. Always a champ, eh buddy?"

"Always a chump, you mean?" laughed Jimmy, holding his arms above his head in a champion's pose as he backed away, turned and made off into the night.

I watched him walk for a couple of seconds then made my way round to my side of the car and climbed into the driver's seat. Within seconds of the ignition kicking to life and us skidding off down the street on a blanket of ice, Richard was lit up and insufferably off on full blast:

"Oh my God, thank you so much… You were so fucking cool in there man… I can't believe my folks threw down two grand… Are they pissed? I bet they're really pissed? … How did you find them? My mum can be a bit wet but I love her… Do you think my dad is an arsehole? People tend to think he's an arsehole but he's alright, actually… I mean, they'll let me sleep this whole shit off when you drop me back because it's late and what not but, maaaaan oh man, they're going to be lecturing me all day tomorrow…. They'll get over it though. They will… I just hope I can talk them into not throwing me into rehab again until after Christmas… Have you ever done rehab? Rehab sucks, man… Rehab at Christmas is something else! Orderlies with Christmas hats on and shit? Forget that right now! … So how did my parents find you?

… I think they broke my nose, you know? … I guess they could have done worse though, right? … I didn't throw that lass down the stairs, you know? It was totally an accident. She thought I was going to hit out at someone so she tried to grab me and I pushed her off me and… I don't hit women… I don't. She lost her footing and next thing she just disappeared down a hole in the floor. That was it… That was all it was… I'm not a violent thug… I mean, honestly, I'm an addict. It's not what defines me as a person. I swear. But I absolutely should not have been given a line of credit… It's not that it's not *not* my fault, you know? But really we wouldn't be in this position if they'd cut me off at the first possible point!... What's your plans for Christmas? … Do you have kids?"

I drove in silence.

My mind was working overdrive to drown out everything and anything he had to say. I thought about how this job tonight would hold the wolves at the door for another month financially and that was no bad thing being two and a bit weeks out from Christmas. I thought about the fact that I couldn't really remember the last time I'd slept in my bed, alongside my wife with her cold breath blasting away on the back of my neck, instead of always snatching an hour here or an hour there on the sofa at home when the kids were at school or the sofa in the office when my sidekick Psychic was quiet enough to just let me be. I thought about what repercussion my lies were going to have on Ryan's relationship with Bobby and what Bobby meant when he told me I "owed" him as he snatched that two grand from my hand. I was in the process of thinking about the last time I'd had a drink of Jim Beam… and how it had been a long time since I'd missed it but I was missing it badly tonight… when we arrived at what would be my final destination with Richard.

He'd been flapping his jaw and intensely staring into the side of my head for so much of the drive that he'd never taken note of the fact I missed the turn-off to head to his parents a while back and that we were now instead pulling up on double yellow lines right outside of the only police station I knew in the city that still operated twenty-four hours a day.

"What the fuck…" Richard spat.

I silently held a finger to his face whilst pulling my mobile phone from my pocket. With one hand I accessed my contacts book and pressed the dial button. With the other I took a tight gripped hold of Richard's seat belt, making sure he had no chance to disconnect it and flee. "Don't you move!" I whispered to him.

The call connected.

"We're outside!" I said.

And that was the length and breadth of the call. It was all that was required.

Seconds later the automatic double doors of the police station opened up spilling light onto the pavement outside and with the light came Richard's parents – and two uniformed police officers walking behind them.

You see, not everything is chuff. But like feeding medication to a dog, sometimes you've got to coat the hard-to-take in a more palatable texture. In this case, I hid Richard's fate inside a coating of the chuff, lies and double-douses of good old 'verbal bumwater'. But his fate was always sealed.

Richard started to panic. He looked left. He looked right. He started to punch the dashboard of my car.

"Get out or they're going to drag you out!" I said whilst looking coldly straight ahead.

Mr and Mrs Willis stepped back immediately upon arriving at my car. The two officers moved into position with one opening my passenger door and the other blocking Richard from going anywhere other than straight into the handcuffs waiting in the officer's grasp.

Richard got out and was swiftly cuffed and dragged away.

Mr Willis leaned down into my car through the open passenger door. He stared at me silently. He had something to say but the words weren't there. I saw Mrs Willis' hand gently place itself on his back and suddenly he quietly but affirmatively whispered to me.

"Thank you. Sincerely. Thank you."

I nodded as he stepped back and closed the door.

I offered a wave in Mrs Willis' direction as she fell into her husband's arms and I heard her begin to sob even ten feet away and through a closed car door.

I turned the engine over and snatched a quick glance at the clock on the dashboard in the process. The time offered me the rather tempting possibility of snatching three hours sleep before the kids woke, lit up my world and sent me straight back out onto the streets again to work.

I'm going to tell you my story, I promise. I'm going to tell you everything. But to really understand how big that sack of hurt is and to truly at least be able to empathise with me as to why I picked up that gun, you've got to be able to understand the context.

And to do that you're going to need to know about Jane.

And you're most certainly going to *have* to know about Mick fucking Hetherington.

## [2]

## or

## "Jane..."

*"♫♫ ... Some people, they like to go out dancing. And other people, they have to work, Just watch me now! And there's even some evil mothers. Well they're gonna tell you that everything is just dirt... Y'know that, women, never really faint. And that villains always blink their eyes, woo! ... And that, y'know, children are the only ones who blush! And that, life is just to die! And, everyone who ever had a heart. They wouldn't turn around and break it. And anyone who ever played a part. Oh wouldn't turn around and hate it! ... Sweet Jane! Whoa-oh-oh! Sweet Jane! Sweet Jane! ... ♫♫"*

*Sweet Jane – The Velvet Underground.*

*Written by Lou Reed. From the Album 'Loaded' (August 1973)*

**I** met Jane fourteen years ago. Or was it thirteen? I'll need to ask her.

I was a probationary police officer, fresh off the production line so to speak. Three weeks out of training school at twenty-three years of age and out on the streets with my assigned mentor.

Jane was twenty.

She was studying to be a teacher at university, a recalibrated career choice after a brief misstep studying to be a solicitor for a year or so. She studied by day and did bar work by night and weekends like many a student. And just like everything Jane turns her hand to, she excelled at it so well they made her duty manager in a short amount of time.

The bar Jane worked at was one of the seedier ones, shall we say. It wasn't down the Bigg Market – which believe it or not was still a thriving part of the drinking scene back in 2006 – or anywhere near the Quayside which was starting to really boom back up there as the go-to-destination for bars and clubs in Newcastle. It was right outside of Haymarket at the top end of town. Her shift generally started with students leaving digs or coming out of the metro station to start their night out and work their way down to the Quayside getting more inebriated as they went, and ended with smashed up cheapskates finishing their night earlier to get the last metro home who'd stagger in for "one last one for the road". On match days of a weekend, which Jane continually and unsuccessfully tried to avoid, her pub was hell on earth.

It was a match day when we met.

Football season started mid-August as usual. Nobody had the highest of prospects for Newcastle United back then. The golden Bobby Robson era felt like it had disappeared into the ether even though it was but two years ago or something. Glenn Roeder was manager... and I pretended to give a single shit about Newcastle United and the hopes and dreams of its fans purely because I didn't think I'd have anything to talk about with my police colleagues if I didn't.

Beyoncé and Jay-Z's 'Déjà vu' had replaced Shakira's 'Hips Don't Lie' in the charts. Justin Timberlake was still a week or so away from unfortunately bringing 'Sexyback'. All of this meant nothing to me back then or even now, really. I had a scratched up version of Journey's 2001 album 'Arrival' on obsessive repeat because I was a true committed fan from childhood who didn't just jump on the fuckin band wagon because 'Don't Stop Believin' got covered on some American kids soap opera or something. But anyway, I digress once again. I apologise.

I couldn't tell you one single news story for anything occurring anywhere around the world at that time. But I could tell you that Snakes on a Plane was still inexplicably in cinemas and, round these parts, doing surprisingly well for some reason. Michael Mann's big screen version of Miami Vice had cratered at the cinema because someone somewhere had seriously overestimated the appeal of a coked-up Colin Farrell as a cinematic version of Sonny Crockett.

I'd been on duty for about three hours. It was a Saturday night shift and I'd not slept all day from the previous night shift due to my then neighbour getting work done directly next door to the flat I shared at the time with my buddy, Andy, who I'd met in police training school.

And if you're thinking at this point that maybe the flatmate 'Andy' could be the 'Andy' that was referenced way back in our prologue then, you know what, well done you. That's some good spotting and tracking of characters. I had a low opinion of you guys initially but this just shows we're connecting and you're paying attention so... yeah, wow.... Good going, peeps. Let's crack on...

I just wanted to keep my head down and walk the beat, attract not one single job to attend and get my arse home the minute my shift ended come Sunday morning. These were unrealistic expectations, being a probationary police officer in Newcastle on a Saturday night but I had them nonetheless.

Newcastle's match had finished a good two hours before I'd even started my shift but the fans were still out in force, drowning their sorrows after an embarrassing defeat within the opening weeks of a new season. A call came out over the radio that a bar brawl had broken out at this piece of shit pub outside of Haymarket metro station, we were round the corner on Northumberland Street so off we sprinted.

Cut to the chase: Folk got arrested, batons got used, back up was called for and across the carnage was the most beautiful woman I'd ever seen in my life. Everything went into slow motion as we locked eyes – even the blood that was pumping out of the wound on her forehead from a glass that had been thrown at her when the carnage got underway.

I was tasked to get her details and meet her up at the hospital just round the corner later on in order to get a statement from her about who threw the glass and.... and... Sorry, I get distracted and go off into a lovely warm daze just thinking about the moment Jane and I met.

I got her details. I got the statement too. I was too scared to ever call her using the details I'd secured in my role as a police officer because you hear about dirty scumbag coppers doing shit like that all the time. So instead I took to visiting her bar every chance I could get. To the point I began to worry that she thought I was some burnt-out alcoholic cop or something. And to avoid her thinking that I switched to drinking Appletise instead because I'd overheard her tell one of her workmates that she loved the stuff. It gave me crippling heartburn that left me gagging bile for the rest of the evening. But we suffer for love, right?

I asked her out across the bar as she handed me my change one quiet Sunday afternoon. Well, I started asking her out but aborted half a sentence in. Luckily she picked up the baton and put the words out there and I accepted. We went to the cinema and for drinks that very night, the minute she finished her day shift and went home to freshen up. I remember that we watched some Michael Douglas movie about a Secret Service agent framed for a murder who has to go on the run. Man, the name escapes me. That's going to piss me off. I know that I wanted to see the Jason Statham movie Crank but that I picked up Jane's disinterest when I got to the "He plays a hitman who will die if his poisoned heart drops below a rate of…" part of its description and I let her choose instead.

We held hands in the cinema. I remember that. I also remember she had salted popcorn and I had sweet and she wanted to mix our boxes "because mixed popcorn is amazing" and I thought that was the scummiest thing I'd ever heard in my life but I shut my mouth because I thought she had the most gorgeous smile I'd ever seen.

Jane hates her smile, by the way. Detests it in fact. She thinks her teeth are too small and her gums are too big. She tries to smile with her mouth closed all the time but can't maintain it and her grin always breaks wide instead. I think her smile is perfect.

We kissed within half an hour of the film finishing. We'd just got settled in a bar up by St James Park that she'd heard played classic soft rock which showed she'd picked up on the sort of music I liked when we'd walked to the cinema earlier. I brought drinks over to our table, sat down and asked how her head was because I noticed it was starting to heal over now but she was still trying to self-consciously cover it with her hair. I remember she asked if I'd like to feel it because she thought it was going to heal all raised and ugly. I stroked my index finger across that tiny scar on the corner of her forehead and… get this for 'smooth moves and grooves' all you gentlemen out there looking for 'love tips'… I kept my finger going, brushing the hair back behind her ear and letting my hand fall to the back of her neck. She smiled, bit her bottom lip as she leant forward towards me and…

… We clashed teeth hard causing us to both open our eyes and spring back in our seats. We both laughed nervously, leant back in and butted heads. I'm not kidding. We finally got there in the end but our first kiss was dreadful, man. Honestly.

But our second kiss?

Our second kiss at the end of the night was the game-changer.

That was the kiss that made me see her four times more over the course of the next seven days wherever my shifts would allow. That was the kiss that made me move in with her eight weeks later much to Andy's fury.

That was the kiss that made her my wife two years later.

We honeymooned in San Francisco, getting drunk every day and verbally abusing seals down by the Pier. We visited Alcatraz in the day. And again at night because Jane wanted to know "if the tour was scarier in the dark".

Our children, Jack and Jonathan, followed a year and three years respectively after that too. Yes, our house is full of J's. No, it was not intentional or pre-designed. Jane thought it was. She thought I'd suggested Jack and Jonathan as names because "it would be cute to see Christmas cards signed 'To All The J's'!" or some shit like that. In fact, I think she didn't speak to me for like a week when she found out I suggested those names because they were the characters Robert DeNiro and Charles Grodin played in Midnight Run. And screw you and the horse you rode in on if you don't think THAT is a straight-up American classic of a film!

If everything I've just told you right now doesn't give you a clear indication of how much I love Jane and the family she's given me, then I don't know how else to sell it to you.

We had the perfect life.

A beautiful home, good money and fantastic kids who thought their dad made money "being a hero". I was going to go for the detective's promotion after the last couple of years of getting my arse kicked as a plain clothes officer on the robbery squad unit, Jane had just been offered a deputy head's position at a lovely little school down near the coast.

And then my police career ended.

With it, everything I thought I knew about what was right, what was wrong… about trust… friendship… You name it. Everything changed. My marriage certainly did.

I love Jane with all of my heart but I think she's done. I think I've broken her. Whatever love, tolerance, patience and all that stuff that she had, it feels like I've burnt through it all. I think she wants to leave but she knows I'd die without her.

Not from a broken heart or anything although my heart would most definitely break.

Just incompetency.

Last week for example she asked me to feed the kids, put them to bed and tidy the kitchen as she was staying late at school for a parent's evening. Cut a long story short, I couldn't work out how to open the washing machine door. So I put the kids' dirty clothes in the dishwasher as a substitute option because, you know, think outside the box and all that eh? I broke the dishwasher, flooded the kitchen, slipped in the mess and broke two fingers.

This isn't a joke. Seriously. They had to be all strapped up and everything.

But… yeah… laugh all you want, things aren't good.

I keep failing, Jane keeps picking me up.

That seems to be the status quo of our relationship nowadays. But I think Jane's back is starting to hurt now and I don't think she's got it in her to keep bending down to reach me.

## [3]

## or

## "A Sworn Promise That This Is The Last Run Of Exposition You'll Need."

Jane came up with the name 'Lehman's Terms' for the business.

I had a very specific idea about my PI company being a separation from the phone-hacking, shadow-skulking, law-bending types that seemed to always be advertising on Gumtree and the free listings sites. I wanted to put my knowledge of the law and evidence gathering to proper use and build really strong case-files for court. I had visions of being the go-to-guy for insurance fraud investigations… and defence investigations… and…

Let's just say it didn't work out *quite* like that.

From the get-go 'Lehman's Terms' struggled and has never really stopped. I think it would have struggled regardless but the stupid name Jane chose certainly didn't help. It doesn't tell anybody anything about what it is we actually do as a business and, yeah, even in its original form a 'layman' is someone who is not trained to a high or professional standard in a particular subject so… it just isn't screaming *"Oh this guy is a great investigator – use him!"* is it?

I couldn't compete with the big investigation and surveillance company down the road with all their state of the art cameras and telephoto lens. I couldn't conduct traces in bulk at the discount rates some of the huge firms were offering. So I just got to scrapping around, keeping busy, taking anything I could get to keep my mind off drinking again and to make Jane look at me once more like I was the man she fell in love with.

Work came in here and there – hunting down and serving court papers on all the people no one else would touch, looking for people's missing dogs and shit like that. I kept the overheads as low as possible and in the early days I worked as hard as I could promoting the company and going to stupid, cringe-worthy business networking breakfasts and all that shit. Sometimes it paid off just enough for me to bring a couple of hundred quid a month home as a wage for the family that I was deeply embarrassed by but Jane would champion as a "huge achievement considering who we're going up against".

She always said 'we'. She always purposefully reinforced that my business was our business and we were in this together. I liked that. Even though every day felt like I was dragging her down to the depths with me.

The stamina to always be out there promoting who we are and what we do faded over time. I started to just get sick of the sound of my own voice saying the same things about who we are at 'Lehman's Terms', what we do and what we stand for… Then seeing nothing come from it except the pile of business cards for people who'd never taken my follow-up call grow bigger and bigger each fortnight. Eventually I just took to the office and hoped the phone would miraculously ring or the inbox would just ping with self-generating jobs.

At home we just kept cutting the cloth until there was no more cloth left to cut. Jane and I slashed our date nights down to once every three months. Every single unnecessary expenditure went out the window - which means in our house a request to "Netflix and Chill" translates as "Chill" – and whatever the supermarket brand is below the supermarket's cheapest brand is usually the one we buy. Hell, there's tins of food in our house that don't even have shitty quality labels on them. There's just the words "Guess what this is, motherfucker!" scrawled on it in marker pen.

The kids are each another few years away from ever working out that we're essentially a one wage family because their dad is just phoning it as a PI no one really hires that much. They'll soon spot too that despite it being a good wage, Jane's earnings don't stretch that far at all. They didn't before the country had its collapse and they certainly didn't afterwards.

I eventually landed a huge job after a year that took me over to Australia.

Impressive, huh?

Except it proved so traumatic that it caused me to fall off the wagon and start drinking again. Which in turn led to Jane having to pick up the pieces.

But that's a whole other story.

Seriously, I'm talking like a whole other book. How's *that* for a threat?

I hung on in there as an investigator long enough to land that Australia job we'll not get into right now and came back from that a broken man. The only good thing that came from it really was the office in which 'Lehman's Terms' is now based in, permanently and forever for as long as I want it.

Completely free.

Courtesy of the client who commissioned "that Australia job we'll not get into right now", I now have an open-plan studio office space above a large accountancy firm smack bang in the middle of the illustrious Grey Street in the centre of town in a listed building the client owns.

Pretty sweet, huh?

All I have to do is pay the running costs. The office itself is free.

And even with this prime location, I'm still struggling to keep my head above the waterline… I assure you, I'm a better investigator than I am a businessman.

I thought "that Australia job we'll not get into right now" was going to get international attention and break 'Lehman's Terms' out big time. I thought everyone would want to work with me after that – the first time I learnt to sleep properly again after it all happened, I dreamt there'd be news interviews, book deals or at the very least retainerships with the country's leading law firms.

There was none of that.

Not one bean.

Just a free office in the centre of town and a very large invoice paid early and in full that was big enough to keep the business' comfortable for a little while.

Then the country cratered.

And I mean absolutely fucking cratered – Not like 'oh the North had it worse' type cratered. I mean the whole country all went to pieces in the blink of an eye and then crumbled to dust thereafter.

The pound was shot.

Unemployment went through the roof.

Our government shut the doors and turned their backs on us to get on with it.

It was crazy. People were taking to the streets and screaming into a void.

The sad thing was we saw it all coming. We watched the government make bad choice after bad choice and the country kept getting more and more isolated from the rest of Europe and the world. We saw it coming and we did nothing. We tweeted and we Facebooked and we shared articles about conspiracy theories at the heart of what our government were doing to us, like how our Prime Minister was making deals that seemed to serve her own personal interests for investments we knew her husband's firm were handling.

We all vowed she had to be stopped.

And we did nothing.

I think we all believed there was going to be an intervention. There was talk of the PM being overthrown by her own party in the interests of the country. Or a snap general election. Ideas were continually thrown around and the British masses bought each and every one and naively believed the next one was going to be implemented to stave off the repeatedly harmful decisions that were being made.

But none of them happened.

And when the landslide of ramifications from the Prime Minister's corrupt dealings hit home, they all hit home at once.

The small and medium business market died very nearly overnight.

Our country's import and export dealings were strangled to death by petty bureaucracy and left unfixable by too-little-too-late interventions.

The cost of living kept rising and rising… and rising. There were kick-offs at petrol stations, riots in supermarkets… No one could afford to live anymore and there just wasn't enough work to help provide.

Then the medicine shortages started and the property marketed exploded and repossessions had a stratospheric increase at a level not seen in British history. People were dying – and dying from things that no one should be dying from in the twenty-first century. Diabetics couldn't get insulin. The elderly weren't getting the heart meds they depended on.

CEOs of major, imperative firms were left completely unchecked and kept throwing themselves big bonuses out of whack with the earnings of the staff below them and especially so in terms of the profits available, driving their firms into the ground.

Those big companies that survived? The ones that were the foundation of thousands of jobs around the country upped sticks and moved elsewhere in the world making a cavalcade of middle-managers and pen-pushers immediately redundant. The only jobs out there were the minimum wage, thankless piece of shit jobs these very same people would have turned their noses up at in disgust and considered them as twenty-five stories beneath them just a year or so earlier. But optionless in the face of hard times, these over-qualified types started chasing the shitty jobs, pushing the lower working class who relied on such jobs into a position of having no options left for themselves.

By the time over two million people marched on mass into London to protest it was too late. There was no truly effective government left in power in my eyes. We were a country dead in the water. The Prime Minister had quit and fled to a holiday home she held in Venezuela with the millions her husband had secretly creamed off the back of her corrupted decision making and national deals. A revised definition of cowardice may lie in the fact she informed the nation of her resignation and flew out of the country within the same hour. Her deputy stepped into the breach before resigning four weeks later. On and on the musical chairs of leadership occurred with no legitimate rival party of any worth to make a stand against them.

Up here in Newcastle it was awful to watch the painful crumbling of our city; our public transport system was stripped back to minimal services, our police stations and doctors surgeries, barely standing as they were, shuttered to just one or two per county. Food banks were now two or three to every high street and had voluntary security guards posted outside but normally closed their doors within two hours of opening due to running out of stock. Most folk couldn't fit on the overpacked and underserved buses and metros so were taking to trudging everywhere to get anywhere in all weathers. There was more people out on the streets at all times than ever before.

Our roads and infrastructure started to fall to pieces with no money to replace them. People queued like zombies outside of job centres like it was the 1980s again, because they didn't know what else to do even though there was no more jobs to reach out and grab. It was too expensive to heat or light your home outside of exceptional circumstances – if you even still had energy supplies you could afford.

We'd been rolled back to the late seventies and early eighties again and no one really got their head around how it had happened. There was a very brief period where all of this was great for 'Lehman's Terms' I guess you could say. Because with all this going on, mortgage payments were missed, businesses fucked creditors over and court orders and statutory demands were being passed around like they were bank notes.

I was doing very well out of all of the misery and burying down deep the pain that came from having to do this to people in a state of distress in order to keep my own head above water. Then people stopped being able to afford solicitors too.

And the flow of demands needing served slowly ebbed back down to a trickle for me.

If you had money and your investments and savings were protected then you were okay and you were one of what I classed as the five percent that could drive through the streets of Newcastle with your windows tightly rolled up turning your head away from the masses that struggled along, looking each and every way for their eyes to land on a break whilst you prayed you weren't going to get hijacked by them.

Stephie Jay's parents were one of those types.

Sue George and her modelling company were inexplicably one of those types too. (How does a major North East based tool manufacturer with international reach die in a fortnight and make 1700 people redundant, but a tiny regional bloody modelling agency stay afloat whilst we all go to hell in a hand basket? I mean, come on?)

Our city's 'Mayor' was another one... But of course he was.

And Bobby Maitland seemed to do alright too. Because it seemed that no matter how poor we all got and no matter how bad things kept getting, everyone still had the money to go and get smashed in one of Bobby's venues.

Every morning I have the same routine:

I get up from wherever I've dropped coming through the door the night before and I make breakfast with the kids. We sit and talk and I get a rundown of what they've got planned for school that day and whether their homework is all completed. Sometimes it's a chore, sometimes its inane and sometimes I flat out love just sitting and shooting the shit with them. But the important thing for me is that I do it. I've got far too many missed mornings or phoned-in interactions from my alcoholic days to make up for.

Once they're out the door to school with Jane dropping them off on her way to work, I shower and dress whilst looking over my calendar for the day. I like to do this so I can pretend that there's something I need to be rushing for but there's very rarely an occasion where this is the case. There's the odd day where I will need the car for some job in which case I'm out the door to do the drop-offs but most mornings aren't like that…

… I'm throwing off tangents to not have to disclose the next bit because I think I look terrible enough without further admissions of awfulness but, you know, we've come this far together and we're not even underway *technically* with the actual story (I know, I know) and I don't want to start lying or withholding anything from you because…

… Well… I feel like we're bonding, aren't we? There's something building here between us don't you think? I mean, I'm hoping you're getting a feel for whether you like me and want to stay invested with hearing the story of this whole sorry saga. Because I think I like you and I'm talking about 'like' to the sort of level that when you write *your* book I'm going to commit to reading it in full and not sack it off after three chapters because the protagonist/narrator was a procrastinating addict.

There. I said it.

I'm an addict.

Jane doesn't know. Or at the very least she does and she's just stopped caring and decided to just use the last of her energy to insulate the kids from it. But, yeah, the alcohol has been replaced by pills just like a psychopath downgrades serial killing to the odd occasional stabbing.

Now, don't get me wrong, I'm an addict but I'm not a junkie. To me, there's a difference. I'm not in denial about the fact I'm an addict. I'm not hurting anyone in order to get a hit. You're looking at me right now and making your own judgement. I can't stop you. But I know there's a goddamn massive line between the likes of what I do to get through a day and what scumbags like Richard Willis do.

I'm not hurting anyone popping a couple of pills once or twice a day. I'm just enduring. That's what I've got to do, man. I've just got to endure until I'm six feet under or until things are made right again.

I was prescribed Tramadol for the injuries I picked up on "that Australia job we'll not get into right now" and, like any good addict, I parlayed that short-term prescription into a long-term solution to the arthritis they lumped in amongst the diagnoses they were throwing out at me that day. I've got a pretty good supply gig going now by simply picking up a good feel for when one doctor thinks I've been on them long enough… and then I fuck the fuck right off as quickly as possible next time round to another doctor. I've got a list hidden in the note screen of my phone of the doctors that really, really don't give two shits and whenever I ring for a top-up, I make sure I book in with one of them.

As I say, every morning I look over the calendar whilst drinking a black coffee with two sugars and throwing down two Tramadol tablets. I hang around tidying the kitchen or putting the kids toys away, whatever kills the most amount of time in order to give the caffeine, sugar and opioid time to meet up, discuss things and decide to kick the day into gear.

I get hot fingers and they start to tingle. When I find myself rolling my index fingers and thumbs off each other in little fast circles I realise that I'm getting the buzz I need and I leave the house.

I take a packed metro ride into the city on a medicinal high, people-watching and still delighting in my developed skill of being able to 'call shit from a mile off', whether that be the commuters with an unspoken crush on each other, the cheating husband who's texts I sneakily read over his shoulder or the rude scumbags who don't give their seats up to others less able than them or the elderly. Everyone has a story and I like to fill the dreadful, stinking, shaky morning commute by trying to uncover them or write them in my head.

You'd think the painkillers would affect my ability to do my job but they don't. They *accentuate* it, actually. Which is proper 'addict' bullshit isn't it? But it's true. It really is. I am full of so much anger and hate for how my life has ended up and how powerless I feel being scapegoated and having my dream career pulled away from me. It consumes me. The anger courses through me at such a rate and level, I don't actually know what my body would feel like and what the world around me would look like without the hate imbued in me.

The painkillers strip that back. They dull the edge off the hate and the anger and the resentment and they clear things back a little in order for me to focus on things. Because, honestly, when I'm focused I'm good.

Very occasionally I get within reaching distance of potentially great.

So… I'm normally in our office by around nine.

I lug our old, battered portable street-sign with its weighted bottom down into the street and put it out for the masses to either ignore or trip over and threaten to sue, then I get the kettle on for my second coffee and to sink into the buzz that's starting to kick nicely into gear in my head.

I was given an open planned space by our benevolent benefactor of an ex-client and for the most part it still is. There's a hastily placed makeshift plasterboard partition and door that a handyman client I once had did as a favour to me and its within there that I base what I call my 'private' office and meet clients should one ever walk through our doors. But the main floor is taken up with two large sofas and a desk for Psychic who is forced to continue to be the company's front-facing receptionist of sorts, especially if he wants to keep working for/with me. The second sofa closest to my office-of-sorts is where I kick back and look over existing or outstanding case files or miraculous job requests until Psychic arrives.

You heard me say 'our' office earlier by the way and that's sort of the case because I don't work alone. I now somewhat reluctantly / somewhat lovingly share it with Psychic.

Psychic isn't actually psychic.

That's what sort of makes the joke all the more brilliant really.

Psychic's name is actually Robbie Dayer. He turned up at my office one day looking for work and I didn't have any. But then he turned up the next day. And the day after that.

He was really into "private investigation" and kept saying that he'd volunteer if I'd train him. I didn't bite for the longest time until one day when Robbie turned up as I was struggling to fix a broken covert camera. He got to work on it, got it going in twenty minutes and he's never left.

What's more, Robbie got a lot of money as a result of getting knocked over by a police car that was travelling without due care and attention a few years back. So he's not short of a few quid. You could pull out that list that Maitland, Hetherington etc. were on and then add him to that… really, really, really, REALLY far down at the very bottom of it though.

Robbie only wants paid for the cases we work on. The rest of the time he comes in and 'hangs out'. Which, look I'm not going to lie, is pretty cool because he's a great guy and he's got some really good craic. And I couldn't afford to pay him a full time living wage anyway.

There is no craic greater than how Robbie became 'Psychic'.

You see, once we agreed Robbie was going to become a semi-permanent fixture and he started hanging around working with me, I started affectionately calling him "Sidekick Robbie" and in time I shortened that to just "Sidekick". After a few months, he came to me and asked if he could clear something up. Then, really earnestly, he looked me dead in the eye and said "I don't want to lead you on, Jake mate. I don't have any psychic ability!"

I was all like "What the fuck are you talking about?"

It turned out that all that time Robbie thought I'd been calling him 'Psychic', not 'Sidekick'. And thus his stupid nickname stuck and has officially replaced his actual name as far as I am concerned.

He's a good looking 'Page Seven Fella' type is Psychic. Other than the dropped shoulder he carries in his gait as a result of that accident with the police car, he's the guy that turns a lady's head when he walks down the street. Me? I'm the bloke she walks straight into because she's too busy looking back at Psychic then mutters "Eurgh. Watch where you're going!"

I'm an analogue man in a digital world, born completely out of time, and he's a bit of a tech-head so we work well together. On top of that, we've been in each other's pockets for a couple of years now so he's very quietly and non-judgementally come to cover for the pill-popping that goes on in order for me to get through the day.

Psychic and I like to sit and cut through the shit on what we feel are a lot of myths about investigations, PIs and all that which stem from TV and movies. Probably one of our biggest shared frustrations is the fact that it would all be much easier if in real life you were given a chance to do what we've nicknamed 'The Richard Kimble' but it never happens.

Remember that Harrison Ford movie The Fugitive?

Ford plays Dr Richard Kimble, framed for the murder of his own wife and forced to go on the run. Remember? And whilst he's on the run and evading Tommy Lee Jones and what not, he uncovers a conspiracy involving his medical colleagues and learns his wife was killed in error by a one-armed hitman who was intending to get Kimble himself in order to cover up the results of this medical trial that…

… Anyway, if you've seen it you know what I'm talking about and if you haven't then I'm sorry but I've pretty much just ruined The Fugitive for you.

But yeah, Kimble realises his best friend Dr Charles Nichols is the mastermind behind the medical cover-up and arranging the hit-man and all that. He's right in the middle of being honoured at this big awards dinner and Kimble evades the authorities and gets inside of the venue. In front of the whole crowd of startled patrons, Kimble starts striding through the tables shouting "You almost got away with it, didn't you? I know about it. I can prove it!" and Dr Nichols is all like "Ladies and gentlemen, my friend Richard Kimble doesn't feel… well, obviously. So, if you will just go on with your dessert and coffee, I'll be right back!"

But Kimble keeps going and in front of everyone he says "You changed the samples didn't you? Huh? You switched the samples… after Lenz died! After Lenz died, you were the only one who had the access. You switched the samples, and the pathology reports!" The crowd gasps and Kimble shouts "Did you kill Lenz, too? Huh? Did you?" and then he turns to the crowd and he says "He falsified his research. So that RDU-90 could be approved and Devlin McGregor could give you… Provasic!"

Man, The Fugitive is such a great movie!

Anyway, it's a great scene where the main hero character gets to monologue away and stitch together all the facts he's collected along the way and get the audience all caught up with where we're all at now in the film. It's so neat and tidy and… you never get that in real life!

As PIs especially, we skulk in the shadows and we chase the facts then we put it all into a report and give it to the client. Sometimes, if we're lucky, the client might get back to us with an update as to what ended up happening as a result of our report. But generally, we never see the end result and we never get to confront the bad guy and 'Richard Kimble' the shit out of them in front of a crowd, showing how clever we are at having worked it all out and caught them bang to rights. And that's really frustrating – because Harrison Ford makes it look like that would be a *lot* of fun.

The reality of being a private investigator is really nothing at all like what you see on TV and in films. My experience of it isn't anyway. We don't hack phones and computers – at least the ones that want to stay out of jail don't anyway.

No, we don't go beat people up who owe you money and access their criminal records through miraculous 'dark means' or a 'contact they've got on the front desk down at the police station'.

No, we don't hide in wardrobes to film your wife having sex with someone else.

No, we don't have trench-coats and…

Well, actually I do own a trench-coat. But I had it before I was a PI, in my defence.

Psychic and I also have some of the best conversations that stem from days sat in an office, waiting for the phone to ring and in between "brainstorming sessions" thinking up the next best way in which we can market the business to bring in more work and compete with the big players out there.

Possibly not sitting around talking inane shit and instead being relentlessly proactive and hungry every day in chasing work would be a *really* good way in which we could bring in more clients and cases...

Oooh, maybe I should write that down?

That seems like a good one that has some legs to it doesn't it?

Our conversations range from the sublime to the completely ridiculous. One time we spent an entire day, and I mean an entire day, sat discussing what song would be used over the opening credits of a reality TV show that was made about me and him going about our jobs as private investigators. We took it really, really seriously too. I cleaned off what was no longer required on the white board in my part of the office and we got down to listing tracks that would work and what sort of songs would be best suited to what credits – cheesy, retro, action-packed, serious. We had it all covered.

Psychic is seven years younger than me and it showed in his choices. He fought hard for Kings of Leon tracks and Metallica and shit like that. I mean, he did admittedly come good in putting forward 'Walk of Life' by Dire Straits and something by Talking Heads but that was after some serious arguing.

Ultimately we got it shortlisted down to either 'Jungleland' by Bruce Springstreen (on the grounds that it is, by my estimation, "one of the best songs ever written and recorded") or 'Alright' by Cast because both Psychic and I agreed that it would look pretty cool to have action-packed shots of us serving court documents or running and missing a metro and all the other shite we do in a day, all soundtracked to that classic.

The best time-killer conversation we have ever had is the one that got Psychic so angry that I swear to God he stormed out of the office, went home and didn't speak to me or come back to work for three days. It was such a good wind-up that all sprang from some banal discussion about what the greatest movie of the 1980s was (… and if you didn't immediately silently mouth the words "Midnight Run closely followed by Die Hard, obviously!" then you should put this book down because it isn't for you! I'm not for you and you're definitely not for me!) and how the 80s were an underrated decade for cinema. I'll present the whole transcript to you in full:

Him

The Karate Kid was the greatest movie of the 1980s! Hard fact!

Me

It is a great movie. I'm not arguing with you there. But the greatest? The greatest of that decade? I don't know. I don't think I can go with you on that.

Him

You're wrong! It has everything – It's got romance, drama, a great message about good triumphing evil, it's got that great Bill Conti score, that 'crane kick' and…

Me

It <u>is</u> good. It is. Especially considering it has such a pretty awful subtext, you know?

Him

What are you talking about?

Me

Well, you know? The whole paedophilia thing?

Him

What? There's no paedophilia thing in The Karate Kid!

Me

There is. It's well known. People have written books about it. Seriously.

Him
There are no books about paedophilia in The Karate Kid. Stop it. This is a wind-up.

Me
It isn't a wind-up. I'm serious. Are you telling me you've seen that movie as many times as you have and you've never picked up once on the fact that they're pretty bloody clear about Mr Miyagi being a paedophile?

Him
MR MIYAGI IS NOT A PAEDOPHILE! HOW FUCKING DARE YOU?

Me
Don't get angry with me. I didn't write the film. It's true though – look at the facts, right? Fact one, he takes this young teenage boy under his wing…

Him
For the purposes of training him in the art of karate!

Me
Yes, yes. That's what he *lures him in with.* But if you look, initially all the 'training' he gets Daniel to do is just coming to his house and doing menial jobs whilst stripped down to his vest and getting all hot and sweaty in the baking sun…

Him
HE'S TEACHING HIM ABOUT DISCIPLINE AND HE'S TEACHING HIM ABOUT STRUCTURED DEFENCE TECHNIQUES BY GETTING HIS BODY USED TO ADOPTING SET POSITIONS VIA LABOUR-INTENSIVE TASKS!!

Me
He doesn't initially show any interest in the kid until his mum goes out of town. And he throws the kid off a boat just to see him wet. He doesn't approve of Elizabeth Shue's character…

Him
SHE'S A DISTRACTION TO HIS TRAINING!

Me
And let's not forget that his entire bullshit strategy for helping Daniel get back on his feet after a serious injury in competition, is to simply breathe heavily, clap his hands together and rub the boy's leg in an area I'm still not entirely convinced was the area that he actually injured!

Him
HOW DARE YOU?

Me
It's all there, Psychic! Mr Miyagi was a paedophile. Why do you think he spirited Daniel straight out of the US and over to Japan for the sequel? Less stringent laws around that sort of thing over there and…

Psychic got up and left.

We didn't speak for those aforementioned three days.

On the fourth day I came into work to find he was back at his desk and that the framed Last Boy Scout poster in my office had been defaced with the word 'Paedo' on Bruce Willis' forehead.

The poster got taken down and together Psychic and I found a way to move past this difficult incident and build a stronger future together. Until one day I suggested that the reason Mr Miyagi started hanging around with school girls in the fourth movie was because Daniel had outgrown his tastes. Then everything got opened up all over again.

But you don't need to worry about that.

## [4]

## or

## "The Instigating Act You've All Patiently Waited For..."

**I** get what you're thinking already.

You're all like "Four chapters and NOW he decides to get going telling this stupid frickin' story about blowing up the Metrocentre or something!"

And I get your frustration, I really do.

But here's a couple of things:

This isn't a story about me setting fire to what was once the North East's premier shopping location and the biggest shopping outlet in the whole of the UK, no less. It's a *much* bigger and more heart-breaking story than that.

Most importantly though, everything you need to know is all set up for you to best understand what happened and why I did what I did – The fact that I'm willing to do anything to get Jane to look at me the way she used to when I was a police officer? Check! You know now that I love her with all of my heart and it scares the shit out of me that I'm forcing her away with my repeated 'fuck-uppery'.

The fact that Bobby Maitland is a full on crazy gangster scumbag? Check! That's important because it's my experience that nothing bad happens in this city without his finger prints all over it and boy are we about to introduce something awful!

The fact I'm a recovering alcoholic turned painkiller addict, two shades shy of a nervous breakdown and struggling to make a living as a bottom rung PI in a city that has gone to serious shit? Check, check and double check, yeah?

So, with all that in mind....

*Away.*
*We.*
*Go.*

I'd grabbed maybe two hours sleep at best on the sofa having crashed through the door from dropping Richard Willis' stinking carcass at the police station. I woke in a startled daze to find Jonathan jumping on my stomach and leaning in to kiss my stubble.

Jane asked me how I'd got on as she passed through to put the kids' school lunch together. I told her I'd come good - as good as a result could be in that situation but that there were no winners really. I then hastily added that if there was though, it was me because I got paid. She smiled but didn't follow through to say anything.

We didn't really *talk* that much anymore.

Then again we didn't make the time, I guess. We passed each other more than we hung out with each other and our quarterly date nights were taken up with her getting me up to speed on things about the kids I'd missed out on through not being at home or able to make one of their school events. We were normally done, home and in bed asleep all within three to four hours.

We certainly didn't talk about *us*, I felt.

The kids ate breakfast, busted my balls a little and left for school.

I switched the routine around and had two strong black cups of coffee, jumped in the shower, popped a handful of tramadol mixed with naproxen and ibuprofen because my head was starting to thump and my joints felt like they were seizing up.

I have a set pile of stuff in the drawer my bed – wallet, watch, mini-leatherman, pen and hardbacked notepad… and underneath all that an old, battered tin lined with bubble-wrap that I keep my Tramadol in. Why the bubble-wrap? Because I don't want to rattle when I walk like a goddamn junkie. Because I'm not a junkie. I'm an addict. There's a difference. We've talked about… You've got me sounding all defensive here. Forget it.

I grabbed all the things from my bedside drawer like I do every morning and I was out the door to survive the hellish, packed metro ride into the city not that much later than usual but I still arrived late enough to find Psychic at his desk, furiously typing away and looking exasperated already. The working day wasn't even an hour old.

"How'd we get on?" he asked.

"Good. Good. Bobby took the deal. Richard was put into police custody. Clients seemed as happy as they could be under the circumstances."

"It seems. The invoice was settled in the early hours by BACS and the money is in already!" he replied.

"Well, that's good too. That gives us breathing space for over Christmas, no?"

Psychic slowly turned in his seat and looked at me. There was sadness in his eyes, suggesting he didn't really want to say what he was about to say.

"No. You've forgotten we were behind one month on all the bills for here and there was money on the credit cards too. We're clean and even again now. But we're back down to zero in terms of…"

I interrupted him with an organ-rattling scream of "FUCK!" and flopped down into the sofa directly behind me. The cushions let out a shocked and enormous hiss upon my impact. I put my head in my hands.

"I had such grand plans!" I muttered, almost to myself.

"With the money?" asked Psychic.

"No. For the day. I'm absolutely shot, mate. I was going to go lie down, catch up on the sleep I missed last night and then me and you could go get a celebratory pint of Sprite down on the Quayside."

"And instead?"

"Instead I'm going to have to go on the beg!"

‘The Beg’, as Psychic and I called it, was something neither of us enjoyed. It was in fact something we both detested with every fibre of our beings. Which is why no matter how bad things got, we tried to avoid it like the plague. It was embarrassing. It was degrading. And Psychic always without fail managed to escape having to do it after his first experience by simply reminding me that he pretty much works for me voluntarily these days so I shouldn’t force him to do this. That’s a hands-down, mic-drop, award-winning argument ender right there isn’t it?

I keep a clean, pressed shirt and a tie on a hanger in the corner of the office for the extremely rare occasion in which I land a meeting with an important prospective client… or when I’ve got to do ‘The Beg’.

‘The Beg’ is simple enough. It’s just horrible.

There is a half a mile stretch in the centre of Newcastle city centre leading down onto the far corner of the Quayside in which pretty much all of the leading law firms have their office space. Mixed in amongst these leading law firms is smaller boutique offices and on the cheaper top floors above them are the scummy ambulance-chasers and ‘no-win-no-fee’ whiplash-obsessives.

Thirty to forty potential clients all stacked up neatly alongside each other for half a mile straight. And you’re probably thinking “So why haven’t you been hitting them up every bloody day if things are that bad?” and to you I say don’t be so hasty to judge me as lazy – I used to be at each of these guys’ doors every day at one point! But the continued rejection and pitiful looks started to break me down, if I’m honest. I pulled back. Now I keep it as a desperate last resort, going cap in hand… or business cards and leaflets in hand, I should say… to see if anyone has any trace work, process serving or defence investigations just, you know, casually lying around or something.

Today is that desperate last resort kind of day.

The idea that I can’t give my boys a good and comfortable Christmas alongside Jane’s earnings - because the money I had planned to put away has now been pulled out from underneath me – has pissed me off enough to knock the daily inertia out of me.

I asked Psychic to set me up with another coffee whilst walking into my office space. I pulled off my should-have-been-thrown-away-years-ago ‘retro’ Journey: Live In Concert t-shirt and threw it on my chair, begrudgingly pulling on in its place the starched white shirt and navy tie that is meant to scream “Professional Investigator: At Your Service” but realistically just says “You can put a ribbon on a turd but it’s still a turd!”.

I picked up a handful of business cards and stuffed them into my pockets and grabbed a pile of old, curling ‘not-been-updated-in-a-while-because-funds-haven’t-allowed-the-expenditure’ leaflets advertising what we do here at ‘Lehman’s Terms’. I headed out the door having downed a good few mouthfuls of coffee as I moved, angrily barking “See you in a few hours!”

“Don’t come back without a job, darling!” laughs Psychic.

I stuck my head back round the door and sourly shot back “Not helpful! Dickhead!”

It took me fifteen minutes to get up the street and across to the top of what we've nicknamed 'Solicitors Row'. The drizzle had changed to large thumping, intermittent rain that smashed like clumps into the pavement as I walked. There was yet another thirty to forty person 'outrage' campaign going on against Scheider Bank that morning – the news having broken just that week that 'fat-cats' had plundered it and practises had been conducted against banking regulations with the short version of the story ending with the bank going under and taking millions of people's savings, pensions and the like with it.

Whilst the thirty to forty odd people wasted their time hoisting placards and shouting at closed windows of which no one actually responsible for this crisis was sat behind, a hundred or so queued furiously to get through the doors and strip their accounts of every penny they could get out before the bank sank once and for all.

I pushed through the crowds, shaking my head at the angry chants as their sound violently smashed into the temples of my head. "What do they think?" I asked myself. "Those scumbag CEOs are going to hear them all the way over there in whichever sunny holiday home they're hiding out in and come rushing back to return every penny they stole? What's the point?"

I could feel my bones give off that familiar little ache that suggested I could maybe do with topping up the Tramadol kick. I only had a handful of pills less than three hours ago. Surely I couldn't be needing more already? I had my supply carefully measured out and set inside my 'safety' tin that stayed pushed down in my jeans pocket. If I took an extra kick now, it would ruin my daily lay-out! *Plus* I couldn't start trying to engage people professionally at the exact moment a top-up run of drugs kicked in and started chilling me out…

… I pushed on, driving my hands deeper into my pockets, curling my upper body into a tighter ball as I walked and crunching my jaw tight to brace against the pain in my head that was now starting to shoot down my spine with every hard, purposeful step that slammed into the wet surface beneath my feet.

I was eleven visits into 'The Beg' and already sickening of hearing myself politely ask if there was any court orders lined up ready to go out, whether anyone needed help with litigation enquiries or people tracing and could I leave a promotional leaflet…

Then I landed on Dreyfuss & Associates.

Dreyfuss & Associates were the 'big boys' in the city. They were a huge firm housed in a big, five storied, glass-fronted building down by the law courts who pretty much were the appointed legal representatives for every big contract, property deal and high value law-suit that went down in the city. They prided themselves on being "local solicitors with local knowledge for local people" and I guess they just hoped no one realised very few of their solicitors were Geordies and that all of them oscillated between the offices here and in London… and in Edinburgh… and in Manchester too.

Through the automatic rotating doors lay the gargantuan glass and metal foyer with what felt like a twenty-five mile walk across a cold, solid, gleamingly polished tiled floor to a three-person receptionist desk on the far side. Wrapped against the wall in a U-shape, branching out from behind the reception desks were a series of conference suites purposefully positioned there and always kept busy so visitors could see these expensively-attired solicitors 'in action' like going to the monkey enclosure at the zoo to watch them fart on their hands and sniff it.

I'd been here a couple of times doing 'The Beg' and it always amazed me that I got as far across the foyer floor as I did before they called security on me. Maybe the receptionists' concern as to whether I was some sort of homeless threat that had wandered in off the quayside was internally overwhelmed by a strong sense of pity? Who knows.

I was two or three sentences into my spiel when one of the conference room doors spun open and out walked Katherine Banks.

Katherine Banks was in her late twenties and kicking some serious arse as a solicitor on the rise. She was hand-picked by Dreyfuss & Associates' rivals straight out of university, built for greatness and poached directly by Dreyfuss & Associates themselves two years later.

Banks looked and dressed like someone who lived the dream of being able to afford expensive suits, frequent hair treatment and regular upgrades on her choice of watch.

I am always quick to get a measure on a person by the watch and shoes they wear. You can get a lot of information drawn off a person from assessing those things. In my line of work, you can certainly get a pretty accurate feel in a consultation as to whether they're going to be able to afford your services or not.

Katherine Banks was wearing a ladies Omega Constellation Quartz watch. A very simple silver band design that looked no different to the most basic of metal band watches you get out of your local Argos catalogue. The difference being that Banks' watch didn't sell for less than £2,280.00.

So if you want to get a measure on the types of fees this lady charges and the type of company she works for in the simplest possible terms, take note of this: She is not even thirty years of age yet and she's in a position that affords her the ability to wear a £2,280.00 watch that looks like a £29.50 supermarket knock-off. She didn't buy this watch to flaunt it on her wrist. It isn't ostentatious enough. She bought this because she could - so she did.

This lady will make senior partner before she's thirty-five. Just you watch.

Banks was the 'client contact lead' at Dreyfuss & Associates for a lot of heavy-hitters and pretty much every member of the Newcastle United footballer team. I'd done a few odd bits of process serving for her directly in the past. I'd also done a bit of cheating spouse surveillance work for her… but all that was a few years back.

It had been a while.

I was reminded of that by the fact that Banks pulled open that conference door and bounded towards me but the speed of her gait slowed and her eyes narrowed as she got closer to me.

"Lehman?"

I turned, smiled and nodded. "Katherine, how you doing?"

Banks feigned a smile in return. "Jesus, Jake! I don't mean to be cruel but are you living out of your surveillance van nowadays?"

I laughed. "Something like that!"

Banks cautiously put her hand to my elbow and her face flinched like she was going to catch some mutated virus from my jacket. She gently led me away from the reception desk and out of earshot of the clearly eavesdropping receptionists positioned there. She began to whisper.

"Listen, I'm sat here with one of my top clients. Like top, *top* tier. You know Margaret Jason of J&J Ltd, right?"

I didn't but I nodded anyway then thought better off it and started to shake my head.

Banks clocked this and continued to talk at the exact moment the head shake devolved into a shrug of sorts.

"Margaret and Matthew Jason run J&J Ltd. They are the biggest property developers in the North East and North West. They are… they are *big* money!"

"That can't be true!" I laughed. "No one has any money any more. Have you seen the news lately?"

"Oh trust me, they've got money! They've got nothing to worry about there. What they do have to worry about is their daughter!"

"Missing?" I asked.

"Dead! Have *you* seen the news lately?" Banks shot back.

"Their daughter's death made the news?"

"Jesus, Lehman! Their daughter was Stephanie Jason. As in Stephie Jay?"

I stood in silence.

"Stephie Jay? Stephie Jay from Snog On The Tyne? The model? Have you been on a night out in town in the last few years, man?" she gasped.

"I've been staying in a lot. You know? Washing my hair and doing skin treatments and stuff like that!"

"It shows!" smirked Banks. "Stephanie was Margaret and Matthew's only child. She killed herself about a month ago. It was all over the news. What is *wrong* with you? But anyway, forget that. I deal with all of the Jason's contracts, oversee all their deals and I basically make sure that their financial management people don't so much as look at a penny of the Jason's money without my oversight."

"Okay?"

"Margaret Jason is in that room right there!" motioned Banks. "She's here this morning because she wants me to assist her in starting an investigation into her daughter's death and what she thinks is the police's incompetence in handling it. The Jason's do not believe it is suicide."

"Okay!" I started to smile, because this sounded lucrative and boy did we need lucrative right about now.

"Don't get ahead of yourself!" Banks cautioned. "As her legal representative and guardian at the gate, I *don't* want Margaret to go ahead with this. I think it's a fool's errand. I think it will go nowhere and I think it will delay both her and Matthew's ability to process what's happened and mourn properly. What they don't need right now is false hope."

"And spending money you'd rather went on your fees, right?"

"Don't do that, Jake! Don't make me regret the offer I'm about to make."

I fell silent.

"I'm going to introduce you to Margaret now, okay?" Banks said. "I'm going to let her explain her needs to you and then I want you to go through some exaggerated pitfalls with her, generally talk her out of pursuing this and help me shut this down."

"Why do you want this shut down? What does it matter to you if they want this to help them with closure? They've got the money to comfortably handle this, right?" I replied.

Banks took a step back. She went to put her hands on her hips, considered this to be confrontational and went with her arms half-heartedly crossed over her chest instead. She took a breath.

"I care about the Jason's. I've represented them for a long time. I even handled all of Stephanie's contracts when she got famous. So I'll reiterate - I don't want them to go ahead with this. I think it will go nowhere and what they don't need right now is false hope! I say this as their friend and their solicitor!"

"So… you want me to go in there… and talk someone out of giving me work… when I'm specifically here begging for work? What is in this for me?"

"Two hundred pounds!" Banks immediately shot back.

"Two hundred quid? Forget it."

"What about we locked you in on some sort of retainer too? You know, twenty hours of litigation support a month for… I don't know…"

"A thousand a month?" I offered.

"Fuck that!" gasped Banks before realising this was both somewhat unprofessional and had also echoed around the foyer. "Five hundred?" she shot back in a whisper.

"Five hundred for twenty hours. I want it locked in with the partners before I leave today too!"

Banks stopped. Her hands slid to her hips as she looked up to the top floor of the building, where clearly the decision-makers of the firm were stationed.

"What if I can't lock that in today? That'll take time to…"

"Then I'll put a trace out for Mr and Mrs Jason's home address, go to it, tell them I've reconsidered and…"

"Okay! Okay! Okay!" spat Banks. "Five hundred for twenty hours work a month. For *one year*. No mileage inclusions. No expense account. And in return you go and close this off for me in…"

She checked her watch.

"… Forty five minutes or less?"

"Deal!" I offered her my hand.

She looked down on at it then slowly took it and gripped it tight. "You need to get some sleep, Lehman!"

She then pulled on my hand and led me off towards the conference room.

I pulled my tie up tighter around my neck, smoothed down my shirt and adjusted my posture to a position that didn't scream 'broken-up old fuck' as I strode into the room with a confidence that I didn't have, rolling the numbers in my head as I walked behind Banks.

Yes, this was an affluent potential client but there was a risk this could go somewhere or nowhere. I could make my average daily rate of about a hundred-and-eighty and that might last a few days or it could last weeks and months.

It was a punt. I wouldn't know what I was looking at until I'd already committed to taking the job and starting to discuss budgets. Rich people can often be the most frugal. That's what makes them rich. What price was this lady willing to put on having her daughter's suicide re-investigated?

But a guaranteed five hundred a month? For twelve months?

That was a six thousand pound secured run into the business. It more than covered our low overheads. It meant that every single penny 'Lehman's Terms' brought in over that year went directly into mine and Psychic's pockets.

Six thousand was *nothing* to a business like Dreyfuss & Associates.

It was everything to me.

Simply because it was six thousand that the business didn't have currently.

That was what I was thinking about so hard that I missed Banks' introduction of me and Margaret Jason was already on her feet on the other side of the conference table, extending out her hand for me to shake.

Her rose gold and stainless steel bracelet watch was purposefully fit loose to jangle on her wrist, possibly to draw a person's eye line to it – so that they would catch that it was a Raymond Weil Geneve Freelancer, which retailed at £1,795 on its release and had now aged into being a 'collector's piece' probably worth double that now!

Margaret Jason's handshake was soft but purposeful. She was in her late fifties, early sixties maybe but she was wearing it well. Her entire look screamed of someone who'd done well enough in business to now enjoy the luxury of gym workouts and sauna sessions before starting her day. She was a beautiful woman who age seemed to be treating very favourably.

"… I was just telling Mrs Jason that I would give you a call when you appeared right in front of us in the foyer!" lied Banks. "Jake Lehman runs the best private investigation company in Newcastle. I use him frequently. He's a God send."

I let the broadest, fakest smile break across my face as I stared hard at Banks.

"It feels like I'm never out of the place sometimes!" I said through my grin.

Banks smiled back hard and let out a short, fake laugh.

"I was just giving Jake a brief rundown of…"

"Thanks Katherine," Margaret Jason cut in. "Is it okay if I take it from here?"

Margaret's voice trembled. Her physical appearance reflected a confidence that was not matched by the manner in which she spoke. She seemed nervous, almost like she was about to burst into tears any second.

Katherine gently nodded and Margaret cleared her throat.

"Mr Lehman, four weeks and five days ago my daughter Stephanie was found dead in a warehouse in Hebburn. She was twenty-four. The police and coroner state that she hung herself. Her death has been classified as a suicide despite there being nothing in Stephanie's life to suggest she would do that or why she had any need to or..."

Margaret's voice started to break.

"... There was no note. There was nothing in her life in the lead up to her death that suggested she was troubled. We were laughing and joking with each other literally the same day she died. I have so many questions, Mr Lehman..."

"Please, call me Jake!" I said softly.

"Thank you, Jake. I have so many questions. The police won't answer them. The coroner's office say their report is final... Stephanie had never been to Hebburn in her life. There's no rhyme or reason as to why she would suddenly go and kill herself there. And if there is a reason I need to know. I *need* to."

"Katherine mentioned that Stephanie was famous in some capacity?"

"Yes," replied Margaret. "She was on a reality TV show a while back called Snog On The Tyne. Have you heard of it?"

I shook my head.

"It's not mine or my husband's cup of tea, frankly. We were aghast that she went on it and didn't continue with the career her degree would've afforded her. But she did very well out of it. She became a model and some sort of... I don't know what it is exactly... a social media influencer, they call it. She was very popular, very loved and..."

The tears started to fall.

"... They didn't investigate her death" Margaret sobbed. "They had it all wrapped up and written off in a week. If *that*."

Margaret looked to Banks who nodded solemnly and supportively.

"My daughter was popular and loved. She was designing things and setting up charities and then she was gone and everyone has moved on within a month like she never existed."

My mouth started to move. "I'm sorry." I whispered.

Margaret nodded.

"I need someone to look into her death. I need someone to answer the questions my husband and I have. Well, I say my husband... This has broken Matthew. He's not left the house since she died. He just drinks and stares out into our garden. I'll bc amazed if he survives the year, if I'm honest."

She began to sob heavily.

Katherine got up and went and put her arm around her. Whilst Margaret composed herself, Katherine shot me a glance from behind her head. Her teeth gritted and her mouth widened. She silently shaped the word "SPEAK!" at me.

My mouth opened but nothing came out immediately.

"You see…" I started. "The thing is…"

Margaret looked up and wiped her eyes dry. She cleared her throat once more and recomposed herself.

"I have no one left to turn to Jake. The police won't return my calls. The coroner has ceased communication. We've heard nothing from our requests for an independent review. Katherine here only meets with me now because it's financially beneficial to keep me sweet…"

"Oh no, Margaret! Not at all!" Banks quickly squealed in shock.

"Please Katherine! I'm not daft! Come on now!" replied Margaret swiftly.

I was beginning to like Margaret even more.

"All I'm asking is for someone to spend a few hours with me, Jake!" Margaret said. "I will pay for their time just to listen to me… just to walk around Stephanie's flat with me and hear what my concerns are. Then make a judgement on whether I have a case or whether I'm just a grief stricken old fool."

She let out a big, deep, pained breath.

"I'm going to put my trust in you Jake. I'm going to put my trust in you because I don't have anyone else to put my trust in. I'm going to ask for your help. I have no idea whether you're good at what you do, whether you're a honest man. But I really don't know who else I can look to help me…"

I wanted to be good again.

I wanted to be an honest man again.

"Will you give me a few hours of your time?" Margaret asked.

Banks' look got harder and more fierce.

My head was counting the pounds that came with a one year fixed minor retainer from just smiling politely and stepping the fuck away from this but my voice was already uttering the words "I guess I could walk things through with you…"

Margaret smiled as best she could. "What is your daily rate, Jake? What is it you charge?"

"Well…" I started before stumbling. "There's a lot of different… erm… complicated factors, you see. And… there's…"

"Rough ballpark figure – what's your daily rate?" replied Margaret, the confidence in her voice forming back up and round on itself.

I was a scrapper of a PI. I was at the bottom of the rung. I knew this. I'd be lucky if I was able to clear a hundred and fifty quid on a good day for ten hours work. So I shot for the sky with all the misbegotten, half-baked, underselling confidence of a journeyman boxer who didn't know his worth.

"I charge… a hundred and seventy five a day, basic!" I said with a complete absence of salesmanship.

Margaret lent forward in her seat and met my eye line. "If you visit my daughter's flat and listen to me for one hour tomorrow I will pay you one hundred and seventy five pounds for your time…"

She put out her hand.

It hung there.

Banks stood behind Margaret. Her face was curling into a grimace. She began to shake her head and widen her eyes once more.

I don't know why. I can't explain it exactly but for the first time in far too long my head cleared of pain, the veins in my temples seemed to relax and I took hold of Margaret's hand.

It suddenly dawned on me that this wasn't about the money.

This felt to me like it was about the pain in Margaret Jason's eyes.

There was something else building in my gut here that I couldn't quite explain.

She could've rang around and had the big firm down the road with the state of their art surveillance vehicles and trumped up invoices take her on as a client. There was never any normal version of this situation in which I should've and could've been able to get in the room and get an opportunity with a client akin to Margaret Jason.

Yet here I was.

A broken pill-popper with Sherlockian delusions of grandeur, dreaming of a second chance at being worth something again standing in front of a highly successful business woman wrecked with grief who was asking *me* to trust *her*.

As the words left my mouth I realised that the money wasn't what was making me say what I said. It was something else entirely.

It would just be a few weeks before I realised exactly what it was.

I took hold of her hand and said "What time would you like to meet tomorrow?"

## [5]

## or

## "Hopefully this will intrigue you…"

Once I got home that night and the kids were in bed, I decided to do something unusual – I decided to forget all the bullshit lies about needing to clear some paperwork upstairs when really I just wanted to pop a couple of pills and zone out, pretending I was doing something that earned money… and instead I decided to put my actions ahead of whining about the state of my marriage.

I sat down with Jane and asked her if I could tell her about my day. She paused what she was watching, put down her phone and smiled warmly.

"Please!" she said.

Good start, right?

I told her all about getting out there on 'Solicitors Row' and doing 'The Beg' and she nodded and intermittently said "Good!" in the way that when Jane does it, it feels supportive and intended as encouraging but if someone else does it it'd be obnoxious and patronising. I told her about my visit to Dreyfuss & Associates and landing some face to face time with one half of J&J Ltd. She kind of shrugged at their mention exactly as I thought she would.

"They're the parents of Stephanie Jason?" I offered.

Jane shrugged some more.

"She went by the name Stephie Jay?"

Jane's face lit up.

"The party girl!" Jane gasped.

"I don't know what that means?" I replied.

"Oh, you'd have hated her!" Jane salaciously said, leaning forward in the seat towards me. "She was on that show that I used to watch and you hated – the one where the lads and lasses had to team up for drinking games and they all just ended up essentially shagging each other on TV and what not?"

"It sounds awful but go on."

She laughed. I laughed. It was nice.

"She was on that show and then she did the reality TV rounds but she was big up here for all her modelling and Instagram stuff. She was like a Kardashian. But a Geordie version, you know? Big ego, small pond. Something like that!" Jane paused. "She killed herself though, right? A couple of weeks ago or something?"

"A month!" I clarified. "Her mum doesn't think it's legit though. She wants an independent set of eyes to look things over."

"Are you going to take it?" Jane asked.

I explained about my meeting with Margaret Jason the following morning and how Katherine Banks didn't want me to take it but I felt drawn to at least trying to help in some capacity to find closure for the parents.

"Obviously be careful not to exploit their grief, Jake. Which I would never assume you would anyway. But… you know… this could be good for you. Hanging around with a better breed of clientele, don't you think?"

Jane leant forward and ran her fingers through my hair whilst taking the coffee cup from my hand. She smiled. "Go get an early night. You need it."

I nodded and got up from the sofa. Half way across the room I turned and looked back at Jane. She caught me looking and smiled back before her face gave way to inquisitiveness.

"You okay?" she said.

"Yeah. Are you okay?"

Jane nodded, got up from the sofa and walked across to me. She kissed me softly on the mouth and smiled again. "I am… And thank you for remembering to ask."

I arrived the next morning outside the Baltic Quay apartments, across the Millennium Bridge and just down from The Baltic Centre For Contemporary Art. I was early and already wired so found myself stuck in the position of a) knowing that slipping off for another coffee would be a terrible idea, b) not being able to smoke because I'd been off them for over ten years now and c) well, I'm a recovering alcoholic so killing time on my own in any bar I could find open was a terrible idea.

It was cold but not biting to the point of discomfort on par with when I was out in the early hours a few days back. So I took myself down onto the Gateshead side of the quay and looked out, taking some time with my thoughts and looking across to the mouth of the Tyne itself on my right.

I was deep in thought about Jane and I, and how just twenty odd minutes together shooting the shit last night added more warmth to our marriage than the last twenty months. I saw something in her eyes as she talked with me that suggested maybe she wasn't as burnt out on me as I was telling myself. Then I asked myself the hard question: "Is what's killing your marriage in the long term the lies you hide or do you hide them because you know that the truth would kill it immediately?"

I didn't get a chance to start processing the answers to that because I felt a tap on the shoulder and found Margaret Jason standing behind me. She looked stylish yet suitably wrapped against the cold.

There was a Michelle Pfeiffer type quality to Margaret.

Like, you know she was a formidable stunning beauty in her youth which time usually takes a delight in smashing to pieces by adding weight and loosening up skins and all that bullshit. But time can't seem to get its claws dug into Michelle Pfeiffer. She remains as quintessentially fuckable in her sixties as she did in her twenties.

Margaret Jason had that fuckable older lady Pfeiffer vibe going on too. I am making a presumption that like Pfeiffer she was a beautiful young woman who'd aged well. I mean, it's hardly likely that she was a total troglodyte and then blossomed into a sexy sophisticated woman at sixty or something, is it?

Margaret smiled at me and I made a mental note even as a loyally married man to take out my list of 'gorgeous women that are still sexy the more they age' that I keep stored in amongst the clutter in the back of my brain and add her to it alongside Susan Sarandon, Halle Berry, Julia Louis-Dreyfuss, Sharon Stone, Elle Macpherson, Mary Steenburgen, Shania Twain, Diane Lane, Elisabeth Shue and of course Judy Judy... And if you're looking at that list right there and thinking "That's a pretty bloody extensive list you've got going, Jake. Maybe you've spent too long thinking about this?" To you I say "Shit like this deserves to be taken seriously!" and also "Do you have ANY idea how slowly time ticks when you're doing surveillance alone or waiting for a job to come in?"

Margaret pointed to the mouth of the Tyne.

"Beautiful isn't it?" she said.

I nodded.

If Jane had left me already I'd have gone with adding "But not as beautiful as you!" on the end because... I'm kidding. Of course I'm kidding. I'm a mess. I'm not a sleazy mess.

Margaret nervously filled the silence some more. "I think a lot of people take it for granted and a lot of people forget it's there. When we talk about the quayside everyone just immediately assumes bars and restaurants, you know? But the lip up there on the North side is a fantastic spot with great views. We bought and developed a lot of property up there for that reason."

I nodded some more.

"Sorry," she laughed. "You're going to think I'm trying to sell you a property. God, no. I've not done that directly in many a year... I don't want to take up anymore of your time then what we agreed."

"It's okay. I'm all for a bit of small talk, I'm just terrible at it." I replied.

She smiled. "Let's head in."

'Stephie Jay' was the woman Stephanie Jason became whenever she finished visiting her parents on a twice weekly basis. To them, she was Stephanie. To the rest of the region and anyone with an internet connection she was Stephie – the gorgeous blonde party girl who dripped perfection.

Stephie lived on the top floor of the Baltic Quay block, in a two bedroomed apartment located on the very far corner which meant her balcony provided her with exquisite views up the Tyne right from the mouth all the way until it bent out of sight over in Gateshead.

I noticed Margaret used a key fob to open the external door before leading us both through the foyer and to one of two communal lifts which again required a key fob or a code in order to access it. Margaret used the key fob once more and took us both in the lift to the top floor. As the lift ascended, Margaret spoke. She talked about how she and Matthew were knocked out of bed in the early hours of the morning on Sunday the ninth of November to be informed that Stephie had been found dead. She talked warmly of the uniformed officers that sat with them after breaking the news but who could tell them nothing really.

She continued talking as the elevator pinged at the top floor. We stepped out and Margaret gently guided me to the right and straight ahead to an apartment door in the far corner. She got to the point in her recounting of the events of that night where she described her and Matthew going to view Stephie's body and the pain of the memory overwhelmed her. She gripped the frame of the door hard and began to sob.

I put my hand on her shoulder and gently whispered for her to take her time.

She composed herself ever so slightly and turned to look at me. "Do you know what words make me feel physical just to hear them grouped together now?" she asked.

I softly shook my head.

"It can't be!" she replied. "Over and over again I said them, shouted them, screamed them, reiterated them to anyone and everyone. To the police that night...To the so-called investigating officers who blew us off within a day...To the coroner's office who told us there'd be no inquest. I hear those words now or I remember them and I retch."

"Explain the timeframe of the investigation into Stephie's death being closed off?" I asked.

"What 'investigation'?" spat Margaret, her eyes lighting up with anger. "They told us it was being handed over to the coroner for consideration before we'd even finished confirming that was her on the slab. They said there was nothing suspicious about the scene or how she was found. They hadn't spoken to us or asked us anything about her mindset leading up to her death. They hadn't gone and looked at her home or questioned any of her friends. They couldn't tell us where she'd been or who she'd been with leading up to her death. We rang them for two days straight, begging them for answers and asking why it wasn't being looked into. We just kept getting told there was nothing suspicious and that this is what would be concluded in their report and it was for the coroner to decide otherwise."

"Who was telling you this?" I said.

"Some man called Tidyman. DC Tidyman. He came out to the house about four days after Stephanie had died. He didn't realise her car had been released and cleared after being moved from the scene and had been brought to our place. He wanted to check it over. We let him and then when he was finished that's when he said that he'd cleared all his lines of enquiry and he'd be concluding the report as suicide. He said that the coroner would decide here on out if they thought differently... Then the coroner backed them. It was a joke. The coroner concluded no further enquiries needed to be made. The bitch down at their offices couldn't even tell us if Stephie had alcohol or drugs in her system. That's how glossed over this whole thing was. Like, right, she's dead, move on, next!"

"He checked the car over? Did he find anything or take anything away? What did he say he was looking in the car for?" I asked.

Margaret shook her head. "He didn't take anything away that we saw. He turned the car on, he pressed through her navigational system and dashboard screen. I think he was trying to see what routes she'd driven but it was busted and didn't work. I remember he said that and we said that nothing stayed functioning in Stephanie's hands for long and that she was always like that. He didn't seem particularly taken by anything with the car. I think it was just a box ticking exercise for him."

"What about the coroner? Have you contested this coroner's decision?"

"Oh yes." Margaret sighed, now leaning hard against the door it felt obvious she wanted to do anything possible to avoid opening. "We sought legal advice from Katherine at Dreyfuss & Associates. She recommended we put in a Section 13 complaint or review or whatever it's called under the Coroner's Act. That went nowhere almost immediately. We were shocked at how fast that got thrown back at us. We got told we couldn't go to the Judicial Conduct Investigations Office about the coroner's decision but we could about her personal conduct, so we tried going down that avenue because... well... I thought she was a bitch, as I said."

I gently smiled. "I'd have thought that might work."

"It didn't. It went nowhere. We wrote letters and made phone-calls to the Chief Constable of the police..."

"Hadenbury?" I clarified.

"Yes. That guy. His office wrote back and blew us off." She said.

"What next?"

"You're what's next? We had a month's worth of rejection which amazed us because we thought all of these appeals and complaints would take time or there'd be a queue or something but no... We were getting stonewalled almost immediately from being afforded any options. It shocked us greatly, as I said. So we went to Katherine and said we wanted her help in looking into this privately and getting some answers without police support and all that, you know? ... And you're what fell into our laps when she shook the tree!"

She attempted to smile.

"Ok." She said. "Enough procrastinating..."

Margaret unlocked the door and took a deep breath. She forced a smile upon her face and stepped into the apartment as if she was going to meet with Stephie herself. I walked in behind her. She stopped just inside the front door after closing it behind me.

"Stephanie owned this apartment outright. She bought it with all the money that came from Snog On The Tyne and her endorsements. How many twenty-four year olds can say that?"

"So... Snog On The Tyne?" I asked.

"Awful show!" muttered Margaret. "*Awful.* We demanded she didn't do it. And of course that just made her want to do it more! I can't understand why anyone would watch it."

"My wife did."

Margaret smiled weakly. "You're married? That's nice. Do you have children?"

"I do. Yes, two wonderful boys."

"How lovely."

Margaret took another deep breath and finally moved off away from the front door and down the corridor. I cautiously followed, giving her the space to move and take me where she wanted us to go.

The flat was beautifully decorated in cream and hard wood as far as the eye could see. Either this girl had a keen eye that bellied her twenty-four years of age or she'd had an interior decorator come in and set this all up for her. The flat was clean and minimalist in its set-up but there were still corners of the room stacked with the latest tech gear and a huge flat screen television.

Stephie had one room set up as her bedroom with nothing more than a bed, a night stand and a large mirror panel that ran across one entire wall of the room. Billowing curtains led out onto the balcony that overlooked the Tyne and wound back around to a second entrance door to the apartment from the living area.

The second room was set up almost in three areas definitive to their intent.

On the far left of the room the entire wall was set up like a giant open wardrobe with racks upon racks of clothing, shoes and bags that all seemed to be hung and filed in a manner very specific to Stephie herself. Across from this was a treadmill, cross-trainer and sets of weights none of which had the sort of cobwebs on them that lay across the exercise equipment in my garage at home. And finally in the far corner of the room was a large dresser with a huge vanity mirror positioned on it and mounds upon mounds of make-up and make-up utensils stacked around the surface.

Where there were things hung on the walls as I was led around the flat they were framed or canvassed professional photographs of Stephie as part of her modelling career or Stephie on night's out with people who were very clearly celebrities in this day and age but who meant nothing to me. I stopped giving a shit about famous people when it turned out that Bruce Willis was an utter cock… That broke my heart, man.

Without realising it I'd clearly come to a stop in front of one particular picture of Stephie and become more drawn to it than I realised because Margaret turned to go into another room, realised I wasn't behind her directly and came back to stand with me. I had no idea how long she'd been stood with me when I heard her very softly say "She really was beautiful wasn't she?"

"Extremely!" I found myself saying, somewhat trance like.

Because Stephie or Stephanie in whatever form you wanted to put her really was an *exceptionally* beautiful young girl. Her figure was perfectly toned and bronzed in all the ways you would expect from someone who was selling themselves physically as a model. Her blonde hair was perfectly kept and blown out in a seventies Farrah Fawcett style that seemed to be on the way back and, for children of the 80s like me, made my penis feel funny at the provocation of memories of syndicated re-runs of early episodes of Charlie's Angels and repeated viewings of Saturn 3 and The Cannonball Run. She had the most perfect green eyes with just a hint of brown but her smile had been tainted by lip injections and what looked like repeated whitening treatments on her teeth. It said a lot though that not even such alterations could truly hide the fact that behind all that lay the foundations of a natural, beautiful, *perfect* smile.

I guess you've picked up on it now, right?

Stephanie Jason's Stephie Jay was, if judged on the photographs that hung around her home, positively perfect.

There were shades of Stephie in Margaret.

You could see that in the eyes and smile. Age had tried to dull it back but you could definitely see Stephie was her mother's child.

"I can see a lot of you in her!" I said.

I've probably led you to believe that I was hitting on her here because of the whole 'sexy older lady' tangent I went off on earlier. But I wasn't.

Honestly.

Stephie really did have a lot of her mother about her, judging from this photo.

"Oh, stop it. I should be so lucky." She laughed. "She's got my eyes, maybe… Thankfully she's got her dad's head for business!"

It would take a special sort of evil bastard to correct a grieving mother on the tense in which she spoke about her dead daughter. I have many a failing as a man. I'm not quite at the 'evil bastard' level.

"How is your husband?" I gently enquired.

"Oh this has killed him, really." Margaret said in an almost painful whisper. "She was our everything but she was absolutely daddy's girl. He adored her and he's essentially stopped living without her. I manage to lead him upstairs to a bath every now and again and I get away with sliding a plate of food in front of him every other day. But essentially he sits in a chair in our conservatory and drip feeds himself bourbon all day whilst staring into our garden. I can't get him to speak. I can't get him to leave the house…"

Margaret stopped, buried her face into her hands and let out a big painful gasp of air that had the aura of a dulled and silent scream. She pulled her head back and ran her fingers through her hair, pulling herself back into a forced upright position.

"I'm in a living nightmare!" she said, almost to herself before turning and walking on around the flat. "There's many a young person out there right now with not a clue where their next pound is coming from or how much longer they are going to be able to afford their rent." Margaret continued. "That wasn't Stephanie. Stephanie had money. She was well looked after by us. She had a trust fund that had just come into effect. But she never touched it because she never needed to. She was doing really well as a model and whatever an influencer is."

"It's someone who is paid to post about things on social media in order to entice their followers to buy the thing – clothes, make-up, that sort of thing." I said.

Margaret looked at me with a quizzical expression.

"I looked it up since we last spoke!" I smiled.

Margaret returned my smile and continued.

"What I'm saying is Stephanie had money. She was doing very well for herself. She'd just got into designing and she'd got a patent on this bag thing she was working on. If anyone is going to say she killed herself because of money woes than I cannot and will not believe that. We're happy to open up her accounts to scrutiny. She was not in debt."

I nodded whilst pulling my notebook from my pocket and began to scribble a few key words down of what Margaret was saying. Seeing me do this seemed to give Margaret hope. I saw her face start to relax as I wrote.

"Boyfriends?" I asked.

"She was never short of offers and attention." Margaret replied. "It had been a while since her last long term relationship. Up here she seemed to have an attitude that men were beneath her and just wanted to brag they'd bedded Stephie Jay, you know?"

I could see the appeal in such a victory.

"Down in London though? Whenever she was there on business or doing some stupid show, she always ended up in my magazines as being touted like she was in a relationship with some other reality TV numpty!"

I let out a little chuckle.

"She'd been on a couple of double-dates with a lad called Max who plays football for Newcastle but… that was nothing. It could've been further down the line. Who knows?"

I noted down 'Max'.

"Answer me this, Jake. We've been out and stood on that balcony over there, right?" she said. "That's quite an almighty jump isn't it? If you cleared ten to fifteen feet off the railing you'd hit the Tyne itself. Stephanie wasn't *that* athletic. So she'd have been secure in the knowledge that one big leap would have taken her straight down onto the railings below. And if she'd missed them she'd have surely met the concrete."

"That's all probably correct." I replied.

"So why would she need to take herself out to some god-awful warehouse in the back-ends of Hebburn in order to do it? She's never even bloody been to Hebburn as far as I know. She's been everywhere else in the world, getting photographed. She's never been to bloody Hebburn."

Margaret could feel something rising that she didn't want unleashed. I could see that. She took a step back, almost from herself, and started to take deep breathes.

A few seconds passed before she spoke again.

"She couldn't tie her shoes properly, could my Steph!" laughed Margaret. "She certainly wasn't tying noose knots in the pitch black strong enough to snap her neck and crush her wind-pipe, I can tell you that much - but that's as much as I can tell you because it's just about all the coroner would tell us!"

I quickly noted the words 'Hebburn', 'warehouse', 'neck injuries' in the notebook. As I did Margaret began to talk about how Stephie was loved by everyone and that there were whole hashtags on social media that referred to her as the "Queen of Newcastle". Apparently Stephie was idolised because she was starting to use her physicality to lead the charge on getting people to pay more attention to what women her age wanted and were asking for – better opportunities, equality and so on.

"She was my little warrior!" said Margaret, her voice breaking beneath the words.

As Margaret composed herself, my eyes were drawn to a small unit placed against the wall in the living room. There was a phone charging station, a framed photo of Stephie with her parents, a small ceramic pot with some keys in and beneath that was a receipt that sat atop a hard-backed A4 diary filled with pieces of paper and colourful leaflets.

I picked up the receipt. It was for some engraving that Stephie had paid to be completed. It wasn't torn down the right side which normally denoted that it had been picked back up. I looked at the date on which she'd commissioned the engraving.

"Stephie... Sorry, Stephanie died on the eighth, is that correct?" I asked.

"It's believed in the late hours of the eighth into the very early hours of the ninth, yes. She was found on the ninth but..."

Margaret stopped herself.

I simply nodded and then placed a hand on her shoulder. We stood in silence for a few seconds. I broke it by pointing at the hard-backed diary on the unit.

"May I?"

"Please!" Margaret responded, picking up the diary and handing it to me.

Margaret then walked over to the sofa and sat down. I joined her on the adjacent single seat and the first thing that fell from the diary was a coloured piece of paper. I caught it as it dropped and turned it over in my hand.

It was a leaflet advertising Paradox, a nightclub over on Moseley Street in town. There was a big photo of Stephie Jay emblazoned across it with the words "Meet The Queen" in horrendously garish lettering above her head. It had bubbles around the sides with text in each one listing her reality TV 'credentials' and at the bottom all the information about where, what time, what day and offers on drinks.

The date of the eighth stood out to me once more.

The time too.

Ten o'clock that night doors were opening with a "live appearance and beat selection from Stephie herself, eleven o'clock onwards"... Whatever the fuck a 'beat selection' was!

Surely Stephie can't have actually gone to this, right? Because if she did she nipped off after forty-odd minutes or so in order to get herself across the river and gun it down to Hebburn in order to kill herself?

Margaret took the leaflet from my hand and started to look at it for herself. I made more notes then flicked the diary open. I checked enough pages on my way to the eighth and ninth to be able to see she seemed to make a lot of commitments and appeared as popular as her mother suggested.

Then I landed on the page for the eighth.

The day Stephie died.

The appearance at Paradox had been listed. She'd written the word *"Alia??"* next to all the details... but then a wavy scribble crossed it all out and above all of it, in big capital letters, was *"9pm. 'Toccare'!!"* instead.

"Does Alia mean anything to you?" I asked.

"That's Stephanie's best friend." replied Margaret. "I can get you her contact details if you'd like to speak to her?"

I nodded my head. "That'd be great, yes please. What about 'toccare'? Does that mean anything?"

"To care?" clarified Margaret.

"T-O-C-C-A-R-E!"

Margaret took a few seconds. She looked at the floor. She looked around the room. She eventually shook her head at the exact moment the door knocked. Margaret was startled by the sound. She excused herself and left to answer the door.

I used the time to write down "9pm" "Eighth" and "Toccare" (underlined twice) then continued to flick through the diary in front of me whilst listening to the conversation at the door between Margaret and the visitor.

"I saw you come in with a gentleman... I didn't want to disturb you... I took this package in for Stephie a few weeks back now... I've been at a loss as to what to do with it... I'm so sorry for your loss... She was a lovely girl..."

I heard the door slam and Margaret returned to the room carrying a shoebox-sized cardboard box with Amazon Prime tape wrapped around it, sealing its edges and flaps shut.

"It was Stephanie's neighbour. She'd took a package in for her." Margaret confirmed.

Margaret looked at me, then at the package.

I looked at the package, then at Margaret.

Margaret started pulling at the tape with her bare hands and had the box open in a matter of seconds. She lifted up the packing paper, took one look at the contents and tears started to forcefully pour down her face.

Margaret sunk back in the chair. I leant over and looked at what was inside.

It was a garden gnome, dressed up to look like Santa Claus.

"This was a gift for me." Margaret explained through her tears. "She hated my Santa gnome and made fun of it all the time. We were out for lunch a couple of weeks before she died, talking about Christmas plans and traditions and all that. She started taking the mick about when I was getting my Santa gnome out and I said I was really upset because the dogs broke it after getting into the storage boxes in the shed and..."

Margaret started to sob hard. The hardest I had seen her cry yet.

"It's okay..." I stupidly said.

"It's not!" she cried. "It's a living fucking *nightmare*."

I reached over and took the box off her knee. I could see the paper invoice folded up inside the box, pushed in alongside the ugly looking Santa gnome. I pulled it out and unfolded it. I didn't realise I had audibly let out a suspicious hum but I must have done because Margaret pulled her head up slowly, aggressively wiped away her tears and said "What? What does 'Hmmmm' mean?"

"Well," I began. "This was ordered the day of her death too. With next day delivery selected. Then there's the engraving. That was put in on the same day too. And paid for in advance. That doesn't seem like the behaviour of someone who was going to kill themselves that night, does it? Ordering parcels you know you're never going to receive, booking in engraving you know you're never going to pick up."

Margaret slowly started to nod her head in agreement.

I pushed on. "… And she cancelled an event at Paradox the night she died to attend something to do with 'Toccare' at 9pm, two to three hours before her death, with her best friend? What's the best friend said in all of this?"

"We've not heard from Alia since Stephanie died. She sent some lovely flowers to the funeral though she didn't come herself. We're told she's as broken by all of this as we are. They were very close, after all…"

Margaret took a breath and slowed the anger that was clearly billowing up from the next line of thought.

"… Look, I'm sorry to bang on about this but I want you to understand just exactly why you've actually been brought in on this - the police have considered none of this because they've not looked at any of this. They had it closed off as a straight suicide within a day or so. They've never visited this apartment, for Christ's sake. The coroner has been worse than useless. We're shouting at the top of our voice that this isn't right and it doesn't make sense and no one can hear a word."

It felt bizarre to me that the police hadn't checked out the deceased's apartment once identified. It felt even more bizarre that they'd made no enquiries into her movements in the lead up to her death.

Maybe Margaret had it wrong? I didn't have the highest opinion of the police and I say this as someone who used to be one but that seemed crazily inept. As I was thinking this, Margaret lent forward and tipped her head to meet my gaze whilst I stared down at the diary and leaflets in front of me. She pulled out an unsealed envelope containing bank notes and thrust it into my hand.

"This is for your time today, as agreed!" she said. "I'll raise your daily rate to two-hundred and fifty pounds plus expenses if you take on my case, Jake."

I folded the envelope and pushed it into the inside pocket of my jacket pocket.

I nodded my head and took hold of her hand.

We shook hands.

She smiled.

I never said that I'd already decided I was taking her case before I'd popped my first Tramadol and left the house that very morning.

All the meeting today had done was reinforce I had good starting grounds for having pre-emptively made the decision.

## [6]

or

"The Ballad of Stephie Jay."

***S****tephanie Melinda Jason was born at 0443hrs on the fourth of August 1996 to Margaret and Matthew Jason. She would be their only child. They both agreed they liked the name Stephanie. Melinda was something Matthew fought for as a middle-name and Margaret went along with begrudgingly; Matthew wanting to pay 'tribute' to his Aunty Melinda who helped them get their business off the ground in the early 1990s via a donation of a large sum of money.*

*Margaret wanted more children. Matthew was open to more too though it didn't matter as much to him as it did to Margaret. But life got in the way and it seemed it just was not meant to be. The more their business grew the bigger a distraction and an obstacle it became to expanding their own family.*

*Margaret and Matthew started J&J Ltd in the early nineties, with Aunty Melinda's money, as a letting agency in the West end of Newcastle. They first started to expand their offices around the city before getting into property development and as that become more and more successful they dropped the letting side of the business entirely.*

*By the time Stephanie was four years of age, her parents were millionaires and J&J Ltd was one of the most highly regarded property development firms across the whole of the North East, North West and Scottish borders. They were continually courted to get into the London scene but repeatedly resisted the offers. It didn't appeal to Margaret at all, Matthew was put off by the Russian oligarchs they'd met with and it all carried far greater a risk than either of them were comfortable with.*

*Their development portfolio expanded just nicely in the ways Margaret and Matthew wanted it to, affording them their £1.1 million home on 'Millionaires Row' in Smallburn, near Ponteland, with the owner of Newcastle United neighboured to their left and British actor Robson Green's 'city' home to their right. On top of that there was the beautiful £875,000 holiday cottage in Millom that they kept for weekend breaks and for when they were in the Lake District overseeing their latest developments in Seascale and Ulverston. Not to mention the three-storied villa they owned in La Savina, Formentera, with its own built-in port for boat-rides over to Ibiza whenever the mood took them.*

*The Jason's most important and (to them) worthwhile expenditure was the £6,300 per term they spent for Stephanie to attend Accrington Academy, a prestigious private school up in Northumberland. It was there that Stephanie first started to realise that she didn't look like most girls and that with her beauty came a degree of power over hormonal boys and a whole host of responsibility to not lord it over smaller, fatter, less sure girls in her year. Stephanie was very quick to become aware of the cliché that came with being this beautiful and she was determined not to be the stereotypical 'mean girl'.*

*During her A-level studies she'd been introduced to the illustrious Sue George of 'The George Platform', a modelling agency in Newcastle that had national reach and had been responsible for a handful of some of the biggest supermodels of the last few years. Sue snapped Stephanie up on sight, against Matthew and Margaret's hesitations and Stephanie was allowed to go ahead with the odd modelling assignment "to bring in a bit of extra pocket money" as long as it was restricted to one job a month and it never interfered with her studies.*

*Stephanie's parents need not have worried because her academic success matched her popularity and she left Accrington with many a friendship and three A-grade A-levels which gave her the scores and leverage she needed to study law at Cambridge University.*

*By the sixth month of her first year at university though, Stephanie knew that law was not for her. Neither was Cambridge. People there were mean and she missed the warmth and friendliness of the infamous Northern wit. She was sneered down upon because of her looks with many a snide comment made about her being a "bimbo" or having "fucked [her] way into Cambridge".*

*She wasn't and she hadn't. But people seemed to have made the instant opinion that women who looked like her did not have to work hard for anything.*

*Stephanie missed modelling.*

*She liked what she got from it both financially and emotionally. Law didn't hold a torch. She tried to broach the subject with her parents but it only resulted in Matthew talking her into her seeing out her first year and seeing the lay of the land after that.*

*It didn't matter.*

*By the end of the year, Stephanie wanted to leave Cambridge. Matthew thought he'd succeeded in keeping her on track by getting her to move back up North and carry on her law degree in her second year at Durham University instead. It was a plaster over a wound in need of stitches though and just like the plaster, it didn't hold.*

*Stephanie increased the number of assignments she took from The George Platform at a rate directly comparable to the number of classes she decreased attending at university and, within six months, she was preparing to take her parents out for a meal* <u>*on her*</u> *at their favourite restaurant – where Matthew's end-of-evening Remy Martin cognac went for £250.00 a glass – in order to break it to them 'gently' that she'd left her law degree entirely behind and she had been accepted as a 'contestant' on MTV's Newcastle-based semi-notorious reality TV / competition, Snog On The Tyne.*

*Matthew left the restaurant alone that night and didn't speak to his daughter for two whole days. Margaret was inconsolable.*

*Snog On The Tyne was another entry in MTV's blow to anyone who still thought that the channel would make a return to showing music videos one day. Now a platform for launching the most low-brow cavalcade of reality TV programming, '#SotT' – as the kids called it – was another example of what the broadsheet media referred to as "debasement television":*

*Eight twentysomething individuals local to the North-East, made up of four males and four females, were shortlisted from an audition list of thousands based on the size of their breasts (for the ladies) and the tightness of their six-pack (for the boys). If their moral compass pointed lower than their IQ and their BMI then they were the perfect contestant for this 'competition'.*

*Together the eight 'contestants' were housed for sixteen weeks in a converted, luxurious studio apartment space down on the Ouseburn outside of the city. They were partnered into four mixed-sex pairs and every night set loose around Newcastle's pub and club district to compete in as many drinking games and challenges as the '#SotT' team could think up behind the scenes. The more debauched the better.*

*The pair that collected the most points from the challenges and got back to the apartment space first was that week's winner. The team that had won the most over the sixteen weeks got a £100,000 cash prize to split between them. MTV cared not one jot about the point collecting, collating and ultimate winners. They cared about the footage that was getting returned each week of what went on 'after dark' when eight extremely drunken attractive twenty-odd year olds were all returned to one set location with a readied hot-tub and an overflowing, ever-full fridge containing every beer and spirit you could want.*

*They were never let down in that regard as contestants swapped their competition partners for different sexual ones, played fast and loose with their sexual preferences and stirred up loads of televisually-perfect drama for the gaping, horny masses that were tuned in and watching.*

*The first series had been an immeasurable success if success was to be judged by the size of both the outrage and the conversation across social media. Nobody believed for one second that there would be a second series once it was announced that two contestants were being investigated by the police for publicly indulging in heavily inebriated anal sex on Byker Bridge in one episode and that OFCOM were dropping record-level fines on MTV for broadcasting the act with insufficient blurring and censorship.*

*But a second series was commissioned once the dust settled and Stephanie was pushed hard by Sue George to go for it despite the fact that Stephanie was far from a match personality-wise for this type of show.*

*Stephanie was fast becoming Sue's most lucrative and favourite model that she had on her books and she promised Stephanie that with the contacts she had on the show, she could almost guarantee her a slot on the next line-up if she wanted to go for it... And Sue really thought she should go through with it, believing that it would send Stephanie's national profile through the roof.*

*Stephanie auditioned under the name 'Stephie Jay', believing naively that she could create a separation between her modelling work and whatever 'goes down on television', should "the TV edit not go in [her] favour".*

*Stephie Jay was "born".*

*Stephie took Sue at her word and reluctantly booked a role on the new series of Snog On The Tyne, much to Matthew and Margaret's aforementioned disgust. In time, they tried to be supportive of their only child's new endeavour. But by the time MTV broadcast a very drunk 'Stephie Jay' rolling around on the floor of Captain Bucks night club in The Gate with her allotted TV partner Greg (a Jesmond-based gym-junkie meathead with an allergy to shirts), trying to apply fake tan to a naked obese lady on all fours whilst a crowd of clubbers brayed drunkenly, Margaret and Matthew switched off and decided this was too painful for them to endure.*

*Their dreams of seeing their darling Stephanie graduate from Cambridge and eventually go on to open up her own law firm with Robin and Maureen Banks' daughter, Katherine, now seemed completely dashed...*

*Who would want to hire a legal representative who's "best bits" were on the internet forever – and had little to do with law and everything to do with her rolling around in a two piece bikini with a fat lady on a nightclub floor whilst hundreds of people shouted obscenities?*

*The naked obese lady was paid £150.00 for her chance to appear on TV.*

*The crowd got to drink for free "in order to help create the right atmosphere".*

*And Stephie and Greg went on to win the series, splitting the prize money and disappointing the show's producers because Stephie was "one of the more boring contestants seeing as she wouldn't put out on camera".*

*The winners parlayed the experience into a post-series 'show-mance' that they shopped around the tabloids and weekly women's magazines in order to net a further quarter of a million pounds each in 'kiss-and-tell' type stories about their "great love" for one another. The story of their engagement earned Stephie and Greg £120,000 from Hello! magazine alone. The particular issue announcing their intention to marry with a nine page photographic spread stayed on the newsagent shelves longer than Stephie and Greg stayed engaged.*

*Greg spent all of his accrued fortune on a series of terrible fitness-wear and protein supplement deals and he was eventually declared bankrupt; resurfacing years later in a 'Where Are They Now?' online article that identified him as now being a personal trainer in New Zealand.*

*Stephie had done well to follow her parents and invested some of her earnings in property and it was paying off nicely. Modelling assignments were stacking up too and she was soon the face of a lingerie brand, a beer and a fitness app. She occasionally boosted her profile too by, at Sue's insistence, dropping in on 'youth TV' comedy panel shows and high concept reality TV programmes.*

*Sue now worked in "complete alignment" with Teddy Steiger down in London who was Stephie's "TV agent". Teddy's tastes and Stephie's were quite a far reach from one another. She had dreams of being on Strictly Come Dancing and "showing a new side" to herself. Teddy was more interested in getting her short-listed for Celebrity Big Brother but the producers demanded "accidental nudity" if she was picked, and Stephie flat-out refused.*

*Stephie came second – behind Bobby Ball of Cannon & Ball - in the fourth series of Bear Grylls' Celebrity Survival which required her to survive in a jungle wilderness for 21 days only on the food she could forage for herself, with "drop-in mentorship from Bear Grylls himself". The tight non-disclosure agreement she signed with the production company meant that whilst viewers at home believed from the swooping drone footage that she had camped out in the wilds of Borneo, she had in fact never left a studio in Dagenham kitted out with foliage and shot from deceptive angles.*

*Teddy forced her to take everything they were offered "because 15 minutes is not a whole lot of time" in his professional experience. Stephie detested doing anything with Leigh Francis and any of his new shitty half-baked 'characters' because it was always immensely crude and misogynistic but she repeatedly reminded herself they were the most-watched and therefore ultimately the most lucrative for her. She'd come to accept that having Francis ('in character') stick his hand up her skirt and pretend to work her like a puppet was worth the extra two to three thousand calendars of herself she'd shift that year.*

*Stephie sickened of her television work before it ran out and eventually cut everything back to 'straight' modelling work which continued to roll in, alongside 'trend leader' nights in bars and clubs around the North East: Venues would pay Stephie to attend and heavily promote their upcoming events on her social media platforms and post photos of herself at their themed nights, drinking specific drinks and sharing certain hashtags. They paid her thousands at a time to do this.*

*She became known as the 'Queen of Newcastle' off the back of this and leant in hard to the title.*

*You would assume a backlash would come but Stephanie was so careful to always be so friendly and inclusive to each and every person she encountered that it was very difficult for anyone to get a hate campaign going. She put faith in each venue's security teams to protect her from the most handsy or drunken revellers and she'd yet to have that faith broken. As a result, every person who responded to her 'suggestions' on night's like this was a "friend" and deserved to be treated as such.*

*Her popularity soared accordingly.*

*The 'Queen of Newcastle' label stuck hard and Sue George took to exploiting it as best she could for the benefit of The George Platform. Sue started to encourage Stephie to include "smaller much more intimate gatherings" on her roster of bookings; places where visiting businessmen to the city wanted to spend quality time in good restaurants and VIP club rooms with the models they'd previously masturbated to in some nameless hotel suite in some faceless city after a hard day sat in conference rooms talking about share prices.*

*Stephie was very clear she would never have sex with any of these people and that she was not an escort - and Sue was very clear that she was not asking her to be one. This was "just another paid appearance by a celebrity, meeting a fan".*

*Stephie never felt entirely comfortable but the money was fantastic and eventually she managed to orchestrate such 'gatherings' to always include one of her own model friends on the guest lists because they got to share in the riches and she got to feel a little more safe... They'd stand around drinking very, very expensive bottles of champagne, pose for the occasional picture pouting next to some CEO of some company they didn't give two shits about and then have their hosts' driver drop them back off in Newcastle city centre for one last dance and drink at whatever club hadn't yet died for the night.*

*Stephie had hired the exact financial advisor that her parents had told her to and she'd even started to put some money in property development schemes they themselves directed her to. She was doing very well but, most importantly of all, she'd done as she was told and made sure a lot of her money was overseas and protected well. When the UK cratered, Stephie didn't have to flinch. The nightclub gigs quietened down here and there because there was less people going out nowadays, but that was about it.*

*By mid 2019, Stephie was starting to get restless.*

*She'd lost out on a few longstanding modelling contracts to newer reality TV stars and she was starting to feel a bit empty. She wanted to have stronger foundations then this. She wanted to have children too. Her lifestyle didn't really afford her the latter right now.*

*So Stephie started developing an outreach charity, specifically targeting young girls in the region for support around building careers for themselves, gaining scholarships and promoting anti-bullying strategies amongst their own social circles. By the Autumn of that year she had charitable status secured and headquarters set up in an office complex down on Team Valley in Gateshead.*

*All in her name of Stephanie Jason, no less.*

*On New Year's Eve, twenty-five minutes before midnight, Stephanie drunkenly started complaining to her best friend Alia that she was sick and tired of having to pull her phone out of her bag every time she wanted to take a photo of the two of them. She said that if she had her way she'd snap the selfie-stick in half and design a clutch bag with a lens hole that held your phone in a compartment inside and you just pressed a tab near the zipper and it took a photo from inside the bag. Alia felt it important to treat the idea with the drunken contempt it deserved.*

*... The next morning Stephanie woke up and started designing a small, trendy clutch handbag with a lens hole and a cable on the inside that was operated by a flick switch hidden on the outside. As far as she was concerned, it would be as simple as connecting your phone inside a special compartment lining at the start of the night to a cable that enables your phone inside the bag to be worked like the equivalent of a selfie stick: You take photos without ever taking your phone out of your bag.*

*By May of that year she had a fully functional prototype that she was putting to the test on every night out she went on. She hashtagged relentlessly about it and eventually got a groundswell of people asking where they too could get such a 'hot' item. In early October she started booking meetings with "all the right people" about funding with ownership percentages she herself "didn't find all that offensive".*

*At the start of November Stephanie started excitedly talking to her mother about the months ahead – there was going to be a large-scale advertising campaign for her charity starting after Christmas, a company down South wanted to go all in on her "silly camera bag" idea and if that deal came together the way it was being talked about at that time it could stand to make her millions and, Stephanie decried most importantly, she'd been on a couple of double-dates with Alia, her professional footballer boyfriend and his team-mate Max and they'd "gone really well". Stephanie told Margaret that she had a couple of 'trend leader' gigs and "groupie gatherings" that weekend that Sue had arranged and then she and Max were going to have their first official one-on-one date.*

*Stephanie was happy.*

*Stephanie was starting to feel less restless.*

*And at thirteen minutes past midnight on the ninth of November that year, four days after talking about her plans with her mother, Stephanie Jason – also known as Stephie Jay – was dead.*

## [7]

## or

## "Right you patient fuckers, let's REALLY get going..."

"Two-Tramadols-and-a-quick-black-coffee-to-get-my-head-together-and-look-over-my-notes" later and I was back in the office following my meeting with Margaret.

I needed the Tramadol because the self-doubt had kicked in before I'd even got all the way across the Millennium Bridge onto the North side of the city. Two-hundred and fifty a day was a lot of money for me, but it was nothing by the standards the 'big boys' in the industry were charging. They were faster and more effective too. They had better equipment and more substantial contacts…

… Maybe if I was all about 'doing the right thing' then I should have told Margaret about those guys so she'd have had the full roster of choice? Maybe I shouldn't have been tricking her into 'settling' for 'Lehman's Terms'? Maybe this is why my business sucked because I'm prone to thoughts like this and sometimes even acting on them?

Honestly, which businessman have you ever heard of who's stayed in business as a result of a client literally getting dropped into his lap only for him to say 'Actually, there's bigger and better companies down the road with a far greater reputation – Why don't you go see if they're free and if not pop back to us and we'd gladly take your case on!'

My head hurt and my back was starting to throb.

I stopped at the end of the bridge, took a second to catch my breath and leant on the railing to look back out at Baltic Quay Apartments on the other side of the Tyne. 'I'm a good investigator', I told myself. 'I'm just a mess of a human being. But I *can* do this. I can do this job. I know I can.'

I stared up in the distance at what I now knew to be Stephanie/Stephie's apartment. Margaret was right. Why didn't she just jump? Why drive herself over to an all-but-abandoned warehouse in Hebburn and hang herself?

I pushed myself on a couple more steps across the road and hit the Greggs outside of the law courts, slumping into the first seat I could find and taking full advantage of being enough of a regular in this particular branch to be able to just raise my hand at little old Dawn behind the counter and blow her a kiss – minutes later a steaming black cup of coffee and two sachets of brown sugar were brought over and I slipped her the exact change with a smile and a thank you.

The Tramadol started to meet the caffeine as I talked to Jane on her lunch break.

I was walking back from Greggs, along the quay and up Dean Street towards my office gabbling words out of my mouth and down the phone as fast as I was thinking and I was thinking very fast. I was possibly running my mouth even faster because I remember Jane saying "Slow down. Slow down. I know you're excited but slow down!"

I must have said "It stinks Jane, it stinks! And I haven't even started digging in just yet!" at least twelve hundred times in an eight minute phone call. Jane told me she'd speak to me properly that night. Which was probably the politest possible way of avoiding saying "I've got to go. You're making my ear bleed."

The truth though was that it *did* stink and it stank without me ever having started to dig into Stephie Jay in much detail at all. I bounded up the stairs to my office and I hadn't even got through the door at the top before I heard Psychic shout "PLEASE tell me we've booked this!"

I stepped through the door. "We booked it!"

Psychic punched the air before exclaiming "I knew it! I could tell from Katherine Banks' voicemail message!"

"What message?"

Psychic smiled before leaning down on his desk, pressing the speaker tab on our office landline and then punching in the answer phone code. The beep was followed by the office being filled with the amplified sound of an angry voice:

"EXPLAIN TO ME WHY I'VE GOT A FUCKING MESSAGE LEFT WITH MY FUCKING PARALEGAL FROM MARGARET FUCKING JASON ASKING FOR A FUCKING PERMISSIONS LETTER TO BE PUT TOGETHER FOR YOU TO GO FUCKING ACTING ON HER FUCKING BEHALF, DIGGING AROUND INTO STEPHIE'S DEATH? CAN YOU EXPLAIN THAT TO ME? BECAUSE I WAS UNDER THE IMPRESSION THIS WAS MY SHOW AND I BROUGHT YOU ON AS A ONE-LINE FUCKING GUEST STAR AND YOUR ONLY FUCKING LINE WAS TO SAY 'THANKS BUT NO THANKS MARGARET!' AND THEN TAKE THE FUCKING DEAL YOU WERE GENEROUSLY OFFERED? FUCK YOU JAKE! I DON'T KNOW WHY I BROUGHT YOU INTO THAT ROOM. I KNEW YOU WERE A CLUELESS TIT. YOU'RE ABSOLUTELY FUCKING BLACK-FUCKING-LISTED…"

Psychic and I stood looking silently at one another. Was she done? That was Katherine in full flight but now she wasn't saying anything and… Oh, no. There's more:

"… You'll have your letter by close of business today. Don't take the piss with this Jake. Get her the answers she needs to sleep better and then close this up. I'm warning you… THEN YOU'RE FUCKING DONE WITH ME!"

A permissions letter is something we often get from our clients or where possible get their solicitors to provide one for us. It's basically something that says we're acknowledged as private investigators to be working on their behalf. We make a fair few copies of it and we stick it in with every Freedom of Information request we make or we pass it across the table when trying to get evidence. We've found it speeds up the process so that people don't try and block us from the outset with the whole "We'll need to get such and such's permission before we speak to you!" or "We can't disclose that without such and such confirming they want us to first!" It's not a guaranteed door-opener or anything like that. It's not a legal guarantee. But it's a bureaucratic assist in a lot of ways.

I didn't return Banks' call.

"Katherine seems well, huh?" I smiled.

Psychic shrugged. "Fuck her. It's not like she's our numero uno client, is it?"

I deemed now a bad time to tell Psychic about the alternative offer of a fixed one year retainership with the biggest law firm in the region. Instead, I nodded and started to undo my coat and head towards my part of the office.

"I know this is a bit sexist," Psychic said. "But I find it very unfeminine when a woman swears like that!"

"Ring her back and tell her that!" I laughed, hanging my coat up in the corner as I opened my door.

Psychic and I moved into my office space.

I ran through everything Margaret and I had discussed, the timings of things and the fact that the police had completed zero in the way of enquiries into Stephanie/Stephie's life. Psychic seemed as shocked as I hoped he would be.

"What are we going with for the girl then? Stephanie or Stephie?" he asked.

"My gut tells me 'Stephie' was what was most likely to have driven her to kill herself or got her killed so let's stick with that. We know who we're talking about regardless, right?"

Psychic nodded.

The adrenaline, the opioids and the caffeine converged in a perfect, gorgeous 'kick' and I lit the fuck up; wiping my whiteboard clean and pulling out my notebook as Psychic jumped into the seat behind me.

"Okay, as soon as the permission's letter lands I'm going to head straight out and start getting up the noses of the police who handled this." I said, whilst writing both Stephie Jay and Stephanie Jason in big capital letters at the top of the board. "Whilst I'm doing that I want you to pull every social media profile you can find under both of these names, assess how heavily she was trolled or bullied online and on what dates, by who and try and get pinned locations for them where possible."

Psychic scribbled on a bit of paper and nodded as he wrote.

"She apparently double-dated with a guy called Max who plays for Newcastle United?"

"Max McNae? Defence?" proffered Psychic.

I shrugged.

"How many Max's play for Newcastle? I don't know shit about any of that stuff!"

Psychic smiled. "There's *one* Max. Max McNae."

"Okay, cool! See what you can dig up on him – call it as you see it, is he a dickhead or what? We're going to want to speak to him so see if you can get me a lead in on that, yeah? Also, her mum was very clear about how secure she was financially but not everyone is as transparent as people think they are and who tells their parents everything, right? What's more – who's truly financially secure these days? Debt is a huge cause of suicide, depression, all that. Get me a look at her credit rating, level of debt, insolvency register appearances… Anything… *Everything*!"

I wrote bullet point variations of all of that under her name as Psychic speedily took notes for himself.

"Got it!" Psychic said. He sat back in the chair and smiled. "Jake?"

"Yeah?" I replied.

"Are we going to lower ourselves to playing this out for a much-needed pay day or… you know… Do you think she really *didn't* kill herself?"

I stepped forward and took a seat on the corner of my desk. I rubbed my eyes and felt the skin almost harden under my touch. I sighed and leant back.

"Her parents deserve more answers than they've been given. We're going to help them try and get them… and, right now, that's about as much as I can say."

Margaret's permission letter, formally notarised and accompanied by an official Dreyfuss & Associate instruction letter making clear we working in partnership with them on behalf of their client, arrived a couple of hours after I'd briefed Psychic and set him loose.

With both documents printed I headed over to the central police station on Forth Street to see if I could draw out some information and get in front of the officers that had been in charge of Stephie's case. I had a good rapport with the civilian front-of-house station officers down there and was often able to get them to disclose more stuff to me on cases I was working on then they realised they probably should.

All of our conversations usually ended along the lines of them saying "I'm sorry I couldn't be of more help but, you know, Data Protection and all that?" and me replying "It's okay. No worries. I'll try writing out to your Freedom of Information team or something!" whilst secretly dancing inside that they'd read out more off the screens in front of them then they were actually allowed to.

I wasn't going to have to push, flirt and throw down the craic as heavy as I usually would on this occasion because in discussion with Margaret on our way out the door of Stephie's apartment, she'd confirmed once more that her point of contact on the case so far had been a Detective Constable Billy Tidyman. All I wanted from the civilian front-of-house station officers down at Forth Street was for them to get me an appointment with him in some sort of manner that didn't set off the police's legal team demanding he not grant "interviews" etc. without a police solicitor present or any of that blather.

Or set enough alarm bells ringing that it put me in the path of that scumbag Detective Inspector Andy Andrews.

Yes – *that* DI Andrews!

Basically the way to avoid all of that was to avoid putting anything in writing – which was the police service's standard bullshit response to every request – so that it could be passed up the line and cut down by some senior solicitor for the police as "not required by law" for the officers to attend and discuss. My aim today was to get that appointment without ever technically asking for it directly, *especially* in writing.

I hit the crossway outside of the police station at the exact moment a chain of police van doors sped in unison through the secured gates down the side of the main building. They all came to a stop and I held back to watch through the chained fence as uniformed officers climbed out of the vehicles and pulled open the doors. Three to four campaigners per van were forcefully pulled from the vehicles and dragged, handcuffed towards the custody suite. Two officers held back and pulled placards from each of the vans, piling them up on the ground in one stack. I saw "WHERE IS OUR GOVERNMENT?" on one. I saw another that said "KNOBS TOOK OUR JOBS!!' and a final one thrown on top of all the others that said "HETHERINGTON IS ROBBING OUR CITY!"

Anyone who knows me would know how strongly I agreed with that last one out of all of the placards.

This is where we're at now in society. People are displaying what was once their democratic right to express their voice, regardless of whether it was ultimately hollering into the darkness. And they're being crushed down, arrested and dragged off the streets into custody. These people have no jobs now, possibly no future prospects. A lot of them didn't know where the next meal for their families was coming from. Was it really that imperative that their voices were taken from them too? Were they really offending the upper echelons of the local authority headquarters they'd obviously been protesting outside of?

I shook my head in disgust and headed into the station, slowing my pace down to get a good eye on who was working the front desk that day.

To my luck it was dear old Lesley.

Lesley was a big old rump of a lady, very much mutton dressed as lamb. An old-fashioned, take-no-prisoners type who used to run the payroll department down on the Swan Hunters boat yards but in the twilight of her years switched it up to take a station officer job in one of the last standing and thus busiest police stations in the city.

She was straight as a dart, tremendously brutal and I loved her.

"Hey Lesley," I said as I slid on up to the perplex-glass counter that separated the two of us. "How's it going?"

"Oh Christ! Just when I thought my day couldn't get any worse. What's up 'Magnum PI'?" she laughed.

"You're looking good these days, Les'? You still doing your juice cleanse?"

"Shut up, I've put a stone on you clueless shite! How you doing?"

"I'm good. I'm good. I'm hanging in as best I can, you know?" I replied. "I just popped in to see if you could help me?"

"Well I know you didn't pop in to see if I was divorced and free for the taking so… what's up?"

I smiled. Lesley was no Margaret Jason. This afternoon there would be no late additional entry being made on my list of 'gorgeous women that are still sexy the more they age' that I keep stored in amongst the clutter in the back of my brain.

"Do you know Billy Tidyman?" I asked.

"I know Billy, aye!" she replied. "He's a DC upstairs."

"I'm trying to get a hold of him on this thing I'm working on." I said.

And now… for the chuff:

"I got given some direct contact details for him but they don't seem to be correct." I said, looking down at a page of notes that had absolutely nothing to do with anything I was there to discuss today.

Lesley checked the laminated sheet to her right, behind the glass.

"Have you got extension 3820?"

"Oh, that's what it is!" I lied some more. "I've written the eight as a zero! Can I just check his email address too? It's still just his shoulder number and then the 'at' symbol followed by the usual server address right?"

"Yeah, so you're looking at 454 then the usual server address. You got that correct at least?" she asked.

"Yeah." I lied even more. "That's what I've got written down here. Is he in upstairs, do you know?"

Lesley smiled as the realisation she was being played a little bit started to kick in. She winked at me and picked up her phone. I idly pretended to check through my notes whilst straining an ear to hear her speak to whoever was on the other end of the line. By the time I'd worked out what I thought I'd heard, she was already off the line and tapping the glass to get me to look up. She pointed her index finger in three forceful jabs towards a room in the corner of the foyer.

"I'll buzz you into Interview Room 2. He'll be down in five minutes."

I gave her a wink and blew her a kiss. She caught it and mimed throwing it away.

"I don't want people starting to talk about us, Jake!" she laughed.

DC Tidyman's 'five minutes' were more like 'thirteen'.

He arrived through the interview room door on the station side with the bluster of someone who timed his working day to the exact minute and he had not allotted any time for this. The cut-to-fit trousers and slim-fit shirt with the top button done and a no-nonsense jet black tie suggested he was an everything-is-serious, graduate-entry fast-tracker who already knew this police service was going to be better once they saw some sense and made *him* Chief Constable.

His ice-breakers needed a lot more work though.

"*The* Jake Lehman!" he said, extending his hand as he came over to the desk.

I stood and shook it.

"I'm famous?" I asked curiously.

"Well, more like *infamous*!" he clarified. "There's a few DI's here who talk about you as the living example of burning out fast and bright or something…"

I could feel my anger rise. It was this exact sort of shit that lived as a crushing weight on my soul each and every day – The total disconnect between who I was and who I was perceived to be. I was going to let it slide. I had to let it slide. And just as I was letting it slide I found words falling out of my mouth faster than I could stop them.

"It wasn't so much as burning out as it was getting found out, really!" I shot back.

"What got found out?" Tidyman smiled politely.

"That I had a quality not suitable for the police service!"

"What was that then?" he said with genuine curiosity.

"An inherent sense of human decency!"

Tidyman didn't see that coming. You could tell on his face. His body stayed fixed but his head rocked back a little. Meanwhile, inside my head the little voice took on the form of a tiny little marionette boy and the strings pulled themselves in order to perform the most glorious of victory dances. A victory dance completely disproportionate to the 'adversity' that had just been 'overcome'.

"Yes… Very droll!" sighed Tidyman. "So what is it I can help you with today exactly?"

"I'm representing the Jason family in reviewing the Stephanie Jason case."

Tidyman stared at me blankly.

"Stephanie Jason – also known as Stephie Jay?"

Tidyman continued to look blank.

"You worked on it just over a month ago, Detective Constable!" I offered further. "Margaret Jason says you were her point of contact?"

Something clicked.

"Oh. Oh. No, I was just the dogsbody on that job. I wasn't the investigator or anything. There wasn't anything really to investigate anyway. I can't remember any…"

Tidyman stopped himself. It was almost like he realised that the things he was saying ran completely contradictory to the public-facing aura of excellence he wanted to continually exude at all times.

"Look, give me a second. Let me go pull the file and familiarise myself with something and then I'll be better placed to tell you what I can and can't help you with, okay?"

I smiled. He nodded then left the room.

I sat silently, patiently looking around the interview room. There was a fixed CCTV camera in the corner that didn't seem to have been activated for purpose today. They didn't have them as standard back when I was in the police. And it was that one stray thought that led me down the path of thinking how different life would be now if I was still in the police. I'd be on the other side of this desk…

… I'd be better prepared than this fool I was having to deal with.

… I'd most definitely have been his rank manager, that's for sure.

… I'd probably not fit into a shirt half as well as he does though.

The door flew open at speed and Tidyman was back in the room, clutching a thick green cardboard file in his hand. He dropped it on the desk and pulled up a seat once more.

"Right," he said, clearing his throat. "Stephanie Jason. The suicide... Hanging, is that correct?"

"It is, yes. I was..."

Before I could finish speaking the interview room door burst open a second time and there stood DI Andrews.

DI Andy Andrews.

DI *Andrew* Andrews.

The scumbag of scumbags.

He made direct eye contact, scowling but never communicating directly to me. It was every bit as weird as you'd expect from someone talking to the other guy in the room whilst looking straight at you and grimacing.

"DC Tidyman? A word! *Urgently*!" Andrews said.

Tidyman looked back in shock. He nodded then quietly excused himself... leaving that file on the table behind him. My iPhone was out of my pocket, underneath the interview room table before Andrews had even slammed the door. I had my phone unlocked and the notes screen open before the clasp on the door clicked shut.

Now, here's the thing:

A dipshit private dick with no scruples would've opened that evidence file up and stole as many pages from it as possible and hoped that he'd get away with police officers not noticing it at least long enough to make notes or photocopy it or something. That's what a rookie would do. It's ridiculous. Top tip: *Don't* do that!

A fast-thinking but morally dubious private eye with some degree of nuance about them would've pulled their notebook out, grabbed the file and quickly tried to squirrel down as much notes as possible before anyone re-entered the room. That's what an old sweat of a PI who's been around the block would try to pull off. Here's the thing: You don't write anywhere near as fast as you think you do. You're going to get two words at best down before getting caught right in the act! Don't do that *either*!

A master private investigator who doesn't trust the police to do fair and frank disclosure... and who lessened the amount to which he gives a shit anymore as more and more pressure is placed on his business nowadays for trying to survive on the principle of 'doing the right thing'... and who REALLY hates DI Andrews... and who learnt this very technique only six months or so earlier when Psychic showed him how... forgoes all of the above and instead uses the 'scan' function on his iPhone notes app to copy as many documents as possible in their full, original form straight onto his smart phone!

And that's exactly what I did whilst listening to the raised voices outside the room.

"Who told you it was okay to meet with that piece of shit?" blustered Andrews to Tidyman, through the closed door on the other side of the room.

I scanned the summary sheet that lay as the front page inside the file straight onto my phone.

"What exactly were you thinking, disclosing informally like that to a just-rolled-out-of-the-gutter PI like him?" growled Andrews.

I scanned two of the scene of death photos onto my phone.

"You do not take one of my files for a closed case and…"

I scanned the first page of the coroner's report onto my phone.

"Where's the file?" barked Andrews. "Where's the fucking file? You left the file in the room with HIM?"

Time's up!

I slid the file shut and slipped it straight back across the table to where it was – just as the door smashed open once again, smacking hard against the wall and bouncing back on itself. Andrews was already clear of the impact as he strode forward and grabbed the file. Behind him, the door hit Tidyman square in the face and knocked him off to his right.

As Andrews turned to Tidyman, I was already pretending I was still distracted by my phone. It's funny how easily you can make the act of emailing a load of documents straight over to Psychic look like you're texting your wife to say you'll be home late.

What I'd just pulled off was ruthless and unprincipled. It was unprofessional too. But it was also superbly quick-witted and smart because when it comes to DI *Andrew* Andrews, all bets are off. I should have smelt that his fingerprints would be all over this thing from the minute Margaret Jason started talking.

"LEAVE!" Andrews screamed at Tidyman as he himself took a seat in front of me, lifting the file above his head for the DC to take with him. Which Tidyman duly did.

The door shut and Andrews and I were alone.

"That was a confidential series of documents. That goes without saying. I take it that file went unmolested whilst we were out of the room?" sneered Andrews.

"Poor choice of words, given our history don't you think?" I spat.

Andrews stared at me. Hard.

"What is your interest in this case?"

"I've been hired by the family…" I said, reaching into my inside pocket and removing the neatly folded permission's letter and accompanying document from Dreyfuss & Associates.

"I don't give a single fuck about your letter from your bloody mum excusing you from PE or whatever the hell that is, Jake!" Andrews snapped. "What is your interest?"

I re-folded the letters and put them back in my pocket.

"Mrs Jason feels like she still has unanswered questions…"

"Of course she will feel that way!" Andrews sneered. "There was no note left by the deceased. It's common for the family left behind to feel lost at sea in their grief. We have been more than patient with the Jason family. They don't like the decision that has been reached by myself, my team and the coroner's office. It is as simple as that."

"What enquiries were made into Stephanie's life by your team? What made you think that suicide was so…"

Andrews fist landed hard on the table.

"What on God's green earth makes you think I or any of my team have to explain themselves to you? *You*? Look at you…"

He was going to get personal wasn't he? Oh, you can tell in his eyes he was. He was going to think he was crossing a line to provoke me without realising he went so far over the line all those years back that he's existed ever since in a state of being two shades shy of me murdering him every time I lay eyes on him.

"How Jane can still bare to look at you, I don't know. Or has she seen sense and pissed off?" he said with the cruellest of smiles.

"Don't you mention my wife, *Andrew*!"

"My name isn't Andrew! Just look at you, man. You're a total laughing stock. Do you honestly think there's a single person in this sorry city that takes you remotely seriously? The gobby ex-copper, thrown off the force and bumbling around trying to make it as a private investigator! You're a shit 80s action comedy no one wants to watch that's come to life."

Andrews started to laugh.

"What were you earnings after tax last year? Go on, I could do with being cheered up. How much does a Jimmy Nail wannabe like you clear eh? Judging from the state of you I'd say you'd be lucky to take home two hundred quid per annum!"

Andrews was exactly the sort of two bit shitbag who thought he was being clever throwing out a reference to an early 90s TV show in usage as an insult and getting it completely wrong.

"Okay, hold up." I said, leaning forward in my chair. "There's four extremely important things that need to be made clear here before my resolve is broken and I beat you to death with this very chair I'm sat on… One, Spender was an amazing television show. Jimmy Nail chased a metro on foot, for Christ's sake. So if you're throwing that show down as an insult against me then it doesn't really work because it was awesome. Unless you were actually making a Crocodile Shoes reference, in which case I'm sorry but you've lost me. Two, sticking with the Spender thing. Spender was a police officer – not a PI. So the reference definitely doesn't work. Three, you closed off your investigation into Stephanie without making any enquiries, without speaking to any of her friends according to her family and you had it all sewn up and boxed away with the coroner in a week or less. If you're *that* secure that you've ticked all the required boxes, made all the right judgement calls and what not you'll not have any problem with me having a sniff around then? Finally four, it pleases me greatly to see that you are still the walking talking exemplification of what happens when a penis makes a wish to be turned into a human and get given a warrant card!"

I sat back in my chair.

Remember that little voice that took on the form of a tiny little marionette boy inside my brain earlier? Well now it was doing mic-drop motions and throwing its goddamn hands in the air… like it *just don't care*!

I'd flamed any chance of police assistance but I was never, ever going to get it wherever DI Andrews was concerned. At least I'd gone down swinging and not got knocked out with one blow in the opening ten seconds of the fight.

Andrews folded his arms across his chest and looked me up and down.

"Do whatever you need to do in order to line your pockets with the money of grieving, exploited parents." Andrews said slowly and coldly. "You will receive no assistance from this police service. My team will be told to deny all Freedom of Information requests that are placed before us in relation to your enquiries because I believe your intentions are illegitimate and exploitative. There is nothing with the case of this poor, tragic young lady that requires further investigation."

Andrews stood up and walked towards the door.

"Hey, DI Andrews?" I said loudly.

The door was already open with Tidyman standing waiting patiently in the corridor with fear etched into his face, well within ear-shot of what I was about to say.

"Yes?" said Andrews.

"What is worse as far as you're concerned? Lining your pockets with money from grieving parents or lining it with the hush money from child molesters?"

I watched the colour drain from Andrews' face in unison with Tidyman's jaw as it dropped and his eyes fell accusingly on the back of DI Andrews' skull.

I might be a joke and a loser to everyone in Newcastle.

But I was a joke and a loser who doesn't forget.

## [8]

## or

## "Toccare..."

**I** woke up feeling like someone had parked a car on my upper torso. I went to bed overwhelmed with anger at my interaction with Andrews and it had festered to the point of preventing me getting to sleep. I just lay there hour after hour, feeling my jaw get tighter and tighter as I locked in the tension. Eventually, at around three am, I had slipped out of bed and quietly pulled my battered tin from the drawer next to it.

I went downstairs and downed a pint of water, two tramadol's and two naproxen's in the hope they'd dilute the anger and afford me some sleep. I spent a few minutes sitting staring out of the dining room window, waiting for the tablets to kick in a little bit. I thought about Stephie. I'd looked over the scene of death photo that I'd printed out properly when I'd got back to the office after my confrontation with Andrews. It was still clear enough on my mind that I was able to close my eyes in the darkness of the dining room and I could see the dilapidated warehouse, the big steel barrel on its side near to her corpse and the body of Stephanie Jason/Stephie Jay hanging from a thick wire cord wrapped around an iron rafter fifteen to twenty feet above her.

I remembered she was barefoot in the photo. Her shoes were nowhere to be seen. The parts of the summary report I'd scanned made no mention of her barefoot imprints at the scene or where her shoes were found if they were found there at all. If I was just thinking that up now in the drug-addled state I was in, shrouded in the shadows of my dining room with no file in front of me then why hadn't an officer on the case given it this consideration and shown to have done so? If it was in the report it would be in the summary…

… I couldn't stifle the yawn. It was the sign I'd been waiting for so I slumped off to bed and was asleep within minutes.

Unfortunately the timeframe of such opioid consumption and my required wake-up time was far too short which landed me with the after-effects of rising from the bed like I was submerged deep underwater and being forced to move in slow motion.

I made my way downstairs to find the kids running manic at the news there was a burst pipe at the school and they were being given an impromptu day off. Jane looked helpless and spent all ready. Being the 'project manager' of the family in every way she'd already rang her own work and taken the day off to cover the childcare, making the decision all on her own that she didn't want me to stop before I'd started on the Stephie Jay case.

Jane took one look at me and made an unsteady step back.

"Are you okay?" she said in semi-shock.

"Yeah… I just took a sleeping tablet too late and…" My voice trailed off.

There was an expression slowly building on her face.

"What?" I asked.

"Nothing. Nothing… Listen, we've got 'Date Night' coming up soon, remember? And there's something I want to talk to you about without the noise of the kids banging away over the top of us so… how do you fancy me moving 'Date Night' forward a week or so?"

"What do you want to talk about?"

Jane took a steadier step forward. "Nothing bad. Don't start overthinking. Just adult stuff… Kid-free conversation type stuff!"

I looked at her and scrunched my face suspiciously.

"Have you done something you should be feeling guilty about Jake?" she said with a straight face.

The addict in me took full control of my brain, grabbed the loudspeaker and screamed "SHE'S FOUND YOUR STASH – RUN!" but externally I fought against that and shrugged. "I feel guilty every minute of every day about something, Jane! That appears to be the Lehman's Terms of Service!" I smirked.

"Cheesy!" said Jane, leaning into me and kissing me on the cheek.

Fifteen minutes later I was washed, dressed and out the door with a travel mug of black coffee that helped dissolve the two Tramadol's I gunned down my throat the minute I was clear of the house.

I sat on the metro that morning reading over my notes and staring intently at the Paradox nightclub leaflet. What caused the 'meet and greet' night there to get crossed out in Stephie's diary? What took its place? Whatever it was would hold a pretty strong account of her mood and her movements directly leading up to the time of her death… Man, it felt *good* to start digging my teeth into something like this again.

Before the metro went into the tunnel and dropped out my signal, I scanned the Google results that came from searching 'Toccare'. I was desperately trying to land the name of some bar, club, restaurant, etc. by that name that I could use as a lead. I mean, wouldn't that be great huh? Google just shoots up the name of some place called 'Toccare' that we link up with Stephie's diary entry, go there and just get handed all the clues and witnesses we need? It's *never* like that though.

There's never a big, immediate smoking gun. That's just bullshit. It's never that simple. You don't fall across something in the first instance. If you did all PI dramas would be ten minutes long and all private detective books would be five pages. You've got to get out there and chase down dead ends and consider everything to be anything before it becomes something. There's a reason all private investigator tales are referred to as "shaggy dog stories". It's because they've got to ramble through all the inconsequential stuff they worked the angle on to show how they landed on the eventual reveal that tied everything up.

*If* it ever gets tied up.

Because sometimes there's no answer.

Sometimes the bad guys get away.

And the good guys get their careers taken off them in the blink of an eye.

… And end up as Tramadol-addicted PIs trying to eke out a living in a city falling apart at the seams. I threw that last bit in just in case I was being too subtle and you didn't pick up on the fact that I was referring to myself. Maybe I'm underestimating you lot?

I landed through the office door and Psychic hit me before I'd fully stepped inside.

"Mrs Jason has been on the phone – she's provided contact information for Alia Marcus, Stephie's best friend… I've tried calling. There's no answer!"

"Did you shit the bed this morning?" I smiled.

"I'm on fire, Jake baby! This is what we've been waiting for. We deserve this case and we're going to make good on it – right?"

"Absolutely!" I removed my jacket.

"Now, go grab a seat because I'm going to knock you on your arse with what I've managed to gather up so far!"

I flopped down onto the sofa and Psychic immediately handed me a cup of black coffee. He smiled. "Buckle up!" he said, spinning in his chair to get eyes on the computer screen on his desk.

"Right… Max McNae is a dead end so far. Newcastle played away the weekend Stephie died - Tottenham Hotspur. They lost 3 – 0. Max was down in London three days before the game and he stayed in London two days afterwards. It would appear from his social media feed that he learnt about Stephie's death at the same time everyone else in the country did. I've got his agent's details and I *think* Max may be amenable to speaking to us should we have a need to but…"

Psychic stopped and shrugged.

"No, at this stage I'm not sure we need to pursue this!" I said. "They went on a couple of double-dates, were never alone together from what I can gather and he's got a pretty tight alibi, I'd say."

"Well, he was live on Sky Sports playing football in London that afternoon then photographed falling out of a nightclub down there at the same time Stephie died up here so… I'd say *very* tight?" replied Psychic.

"Ok, what else?"

"Social media stats? She had 92,000 Facebook 'followers' on her public page and no traceable private page. In terms of Facebook her private life *was* her public life. Twitter? 385,000 followers! On Instagram, she had just shy of half a million."

I whistled. All of that sounded impressive.

"How many do *you* have?" I asked.

"How many do *you* have?" Psychic fired back.

"I think I have like ten people on Facebook or something. Maybe one on Twitter and that's Odeon Customer Service Team – I complain a lot, you see – and I don't know what Instagram is. *Should* I be on Instagram?" I replied.

"No. No you should definitely not be on Instagram, Jake!" laughed Psychic as he clicked a couple of tabs on his monitor. "Now… here's something that surprised me. She has very little in the way of trolling, bullying or adverse interactions on any of her platforms across social media. Especially around the time of her death and leading up to it."

"Ok. That definitely was an angle I thought we'd get a lot of traction on, if I'm honest." I said, finishing off my coffee.

"Maybe she was ruthless in just blocking these weirdos at the first available opportunity, I don't know!" Psychic suggested. "But there was one interesting character I managed to get a track on – 'SOTTfan1999'! They made a death threat to Stephie Jay online around the time that Celebrity Survival or whatever it was called aired on telly and she was on it. So, we're talking a good couple of years before she died…"

"But still a death threat?"

"Yup, still a threat against her life!" said Psychic. "He was blocked, came back with a new account and bragged to her that he was the same guy and that, quote unquote, 'no blonde rag is going to shut him up'!"

"When was that and what's the new account?"

"That was a year and a bit from when she died! And get this, the new Twitter account is 'Professor LickHerSpine'!"

"Ok. Classy. He's maturing it seems."

"But she didn't block him second time around. Maybe she had him muted on there instead because…"

"You're going to have to slow down here, Psychic." I grinned. "I'm on Twitter but I don't understand Twitter. How is muting different to blocking?"

"Muting is what you do if you would like to stop receiving notifications from a specific Twitter user about a specific conversation. If you want to see them you'd have to go looking for them. Celebrities do it all the time to dull out the noise of repeated haters."

I sat and pondered this then shrugged indifferently.

"I can see I'm losing you here Jake so let me jump straight to the crucial bit – Two weeks before her death a 'Professor LickHerSpine212' pops up in her feed on a separate chain of Twitter responses to her advertising some random club night and simply writes 'Why aren't you dead yet?'"

I rocked back in my seat.

"Oh – he's *mean*! Please tell me that…"

"Already ahead of you; there's enough cursory checks that come back positive to say 'SOTTfan1999', 'Professor LickHerSpine212' and 'Professor LickHerSpine' are all the same person being ran from an account tied back to the same email address."

"I want this bloody guy!" I gasped. "I really want to talk to this guy!"

"I'll get on that! You happy for me to move on?"

"There's more?" I said. "Did you go to bed?"

"The monkey can't dance if the organ grinder doesn't grind the organ!" replied Psychic.

I laughed. Then stopped. "Wait? Am I the monkey or the organ grinder?"

Psychic winked. "Right… Mrs Jason has been more than helpful and that's assisted me in jumping past a lot of the usual obstacles when looking into finances of subjects. With Stephie, I'm going to come straight out and say I don't think financial issues were what drove her to commit suicide."

"Go on…" I said.

"Her financial lifestyle is high end and you or I would probably think crazy irresponsible or whatever but for her and the life she leads it all works out and evens up where it needs to. She had nothing in the way of crippling debt. She owned her apartment outright. She had credit card bills that would make your eyes water but the pattern was always a build-up and an outright pay out. She never seemed to accrue a credit card balance that was outside of her means to handle it."

"So far, not so crazy irresponsible!" I smiled.

"She had outgoings of roughly four and a half grand, basic."

"What the fuck?" I gasped.

"That's not taking into account the mortgage deals and leaseholds on some of her properties. That was in a separate company set-up. I'm talking Stephie Jay, personally. She literally had close to five grand in outgoings a month."

"On WHAT? She owned her apartment!"

"It clearly costs a lot to look like she did. She had treatments almost weekly that racked up over the month. She bought a lot of clothes and shoes. Like, a *LOT*. She had an Audi R8 on a rolling hire and drove a Range Rover Sport as her 'day' car – which she owned outright!"

Psychic paused for effect.

"You're not impressed? She was driving around in a sixty-five thousand pound Range Rover as her day car. And she hadn't reached twenty-five years of age!"

"Yeah…" I said frostily. "Well, I'm thirty-seven and I have a metro pass so…"

Psychic laughed.

"She's got a good return on the property investments she's made." He said, barrelling on. "She still gets a lot of modelling work. She was getting about fifteen hundred to two grand a night for going out drinking in specific bars and clubs. And she could clear anything from five hundred quid to three frickin' thousand pounds for a single Instagram product placement post! This was not a high stress lifestyle she was living."

"It seems that the country doesn't have any use for industries and tradesmen anymore but it still has money for Instagram and models?" I replied.

I leant forward and picked up Stephie's diary from Psychic's desk and flicked it open.

"I was looking through this." I said. "She certainly wasn't short for bookings in the future going off of her diary, was she?"

Psychic shook his head, agreeing with me.

"The last week before Christmas alone," I said, flicking directly to that part of the diary. "She had two to three bookings a night right the way up to some modelling job at the Metrocentre on Christmas Eve. Even if you took her lowest possible quote, she would've pulled in six lots of fifteen hundred for a week!"

"Nine thousand quid!"

"Yeah, thanks 'Rain Man'!" I said, smirking at the smart-arse before me. "The point being, I think from what you've been able to dig up so far money wasn't a concern for her!"

"No, I don't think so!" confirmed Psychic.

I sat back in the sofa and ran my fingers around my stubble and started to rub my eyes. The 'kick' was dulling already. I didn't like that. Psychic sensed this and gently took the empty coffee cup from where I'd put it down near my feet and immediately started to freshen it back up.

"She was ordering things online and putting things in to be engraved on the day she died. That stands out to me as something a suicidal person doesn't really do." I muttered, almost to myself. "Why put the engraving in when you know you're not going back to pick it up?"

"Do we know yet what the engraving was?" asked Psychic.

I shrugged, opened my notebook and took out the receipt that I'd paperclipped to one of the pages. "I've got the receipt here. It's not been picked up."

Psychic took it from my hand. "I'll take care of that and let you know."

"Then there's this 'Toccare' thing." I began. "She crossed out her thing at Paradox and wrote 9pm 'Toccare' above it. I have been right around Google and out the other side looking to see if I can find a place in the region of that name that she could have gone to. The only definite confirmation I can get is that it's bloody Italian for 'touch'!"

"What if it was a secret member's club thing?" proffered Psychic.

"You mean like an 'Eyes Wide Shut' type deal huh?" I giggled.

"Yeah – and *they* definitely wouldn't be advertising on the internet would they?" laughed Psychic.

Two cups of coffee and another two Tramadol's later, I took a walk over to Paradox nightclub on the far corner of Collingwood Street which wasn't that far from our office. It was shut for patrons but in the process of receiving deliveries at its side door when I arrived down the alleyway that led out onto the Stamp Exchange.

Paradox was once the most popular nightclub in the city. It was the lynchpin and centrepiece of what was known as 'the diamond strip' in Newcastle. The concept of 'the diamond strip' was born out of the death of the city's famous Bigg Market pub district. Collingwood Street developed a run of 'prestige' bars and clubs that seemed to be pushing the idea that it was a 'classier' variation on the Bigg Market… *Anyone* could get into a pub in The Gate or what was left of the Bigg Market, but only *'the best of the best'* could get access to the venues on 'the diamond strip'. It was a façade that lasted all of about a month. After that, the bars and clubs along this route just became bars and clubs for any and every man, woman… and child with a good fake ID.

Paradox was once Bobby Maitland's pride and joy.

Until it wasn't.

He had his hand in so many venues and his fingers in so many pies that he had the ability to pick his favourite based on what was bringing him the most money. Paradox, for a long time, was his favourite venue and The Fire Pit, its 'sister' bar conjoined to it next door, was the very place Richard Willis tried to rob.

I say it time and time again: Newcastle is a big city but a small place – all roads lead into each other's pockets in one way or another. So, it's almost as if there was some sort of method to my madness in opening with that little adventure involving Bobby, the barbell bar and that junkie fuck hanging from the ceiling, don't you think?

Bobby still 'owned' Paradox in the technical sense that most of the money holding it up was his and therefore it was under his protection. But it was run in the traditional sense by Khali Matti, nightclub 'entrepreneur' and estranged son of Ahmed Matti of Matti Inc. a huge architectural and commercial design company with the sort of funds available for Ahmed to back anything and everything his beloved son Khali wanted to try his hand to… until Khali stacked up enough arrests for drugs, violence towards women, etc. for Ahmed to cut him loose.

It was probably for the best. Khali's repeated failed business ventures was costing Ahmed a lot and at time when Matti Inc. were one of several big companies taking hard hits as the UK economy floundered. Nowadays Khali kept himself afloat by running a couple of clubs for Bobby Maitland and trying to keep the illusion of riches and prestige alive in the eyes of anyone who looked his way. The reality was decidedly different.

I arrived at the side door, stuck my head around it and was met with the wall of 'noise' that 'the kids these days' seem to consider music. As Jane often tells me I'm a man born out of time; an eighty-odd-year-old curmudgeon in the body of a thirty-seven year old… who's body feels like an eighty-odd-year-old curmudgeon when it moves.

Nowhere is my 'born out of time' sensibilities more accurately reinforced then when it comes to music and music 'tastes':

I was a child of the 1980s who came of age during the Britpop era of the mid-nineties. Whilst the other kids at school were taking sides in the great Oasis versus Blur 'war' of 1995, I was mourning the loss of synth-pop and demanding to know why songs didn't have saxophone solos in them anymore. When we got old enough to be hanging out in parks after dark - underage drinking one litre bottles of paint-stripper that masqueraded as cider costing one pound fifty - my mates were singing the virtues of the likes of Pearl Jam, Pulp and The Foo Fighters whilst I was trying to 'educate' them on "classic" bands like Journey, Survivor, Chicago, Air Supply and Asia. I still actually carry the scar on my left knee, twenty-two years on, from when Stuart Pennie threw an empty glass bottle of beer at my legs in Wallsend Park because I went on an impassioned and drunken rant about how *"… Bon Jovi were the Rolling Stones of our generation".*

Jane doesn't let me pick the music on long car journeys anymore. My last playlist was a twenty-five track tour of greatness featuring Barry Manilow ("Weekend In New England", of course!), Eric Carmen ("Make Me Lose Control"), Spagna ("Call Me"), The Hooters ("Satellite"), Linda Ronstadt and Aaron Neville ("All My Life") and... We got six tracks in before Jane asked if there'd be any Coldplay featured. I looked at her with distaste. She responded in kind by pulling my playlist from the air with immediate effect.

I guess you're reading this and thinking I'm not a man to be trusted when it comes to music, right? But, seriously, modern music is vile – it's just big long stretches of electronic beats that speed up into white noise or ten year old girls in chaps or hot pants singing about their broken heart and failed relationships. I mean, what the fu... Anyway, it was very much a case of the former blasting away through the loud speakers when I stuck my head around the side door at Paradox.

My pain at the instantaneous exposure clearly caught the eye of the young pissed-off looking bar manager signing off on the boxes of stock that had just arrived.

She looked up and shouted "Can I help?"

At least that's what I thought she said over the horrifying blasts of electronica.

I shouted back "WHAT?"

"Help? Can I help?" she said again.

I shrugged.

She frustratingly pulled a remote from her pocket, clicked it and the music died into instant silence. I smiled.

"Can I help?"

"They make you listen to that?" I asked.

"What? That track? It's great isn't it?" she replied.

"It was certainly *something* – who was it?"

"It's DJ Ki-Yay!" she smiled widely.

"As in 'Yippee Ki-Yay Motherfucker'?" I said.

She nodded enthusiastically. "He's my boyfriend!"

"He's certainly something!" I said condescendingly. "Anyway, is Khali upstairs?"

"Aye!" she said. "Is he expecting you?"

"Yeah, I've got an appointment!" I lied.

"Just head up then. He's in his office!"

I thanked her and walked into the club. Five or six steps in I realised I didn't actually know where I was going. My pace started to slow. The bar manager clocked this.

"Second door up in front of you on the left, stairs straight up to the third floor!" she said whilst lifting to pick up a box of beer bottles.

I thanked her once more and put her directions to use.

I took the stairs slowly. My leg was really playing up badly today and no amount of irresponsible pill-popping was seeming to have an effect. I held the bannister with one hand, pulling myself forcibly up the stairs using my upper body whilst nursing the lower part of my twinging back with my other hand. On CCTV footage I must have looked like a decrepit old man, not some thirty-seven year old.

I knocked on the office door on the third floor once I finally got there, a small headband of cold sweat now starting to congregate across my forehead. But I didn't wait for a response and strode straight in with a faked level of confidence and forced masculine bravado that reinforced exactly what I've been telling you all along about how much of what I do is just chuffing.

… And barging-in.

Now, whilst I will admit I exist in a perpetual state of amazement I've never been shot doing this I do have to say you should never, ever underestimate the effectiveness of a dramatic barge-in.

There's not many movie and television tropes that play out as truth in real life but catching people off guard by bombing in through the door and getting in with your questions before they know what's hit them *is* a solid one. That first reaction to you and your questions tell you a lot more than people will probably realise.

"Khali! How you doing?" I shouted.

Khali sat bolt upright in his seat behind his desk on the far side of the room, a room littered with files and random storage boxes and which carried no personal stamp of Khali Matti whatsoever. I'd clearly interrupted him watching something on the Mac perched on the corner of his desk.

It was probably porn.

If you put bets on the fact it was porn, I'd pay out on it. It was *that* strong a likelihood.

Khali was wearing one of those low-cut, two-sizes too small, cutting off the blood to the brain type t-shirts designed to publicise the fact that he is in the gym every morning before work and he lunches at The Naked Deli before sitting down behind his desk. He had the latest sheered and coiffured hair style and the biggest, chunkiest, jazziest watch you'd ever laid eyes on. The cynic in me thought he'd chosen it specifically because from a distance it looked like a new model £2,300.00 Patek Philippe but closer scrutiny revealed it was simply a highly polished old model Bulova Precisionist – retail price £595.00.

"Who are…" hollered Khali.

Now, here's the thing: You do this line of work like mine long enough and you get a pretty strong feel for idiocy with a fair degree of immediacy. Khali was sat behind an open-fronted desk with his pants around his ankles in an unlocked office, facing out onto the only door in. So Khali is a fucking idiot.

And you can change 'probably' porn to 'definitely' porn.

… And the thing with dealing with idiots is that you cannot give them time to think because thinking is dangerous for them. You've got to be quick and you've got to get them to where you need them to be in any given conversation because they really shouldn't be trusted to get there on their own.

"Sorry to bother you Khali, but I'm looking into the death of Stephie Jay and I thought you might be able to help me." I smiled, sitting down uninvited in front of him.

"Are you with the police? Can I see some ID please?" he stammered.

"I'm not with the police. I'm a private investigator. I've been hired by the family. I'm looking specifically into her movements in the twenty-four hours before she died and I noticed from this leaflet…"

I pulled the Paradox leaflet, now a little curled up and torn around the edges, and placed it determinately on the table in front of Khali.

"… That she was booked to do a sort of 'meet-and-greet' type thing here at your club on the night she died but I…"

"Woah. Woah. Woah. Slow down!" gasped Khali. "Listen, she wasn't here. She didn't show. Her boss lady Sue cancelled her the night before. There was a whole kick-off and everything. But don't be coming sniffing around here. She was never here!"

"Why was it cancelled?" I asked.

"Who the fuck knows the real reason – Sue give me some shit about there being a double-booking and she had to honour the booking that came first. We'd had her booked for over a month so I don't know what shit show they're running over there at her agency. I never even wanted Stephie Jay here. She's like two series of Snog On The Tyne ago to me. This Queen of Newcastle thing is bullshit…"

"But you still booked her?"

"She's popular. Or was. It was pretty grim what happened to her…"

"What? Dying?" I confirmed.

"Yeah. It was… you know… unfortunate for her?"

Khali was a spectacular idiot.

"So… you were saying, you booked her against your better judgement or something?" I said, picking the leaflet back up off the table and putting it back in my pocket.

"Look, we'd had a slump. People aren't going out like they used to. When they do come out they're already off their tits on the cheap Aldi booze they've necked at home and they come in here, stretching their own drink to last the whole night or something. A few of my girls suggested getting Stephie in because she draws a crowd, she gets an atmosphere going and she gets people buying what she's drinking. I didn't want to go back to Maitland and show him the receipts as they were. You know Maitland, right?"

"Yeah, me and Bobby are good friends." I lied.

"Yeah, he's a good guy unless he's losing money and then he's a psychopath."

"How does this all work with you and Bobby then? He owns the place and…"

Khali leant forward across the desk and lowered his voice conspiratorially. "He owns the club but he can't *run* the club, if you know what I mean?" He winked broadly. "Licencing issues with the council and too many incidents of getting under the skin of folk up at council headquarters. So I'm his *representative*… if you know what I mean?"

"I know what you mean!" I winked back. "So… Sue cancelled?"

"Yeah. We got royally fucked! We'd paid for extra drinks stock and we'd paid for advertising and all that so we were 'out' financially. I'd had the posters taken down on the Saturday morning from everywhere I could and we stuck a 'cancelled' banner outside but… yeah, we got stuffed dude!"

"Here's something I don't quite understand about this 'hiring' of Stephie Jay that seems to go on around town." I asked with legitimate curiosity. "She's out drinking in some capacity every weekend, right?"

"It seems so, yeah."

"So what's the difference between Stephie Jay going out drinking with her pals and having a good time and then Stephie Jay being paid by you to come out and drink?"

"Well, when she's out on her own pound I don't care about her." Khali said callously. "She goes out and she can have some VIP area to hang out with her friends in and all that if she wants but I don't give a shit. I'm certainly not sending champagne over to her by the bucket all night long. But when we hire her? She's out there on the floor and she's expected to mingle and take selfies and promote the drinks packages we want her to and play it up for the crowds, judging stupid competitions and shit."

"The line between the two is thinner than I thought, I guess." I replied. "I just don't think I get what's special about a Stephie Jay 'night' when people can sort of see her out and about in the same bars and clubs when she's not 'for hire' if that makes sense?"

Khali sat back and grinned wildly. "I guess you never saw Stephie Jay when she turned it on 'live' did you?"

"I don't think I'm of the age that fitted her demographic!"

Khali continued to smile, his tongue slowly slid out of his mouth and he repulsively ran it across his bottom lip suggestively. "Dude… she was bloody wondrous!"

He paused.

"… And I'm saying that as someone who thought her marketability was shit these days too. So what does *that* tell you huh?"

I wanted to answer "That you're a clueless letch!" but I didn't because… you know… manners and what not. Plus, I wasn't quite done.

"How bad were you put out by the cancellation?" I asked, changing the subject abruptly.

"Sue got us back on the expenses for the flyers and the posters and stuff. But we got left high and dry on the additional stock we ordered in. We're pulling that back now through drinks offers and shit but… when Maitland's guy looked at the books initially he was pissed, no getting around that!"

"How badly then?"

"Let's just say low thousand rather than a few hundred."

I nodded. "And Maitland? How did he react?"

Khali moved forward in his seat and went all in with the conspiratorial tone again. "I never spoke to him. But I did get told by that Ryan lad who's always by his side that the days of Stephie Jay getting comp'd or VIP'd in any of his places ever again was over. He said it was a personal insult and Bobby was going to hit her back hard."

I looked at Khali.

Khali nodded.

He was too stupid to realise the enormity of what he'd just said. If I'd thought him to be smarter I'd have considered the possibility that he was trying to set Bobby Maitland up but, seriously, Khali was *definitely* not that smart.

Plus, I'd seen first-hand back at Coopers Gym what Bobby Maitland was prepared to do to someone who he felt had robbed from him and personally insulted him with their actions.

## [9]

## or

## "The Chapter Where You Should Definitely Be Starting To Think That Something Doesn't Quite Add Up..."

Callerton Industrial Estate in Hebburn was a ghost town now as a result of the economic free-fall that had hit the UK over the last two years. Just up from the Port of the Tyne on the South side of the river, it once housed some of the biggest warehouse units in the North East that were either owned outright or leased by companies responsible for exporting products all around Europe and the world.

Specialist industrial tools? Footwear and accessory production? Vehicles parts? It had been a thriving base of varied operation since it opened its first six units in the late 1980s. Since then it had expanded to twenty-two units before the country cratered. Now, it was going to rust and waste. There was a couple of companies that had stripped themselves back to skeleton staff and barebones production lines and were just about hanging in there. Most had gone bust. There were a couple of businesses on the Callerton estate that had quite literally disappeared overnight – vans were loaded up and the premises abandoned, the commercial equivalent of a 'Moonlight Flit' to avoid/delay contact with the piles of debtors getting prepped to start queuing at their doors.

Hark Roy were one such company. They specialised in designing state-of-the-art air conditioners and air conditioner parts. They were once a proudly North East based firm with local-boys-made-good at the top and who made great efforts to recruit from within the community, offer attractive apprenticeship programmes and give back charitably. Decisions made by the government had a crippling effect on trade outside of the UK and Hark Roy took a hard hit. They fought for as long as they could to keep the company going; cutting staff, slashing away at running costs but it was all for nought.

The warehouse emblazoned with their now-dirt-strewn signage is all that remains of their existence in Newcastle Upon Tyne. It stands at the back end of the Callerton Industrial Estate, the last unit on the far left, barely secured shut and home now to nothing but a dust and mud strewn empty factory floor with a secondary run of abandoned open-plan office space behind that. The latter of which was easily accessible now from what was once the factory floor because all the adjoining windows had been smashed through by vandals many a month back.

Blue Light Security had the contract to patrol and secure the units and land that made up Callerton Industrial Estate. Savvy enough security staff posted there though had quickly realised that there was nothing worth stealing anywhere on the estate so they secretly dialled their hourly patrols back to just one in the middle of their twelve hour shift and one at the end. The rest of the time they stayed sequestered in the security porter-cabin near the entrance and streamed bad action movies off of Netflix on the shared supermarket-brand tablet the Blue Light team had all chipped in to buy for this patch. This security teams' attitude was that you get what you pay for and Blue Light paid one pence above minimum wage with no enhancements.

Davey Brolin was the security guard on shift the night Stephie Jay died. He was the one that found her too. He clocked her Land Rover all but abandoned on a grass verge outside of Hark Roy's now dilapidated loading dock and wondered how it had ever got past him at the gates before remembering that a) the security gates to Callerton Industrial Estate were pulled off and stolen eight months ago, netting some enterprising robber-type a hundred quid or so in scrap and b) he'd slept for nine straight hours of his twelve hour shift. He saw the loading dock side door prized open no more than ten to twelve feet away and shone his torch inside to see who'd slipped in. It was pure luck on his part from the angle he leant at that the first thing his beam of light hit was the torso of Stephie Jay.

Davey was working the shift the day Psychic and I landed at Callerton Industrial Estate. This wasn't well-timed, miraculous happenstance. Psychic had rang Blue Light Security and made some enquiries and they were more than happy to help and change Davey's posting around for that day to put him where we needed him to be to in order to ask him some questions. Davey didn't work Callerton if he could help it. He certainly didn't do night shifts there anymore. It was one of the things his GP supported him in getting Blue Light Security's occupational health team to guarantee before she signed him off as fit to return to work after the trauma of discovering Stephie's body.

Davey Brolin was a little squat man. From a distance you'd think he was the perfect caricature of a Geordie football lout – all forearm tattoos, shaven head and no neck. Up close though he looked like a thumb in human form, a small squat of machismo in a badly fitting company-issued polo shirt and combat pants. The first sign that Davey was not the cliché of the lower working class lout lay in the softness of his voice.

"We should probably be more switched on now the gates are gone!" said Davey as he drew on a cigarette. "Because anyone can just drive in, really."

Psychic nodded.

Davey shrugged.

"But we're just ticking the hours down until we can go home, man. There's nothing to protect here anymore. It's a bloody wasteland. After the last time it got smashed up by young 'uns it just become this joke where we're standing here saying 'We're going to stop you getting to our turd!' and everyone's all like 'We don't want your filthy turd, weirdo'!"

I laughed and nodded.

Davey smiled, sort of thankful that his off-kilter analogy landed.

"So you definitely didn't see her car or any other cars come through?" I asked.

"Nah." Davey exhaled smoke. "The first I knew a car had gone through was when I spotted it on patrol..."

"And how do you think it got through?" asked Psychic, somewhat naively.

Davey leant forward and blew some smoke in Psychic's face. "Well she got through because I dropped a fucking ball, didn't I lad?"

Davey smiled and continued before taking another draw on his cigarette. "But I didn't tell the boys in blue or my bosses that, did I? Because as much as I hate this job, it's a job right now and that's a rarity isn't it?"

"Too right!" I said, smiling warmly, trying desperately to keep the rapport there. "I would guess the CCTV picked up what you missed though, no?"

"CCTV stopped working here nearly a year ago!" said Davey, exhaling more smoke. "Bosses up top never replaced it. They just raised our patrols to hourly. We're here anyway, why not make us more active and why spend more money on monitoring this pile of crap then you absolutely have to? Blue Light have no loyalty to this place. Their contract is rumoured to be up before March next year. There's no money in renewing it. It's one of the last big sites they've got so this place will just be left to the druggies and the homeless to take over and the redundancies at our place will start!"

"So... no CCTV?" clarified Psychic.

Davey's mouth curled at the sides as he looked at Psychic. "No. Was that not clear?"

"And the police are aware there's no CCTV covering this site anymore, yeah?" asked Psychic.

"How the fuck do I know that, kid?" sneered Davey. "You'll have to ask them."

We were losing Davey. I stepped in.

"What time did you nap? And obviously there will be no mention of you napping in our final report, I promise!" I said, Davey eyeing me suspiciously the minute he heard 'report'.

He took another draw on his cigarette.

"I was on shift for eight thirty. I got here about eight. I must have gone to sleep about ten or ten thirty-ish, I think. I tried watching one of those Netflix superhero shows the other lads are banging on about all the time. You'd have liked it..." he said, pointing at me. "... It was about this right looker of a lady who's a private investigator like you!"

I smiled. Psychic decided to steer things immediately back on track. "So you napped about half ten, yeah? And woke up about what time?"

"Maybe three or four. It had to be closer to three I think because I had pressed all the alarm bells going, calling the police and what not at about four so I'd had to have discovered her before then! ... Yeah, actually, I'm remembering properly now. I woke up, felt a bit shit and decided to go walk it off by doing the patrol. I was about five minutes in and I was about to veer right and start down that end of Callerton but then I clocked the car off in the distance. Because that's the thing, you see, when you do this job on this site long enough you do get to know every shape and every shadow. They don't change. Something out of place by an inch would stand out in the dark. So obviously a bloody car jumped right out. I started walking up and that's when I saw the door into the old Hark Roy building was opened up too."

Dave's lip started to tremble. You could see he didn't want to take his mind back any further. He composed himself, throwing down the stub of his cigarette and immediately lighting up a second. I decided to try and pull him back from the upset and settle him down a bit.

"It's refreshing to see you're not a vaper, Davey!" I laughed.

"Oh they can fuck right off can't they!" Davey smiled. "I mean, honestly how many of them do you think have taken the time to do that in front of the mirror eh? Surely if they'd done that at least you'd think they'd have the good sense to realise that isn't right, you can't go out smoking something that looks that ridiculous can you?"

"Everything's all machines and gadgets nowadays, Davey. I can't believe they found a way to 'gadget-up' the act of smoking!" I replied.

"You smoke?" Davey said, pulling the packet from his pocket and offering it to me.

"Ten years off, so thanks but no thanks!" I said politely.

"Ahhh, a smoker who doesn't smoke!" says Davey. "You've never quit, you know? That's the thing with anything addictive. You don't quit it. You just get ahead of it one day and then spend the rest of your life trying to keep ahead of it because when you slow the pace – BAM! It hooks you back!"

Psychic shot a knowing glance my way. I opted to ignore it and keep things light.

"There speaks the man who's clearly been on and off them a few times eh?" I laughed whilst Davey nodded, laughing through the smoke that billowed out of his nose.

The three of us fell silent.

Davey looked at his feet.

"You're not going to make me go back up there are you lads?" he asked.

Psychic and I looked at each other.

"You don't have to go back up there Davey, no. But would you be okay with us going up there with your keys?" Psychic asked.

"Okay with it? I'd *prefer* it!" Davey replied softly.

We took a long slow walk up the desolate road to the far corner where the old Hark Roy building was based. We'd confirmed with Davey before taking his keys that it was, as far as he was aware, still in the same state it was in when Stephie had been found and that according to the log book he checked, no one had been inside of it 'officially' since the police left.

We arrived outside and whilst Psychic pushed the key into the rusted lock on the side door of the loading area, I pulled the copy of the scene of death photos from the back belt-line of my pants where I'd had them stashed in a clear plastic wallet. The weather was such where despite the cruelly cold crispness in the air, it was bright enough to push some sunlight through the large windows that lined the top of the walls of the Hark Roy factory floor. We'd brought torches just in case too.

The minute we stepped inside we stopped right on the spot. Usually when police and emergency services attend the scene of a crime or a death, there's one agreed pathway in from the point of entry to the evidence, body, etc. It helps with the preservation of evidence and minimises contamination. There were lots of footprints here. At first glance it looked like they all came from the same tactical boot print, just in various sizes.

I looked at the floor in front of me and compared it against the floor in the photograph.

Then I repeated the look to the floor once more.

"She was found barefoot, right?" I asked, holding out the photo for Psychic to see.

"Yeah. Her shoes were found in her Land Rover outside. Or at least that's what Margaret Jason thinks as they were returned to her as Stephie's belongings and they are listed as such!"

I nodded and pulled a magnifying glass from one of the many pockets on my coat.

"You carry a magnifying glass?" said Psychic, somewhat startled.

"I carry loads of stuff, just in case."

"I know, but… a magnifying glass? Really? It's a bit of a Sherlock cliché isn't it? I mean – have you heard of zooming in?" he laughed.

I held out the photo. "Show me how to zoom the fuck in on a photograph I've printed out and got held in my hand right now, you absolute utter bellend!"

Psychic held his hands up in mock surrender. "Ok. Ok. Good one… I get you. You win… Crack on, Sherlock Holmes!"

I put the magnifying glass over the photograph and studied intently the ground beneath where Stephie's body hung.

"There's no footprints. I clocked that when I first looked at it but it really stands out now I'm here. There's no footprints. She got out the car barefoot, right? She gets this door open. God knows how on her own but let's just go with the notion that it was already displaced when she got here and that's why she chose this building. But somehow she walks from the car, through the mud and across this floor and doesn't leave a footprint of her bare feet – yet every single person who visited the scene has?"

"You'd really think that would've intrigued the police wouldn't you?" Psychic replied.

"Absolutely – or at least get discounted in the report with an explanation as to why!"

We started to walk around the edge of the factory floor, almost daring ourselves to step in closer to what would have been the central spot in which Stephie Jay allegedly took her life. With each step I kept looking up at the rafters. The wire cord that Stephie had been hung with still rather hardheartedly hung down from them, the only amendment made to it was that the noose that had once been fashioned at its end had now been cleanly cut open.

On the floor, maybe two metres maximum from where the cord motionlessly hung was a huge iron barrel. I mean *huge*. I don't think I'd seen one that big. It lay on its side with drag marks in the dirt that could be traced back to a massive steel pen where another of its type sat pushed against the metal railing, spaces for two or three more existed there too.

"How high up do you think those rafters are?" I said, looking up at the ceiling.

"Got to be fifteen feet at least?" Psychic estimated.

"Yeah, I'd say about fifteen to twenty feet… So we've got to believe that cord was already wrapped around the rafter like that, right? Tell me how she could have got this set up on her own like that otherwise?"

Psychic started looking around the factory floor. There were no ladders or vertical means of assistance. The gap between the rafters and the roof was negligible so let's not even enter suggestions she got up on the outside of the roof, opened up a roof panel, tied cord she'd found inside the building around the rafter, dropped it through, climbed down and then went about her suicidal business… Though that was still more believable than what the police were selling, as far as I was concerned.

"The rope has to already have been hanging when she got here!" suggested Psychic.

"So a lass, North of the river, with seemingly a pretty perfect life and everything to live for drives South to end her life after ignoring the thoroughly suitable plunge from a balcony readily available at her own place of abode…"

"Maybe she didn't like heights?" interjected Psychic.

I smirked. "Well that definitely rules out my thoroughly plausible counter theory that she got up on the roof, dropped the cord in position and climbed down into the building then! … Anyway, stay with me: she doesn't choose the right-in-front-of-her-eyes balcony option. She leaves whatever those new plans were on Saturday the eighth, drives out of Newcastle and comes straight to a warehouse out in the sticks of Hebburn to find a ready-made suicide site with a rope already hanging ready for her to slide her head into?"

"And what made her choose here?" added Psychic. "How did she know about here? The lax security? That this building hidden away out of sight from the main road was the perfect location and…"

"You're saying all the right things to me here, Psychic. You're asking all the sort of questions that make me feel like I'm not alone in thinking this just doesn't add up at all!"

Psychic put his hands on his hips and let out a huge sigh. "You can absolutely see why her parents aren't letting this go can't you?"

"Absolutely!" I said whilst taking to looking down at the photo and then comparing it to the scene in front of me. My attention started to focus in on the cast iron barrel on its side, near to where Stephie's body was found hanging.

"The summary sheet said…" I quickly lifted up the photo to look at the copy of the summary sheet I'd also stolen a copy of. "… that the drum over there is what the police believe Stephie stood on in order to get the noose around her neck and then jumped from or kicked over in order to create the tension in the cord that would snap her neck!"

Psychic looked at me quizzically. "That drum?"

I nodded. "That absolute beast of an iron drum! She climbed up on that, which we can't believe was already in position when she arrived too because we can still see the drag marks of it being moved to roughly where it is now. She has to have jumped. She can't have kicked that over. Surely?"

"They've summarised that they think she did though. How else is it on its side? She knocked it when she was thrashing perhaps?"

I put the papers down on the ground and strode angrily over to the drum lying on its side, collecting dust and dirt. I could see the engraving at the bottom on its underside. I pulled my sleeve over my hand and used it as a duster to smear away all the grime so I'd get a clear look at the engraved markings.

"Listen to these stats, Psychic…" I shouted, not realising he had followed me over and was stood behind me. "…This is a two hundred and twenty gallon steel drum made from both stainless and carbon steel materials… Now get this, the two hundred and twenty gallon steel drum measures eighty-eight inches by one-hundred-and-thirty-two inches and weighs up to two hundred and forty pounds..."

Psychic got his phone out and furiously started typing into it. "Two hundred and forty pounds is about a hundred odd kilograms, Jake. That's just about what I can squat in the gym!"

"So you're agreed that it's highly unlikely she went over and lifted one of those out of that pen over there, dragged it over here, climbed up on it and then kicked it over?" I said.

"Oh, I don't know… there's that whole 'ladies who lift' thing across social media isn't there? Women are banging out the heavy lifting these days. And she was absolutely toned and tight to perfection wasn't she? It's possible she was a lady who lifted…" Psychic replied.

"Barefoot in a strapless cocktail dress?" I snapped, standing up from crouching next to the barrel. I pointed over to the pen. "Humour me okay? Go get that barrel down from that pen and drag it across to here."

Psychic stared at me to verify that I was serious then shrugged and confidently headed off to the pen. I don't want to embarrass Psychic with a detailed description of what happened next but all you need to know is that he was thoroughly unable to get a barrel down on his own and if Psychic really *does* lift and squat one hundred plus kilograms down the gym after what I witnessed, I'm a badger's bollock.

He stood gasping for breath whilst the capillaries in his cheeks seemed to pulsate.

I asked him to go over to the barrel on the ground and stand it upright. His look now was less confident and his move over to it much less assured than when he approached the barrel pen.

He stepped over and grabbed the rim.

There was the sound of heaving and his feet sliding a few inches here and there in the dusty mudded surface beneath him. He tried changing his point of attack. He lowered his knees. Eventually I stepped in and together we lifted it with a little bit of a struggle into standing straight up off the ground. The clank it made upon falling into place echoed horrendously around the empty space. The sound brought water to my eyes and I felt my head start to really push in on itself at the temples. My knee was not responding well to the exertion either.

"Okay," I said taking a much needed breath. "Climb up on top of this barrel and rock it to fall."

"But then I'll fall?" whined Psychic.

"Not if you jump off. Just get a bit of motion going then, don't rock it all the way."

Psychic climbed up on to the top of the barrel with my assistance. He began swaying his legs side to side, trying to build a momentum but the surface beneath which he stood was not moving. It was not remotely moving. He eventually jumped down, leaving the barrel stood exactly where we'd positioned it.

"It must have one of those weighted bottoms, I reckon." Psychic said, now staring at the barrel like it was his mortal nemesis.

"Look, I don't want to be sexist and dismissive here." I replied. "I'll buy completely into the 'ladies who lift' thing and I'm pretty certain Stephie Jay could most certainly bench press, squat and deadlift double what I could... But I'm just not buying that you can't move this thing an inch but a distressed model half your weight and size could?"

Psychic nodded. "I agree Jake."

We stood in silence and then set about photographing the scene at angles and in ways that we felt were important and relevant. The next time we spoke was as we were putting our stuff together and getting ready to leave.

"You know, Psychic..." I said with frustration building up inside of me. "It's not so much that this absolutely stinks to high heaven by just the smallest of glances at the situation. I want to know why the police have called this so wrong and threw it away. This wasn't a straight suicide. There's nothing about this that you could even just casually call 'Death By Misadventure' without asking *some* questions!"

We took a walk away from what used to be Hark Roy, down the path and back out of the Callerton Industrial Estate. As we walked we talked over what the next steps were going to be and Psychic agreed to try and get an appointment booked with the coroner based off the name we had on the copied report. He also said he'd follow up with trying to get in touch with Alia again.

"They keep saying we're in for these blizzards. They've stopped taking bets on a White Christmas too!" said Psychic, pitching 'weather' as the nominated topic of small talk back to the office. "They reckon it's an absolute certainty now!"

"I can't see it coming down, personally." I replied distantly.

He said some other stuff but I can't remember it too well at all. I was too busy thinking about the ringing in my head… and all the questions that were bubbling away having been and witnessed the scene of Stephie's death for myself… and my jaw was starting to feel really heavy with a sort of thumping ache for a Tramadol… and, oh God, did my back ache something rotten too. Not to mention my knee throbbed and felt like it was swelling up inside my jeans.

I'm not telling you all of this to illicit sympathy. I'm telling you so you'll understand that I was a bit distracted in myself. And that's why I didn't initially spot the jet black Ford Explorer, four people deep, that had snail-crawled behind us out of the route we walked from the Callerton Industrial Estate up onto the road where the metro station stood. By the time I did, it did zero to sixty out of my line of sight before I could make a note of any registration.

## [10]

## or

## "Ok, So There's A Possibility Your Protagonist May Have Mental Health Issues..."

My intention, once we got back to the office, was to quickly get my notes typed up that I'd scribbled down at the Hark Roy scene and then have an early finish. I was hurting, I was criminally low on pills in my tin and, to be honest, I had an overwhelming urge to get involved with the kids' bedtime tonight and push to just hang out with Jane a little again.

That intention was immediately way-laid the minute I stepped out of our office and headed up towards Monument to catch the metro home. The square was filled with protestors, holding placards decrying the latest news of more cuts to public services and increases in 'festive' bonuses for the executive management structure at the local authority. I started to force my way through the crowd, bemoaning to myself once again that this was all so pointless.

"You're shouting into a void!" I said to myself as if I was screaming at the protestors. "They're not listening. They don't care. And they're never going to put themselves anywhere near you to be held account…"

I didn't get to finish the thought.

My eyes fell on the railings that were being put up around a makeshift stage with microphones on stands that were wrapped in cheap, chintzy tinsel.

I stopped one of the protestors as they crossed my path to make their way over towards a congregating group of fellow demonstrators lining up against the railing. This wasn't going to go well for whoever they had on the line-up on that stage.

"Excuse me?" I asked this lady with a placard and an expression that suggested she was up for a fight. "What's going on here tonight?"

"We made a vow we would chase down Hetherington and his fat-cat cronies at the council wherever they showed their faces publicly and we're sticking to it. They think they can put up a few extra lights over the streets for Christmas and we're going to forget that they've raised the council tax on us again whilst slashing millions of pounds in much needed services and…"

Her answer was interrupted by a humungous cacophony of boos and jeers that were at a more powerful level than you'd have expected for a group that only numbered about forty odd people but growing.

I looked past her to see if I could source the subject of the vitriol and my eyes fell straight upon Mayor Mick Hetherington walking up onto the stage along with a handful of other carefully selected guests and councillors.

I couldn't help myself.

I flung my jacket open and feverishly grabbed at the small handgun burrowed against the beltline of my jeans. I pulled it out and aggressively clicked a round into the chamber, pushing past the woman I'd just been speaking to who's jaw fell open in shock. She saw the gun and whatever scream she was about to express was drowned out by the gunfire I unloaded in the direction of the stage.

The first shot was carelessly aimed and hit the man standing to Hetherington's left, causing his throat to explode with the force of the bullet. I calmed my breathing a little on the second and third shots, causing them to land right on the person I wanted them to – Hetherington took both shots to the centre of his chest, knocking him clean off his feet and straight into the concrete post behind him.

The crowds were screaming and scattering in exactly the manner you would expect when unprecedented and unexpected gunfire fills the air. I had ten shots left and every single one of them was for that vile piece of shit that had just hit the ground with two holes in his chest. I started striding forward with my arm locked out in front of me, holding the gun tightly. I was fully aware that I was seconds away from being rugby-tackled by some police officer chasing a Pride of Britain Award or some member of the public who wanted to be 'hero for a week'.

Suddenly the air started to fill with the excruciatingly loud sound of the words "Are you okay? Hey, man? Are you alright?"

My vision flashed white and I shook my head to try and clear it from my line of sight. By the time my sight cleared of the blinding flashing light, I found myself stood back in front of the lady with the placard and my arm locked out in front of me. I took a tight hold of an imaginary gun so hard that my knuckle bones were about to burst through my skin. My entire neck and jaw were completely solid and jarred with tension into a cemented position that was unnatural and painful.

"Are you alright?" asked the woman again. "Are you having a fit? Do you need to sit down?"

At the exact moment I heard Mick Hetherington's voice amplified through the microphone over on the stage, I staggered backwards away from the woman and stumbled away, drenched in embarrassment and looking for words to explain the murderous hatred that coursed through my veins.

"Hello Newcastle! Thanks for such a warm welcome!" bellowed Hetherington, his voice noticeably soaked in sarcasm despite it being dialled up to a bone-shaking volume that was designed (yet failing) to hold out over the chorus of boos and heckles working their way into a powerful, uniformed wave of sound.

I lurched my way over to the wall surrounding the stairs down into the metro concourse. I steadied myself against it as I felt a crowd start to increase in size around me and my legs weaken beneath me. There was a bin affixed to it right next to the wall where I slumped. I took tight a hold of it and vomited into its base.

"Fucking drunk!" muttered a man as he was walked past me with his wife.

I paid no heed.

I was too busy wracking my brain over and over.

Was that really the first time I'd seen Hetherington in the flesh in all these years after what he did to me? It can't have been.

Surely?

After all, Newcastle is a big city but a small place and all roads lead into each other's pockets in one way or another… don't they?

## [11]

## or

## "Mick Hetherington."

**I** was a good police officer.

Nah, fuck it. No one else is going to speak the truth so let me have this moment just this one time: I was a *great* police officer.

I'd wanted to join the police since I was a kid. I wanted to be Martin Riggs, John McClane and Popeye Doyle all rolled into one and put out onto the streets of Newcastle.

No kid actually dreams of being a *private investigator*.

I certainly didn't.

I mean, I watched the 1971 version of Shaft as a kid and thought "Well, he walks around a lot, fucks a lot of women and occasionally stops to punch some bad guys – Now, I do like the idea of fucking lots of women. And the punching bad guys seems fun… but I don't know, that seems like a *lot* of walking he's doing!"

I certainly never came away from it thinking that seemed like the sort of job for me.

But life finds a way to get in the way, doesn't it?

I lived, breathed, ate, slept and shit wanting to be in the police - being the guy who people were pleased to see when they were in danger and scared to see when they'd been bad. It really was that simplistic to me. By the time that I hit police training school in the winter of 2005 I had Blackstone's Police Operational Handbook read cover to cover – for fun!

I shit you not.

My police training was residential, meaning I was paid to live in their training accommodation five days a week, bunk with my fellow trainees, eat three square meals a day of stodgy awful canteen food, attend seven hours of classes a day, study in the evening and sit three exams a week – one testing the knowledge I was learning in the classroom around the law and criminal justice studies, the other a physical exam making sure I consistently improved on my fitness on a weekly basis and the final one assessing my ability to carry out handcuffing techniques, take-down and break-away manoeuvres.

I adored absolutely every minute of it.

The more I learnt the more I saw the *art* of investigating; chasing the facts, piecing together a narrative of incidence and looking at the evidence against the lawful points to prove for any given criminal offence. I genuinely began to realise how doctors could come to study and become so fascinated and committed to learning and mastering specific fields of medicine. Stallone's Cobra was not bullshitting – Crime really was the disease and I saw myself somewhat over-earnestly as its cure.

My bunk mate from Day One of training school was Andy Andrews… Yes – just to remind you all - the very same Detective Inspector from the prologue of our tale and the same Andy Andrews from that interview room blow-out.

Yes, that *really* is his actual name.

His parents, one Mr and Mrs Andrews, held him in their arms at birth for the first time, took one look at him and thought "Let's give him a first name that is an abbreviation of his last name because we're zany, quirky little fuckers and we want people to pick up on that whenever they ask us what our son is called!"

Not really - Mr and Mrs Andrews were the driest, most humourless twats you could ever possibly meet. Both civil servants, actually.

I loved Andy from the get go.

He was as completely dedicated to succeeding in police training and ultimately the police service overall as I was. We would sit up late every night giving each other made-up quizzes about the stuff we'd learnt in class that day. He would practice his handcuffing technique on me and vice versa. We'd go for runs every night on the track that circled the training school, repeating the police caution over and over again to each other, lap after lap after lap.

We never argued about anything.

Well we did once, I think.

I mean before the 'blow-out' that killed what we had.

I know we must have argued pre 'blow-out' because that was when I devised the idea of calling him 'Andrew Andrews' for the first time. And I don't know why but it *really* pissed him off to an irrational level when I did that. I hung onto that. I'm glad I did because it rather crazily became a blunt weapon to stab at him with years later whenever our paths crossed and I needed something to replace wanting to smash his teeth in.

We talked about getting a flat together back then.

We knew that the British police didn't encourage or endorse permanent partnering at uniform level like the American police did but we figured that as long as we proved so specifically and irritatingly well aligned to one another, our relief sergeant would find it easier to just partner us up. We were that naïve.

We never doubted we'd graduate though. We never thought for one second we wouldn't end up on the same relief within the same area command. As far as we were concerned it was fated to be this way so that is how it will be.

And sure enough it was.

We graduated in the spring of 2006, rented a flat together almost instantly and turned up on our first day at what used to be a police station on Pilgrim Street smack bang in the centre of town. Every shift ended with us hitting the pub on the way home, falling in through the door of our flat, collapsing on the sofa and watching Band of Brothers pretty much on an incessant loop. We both chain-smoked back then. Our flat was a constant grey haze with a really pungent marriage of smells between Marlborough Reds (his!) and Lucky Strike Lights (mine!).

As our probations ended we started taking every varied secondment going that would give us the breadth of experience in policing needed to convince the panel on the detectives' board that we were the best possible candidates for promotion they could choose. Andy and I always saw becoming Detectives and rising through the ranks in CID, into Murder Squad and Special Crimes as the conjoined route each of us would walk.

… Then everything went to shit one really rainy night in the Autumn of 2011.

I was back in uniform after a long stint in plain clothes on the police's robbery squad unit. I had submitted to take the Detective's exam. Andy was back in uniform after a one year stint assisting in CID south of the river, building up his portfolio of experience to head down the same route. He'd already sat and failed the Detective's exam himself. He passed it the second time but at an absolute scrape. Then he was summarily rejected by the interview panel. He was starting to doubt whether it was ever going to happen for him.

It was a rare and long overdue occasion for us to be side-by-side working together. It was a late shift and we had a marked car to hide out from the rain in. I'd texted Jane and told her I was working with Andy and we'd probably unwind at a dive bar once we clocked off at half eleven, so not to wait up. There wasn't a chance in hell she would have anyway but it felt like the respectful thing to do. Plus, if I'd not been home by midnight at the end of a late turn or updated her I was clocking up the overtime, she'd have already rang the Police Benevolent Fund to find out when her widows' cheque was getting posted out to her.

We were two hours out from the end of our shift, parked up on a street in Jesmond just giving each other shit and talking about all the great times we had living together. Out of nowhere this new model BMW steamed past us at high speed, swerving all over the place on the road in front of us. We started up the engine and with me driving we went after it but before we could even hit the 'blues and twos' that come as standard with the job, the BMW pulled off to the left through a red light and went down into Jesmond Dene. We lost sight of it for a matter of minutes and just as Andy was about to call it in and ask for another units support, I clocked it in a parking pay underneath Jesmond Bridge.

The car was stationary.

All the windows were steamed up already.

We thought we knew what we were looking at here.

Andy called it in and started to do a vehicle check on the registration at the same time that I went over and tapped on the glass of the driver's side door.

Mick Hetherington wound the window down with one hand whilst stuffing his penis casually back in his pants. In the passenger seat, with cheeks drenched in tears that glistened from the illuminating street lamp above the car, was a girl who looked no more than thirteen years of age.

At that.

And I'm talking at an *absolute push.*

Mick is a big mess of a man now. His scaly-skinned borderline obesity is hidden behind carefully sculpted suits that he pays a fortune for and everyone seems to have stopped asking how he can afford them. He was pretty fat when I first encountered him back then, don't get me wrong. But he's disgusting now. It's almost like as his power increases so does any of Mick's friends' ability to say "No Mick. You don't need a third portion. Put the fork down."

He's committed to having his thinning hair cut short and pushed forward to best hide the run of bald spots that lean across the middle of his head like a racing stripe. Back then when I first met him though his head was a mess of wiry splats of hair, balding scalp and combed bits.

The Mick Hetherington of today is the 'grandmaster' and informal 'king' of Newcastle. He was the head of Newcastle's council who continually escaped many, many attempts to be unseated – or 'dethroned' as Mick himself called it. Once he got in as the head of Newcastle council, he continually reinvented himself to suit the needs of whatever voter group he required to keep him in power. Big supporter of the LGBQT community? Enormous believer in helping the elderly around the region? Investor and protector of children's services? That was Mick! That was *all* Mick! Unless you wanted him to *deliver* on all of his talked about promises to all of these people. Then you were high and dry, because you'd already fallen for voting him back in for another few years of running things.

Then came the devolution.

In a nutshell devolution, which is the central government's redelegation of powers down to a regional level by way of administrative decentralisation… Yes, I stole this straight from the Home Office website! Why are you judging me on that? You think I just had the standard textbook definition of 'devolution' for this particular context right there on a certain shelf in my brain ready to pull out and throw out in the most bite-size story-friendly terms? Come on, man. Cut me some slack here. I'm trying to do a massive big exposition-dump here…

Anyway, yeah, devolution came.

And this was our region's equivalent of giving a steroid level injection of demagoguery to a power-obsessed mad man with an innate ability to manipulate masses of people for his own gain. Separate councils around the region disbanded in order to form one 'mega' council representing a larger local swell of area and those council leaders from the local authorities that used to exist would now form a 'committee' working underneath one overall leader of the greater 'new' council for all boroughs.

Of course the leader had to be voted in.

And of course there were "issues" and "concerns" with the voting practices and securities on the night… And *of course* Mick Hetherington was ultimately announced as the new 'Mayor of the North East' despite the "issues" and "concerns".

That was two, maybe three years ago.

And it sure as hell looks like this guy isn't going anywhere any time soon either.

All the shady shit Mick was known for just got blown up to an amplified level the minute he became Mayor in this new form. Contracts for services to run things or fix things or build things or design things? They went to Mick's buddies. Only they were of much, much higher value than ever before. And what was left went to the people who could afford to make Mick feel 'good' about them as an option. Of course what made Mick feel 'good' was money.

And having sex with children.

Because Mick is the biggest paedophile in the North East.

Back then though, I wasn't looking at 'King' Mick Hetherington. I was looking at Councillor "on the rise" Mick Hetherington. A local Labour candidate who took on anyone and everyone in order to protect "the common man" that was "the backbone of what makes Newcastle Upon Tyne great". Those quotes were his, by the way. He really said them. Out loud. At many an event. And he put them down in print on most of his election campaign material. I know this for a fact because I pulled them directly from one of them just now for this paragraph.

I leant down, looking past Mick and at the girl in the passenger seat.

"Are you okay?" I said, my voice shaking more than I would've preferred.

Mick broke straight in before she could even so much as think about how she was going to answer. "This is my niece. She's up in Newcastle for…"

I let my eyes fall back to lock in with Mick's. I slowly raised one finger to my lips then let my eyes roll back to where the girl was sat. "Is this man your uncle?" I asked.

She sat silent.

"Would you like to get out of the car?" I offered.

She slowly started to nod.

"Madeline, stay where you are!" countered Mick assertively. "Officer, you need to understand…"

He started to open his car door. I kneed it shut immediately, unfortunately missing his grubby fat fingers by centimetres.

"Stay in the car!" I shouted.

Andy started to make his way over. He held his pocketbook in his hand ready to do a check against the notes he'd made from the control room's response to the registration. I waved him to be silent before he started.

"There's a young girl in the car here in a state of distress!" I said.

Andy looked at the car, letting his eyes bounce from the driver to the passenger and back again.

"This girl here is called Madeline, according to our driver!" I said loudly. "She's going to get out the car now. Can you take her and put her in the back of ours? Put something down on the seat first. Keep her warm. Don't give her anything to drink just yet. Do you know what I'm talking about?"

Andy slowly nodded. He got what I was referring to. We had that short-hand. There were forensics to consider.

The car door opened unsteadily and with trepidation. Madeline's feet cautiously hit the ground beneath her and she wobbled her way towards Andy. The moonlight and the street lamps converged and lit up the dishevelled state of her clothes and to this day I'll never forget that the left side of her dress was partially tucked into the knickers she had on. Like her dress had been pulled back into place in a hurry with no care or attention paid to what or where it was snagged.

I asked Mick to get out of the car and place his hands on the roof. I asked this as I was unclipping my handcuffs from their holster. Mick started to climb out of the car, eyeing my handcuffs as he lifted himself up into a standing position.

"If those handcuffs touch my wrists, your career is over!" he smiled.

"If I find out your penis touched that girl so is yours!" I shot back whilst spinning him to face away from me and cleanly sliding the handcuffs on.

Back-up was on the way - a second unit to place Mick inside of and take to the station. He'd been informed for what offence he was being arrested for, he'd been cautioned, his reply to the caution was noted – *"Did you like your job? Did you? Was it fun? Are you going to miss it?"* – alongside the time of arrest.

It was a ticked-box, professional arrest. With every urge to smash his face repeatedly off his car roof successfully fought. I wish I'd not fought as hard knowing now that restraint would take me to the same destination as retribution.

The girl was identified as being twelve year old Madeline Mason who lived in a care home under the charge of Newcastle council. On the nights Councillor Hetherington would visit the care home with sweets and magazines and a 'lottery' for who would get to go out on a special night out "bowling or to the cinema", Madeline always seemed to win more than any other girl or boy there.

They only went bowling or anywhere "nice" the first couple of times Madeline "won". After that it was all long drives to desolate car parks "with nice views" where Councillor Hetherington would talk to her about how things were going to get better for her but she just had to learn to trust the right people and "not carry so much anger towards adults". Anger that Madeline didn't even realise she had.

It started with forehead kisses from "Micky" that always seemed to end up with him needing to put his hand on her legs to balance himself as he lent in.

Then the cuddles around the shoulder with the carelessly placed hand.

The cuddles around the shoulder gave way to an awkward cuddle around the waist that didn't really work because of where he was positioned in the car in comparison to her. But once he moved them to the back seat it was easier.

I sat in the observation room as Madeline was interviewed by the Vulnerable Witness team. I stood alongside our duty inspector who silently mouthed the words "Holy Fuck!" over and over again as Madeline bravely gave more and more detail to the abuse she suffered at Mick's hands, using words that were decidedly uncoached and very much unrehearsed.

"I mean, I'd heard a rumour once or twice…" stumbled the inspector. "I heard that he liked them young and what not. But I didn't think he was hanging around the fucking school gates or anything like that."

"Foster homes!" I spat back contemptuously. "He liked them young *and* vulnerable!"

Whilst I stood witness to this horror, Andy was fingerprinting, photographing and generally 'getting to know' Mick Hetherington.

Mick would be front page on national newspapers in a day, it seemed. He'd surely be a central story on the twenty-four hour news cycle within the next few hours. He definitely was facing a pretty open and shut case at court seeing as the forensic evidence had been so tightly preserved on Madeline by Andy and me from the moment she stepped out of the car. Mick would be going to jail for a very…

… And then in a heartbeat, he *wasn't.*

He wasn't looking down the barrel at *any* of those things.

At all.

Mick didn't waste his one phone call on getting a solicitor down to the custody suite. He used his call on Graham Hadenbury. Superintendent Graham Hadenbury of the very police force I worked for.

In less than ninety minutes, Superintendent Hadenbury had arrived in the custody suite in the sort of casual attire you imagined he went golfing in but you also kind of knew cost more than the value of probably all of your clothes added together. He went into a room with our Inspector and closed the door.

Then he went and read the custody notes and our arrest report. He never once made any effort to speak a single word to myself or Andy. *That's* how ultimately unimportant we were on the grand scheme of what was coming next.

After reading through the reports and what not, he went and visited Mick in his cell where voices were raised and apologetic tones were struck. Don't think for one second that Mick was the one apologising either.

Then… BOSH! … Just like that Mick Hetherington was walking out of his cell, putting his belt on and his laces back into his shoes, laughing it up with the custody sergeant about the fact that he can't believe he was so stupid and naïve to think you could be "that innocently generous and supportive to young ones these days especially after that whole Jimmy Savile debacle".

I could begin to feel my skin boil from the inside out. I thought I was going to pass out as I listened to him talk about how "mistaken" and "troubled" Madeline was and that's why he "tried to pay her a bit extra attention, to try and rebuild her trust in adults once again". The vomit rose into the back of my gullet as I watched Superintendent Hadenbury nod supportively as Mick spoke.

Then it happened.

Mick turned and offered his hand to Andy who'd stood behind the exiting party this whole time. "PC Andrews, it was lovely meeting you."

Andy slowly reached out and took hold of Mick's hand which Mick in turn gripped tightly and began to shake vigorously. "I'm sure we'll speak again soon. We've got a lot to talk about, I promise you."

Mick clicked his heels and span on the spot, walking out of custody and straight towards me. He stopped and feigned a look of shock. "Oh, Graham?" he gasped causing Superintendent Hadenbury to look up from typing the exit code into the security door and stop what he was doing.

"You're not going to have to look too far after all, my friend!" continued Mick. "This is most definitely the officer who viciously assaulted me tonight!"

The end of my time in the police wasn't a drawn out affair filled with disciplinary hearing after disciplinary hearing over months and months, with me hanging on in hope that there would be some last minute reprieve and a sudden display of common sense and integrity about the sheer, inexplicable shadiness and corruption that was befalling me.

No, it was fairly instantaneous.

I'm talking like… a fortnight.

That's what was scary. That's how powerful and manipulative Mick Hetherington was back then – and he was barely *anyone* then either; a local councillor for a shitty ward in a shitty part of the city. Yet he seemed to have the ear of everyone.

I was suspended that night.

Mick claimed that I had kneed him in the groin after I dragged him from the car and then I repeatedly kneed him in the head until he fell to the ground. Once there, I apparently kicked him twice in the neck and shoulder.

None of that happened but this was the statement Mick gave within an hour of Graham Hadenbury walking him out of the custody suite that night.

I remember crawling home and sliding into bed alongside Jane and the sheer confusion hit me as to what was happening:

We caught a paedophile.

His victim gave a statement.

My interaction was observed by my partner who was also my best friend.

There was no violence.

There was no assault.

There was forensics though.

This couldn't just be swatted away.

I got to sleep that night purely by repeating all of those things to myself over and over and saying to myself that I would have my chance to be heard. I decided not to worry Jane until there was something to worry about so I kept my head down over the next day or so and just took the hit for being surly with her.

Then things started to get bad… and then they got worse…

I couldn't find a single police federation representative to take my case on. They all took my calls, listened, then heard Hadenbury was deeply involved and slinked off but not before handing me the number of "another guy who can help" because they were, quote unquote, "too busy to take on new cases".

Madeline disappeared – swiftly moved not just out of the care home she was in under Newcastle Council's remit but out of the city altogether… out of the *region*, in fact. Nowhere to be found. Guess what else disappeared alongside her? Her statement! The forensic reports! Everything! It was like someone was rubbing an eraser over that entire night and redesigning it to look completely different.

How could one fat-arsed, sick-fuck, ten-a-penny, local councillor have this much power? What he probably wasn't counting on though was the sheer loyalty and brotherhood that ran through Andy and I and bound us to one another, right? Turns out Mick Hetherington wasn't counting on it because he knew I was being stupid to count on it myself.

I'd rang Andy the next morning and texted him straight after he didn't pick up my call, still a bit weirded out by the fact that he'd not turned up straight at my door the minute his shift finished and he discovered I'd been suspended.

I texted again when no reply came.

And I called again.

And I eventually went round to his flat the minute I knew he was on a rest day and I finally cornered him face to face.

That's when I really, truly realised how much deep shit I was in.

"I didn't see what went on between you two. I had my back to you both!" was one of Andy's proclamations that day. "Dude, I shouldn't even be speaking to you. I was warned. They're going to call me as a witness to give a statement… I don't know what to be saying. It was pitch black and you guys were behind me… That girl didn't seem that upset, man! I don't think it was what you think it was, Jake!"

There was the stone-cold, swinging steel hammer to the jaw right there.

"What the fuck are you talking about?" I gasped.

"I'm hearing that she's disappeared again anyway. She was some homeless girl he was trying to help and it has all got confused. She's panicked and ran off now."

"I know what I heard come out of her mouth at the station, Andy. I saw him putting his dick away in the car. The guy is…"

"Listen, calm down. I'm not going to say that I saw you hit him. I'm not because I didn't. I love you, man. I do. You've got to trust me."

"Andy, I can't even get a federation rep to sit alongside me on this. The entire force has just closed their eyes and turned their backs and you and I know I haven't done anything wrong!"

"They're probably just shit scared of Hadenbury. He's a man on the rise. They reckon he's going to be running the whole of the constabulary in less than two years. And it looks like his best buddy is this Mick Hetherington guy. Just sit tight, man. It's going to be okay."

Spoiler alert: It wasn't.

A hastily arranged hearing was booked in. I attended and represented myself. It was the very definition of a kangaroo court with Mick painting the picture of a wronged man pulled from his car whilst trying to be a good Samaritan on a cold, dark, rainy night by a crazed and violent police thug who beat him to the ground. Andy stepped up on the day and stuck to his promise that he was not going to say that he saw me hit Mick Hetherington.

Instead he said worse.

When asked whether he saw me attack Mick Hetherington, Andy looked directly down at his own feet, gulped air, took the longest possible pause before quietly but affirmatively saying the words "No comment!"

I was sacked that day.

The kids were sent to Jane's parents that night and I sat and sobbed.

I felt so powerless. More so because of the fact that there'd been such a naked abuse of power and I'd been so horrendously hung out to dry by the service I'd given everything to and the man I considered a brother.

Jane and I sat and got very drunk. We talked up plans to go to solicitors and take the police on head first and to get the media involved. We threw hastily drawn up ideas down on paper for how we were going to find where Madeline had been taken and get her to re-testify. Then we fell asleep in each other's arms and woke up with an even bigger problem to add to the messy pile of shit we were in.

... Because I kept on drinking.

I lent hard on booze despite Jane trying to fight me every step of the way. I couldn't stay sober for more than two hours at the start of the day which meant meeting with solicitors was an embarrassment and conversations with journalists turned into angry diatribes that came across like the unprintable 'conspiracy theory' drenched rants of a mad-man. Solicitors shrugged us off and journalists stopped taking our calls. We were completely cast loose and the lie became the truth simply because someone in power said that was how it was going to be.

Jim Beam was my drink of choice... It was like velvet going down.

On a good day, I'd get up and have breakfast with the children and bury the raging hangover for like an hour or something and then head back to bed. I'd clear a six-pack of Pabst Blue Ribbon just watching Big Trouble In Little China (daily!) from under the duvet whilst Jane ran herself down to empty before her day had even started, getting the kids out the door and to school on time. Before her first "What's your plans today?" text had arrived, I'd already taken the empty cans out to the recycling bin and grabbed the Jim Beam from the back of the wardrobe. Her next daily text - suggesting I get showered and go meet her for lunch at the café across the road from her school - was always left unread until hours too late because I was normally having my first crash-nap of the day.

Within a week of my sacking, Andy was made Acting Detective Constable.

Within a month he was a substantive Detective Constable who'd miraculously gone from scoring 35% at his panel interview to 89%, so I was told.

Andy sold me out for a promotion.

Remember how I told you at the start that I hate the clichés and the bullshit and all that? I was betrayed by the worst cliché of clichés – stabbed in the back in order to rise further up the corporate ladder, so to speak.

Andy got a promotion.

Graham Hadenbury rose one more notch up the ranks too.

Hell, even the custody sergeant from the night of the arrest started driving round in a better car and wearing inspector epaulets on his uniform.

Me? I got a drinking problem and the first dent of many in my marriage.

… A year or so later, I came out the other end barely able to comprehend where we were as a family. We'd sold up the house in Gosforth and moved to a much smaller ex-council house that was pennies to take on at auction down near the Tyne Tunnel. Jane got the deputy head's job so as a one wage family we weren't horrifyingly poor but I was drinking the money faster than she could earn it and it was only the children that were suffering.

To such an extent that one day Jonathan hurt himself at school, the headmistress couldn't get a hold of Jane in the first instance so they called me. And of course I was too drunk to get there in any remotely presentable state. I could barely even speak to the school on the bastard phone. Jonathan ended up getting taken to hospital by one of the teaching assistants in his class and Jane's parents were called to attend from there.

They didn't stop to pick me up on the way.

And Jane asked me to leave that night.

I had nowhere to go.

Every single friend I had from my policing days had written me off as an alcoholic mental case. I lost my family at a young age. I didn't know what to do. I ended up climbing the fence in Wallsend Park of all places and sleeping in the recently refurbished Band Stand on the grounds.

Two days later, I cleaned up cold turkey, got my shit together, applied to study for my Private Investigators qualification and set about getting my wife back.

Right, flash forward back to where we are now then?

As you're all probably aware … bit by bit… I've essentially burnt it all down to being a limping, bloated, pill-popping private investigator who's replaced alcohol with drugs and hates himself more than anyone else could and keeps trying to jump in on a game no one wants him to play in.

Quite the catch, huh?

To those currently muttering "Why the hell am I reading *this* guy's story?" whilst about to put this book down with no intention to return to it, all I would say is "Hey, everyone likes a great tale of *redemption*, right?"

Wink. Wink. Nudge. Nudge.

## [12]

## or

## "A Public Ode To The Late Miss Jay..."

Greys Monument Square in the centre of Newcastle used to be awash with festive spirit and activity at this time of year. Festive market stalls and continental food booths were stacked side-by-side in a curved u-shape right the way along the pedestrian walkways on both side of the Central Arcade until the paths would give way to Grainger Street and Grey Street, respectively. This time of year in Newcastle was once so popular it had rivalled York as a Christmas season tourist destination.

Not anymore.

The stalls and food booths were nowhere to be seen. There was nothing to disguise the sight of bordered up shops around the square anymore. The cheer and bustle of the festive season was no longer hanging in the air. Instead it was just boos and cat-calls from the crowd that now numbered over a hundred plus, jeering at the council representatives up on the makeshift stage by the Greys Monument statue.

I pushed my way off and away from leaning on the wall and unsteadily made my way through the crowd. People pushed back against me. There were protestors who treated me as some interloper to their cause and then there was people who'd finished work somewhere in the city only moments ago, just trying to brush through and get on a nearby metro or bus home.

Mick Hetherington was trying to address the crowd but the crowd were having none of it. He spoke about "tough times". The crowd screamed back "BECAUSE OF YOU!" and then united in a chorus of "RESIGN! RESIGN! RESIGN!" He tried to follow up with some misbegotten half-baked greeting card statement that "the thing that defeats tough times is the tougher level of people that are facing them down and there is no city of people tougher than Newcastle!"

That REALLY pissed the crowd off, let me tell you.

Who up there at Newcastle Council thought this was a good idea? To get out here and get front-facing with the community they're wilfully destroying and do this? This was a recipe for disaster. The police clearly thought so too, as eight to ten uniformed police officers pushed their way into position between the baying crowd and the barrier that separated Mick and his guests from them.

I was just starting to get overcome again with the thought of my imaginary gun and the damage I wanted to do to Mick, jumping up on stage and standing over his body as he bled out there and then… with the last thing he ever heard being me screaming into the microphone about the young children he liked to have sex with…

… when I was shaken free by the sight of Bobby Maitland standing with Ryan and three other big, shaved ape type henchmen stereotypes. They stood surrounding him, ensuring that Bobby never once encountered what it would feel like to be jostled by a braying crowd and hurried commuters. Anyone who got near Bobby simply bounced off the brick wall that was the men stood around him.

Just as I was hedging my bets to go over and talk to him and maybe try and casually throw the name Stephie Jay into the conversation, I saw Bobby scowl in the direction of the stage then spit on the ground. "Fucking clueless cunt!" he audibly sneered whilst staring Mick Hetherington down.

Bobby and I should probably get together sometime. You know for light bites and Mick Hetherington 'war stories'? We'd probably have a lot in common, don't you think?

Before I could get close enough to suggest such a thing, Bobby turned and stormed off down Grainger Street and away from the crowds still going strong against Mick and the people up on that stage.

Mick was trying to hold his own too. Clearly shielded by the fact he did not give one single fuck whatever any of these plebs had to say or shout as long as they didn't touch him, he pushed on with gripping the microphone stand tight and selling the message he came here to sell.

"… As you'll see we've extended the festive lighting all around Greys Monument to now include some beautiful, *beautiful* angel symbols in honour of Stephie Jay. Stephie was of course, for many if not all of us, the *Queen* of Newcastle."

Some of the crowd softened their jeering at the mention of Stephie's name. The majority didn't. Most carried on shouting. "WHERE'S THE MONEY FOR THESE EXTRA LIGHTS COME FROM THEN?" seemed to be the most common heckle.

"… It feels sadly ironic that I'm switching on so many artificial lights when the city has lost its greatest most natural one!" said Mick. He paused to let out a false sigh that he segued into a dramatic pause. "We asked Stephie's parents to be with us tonight as we turned on these lights in her honour and take a moment of silence which I hope you'll all honour. Unfortunately they are still very much in pain at the senseless loss of Stephie so I've asked Sue George, Stephie's best friend and agent, to join me instead."

My attention was piqued. *The* Sue George, eh?

Mick held what looked like an index card out in front of his eyes and blandly read the contents out to the crowd. "… Sue will of course be producing her annual festive charity fashion show on Christmas Eve for the fifteenth year running this year over at the Metrocentre. It's free to attend over in the Red Quadrant mall. It'll be a great show for a great cause with free giveaways… and all that. So, Christmas Eve. One pm. Red Quadrant mall, Metrocentre. We hope you'll be there to see some great looking people putting on a great show!"

He hurriedly stepped away from the microphone and up to it in his place stepped a very nervous-looking Sue George – a spindly late-fifties brunette who was fighting the aging process with a splatter-gun distraction of thick foundation, bright red lipstick and what looked like extremely over-complicated 'fuck me' boots.

“Thank you for inviting me tonight, Mayor Hetherington.” Sue said softly into the microphone. The atmosphere from the crowd was a little less toxic but it still wasn’t subduing. “I just wanted to keep it very short and say that Stephie was the best model we had at The George Platform and I am very lucky to say she was my best friend too…”

Sue’s voice broke and it looked like her composure was going down to.

She struggled through the words “… It is an honour to be here tonight for Stephie!” and then sat back down with haste. The crowd were falling a little more quiet and the placards were starting to drop a little bit so Mick seized the moment, giving a quick wave to the side and within seconds a sea of angel lights lit up over every single person’s head.

Mick led a round of applause that no one else joined in on and the crowd kicked off once more, the air filling with hollering choruses of “RESIGN! RESIGN! RESIGN!”

Sue, Mick and a few of the other invited council elite started to make their way off the stage and I took a chance to push through the protestors and get to the point where I would meet them coming off stage and heading for the car waiting to whisk them away from the crowds. It put me closer to Mick Hetherington than my mental health could probably do with, but I needed to speak to Sue and who says ringing for an appointment is better than a cold, hard, unwelcome introduction in the middle of a big, ol’ kick-off eh?

I got close to Sue, assisting police officers be damned and I gently tapped her on the shoulder. She nervously turned and saw me.

“Hi Sue.” I said as non-combatively as possible.

“Hi. I’m not speaking to press tonight. Thank you!” she replied.

“I’m not press, don’t worry!” I smiled. “I’m actually representing Margaret and Matthew Jason…”

Sue slowed her pace and stopped. Mick and his cronies walked on ahead without realising she was not directly behind them anymore.

“Yes?” she said.

“I’m looking into the death of Stephie on their behalf!”

“What do you mean?” she said abruptly, as an air of nervous confusion started to instantly permeate around her.

“Her parents have many unanswered questions.”

“Like what, may I ask?”

“Well, you booked Stephie in for an event at Paradox nightclub on the eighth of November but then it was cancelled for an alternative. Something about a double-booking?” I asked.

“You’re mistaken. There was no double-booking. Stephie asked me to cancel that event as she was feeling unwell. I don’t know anything else that she got up to that evening, I’m afraid. I only wish that I did because maybe I could’ve prevented what…”

The crowd’s volume increased. They edged closer to the pathway the police had made for Mick, Sue and company to get to the awaiting car and leave.

I took my chances. "So Toccare at nine o'clock means nothing then?"

She looked startled. "I'm sorry, I can't hear you."

"*Toccare*? Does the word Toccare mean…"

Before I could finish a large, hard-shouldered man with the thickest, most well-trimmed beard I'd seen up close in quite some time slammed into me and knocked me away from Sue. By the time I got my bearings and reared back round to carry on speaking to Sue, she was being led away by another large, hard-shouldered man and I was left face to face with Mick Hetherington himself.

"I'm pretty sure I have a restraining order in place against you, don't I?" he smirked.

My head started to really hurt.

I could feel my temples pushing in. My head was going to crack. I could genuinely feel the pain of my skull having unbearable force applied to it. I couldn't speak. I stared so hard at him, genuinely wondering whether I could pull his throat out with my bare hands before anyone could stop me.

"I'll let you off this one time. You know, what with it being Christmas." His smile broadened. "What you doing these days anyway, Mr Lehman? Are you still trying to make this Magnum PI cloud-cuckoo-land shite work?"

I stayed silent.

I couldn't move.

Somehow my brain had decided the best self-defence mechanism was just to lock everything down and to protect me from myself.

"I try to keep an observing eye on all my *favourite* people, you know what I mean? But the last I heard on you was that you were out in the land of Oz providing target practise for the Aussies…" he laughed. "I mean, you look like crap. So I'm pleased to see life's treating you how it should!"

He leant forward. I stayed rooted to the spot.

He dropped his voice so it was only just audible over the throng of the crowd's hatred for him. With police officers around him, urging him to move on towards the vehicle, Mick whispered "I never cross a name off my 'Shit List'! Remember that, yeah? Once you're on it, you're in it. The only way you get off it is to die!"

He winked and walked away.

I watched him climb into the awaiting car, a police officer bang his hand on the roof and off it sped away from Greys Monument. I let out a sigh and turned to walk for the metro home.

This was probably something I'd leave out of any conversation I had with Jane later.

I'd maybe taken half a step when I got hit by yet another large, hard-shouldered man. This one was a black guy who held together an impressive business casual outfit.

"Jesus! Watch where you're going!" I said as he impassively carried on walking as if I was a ghost he'd just passed through.

"How many of these American football playing thick-necked fucks is there out in town tonight?" I thought to myself as I angrily stomped on down the stairs to the metro concourse.

## [13]

## or

## "Red Herrings And Bad Guys..."

I'd arranged to borrow the car for work that morning from Jane with the understanding I'd drop it back at her school after my appointment up in Smallburn with Mr and Mrs Jason. I'm no fan of public transport at the best of times but I tolerate it as a necessary evil to be able to get around now we can no longer afford to be a two car family. However, public transport up into the sticks near Ponteland and then a two mile walk to the Jason's palatial country mansion on 'Millionaire's Row' did not appeal to me or my gammy knee one bit.

I was taking my appointment at their home seriously.

I'd set my alarm earlier in order to be able to spend time with the kids but also to pop my daily Tramadol a little sooner so that I got my 'kick' before the appointment – I had been at this long enough now to be able to time the 'kick', the 'haze', the 'comedown' and the 'ache' all rather perfectly... I wanted to be in their company directly after the 'kick' and most definitely before the 'haze'.

It was important to me that Margaret Jason could see that there was worth in continuing the investigation even further still. I wanted her to believe that there was still a lot of avenues worth walking down. I also wanted to make the best impression possible on Matthew Jason, who I'd be meeting for the first time that morning.

I'd summarised all my notes and concerns into one bullet-pointed sheet of A4 and I sat alone in the bath soaking my bad back and legs once the house had emptied following Jane ushering Jack and Jonathan out the door.

I read over the sheet again and again and again.

I called Psychic on the drive up to Smallburn and told him I'd be back into the office after lunch. He asked that I didn't dawdle as he'd got some movement on those 'SOTTfan1999', 'Professor LickHerSpine212' and 'Professor LickHerSpine' Twitter accounts we were looking to identify and he wanted to talk it over.

"Should I be excited?" I asked.

"You should always be excited to see me, buddy. But no, you shouldn't be excited about the Twitter accounts, I'm afraid!" laughed Psychic. "By the way, I picked up the engraving!"

"Oh yeah? And?" I replied.

"It's a gorgeous Rolex with an engraving on the back that says *'I am everything because of you, Daddy! SJ xx'*!" said Psychic.

Ah, man. I didn't need to learn that just before heading through the doors to see Matthew Jason for the first time. I really didn't need that.

I thanked Psychic and drove on.

I arrived at the Jason's home twenty minutes early. My intention was to sit in the car until two minutes before eleven o'clock but the truth was there was nothing but country road with no layby directly outside of their home and to get onto their grounds required me to announce myself via intercom at their security gate. So I went with the idea of being 'professionally early'.

Margaret came out to meet me, looking casually dishevelled in that way women do now where they purposefully fix their hair, make-up and lounge wear to look like they'd just woken up like that minutes ago when you *know* they'd been putting the whole look together for nearly an hour or something.

She smiled warmly and extended her hand. "Jake! Lovely to see you again. Please come on in!"

She led me in through the enormous wooden doors into a foyer area that was bigger than the entire house I lived in with a wife and two children. We talked as we walked.

"How long have you been a private investigator, Jake?" asked Margaret.

"Too long!" I smiled.

"But you're hanging in there, with how things are presently in the country, so that says a lot about how busy you must be, I presume?"

"We're doing okay!" I lied. "A lot of people don't realise that a lot of what private investigators do day-to-day is trace and chase down debtors. And at the moment there's a lot of debtors out there due to the circumstances we're facing in the country!"

"Quite!" said Margaret, she being someone who clearly has *not* had to face the circumstances within the country most of us were dealing with. "So looking into the death of my daughter must be a bit of a break from the norm for you then?"

"Oh, we get up to all sorts at Lehman's Terms." I smiled. "No one day is the same."

That last comment was obviously a lie dressed up as a semi-bluff. Because most days are the same and they generally all involve Psychic and I sitting around talking about films, TV and anything/everything else to while away the hours until we feel like we've put a shift in. But Margaret didn't need to know *that*, did she?

"Well Katherine spoke very highly of you, I must say!" said Margaret.

She won't be from now on, I'm fairly sure of that.

Of course I didn't say that either.

I just continued smiling and went with "That's nice to hear!" instead.

"What's your background then, Jake? How did you get into this?" Margaret continued.

"I was a police officer."

"Interesting. What made you give that up then if you don't mind me asking?"

I inaudibly cleared my throat of the phlegm that was starting to build up and I slid straight into my prepared stock answer that I'd formed and delivered many times over the years: "I just got sick of the shift work and never seeing my children. I was overworked and underpaid with all the cutbacks and I decided I wanted to set my own hours and see more of my family."

“That’s nice. Being your own boss really is wonderful isn’t it?”

I nodded whilst also squinting my eyes at the thought that she was referring to being a boss at a *completely* different level to me.

“I should have really been asking a lot of these questions at the outset and whilst we were at the consultation stage but I was too busy with stating my case and auditioning for you I forgot to get you to audition for me.” Margaret said.

I smiled. She stopped and turned to face me.

“Tell me I can trust you.” She said softly. “I’m fast running out of options, Jake. But right now if you tell me I can trust you I will believe you. I just need to hear that.”

I offered my hand to Margaret and she took it. We shook hands.

“You can trust me, Margaret. I promise you. I promise that I will act with the utmost integrity throughout all of this. And I won’t let you…”

Margaret took her hand and placed it on my chest, almost smelling the desperation I was trying to hide and deciding to put me out of my misery.

“I believe you.” Margaret said warmly. “It’s okay. I believe you. Now, come and meet Matthew.”

We veered immediately left through a living area with a whole wall taken up with the largest in-built television screen I’d ever seen, before coming straight out the other side into an enormous open plan conservatory area where Matthew Jason was sat slumped in a chair.

Matthew looked like two decades of living the best life possible - filled with personal trainers and the best food, holidays and everything else that comes with being very, very rich – had been completely undone overnight by tragedy. He sat, flopped in a chair between two sofas looking pale and totally dishevelled. The tan accrued from multiple sun-drenched holidays a year had faded to a deathly pallor reflective of giving up on eating, stepping outside in sunlight or hydrating yourself with anything other than whiskey. His facial hair was a grey-flecked mess that was another week or two away from making him look homeless.

In his hand Matthew clutched an ice-filled goblet with four generous fingers of whiskey. The bottle that had provided it was within reaching distance, on an antique side table that had been pulled forward and repurposed as his aide.

I smiled at him and introduced myself.

He didn’t look at me. He didn’t turn his head away from looking out into the vast, beautifully kept garden at the rear of the property. His eyes seemed fixed on one small rose bush no more than ten metres from the conservatory door that opened out onto the garden.

“Would you like a drink or anything?” Margaret asked softly.

I shook my head. “I’m good, thank you anyway!”

“Please take a seat.” Margaret gestured to the small sofa on the right.

She sat down on a second small sofa just across from it.

Matthew was there, between us. Present – yet not really.

I nervously pulled out my crib sheet and cleared my throat.

“Please…” Margaret said as her eyes welled up with tears. “… Please tell us you don’t think Stephanie killed herself?”

I slowly shook my head as I put down the crib sheet.

"I don't think Stephanie killed herself."

Margaret began to sob. Matthew's grip on his whiskey tightened. But his gaze never left that rose bush.

I leant forward and put a comforting arm on Margaret's shoulder and then I started to talk. And I didn't stop until I'd told her about the Twitter account with the death threat… and the abundance of questions that sprang up from visiting the scene of Stephie's death… and how I found no logical or physical means for Stephie to have hung herself at that scene unless the police's sole explanation was that she just drove over to this abandoned warehouse unit and found a ready-made suicide site… and also about how the police were wrong to close this off completely within a matter of days and the coroners were doubly-wrong to allow that to happen.

I then talked about what Khali Matti had told me about Stephie's event there getting cancelled on the night she died, that he'd said it was under Sue George's instruction but in the brief conversation I had with her she said that it was because Stephie wasn't well. I talked about how there seemed to be third hand talk that the cancellation angered Bobby Maitland and that I wanted to explore the possibility that he or one of his people retaliated. I talked about still wanting to meet and discuss Stephie's case with the coroner's office and that I was still having difficulty getting in touch with Alia Marcus or any of Stephie's modelling friends for that matter.

I talked.

And talked.

And Matthew Jason never so much as flinched.

I returned to the offices of 'Lehman's Terms' following a quick snatched lunch with Jane at a café outside of her school after returning the car. We didn't talk much about anything other than the kids and my attempts to pull from her what it was she wanted to talk to me about on 'Date Night' fell on deaf ears. She simply said I'd have to wait but that she'd arranged babysitting with her parents for that weekend.

Once back in the city I walked through the doors and had a cup of black coffee put straight into my hand as Psychic said "So… Keith Grounder is a little dick!"

"Who's Keith Grounder?" I asked, taking a seat on the sofa.

"I tried to get some IP tracing going on the Twitter accounts for that Professor Spineless or whatever he's called, right? But I hit a bust! So, get this, I laid a couple of traps and started engaging with him on the 'Professor LickHerSpine212' account using a 'ghost' account I've got going. You know? Shared interests, lots of retweets of his gormless tweets and all that. Eventually I said I had some signed 'Doctor Who' stuff I was getting rid of and did he want it because it's very clear he's into that show in kind of a creepy way…"

"The Professor is Keith Grounder?" I queried.

"Indeed! The guy behind those accounts is one Keith Grounder. He's fifteen and…"

I was disappointed to hear that because I knew where this was going now.

"… he lives with his parents!" continued Psychic.

"Ah man. I *knew* it!" I laughed.

"He's down in Skipton in North Yorkshire. The address and shit he give me is legit. It checks out and so, unfortunately for us, does his alibi on the weekend that Stephie died!"

"How do you know that?"

"Because I rang his parents and grassed him up for the mean things he wrote. I told his mum I was a police officer investigating the suicide of someone and I believed that Keith's comments contributed to her death!" smiled Psychic. "Keith won't be going online for a very, very long time now. And his mum is deeply ashamed of him. She also clarified that he was with her on the night Stephie died… at home in North Yorkshire, watching…"

Psychic checked his notes.

"Please let it be Ant & Dec's Saturday Night Takeaway, the sad little git!" I laughed.

"They were watching an NCIS marathon, she says!" grinned Psychic. "Keith Grounder is therefore a dick. But he is *not* a murderer. And he most definitely wasn't in Hebburn on Saturday the eighth of November."

The next few days passed in a blur of Psychic and I drawing up list after list of what we were drawn to assume were Stephie's friends based on information we'd pulled from social media and from Stephie's mother.

We had a name for the coroner responsible for Stephie's case: Alison Gregg.

We'd tried calling her to ask for an appointment. We'd emailed after tricking one of the people in her office into giving us her direct email address. We even went down to coroner's court on a day we were nearby on an off-chance we could catch her around there in some capacity. We got no response whatsoever. Not even of the 'I don't / can't / won't speak to you!' variety, just to get us to leave her alone. This woman was simply treating us like we were ghosts and our attempts to communicate just weren't getting through from the other side.

The thing with having lived the sort of life that Stephie lived was that her 'online footprint' gave us a connection rarely afforded to looking into someone you don't know or have never met who's died. In usual cases they're mainly just a face in a photograph or a memory verbally presented to you by a person you're talking to about them. There might be the occasional bit of home video footage here and there. But usually they're just a face on a file with a Facebook account to trawl through.

It was very different with Stephie though.

There were YouTube clips galore. And if we ran dry on them there was Snog On The Tyne 'Best Of' compilation DVDs that could be purchased from the HMV up the road. There was an abundance of other reality TV show appearances and interviews that could be streamed on one platform or another too.

We could hear her voice. We could watch her move. We could see her actually develop in confidence across these media forms the more recent we got. The Stephie Jay on her televised audition tape and first episode of Snog On The Tyne was most definitely not the same Stephie Jay who cut Leigh Francis down to size on some diabolical ITV2 game show or who more than held her own with Bear Grylls whilst sitting on a log in a pretend jungle. The growth in confidence and knowledge of how to work the camera was a huge determining factor but so too was the development of a 'style'. With each year Stephie seemed to hold herself differently, her make-up got more professionally applied and the hair went from being naturally long and straight to gorgeously feathered and styled within an inch of its life.

I watched a *lot* of Stephie.

She had a great smile but an even greater sense of humour. She seemed to be a new form of vapid, empty reality TV 'performer' who knew she had to play the requirements of being vapid and empty on reality TV but didn't see why she couldn't take the piss with it and sort of deconstruct what people's assumptions were of her.

I really came to like Stephie a lot.

Remember that bit in Team America: World Police where they take the piss out of movie montages and the song goes "*Show a lot of things happening at once... Remind everyone of what's going on... And with every shot you show a little improvement... To show it all would take too long... That's called a montage!*"

Well, think of those few days in a 'montage' form... Up there with the best of the best in 'movie montage scenes'. You know, like the 'growing in power and riches' bit in Scarface set to Paul Engemann's 'Push It To The Limit'? Or, as Psychic will demand I point out, the tournament scenes in The Karate Kid with Joe Esposito singing 'You're The Best' over the top? Obviously you've <u>got</u> to include *any* of the Rocky movies but *especially* Rocky III and Rocky IV, right? Jane would argue that the 'Hungry Eyes' montage in Dirty Dancing gets a place on the list. I wouldn't fight that. Hell, I'd even include... *whispers it*... the teaching-Chris-Penn-to-dance scenes set to 'Let's Hear It For The Boy' in Footloose too!

Only with every shot in our montage we weren't showing a "little improvement".

We were getting *nowhere.*

We emailed, instant messaged and, where possible, rang everyone we could.

The best and most repeated response we actually got was "We were... like... you know? 'Instagram close'? Not, you know, 'Real Life close'?"

Which meant nothing to me other than to reinforce my long-held belief that with each passing year our human interactions with one another were getting more and more empty and false.

I kept hearing again and again about how I "needed" to speak to Alia Marcus. "She was like Stephie's sister!" I'd hear over and over but I could not get her to return a single call, text or email.

I crossed another 'dead end' name of a list, popped two Tramadol's and downed them with the remainder of my black coffee which had now gone cold and tasted like really bad, stale supermarket-branded caffeine powder mixed in with warm tap water.

I grimaced from the taste and sat back down at my desk with my head in my hands, rubbing my eyes furiously and urging the kick to come quickly.

"It's kind of depressing isn't it?" I said out loud, only half caring whether Psychic was listening or not. "Her life online seems so full and exciting and everyone appears to hang on every word and photo she posts. She died with an obituary in the Evening Chronicle emblazoned with a headline affirming her as the 'Queen of Newcastle'. Everyone we've spoken to as leads so far talks about how beloved and popular she was... but no one actually says they were her 'friend' in the sense you or I would understand it."

"Well, how do you understand it? Because maybe your definition of 'friend' is antiquated now? Your taste in film and music certainly is!" laughed Psychic. "I mean, are *we* friends?"

"I don't know, mate. It's hard because I love you like a brother. I just don't like you as a person, you know?" I smirked and winked.

Psychic flicked his pen at me as I ducked out of the way.

"All I'm saying in all seriousness, Psychic, is that if I'm wrong on this and Stephie *did* kill herself than maybe we're landing on her motive as to why she did? Maybe for all her riches and shit, maybe once the crowds went home and she went back to her apartment overlooking the city... Maybe she was just lonely as hell?"

Psychic nodded. "But you don't think you're wrong do you?"

I sat silently for a minute or too.

"No." I finally said. "And if you asked me to call it right now, based on the purely flimsy and circumstantial guess-work we've got collected up, do you know what I'd say?"

Psychic looked at me, knowing the answer was coming anyway.

"I'd say there may be truth to this thing floating around from Khali that Bobby Maitland tried to send Stephie Jay a message for screwing him over, it went wrong and his guys tried to cover it up by making it look like a suicide."

"Woah!" whispered Psychic. "That's... *something*!"

"Because here's something you overlooked when giving me the breakdowns on Hark Roy and Blue Light Security..."

Psychic eagerly leant forward as I reached for a specific piece of paper in amongst the mess on my desk. Psychic is not someone who 'overlooks' anything. You could see in his face that he found such a suggestion to be an affront. I found the paper, took a glance at it and handed it over to him.

"There's four company directors listed for Blue Light Security." I paused for dramatic effect. "Robert 'Bobby' Maitland is one of them!"

I left Psychic to chew on my theory that Khali had alleged Bobby had motive to strike back against Stephie for abandoning one of his 'meet and greet' nights and costing one of his venues money, that one of his many 'finger in the pie' companies was responsible for the security at the specific venue where Stephie died and that we had first-hand experience of knowing Bobby used abandoned buildings he had some affiliation to in order to torture people that he felt had screwed him over.

I left all of that percolating and headed home to shower, change and head out on 'Date Night' with Jane.

'Date Nights' with Jane now were a completely different beast to what they were when we were first married, had Jack and two steady incomes that had us living quite comfortably – we'd catch a late afternoon film at The Gate, head over for the 'lobster option' at Hana Hana on Bath Lane, get 'ripened up' on sake then go down the Quayside for cocktails, rolling home in a taxi at three am a few hundred quid poorer and dead on our feet the next day when arriving at the in-laws to pick Jack up.

Now? Now the in-laws come to us at tea-time, giving us just enough time to sprint over to the local Italian restaurant round the corner from our house so we can take advantage of the 'two-courses for £8' early bird special. We're back a couple of hours later before the kids are needing to be put to bed because Jane's mum is "too old to be going to war with Jonathan about bedtime routines".

We arrived and got seated, ordering soft drinks with the surly waitress as we threw our coats on the spare chairs next to us. The surly waitress got surlier when we mentioned the soft drinks because she's done this job long enough now to realise that the restaurant really makes its money back on the 'early bird specials' from the overpriced alcoholic beverages and this particular member of the waiting staff has chosen to assume we're cheap and thus bad tippers, rather than miraculously and non-verbally educate herself to the fact that I'm an alcoholic and my wife doesn't drink in front of me to support my sobriety.

I asked what Jane wanted to talk about before she'd even adjusted herself to get comfortable in her seat or the surly waitress had returned with our drinks.

"Jesus bloody Christ, Jake! Give me a second to become one with the atmosphere in here or something, eh?" she said.

I just went straight in. "Do you want a divorce?"

Jane stopped and looked me dead in the eye. "I told you it was nothing bad, right?"

"Right!"

"So divorce isn't 'bad' to you? Is that what you're saying?"

"No!" I said, reaching out to take her hand. "It would devastate me!"

"Good! I said it was nothing bad and I'm not lying on that because ultimately in the long run it won't be. But… I guess… I don't know, in the immediate 'hearing' of it all you're going to think is that it *is* bad. But… I just want you to know that it isn't!"

I sat back and folded my arms defensively against my chest. This sounded like I'd stepped right into a *trap*.

"Okay…" I said slowly and quietly.

Jane took a deep breath.

"You know, what happened to you in the police and afterwards with the cover-up and all that? That was horrible. But the Australia thing? The things you saw? The things you had to do in order to get back home to us? That stuff is going to hang on a man. There's an argument to be made you could have post-traumatic-stress-disorder."

"Oh I don't think I like where this is going." I replied.

"And if it is PTSD then there's medications and counselling and all sorts of stuff you can get professionally prescribed to help you. I've done reading up on it, you see. But popping painkillers like they're smarties isn't the way to keep that shit locked down." Jane continued.

"I don't… pop…"

Jane shut me down. "I found your stash, Jake… I found your tablets!"

My jaw fell open and my heart started to race at such a rate I felt it was going to come loose from the valves.

"Well, you said… what… we had to talk about… wasn't bad." I stuttered. "I'd… definitely say… that's… *bad*?"

"I've known for a few weeks." She said softly but assertively. "I found the first stash and then I waited until you were out and the kids were in bed to comb the entire house and find all the others. I was worried they were in places the kids could find them… and the only thing that stopped me from ending your days over this was the fact that you've been impressively creative and responsible in where you hide them. But I want you to know that I've found what I think is all of them. And I'm going to go through my finds with you later and if there's ones I missed and you lie to me? *Then* we're going to be talking about divorce!"

I sat silent. I stared hard at her. I didn't realise my eyes had moistened up until the first tear dropped down my cheek at the exact moment the waitress returned with our drinks. Jane smiled politely at her whilst she served them and maintained a respectful silence until she was gone.

She took a sip of her drink, leant forward to meet my eye line as it fell with shame and started to speak a speech that I think she'd been running over and over in her head for the last few weeks.

"I was there for you when your police career ended and I did what I had to do as your wife to get you back up on your feet and off the drink. When that Australia thing broke you and threw you off the wagon, I was still right there to pick you up again *and* hold our family together… I know we're in a place neither of us thought we would be and I know it hasn't worked out how we wanted. And I'm proud of you for getting up every morning and trying to help provide for us by doing the shit jobs no one else wants for shit money just to be able to claim a wage for *something*! I am really proud. I know it's breaking you down. But this isn't the answer, Jake. It's not solving anything. It's just numbing it."

I took a sip of my drink, hoping it would ease the painful tension in my throat that came from holding back the tears and wanting to break down sobbing hard.

"These things… these tablets… They aren't making you less angry, Jake. They're not… I've spent the last few weeks keeping a count on your stash. By my estimation you're taking anywhere between eight and ten a day. That's just of the Tramadol I can track down. I have no clue what's going on at the office. But if Psychic wants to keep his bastard ball-sack attached to his body, he's going to help me find out…"

Jane took my hand, squeezed it and continued.

"I've been and spoken to the GPs at our surgery. I've raised concerns… Don't be mad. I had to do it. For your sake and for the family's sake."

I pulled my hand away. Emotionally, I didn't want to at all. I needed to feel her touch. Physically though, my body reacted at the realisation that someone had taken control against 'our' wishes and effectively terminated 'our' supply.

"What you have in the house… along with what you've got in the office, I presume… that's *it*, Jake! There isn't anything else coming. You need to realise that and you need to accept it, okay? Now, I'm going to offer you a pretty reasonable deal that I think you'd be insane to refuse. But then again no one knows better than me how capable you are of random flights of brash insanity, yeah?"

I folded my arms defensively against my chest once more.

"I'm not going to spend the Christmas period fighting you on this. I know how hard it was with the alcohol and I don't have it in me Jake, I just don't. But the alcohol thing and the Australia thing showed me what an amazing fighter I have for a husband. I truly believe that. So I'm going to demand that you fight this too, okay?"

I remained stoic and unmoveable. The idiot in me was allowing the anger to build.

"You do what you need to do to keep your head straight and get justice for Stephie Jay. You run down what supply you've got left however you want. I will make not a single comment over Christmas. But… with the support from the GPs and, I'll be honest, with some financial assistance from my parents… after Christmas you're going to go into a private detox facility and you're going to deal with this."

"I don't need to fucking…" I spat before Jane held up a hand to silence me.

"There is no room for negotiation on this, Jake." Jane said with an admirable and controlled assertiveness. "This is what it is. This is what is happening. I love you and I want to be with you. But I want to be with the man I fell in love with. And I want him to come back to me before it works out that I've actually spent less time with him than I have the shadow of a man he's become… I need you Jake. I can't keep doing life on my own anymore."

And, in typical Jane fashion, she'd clearly got this all prepped in such a fashion that she left the most powerful 'hammer slam' to the end. Because those last few words punched my heart through my chest.

I started to nod and the tears started to fall.

I'd spent so much time thinking that I'd already lost her and that I needed to think of ways to get her back that I was too pilled-up, self-centred and distracted to realise that I hadn't *lost* her… I was *losing* her. She was hurting through yet more disappointment I'd bestowed upon her. Her tone now smacked though of someone who was losing the resilience to keep going in the face of continued disappointment in the man she loves.

"I look in the mirror and I don't recognise myself anymore, Jane… I don't." I whispered.

Jane got up, walked around the table and sat down next to me. She took me in her arms and held me tight to protect my tear strewn face from the other guests in the restaurant.

"You're still in there, Jake. I know it. If I didn't me and the boys wouldn't still be here, I promise you!"

I nodded, only half wondering if that was true.

"I need you to do this for me. I need to hear you say you'll do this for us as a family but more than that I need you to follow through and *do* this. Because what I give to you tonight in grace and patience is all I've got left."

I nodded and dried my eyes.

"We need to start getting more structure together as a family so we can plan things better. The snatched hour or so in the morning before school and then never seeing you until late into the evening or a few days later? That can't keep going on. Nor can you keep coming home spaced out to fuck. We've got to start normalising things again. The shadow of the police thing can't keep hanging over us."

She kissed my forehead.

"So here's where the line gets drawn for you to step over and start helping change the status quo – The kids are in that Christmas concert that they're performing at church on Christmas Eve morning. I want you there, *no matter what*. Okay? I want you there right next to me, holding my hand and telling me they're wonderful… and I want you to sell that lie to me too because they really, really *aren't*. They're actually getting *worse*. If you were around more you'd know that and you'd see they're not getting any better with daily practise! … You being there, next to me? Holding my hand? And not drugged up? That's the sign I need."

I lifted my head and kissed her on the lips.

"I will be there… I will."

Jane took hold of my head and drew it close enough for our noses to touch.

"This case? This Stephie Jay thing?" Jane whispered in my ear. "It's perfect because you so desperately need this to remind you as to who you are and what you're capable of. But at the same time it so desperately needs you too."

She kissed my forehead and we separated. It's at that point that I saw the waitress was standing there, with her mouth slightly agape enough to suggest she'd been stood there awhile.

"Do you need more time?" she said, quietly with a modicum of embarrassment.

"Have you been stood there the whole time?" asked Jane.

"Not the whole time – but a while, yeah!" she replied.

"Why?" I asked.

"Well, you see…" she said, pointing over to the other waiting staff behind the bar who all suddenly busied themselves and tried to look anywhere else but at our table. "… We had a bet on that the reason you were crying is because she's dumped you. And I said I'd come over to sort of cock an ear as to whether that's true or not. But then I just… well… I got sucked in, didn't I?"

Jane and I looked at each other, our mouths agape.

We ate a hurried two course meal and left with our heads down and our cheeks still blushing with embarrassment. We were no more than five or six steps from the restaurant when the doors slammed on a familiar looking jet black Ford Explorer in the car park and four large, thick-necked and broad-shouldered darkly clad men walked towards us.

I clocked the two in front straight away.

I recognised the majestically maintained beard immediately and the black guy that sauntered behind him. These were the same two men from the Greys Monument event a few days back.

"Mr Lehman?" said the beautifully-bearded one. "May we have a word?"

I protectively put my arm around Jane and tried to keep walking but the black guy stepped in front of our path.

"It looks to me like you're not going to give us a choice?" I said. "What's this about?"

"You're investigating matters pertaining to Stephanie Jason? Correct?" said the bearded wonder.

"And what if I am?" I said, pulling Jane tighter.

"We'd like you to stop please." He replied.

I nodded. I looked at Jane and smiled. "Jane, I want you to go back into the restaurant and get a drink, okay?"

"No way, Jake!" Jane shot back.

I fixed a fake smile and stared at her hard. "I want you to go back into the restaurant, grab a drink and a seat by the window and keep your phone tight in your hand. If one of these big, Dwayne Johnson wannabe motherfuckers so much as blows me a kiss I want you to call the police!"

I moved my gaze to fix itself upon the bearded spokesperson. "… Tell them that one of them has a Muslim-looking beard or something. That should stir some shit up with the narrow-minded bastards and get them running over here!"

Jane slowly started to step away, backing up towards the restaurant doors. The two guys at the back, leaning silently against their car bonnet suddenly made a move to follow.

"Ah-Ah!" I shouted. "… *Stay*!"

They looked at one another then over to the man with the jealousy-inducing beard. He nodded at them and they went back to leaning against the car.

"You guys look like you bench-press blokes like me two hours a day, every day." I smiled. "You have all got the whole intimidating 'covert ops' vehicle and hard-man looks down pat, I'll give you that. But you shouldn't underestimate me. You really shouldn't. Because…"

I hadn't thought this through.

I had nothing.

I just wanted to keep them engaged with me long enough for Jane to get back into the restaurant safely.

"Because… Because… I've got chronic Haemophilia. I bleed like a down pour on a rainy day. So… you know… you guys hit me, like just to even give me a warning or something… I'm likely to bleed out all over the place and you'll be on a murder charge. How about that?"

"That would only be a problem if we weren't intending for you to die!" said the intimidating black guy.

"Oh!" I said, realising that I'm throwing down the shittest of chuffs possible and it's most certainly not landing. I decided to go another way – fearless 'Christopher Walken death scene in True Romance' style fake-bravado!

I pointed a finger at the black guy, then at the bearded ring-leader and then finally clicking my fingers at the two over by the car.

"I totally get it now – you guys are the A-Team, right?"

I pointed at the talkative hairy faced one in front of me. "You're the old guy who's hoping your plan comes together. We'll call you Hannibal!"

And here on out, let's do just *that.*

"You!" I pointed at the black guy. "It's not a race thing but… well, it's *totally* a race thing… You're clearly BA Baracus, yeah? And you guys slopping around in the back? You're a good-looking son of a bitch aren't you?" I said looking directly at the man on the right. "So you're Face!"

I clicked my fingers again and clapped my hands together, looking directly at the last unnamed guy. "Which makes your crazy-looking arse-for-a-face the Murdock, huh?"

Murdock didn't like being Murdock.

He clearly thought he was a Face.

So he jumped into a standing position and went to make a move on me. Hannibal raised his hand then smiled at me.

"You've got a quirky sense of humour. I like a quirky sense of humour." Hannibal said. "You're entertaining. But you're distracting. And that's tiresome. So let me swing it back round…"

He took a step forward. I braced for impact.

It didn't come.

"… We would very much like for you to close off what you have and end your investigation into Stephanie Jason." Hannibal said, smiling falsely. "There is nothing further that requires being looked into."

"Says who?" I fired back.

"Says me!" He winked. "And that's all you need!"

"You're looking for suspicion where there is no suspicion!" chipped in BA Baracus.

I squinted in his direction and looked confused. "Did that make sense in your head? Was that meant to come across cool and foreboding or something?"

I shot Murdock a quick glance. "I apologise to you, sir. Because I think this fucker here is the crazy one!"

BA Baracus took a walk towards me. Hannibal held out his arm and blocked him. But BA Baracus shot him the angriest of looks. "What are we doing here, man?" he muttered into Hannibal's ear. "He's mugging us off! Let me bounce his head off the curb!"

Hannibal shook his head.

"See?" I smiled. "Hannibal likes me!"

"For now!" smirked Hannibal. "I don't think the affection will last much longer!"

"I'm surprised you were able to develop some in the first place." I replied. "Most people find me incredibly disagreeable."

"I can absolutely see why!" Hannibal said. "You're very efficient at burrowing under the skin, it has to be said!"

I stepped forward and put a fake pat on Hannibals' shoulder. He didn't move. He didn't flinch. He didn't even look down to see what my hand was going to do. He was both that utterly unintimidated by me and that trustful that his 'team' would have his back should I make any sort of aggressive move.

"Listen, we're bonding here, right?" I said quietly to Hannibal. "So how about you answer me this? You're asking me to leave this Stephie Jay thing alone because there's nothing at all suspicious about it and I'm fishing in an empty barrel, yeah? But do you think this warning is working as confirmation that there's nothing at all suspicious about her death? Because how many Instagram models or whatever have their own post-suicide intimidation squad?"

Hannibal broke out in a broad smile, gently pushed me back on my feet a little to put some space between the two of us and then he slowly started backing away towards the vehicle whilst the other three followed him. They all climbed into the car, whilst he threw his hands up in the air in an overly exaggerated shrug gesture.

"I never asked you to leave this alone because there's nothing suspicious about it, Mr Lehman. I'm asking you to leave it alone because having watched your sons from afar I would hate to have to hit them with my car!"

He stepped inside the Ford Explorer and quickly shut the door.

I was off the balls of my feet and making a run for where he sat, just managing to throw a punch down on the passenger side window, my fist bouncing ineffectively off the glass behind which he sat before the Ford Explorer sped out of the car park.

Jane came running straight out of the restaurant and to my side.

"What the fuck was *that* Jake?" she gasped.

"You got the subtle message about keeping a hold of your phone, yes? Please tell me you picked up on that?"

"Don't worry Jake – I recorded them on my phone, yes!"

## [14]

## or

## "Further Fun And Games With Bobby Maitland..."

**"A**nswer me one thing right now, right here!" said Jane, holding me to the spot in the car park outside of the restaurant. "Did they threaten our family?"

I didn't speak straight away because I wanted to choose my words carefully.

It didn't matter. Jane read the silence in exactly the way Jane has trained herself to do over the years. She instantly grabbed my hand and started striding me home.

We got through the door quick, thanked Jane's parents whilst hurrying them home, chasing the kids to bed with a dominant "Do not fuck with me tonight, boys!" resolve that even Jack and Jonathan were not daft enough to test. I was down in the kitchen washing up the coffee cups left by her parents on the bench when Jane entered, opened the cupboard by the boiler and reached deep into the back.

She pulled out a screw-topped bottle of red wine and shot me an immediate defensive glare. "What? Go on… I dare you!" she said, pouring herself a large glass. "You're the only one allowed a secret stash?"

She jumped up on the bench, effortlessly not spilling a drop as she did. "So… I'm going to pack a few things and take the boys to my parents tomorrow."

I nodded and stepped up to take a seat on the kitchen bench opposite her.

"Just until I get a figure on who these guys are, right?"

"Yeah. And please be quick Jake. I really don't want to spend Christmas away from our own home, okay?"

I nodded once more.

"Now give it to me straight…" she said, taking a big gulp from her glass. "How worried do I need to be?"

When Jane and I married we honeymooned in San Francisco. It was perfect. One of the greatest ten days of my life, I swear to God. We had this lunch at Chowder's on Beach Street because the guide book said that they served the best clam chowder in the whole of the city. It was good clam chowder but the "best" felt a little overstated if you asked me. What made it special was the view from our table on Pier 39, overlooking the bay itself on a really gorgeous day. That and the fact that they served our chowder in a sourdough bowl that Jane somehow misunderstood the concept of the minute it arrived – and took an instant bite out of, burning her mouth and causing the steaming hot contents of said 'bowl' to pour out all over the table and floor.

After her initial embarrassment passed and the ice cubes in her mouth took down the swelling on her burnt tongue… and after the staff had wearily come over and cleaned up the mess… we laughed together about it and, later that night, lying together in our hotel room bed she said she knew that she had made the right choice in choosing me to be her husband because she said I didn't look mortified at her or make her feel like a fool for something so silly.

It became one of 'those stories' we banked and told to people once we returned home. You know? People politely ask how you enjoyed your holiday and what not and you immediately start blitzing them with very specific anecdotes of the 'you-had-to-be-there-variety' that bore them rigid. The clam chowder incident was one such anecdote, one that took on exaggerations with each telling from either of us to the point that if you asked Jane or I now we'd tell you all about the time she bit into a sourdough bowl full of clam chowder and accidentally flooded the entire San Francisco bay.

A few months after "that Australia job we'll not get into right now" when I was at the height of my night-terrors and a heavy re-introduction to Jim Beam and Pabst Blue Ribbon, Jane indulged my fears that friends or relatives from those men from Australia would come over here looking for revenge. So we devised an 'emergency plan' to placate me…

A 'bug-out' bag was put together that was infrequently topped up and refreshed with clean clothes, food, toiletries and the like for Jane and the kids. It also had in it a 'clean' pay-as-you-go phone that only I had the telephone number for. It was stored in the spare-room wardrobe at her parents' house.

Should Jane ever receive a phone call from me in which I ask her how the clam chowder is, she knows to get the kids and get to her parents as quickly as possible. From there she was to dump the car in a nearby supermarket car park and then have her father drive her up to her aunt's cottage situated in Cove, a little village on the Scottish borders.

It wasn't the most highly sophisticated of plans.

But on the test runs we have done of it occasionally over the years, it works well enough to give us security and peace of mind.

I'd clearly got lost in my memories of our honeymoon and our 'protection plan' because Jane flicked her leg out and gave my dangling leg a kick. "Hey? Dreamer? Now's not the time to leave me for Fantasy Land… I said how worried do I need to be?"

I jumped down off the bench and took her head in my hands.

"I've not mentioned clam chowder yet have I?" I smiled, trying to be reassuring.

Jane left the next morning to go stay with her folks until I could get a better read on who these guys were outside the restaurant. Her parents were far from happy. Other than the grandchildren I'd assisted in creating for them, I think they were beginning to see me as a burden and far beneath the expectations in a husband that they'd hoped their daughter would gain.

I couldn't blame them.

I was a recovering alcoholic twice over who was now needing my in-laws to pull from their savings to help get me rehab treatment for a painkiller addiction I'd 'accidentally on purpose' acquired. Not to mention the fall from grace with regards to the police. And the PI business that was just about barely functioning. Or the continued financial and emotional pressure on their daughter on a daily basis. Oh… and now she and the kids are having to hide out at their house for a few days whilst we figure out how endangered their lives are!

I mean, come on now, am I quite the *catch* or what?

I called Psychic the minute I'd made sure Jane and the kids were safely at her parents. As soon as he stepped through the door I handed him two printed screenshots I'd pulled from the footage of Jane's phone, along with an iPad we'd moved the footage over onto the previous evening.

"Tell me if you recognise these guys? Gym buddies? Doormen you've seen when you're out? *What*? What am I looking at?" I said.

Psychic took a long study of the photos and then pressed play on the footage.

"Out of the ones that spoke, none of them had Geordie accents!" I added.

"What accent did they have? Southern? European? What?" asked Psychic.

"I don't know. Maybe London-ish, Manchurian at a push maybe?"

"What are you thinking?" replied Psychic.

"I'm thinking they're Bobby Maitland's hired thugs!" I said.

Newcastle were playing away, the streets were ungodly quiet and I'd never felt the temperature so low. It was like the cold had killed everybody off. Psychic and I took a drive in his car to an old reconditioned pub in North Shields that had been sort of unofficially converted into a private members bar. Bobby Maitland owned it and, we were told, used it most weekends as his preferred 'lounging and unwinding' area of choice.

We parked up outside.

"He has doormen on, look!" pointed Psychic. "It's invite only and we don't have an invite!"

"So we go over and chuff like we do!" I replied.

"You chuff! I never chuff! I don't chuff. I'll stand and nod!" he said nervously.

"It's not going to work if I stand there giving it the chuff and you just nod, man. You've got to get in there with me and back me up, sell the chuff and all that." I laughed.

"I can't chuff Jake! I'm like the computer guy. I'm the bloke behind the curtain. I'm not built that way. I just blush."

"Don't be ridiculous. Watch – we go over there, we say something like 'Bobby is expecting us!' and…"

"What if Bobby's not in?" interjected Psychic.

"Then we just say we must be early and we ask if it's okay if we go in and have a drink downstairs until he shows."

"And then when they say no what do we do then?" he asked even more nervously.

"Well, come on, let's role-play. What would *you* say if they said no?"

Psychic sits silently, contemplating.

"I'm the doorman, right?" I said, helpfully. "We've done the whole 'We're here to see Bobby!' 'He's not in!' 'Can we come in and wait?' 'No'! thing, okay? And you say…"

"Well go fuck yourselves then!" said Psychic with fake-assertiveness.

I looked at him.

He looked at me.

"Stay in the car!" I said, getting out and slamming the door.

I walked over to the pub entrance that had two bored looking old school bouncers standing against the doors.

"Alright lads?" I said with fake, over-exaggerated Geordie good cheer. "I'm here to see Bobby. He's expecting me."

"No, you're not and no he isn't! Fuck off!" snarled the one closest to me.

"Honestly, I am and he is." I smiled. "Could you let him know I'm here?"

"Don't make me say this a third time – you're not here to see him and he's not expecting you!" he replied.

"Jesus Christ, this is like a fucked up Keith Harris and Orville duet isn't it?" I said. "You're standing here going 'I wish I could fly, way up to the sky, but I can't!' and I'm all like 'You can!' and you keep going 'I can't'! This is exhausting!"

The second doormen stepped forward. "Are you saying you want to put your hand up his arse? Is that what you're saying?"

I started to back away slightly. "You certainly took that puppet analogy and ran away with it to quite a dark place didn't you, sir?" I smiled, blindly and pointlessly still trying to build a rapport.

Here's a little thing not a lot of people know about me but I'll let you in on the secret: I find *"With all due respect…"* to be incredibly over-used as a means of passive aggression nowadays. So I've replaced saying that to people when I have no respect for them and don't intend to give them any with a good old, short but sweet *"sir"* or *"m'am"* at the end of the sentence dependent on their sex. Therefore, if you ever hear me call you a "sir" or a "m'am" and you're *not* a "sir" or a "m'am" then you know now that I secretly think you're a total shithead.

"If you had an appointment with Bobby and he was expecting you, you'd know that this isn't the door which his appointments go through. You'd know that because you'd have been told that when you arranged the bloody appointment!" said Doormen Number 1.

Then from out of nowhere a wheelie bin smashed into the side of Doormen Number 2's head, knocking him out cold in two swift blows with the bin. I turned in shock and saw Psychic standing there, adrenaline coursing through his veins.

Doormen Number 1 went to grab a hold of him and I took my chances and threw two full-force, take-no-prisoners punches straight into the side of his temple.

And they did jack-shit!

You know why?

You've forgotten already haven't you?

Let me remind you: Movies and TV lie *so badly*. Walking away from explosions? Jumping off skyscrapers? Taking a bullet without so much as flinching? Remember now?

From the prologue? Go back. Re-read that. I'll wait.

We good? Okay… You know what else you can add to that list?

Clean knock-out punches thrown by guys half the size of the dude they're hitting! You see it all the time in action movies. Henchman steps through a door, the hero's waiting on the other side just out of sight and he cold clocks him straight in the face and the henchman hits the deck like a sack of shit. You never see the reality – which is that the hero smacks the henchman and the henchman turns round and angrily shouts "Ow! What the fuck, man? You don't just jump out and punch people! What the hell is wrong with you?"

My punches on Doormen Number 1 certainly didn't land like a bitch-slap from Steven Seagal in any one of his bad movies… If you're looking for a more specific point of reference on that analogy, let me help you: At the time of writing, Segal has made over fifty movies and only one of them is good – that's the 1992 Die Hard knock-off, Under Siege. So if you're looking for Steven Segal bitch-slaps in bad movies, you've got a smorgasbord to choose from!

… Doormen Number 1 was pissed off now! He grabbed me and pulled me into a headlock just as Psychic wrapped himself around the guy's legs, causing him to tumble to the ground and take me with him. My nose got popped straight off a concrete step in the process. Blood splattered up and straight back across my face. At the exact moment I thought I was about to choke on my blood, the Doormen's grip loosened around my head and I pulled myself loose to find that Psychic had choked him unconscious in a sleeper hold.

I stood up and aggressively wiped the blood away from my eyes and my nose, soiling the entire sleeve of my jacket in the process.

"What the fuck was that?" I gasped.

"I chuffed!" Psychic said, out of breath and struggling.

"That was a hell of a chuff, Psychic! Come on!" I grabbed him with one hand and pulled the doors open with the other, pushing us both through into a pub that was screening the Newcastle game for about forty odd men who's eye line was completely hooked in the opposite direction to where we stood.

Psychic nodded to a door in the far back corner of the pub, where the bar met the wall. It had 'Office' in an engraved metal sign on the door. He shrugged.

I shrugged back.

We walked over to it and opened the door without knocking – landing straight upon the sight of Bobby Maitland sat in a comfy chair off to the corner of his desk, receiving a pedicure from a young lady in a beautician's uniform. He was watching the match on his personal TV whilst Ryan and another man with the look of the recently-released-from-custody about him, kept themselves out of his line of sight, though still trying to catch the game for themselves.

"WHAT THE FUCK??" shouted Bobby as we bounded into the room – Psychic, a quivering stack of adrenaline ready to be set loose, and me, a limping fool with a makeshift beard made up of blood.

"Hi Bobby!" I said. "Don't get up, I'll be quick…"

Ryan made a move across the room, Psychic stepped to block his path but he was effortlessly thrown off his feet and across the room before he'd even known Ryan had made contact.

"Woah! Woah!" I shouted. "Bobby! We're not here for a fight! We're here to ask a question and leave!"

Bobby clicked his fingers at Ryan. "Calm it, Ry'!" he said. "Let me hear what he's got to say and *then* snap his head off!"

I quickly pulled the printed screenshots from my pocket and threw them down into Bobby's lap. He picked them up and looked at them. Then he looked back at me.

"*And*? What? What am I looking at?"

"I want to know why you sent men to come and threaten me and my children?" I said calmly, just as Psychic pulled himself to his feet. He stared hard at Ryan. Ryan simply smiled back at him.

"Stay there, sweetheart!" winked Ryan to Psychic. "I'm coming back to you!"

I stayed focused on Bobby.

"These aren't my men. I don't know who these men are but they don't work for me!" Bobby shrugged his head to one side and let the print-outs drop to the floor.

"How am I meant to believe that?" I replied.

"How are you meant to believe what? How am I meant to give a shit? Why am I sending men to threaten you exactly? I'm at a total loss here, Jake. I really am."

"Why do you…" I started to speak but Bobby stopped me with a hand gesture whilst climbing out of his seat.

"No. You came here with a question. You've had your question. Now, I have a question for you I'd like an answer to… Am I scared of you, Jake?"

I looked at him with perplexity in my eyes.

"I very much doubt you are, Bobby!" I replied.

"So I have nothing to fear in telling you the truth do I, son? I don't have to lie to you. If these were my men, I'd simply tell you they were because your reaction would be meaningless to me. But I'm not scared of you, so I'm truthful with you. Do you see?"

I nodded.

"Good!" smiled Bobby. "Now, you burst in on my relaxation time, banging on about some bloody meatheads being my responsibility. You're in my place. So I get more questions. That's the rules of my place. So… rewind back: Why am I sending men to threaten you exactly?"

"I'm looking into the death of Stephie Jay and I heard that you were pretty pissed off with her for screwing you over on the night she died." I said. "I put two and two together and assumed that…"

"Are you saying you're looking into whether I had anything to do with Stephie Jay's death? Is that what you're going with?"

I stood silent.

"Answer me." Bobby said, stepping close to my face. I could feel the heat of his breath on the end of my nose.

I stood silent.

"You burst in here and tell me I've hired some lads to scare you off looking into that lass' death because I had something to do with it and you're getting too close? Is that right? Am I right?"

I knew the minute I said yes I would never walk out of here.

That's when I realised how terribly this had been thought through. I had absolutely nothing banked in reserve for what would come next after dropping the photos in his lap. Did I really expect to say 'Stop it! Behave yourself!' and then walk out again?

"Cowardice got your tongue, son?" Bobby said quietly, still refusing to take his face away from mine.

"You run Blue Light Security, right? You're one of the directors?" I asked, trying to inject confidence into my tone and deciding to readjust the approach in order to lead with the circumstantial stuff instead. All so I had a route to walk back from if it all went south.

Or should I say *further* south.

"What has THAT got to do with anything?" he replied.

"Blue Light have the contract for the site where Stephie was found dead. She managed to drive her way onto that site without your guys ever spotting her come in. She had stood your guy Khali up at Paradox, leaving you out of pocket. I heard that you were pissed off about that and you were going to teach her a lesson or something. That's all the loose ends around motive that I've got right now…"

"Motive? Fucking motive? Are you serious, lad? You've accusing me of what exactly? Driving that girl to suicide or killing her and faking it?" Bobby laughed. He stepped back out of my face and pointed to the beautician. 'You! Piss off!"

She hurriedly got to her feet and went to run out of the room. Bobby stopped her.

"No. Wait, love! I'm sorry. That was rude. I shouldn't take it out on you. You've done a wonderful job. Thanks for seeing me on a Sunday." He dug deep in his pocket, pulled out a wad of notes and stuffed them into her hand. "You enjoy the rest of your day!"

She opened the office door and fled – at the exact moment that the dumb and dumber of doormen we'd had a ruckus with outside came bounding into the room all swollen and bloodied. They stopped dead in their tracks.

Bobby looked them up and down.

Then he looked at us and smirked. He turned back to Doorman Number 1.

"Did these half-washed twats get past you two?"

Doormen Number 1 went to grab Psychic. "This bastard threw a bin off us!"

"LEAVE HIM!" screamed Bobby and everyone froze. "Here's the thing – Your job is to keep scum out. And as you can see there's scum in my office right now. So you've failed in your…"

Bobby suddenly span on his bare feet and turned his ire to the attention of that recently-released convict son of a bitch who'd remained totally still and quiet up until this point. "DARYL! WILL YOU PLEASE LIVE-PAUSE THE FUCKING GAME, FOR CHRIST'S SAKE! WE'RE MISSING BLOODY GOALS HERE, SON!"

Daryl grabbed the Sky+ remote off the desk and quickly hit the pause button. "Sorry, Bobby!" he said sheepishly.

"Right…" continued Bobby, turning back to what was now quite the little formation in the centre of his office. "Your job, the both of you, was to keep shitbags like these out of my pub, let alone my office. You've failed so first of all, you're not getting paid. Second of all, you're both fired and thirdly, Daryl? Grab a couple of lads from the bar there and take these stupid pricks out the back and show them my displeasure, yeah?"

Daryl nodded, pushing himself off from leaning on the desk and shoving both doormen out the office, closing the door behind them.

"Okay, let's ramble on…" Bobby said, turning his attention back to me and Psychic. "So, here's the thing. Paradox is dead on its feet. I don't give a flying fuck about that place. If Stephie Jay didn't show up there it shows she had taste. Anyone who's told you of my displeasure is talking out of their arse, frankly. Furthermore, the weekend she died I was in Vegas for fight night with Ryan and the boys…"

Ryan nodded in agreement.

"… I didn't find out about her not fulfilling her commitments to Khali's 'meet and greet' until I got back from Vegas which was the Tuesday after she died. You keeping up with me here, son?"

"Yeah." I replied.

"Good! Now… I am or was a director of a lot of things, Jake. A *lot*. And you know why, don't you? And if you don't I'm not going to explain out loud because that's the sort of stuff that if it was covertly recorded it could cause a lot of trouble, you know what I mean, right? Of course you do. So… Blue Light Security? It's just another arm of the doormen and security business I have up and running throughout pretty much the whole of the North East. I don't run it. I put money into it and I get money out. My sister's ex-husband, the twat, is the guy who does all the day-to-day on that. I couldn't even tell you where their offices are. But the companies house listing as a director does a lot of good for me as long as it's doing well. You get me?"

"I get you!" I said.

"Good!" smiled Bobby. "It sounds to me like you're floundering around trying to give that girl's parents their money's worth and you're chasing random bullshit!"

I went to speak, Bobby shushed me down and took a seat. "Now, I'm not judging you Jake. I'm not. Everyone's got to make a living somehow right. But you've chased random bullshit right to my door on one of my rest days. You've accused me of some pretty nasty stuff. You've made me pause the match and…"

"Why did you look so angry at the lighting ceremony for Stephie Jay the other night? Why did you storm off?" I forcibly interrupted.

"Because I can't stand that Hetherington!" laughed Bobby. "He's an absolute scoundrel and, as you know, I am a connoisseur of spotting scoundrels. I've had bad dealings with that man and he's not good for what I'm trying to do in Newcastle. He's not good for anyone in Newcastle, in fact."

"I get that. It seems you and I have a lot in common because I can't stand the man either and…"

"Stop trying to suck up to me Jake. It's unbecoming. You've disrespected me and that misbehaviour needs to be recalibrated. So…"

Psychic looked at me nervously.

"… You know how it works, son. Head or belly?"

"Excuse me?" I replied.

"Head or belly? Choose. Quick. We want to get back to the match."

Psychic stepped forward, boldly said "Belly!" and then braced hard.

Ryan, in a motion faster than my human eye could catch, span on his feet and kicked Psychic square in the stomach, flinging him once again across the room. Ryan didn't even break stride in keep coming towards me after his foot returned to the floor.

"Belly!" my voice squeaked.

"This is for being a shit-stirring prick the other night too!" smirked Ryan.

Then he punched me in the side of the head with such force it successfully attuned my belief about how getting knocked out with one punch is just movie bullshit.

I came round from unconsciousness to find I was slumped in the backseat of Psychic's car. We were parked up in a little spot down in Tynemouth Priory, overlooking the mouth of the Tyne from the point it met the sea. I sluggishly started to pull myself round and sit up.

Psychic was sat in the driver's seat, slowly sipping a bottle of water. "That went well then, Jake. Don't you think?"

His words sounded tinny and almost like they were in slow motion to me. I put my hand to my head and could feel a hard lump just above my right ear. There was some dried blood crusted into my hair too.

"How long have I been out?" I said, groggily.

"About fifteen minutes!" Psychic replied, passing a second bottle of water back to me.

"What we doing here?" I asked.

"I just pulled up to have a think… and because I can't stop needing to pull over and throw up." He replied. "So, Bobby? Dead end or what?"

"I don't know, Psychic. I don't know."

"If he didn't find out about her messing up the Paradox gig until he was back in the country, at which point she was already dead anyway, then he doesn't have the motive that we thought he did."

"No. You're right. And that means Khali Matti was talking shit."

"Oh come on, all Khali Matti does is talk shit." Psychic said. "He's a thirty year old Indian daddy's boy who thinks he's a twenty year old black hip hop impresario. I think retaliation for the Paradox thing is a total false lead."

"Maybe…" I whimpered as I gently tried to sit up more.

I unsteadily reached into my jeans pocket and pulled out my tin, unclasping the lid slowly but with purpose only to discover that I only had two tablets left in the tin.

And only another six, maybe, at home in my stash.

And absolutely no guarantee of whether a GP was going to top me up or not.

"Fuck!" I muttered to myself as I threw the last two down my throat and drowned them down with water.

"What?" replied Psychic.

"I have a problem with painkillers!" I said once my mouth was clear.

"You don't say!" exclaimed Psychic with mock shock.

"And… I think I'm about to run out of painkillers!"

## [15]

## or

## "The George Platform..."

With Jane and the boys not being at home, I slept the night on the sofa back at the office, with an ice pack on my head… and within reaching distance of a packet of Tramadol that I had stashed in the back of my desk drawer.

If ever there was a time when I was justified in popping them like they were sweets, this was it. Not that I ever had a problem justifying throwing them down my neck before. My head thumped so hard and it sent these massive, shooting blasts of pain down my spine and into my leg like a dump-truck was repeatedly slamming itself into a wall.

And my body was the wall.

I use the term 'slept' extremely loosely as at the exact moment I felt my eyes become too heavy to stay open and my mind slow down enough for me to just catch up with it and start closing it down for a bit, the sun broke through the office window shining from over the rooftops on the buildings on the other side of Grey Street. In a hearty 'fuck you' to the concept of rest the sun landed directly on my eyes and by the time I'd frustratingly jumped up, tilted the blinds in the opposite direction to where they'd laid, realised this made no difference, hung my coat as best I could over the window itself to definitively block the sun out once and for all and then settled properly back down on the sofa… I was wide awake.

And cold.

With no coat to put over myself.

I got up, made myself the strongest cup of black coffee possible and sat myself down behind my desk. I kept trying to focus on what I needed to achieve in the day ahead of me and what leads I wanted to chase down but my head kept swinging its way back around to the conversation with Jane and my recounting of it to Psychic as we sat up on Tynemouth Priory.

"You *do* need to get help." Psychic had said. His words echoing like he was right there in the room with me. "I will hold the business up. I promise you that. If the only thing that is stopping you taking some time off and getting clear of this is worries about the business then you don't need to worry about that. I have your back."

I kept shaking my head. I didn't want to be thinking about that right now.

I shook it and rubbed hard on my temple, being careful not to touch the spot where Ryan had slammed his fist into it.

I thought about how peculiar it was for the police to close off Stephie's death in the way they did but how even more peculiar it was that her parents' attempts to appeal it were so summarily shut down so quickly across all other avenues. A month is an insanely short period of time to find out your child is dead, have the police shrug their shoulders, discover the coroner doesn't give a shit, get rejected in your appeals and complaints against both and hire a PI to take on your concerns.

I moved my fingers from my temples to my eyes and rubbed harder.

My thoughts jumped to what Bobby had told us. From a chronological point of view, it's true he could not have been anywhere near Stephie at the time she died and if his story checked out then he didn't come back into the country until after her death. That didn't mean he couldn't have ordered some retribution whilst he was in Vegas though. But did he really have the motivation? Was the motivation we thought he had drastically overstated? Because he certainly didn't come across like he gave as much of a shit about Stephie cancelling her appearance at Paradox as Khali made out.

I took a large gulp of coffee and sat back in my chair.

The thought process jumped straight to Khali Matti. Was he lying about Bobby's ire? That seemed inconsequential in the grand scheme of things if we were to take Bobby at his word. But more importantly was Khali lying about what he was told by Sue George regarding why Stephie had to cancel? And if he wasn't lying it meant Sue George was.

*Why?*

There really was only one way to find out.

The George Platform as a modelling agency started out being ran from the back room of Sue George's sister's bungalow in the early nineties. It got its first set of professional offices in Chillingham Road the same year that Stephie Jay was born and moved into the heart of Newcastle five years later. It blossomed in size off the back of having great success at spotting regional 'talent' and getting them onto the international stage. When the reality TV boom kicked into key towards the end of 2005, Sue astutely hooked into making strong contacts with lots of London based producers and opened her books to suit their needs in filling any and every show with positively perfect, toned, bronzed and pearly white teethed young twentysomethings desperate to "take the next step from modelling to…"

Sue's modelling agency was her *everything.*

She'd foregone children and she'd burned through three marriages in maintaining her passion for running The George Platform and living off the riches and delights it brought her in being able to travel and schmooze with a higher class of people and a certain type of celebrity. She was on the wrong side of fifty-five now and it was costing her a fortune to dress and 'paint' herself in a way that camouflaged this fact. Without The George Platform she was nothing. That's why she worked nineteen hour days, six days a week and religiously spent the seventh at a health spa in Durham desperately revitalising her skin and getting massaged into a state fit to go for another one hundred and fourteen hour working week.

Sue was the first through the doors at six thirty am every morning bar Sundays and she expected her assistant/main receptionist to be there waiting for her. Any member of her team who walked through the doors later than eight am and left before seven pm was someone who "lacked the commitment" and were swiftly dismissed.

She yearned to move The George Platform down South and "really take it big" in London but her business advisors continually fought against that. "The Northern edge is intrinsic to your success!" she was told time and time again. "You're big! But not so big that you wouldn't get swallowed whole by the more established agencies down there!" others told her. So, instead Sue moved the offices down to Hanover Street behind the Copthorne Hotel on the Quayside and expanded the premises into a big, glass-on-all-sides, open-planned 'London style' base of operations that was designed to dazzle anyone who stepped inside of it.

It certainly dazzled me.

Maybe I was more dazzled because I was caught by surprise taking an early half seven walk down to its location to check it out before popping in for a sneaky breakfast at The Copthorne across the road and then come back for 'opening', only to find from looking up that the lights were on and people inside seemed to be hard at work already.

Maybe I was *really* dazzled because the Tramadol and caffeine had kicked in at the exact moment my feet hit Hanover Street.

I stepped out of the escalator that brought me to the top floor and out onto The George Platform to find a bank of desks running down one side of the floor, most of which were empty of people at this time in the morning, and on the other side a series of small conference rooms that had been set up as small photo studios.

Directly ahead of me though was a large mahogany desk with 'The George Platform' carved into its frontage and behind it sat a very tired looking, painfully thin, blonde twenty odd year old who was trying to get her telephone headset adjusted as I stepped up to the desk.

My eyes were immediately drawn to the name tag that was up in front of where she sat. It said 'Holly'. But the 'o' was done in such a way it was shaped to look like a 'heart' symbol. It was quite a cute little design. If this was Holly sat in front of me than it certainly fit the person it represented.

She looked up and shifted her entire body to 'professional mode' and broke out the broadest possible smile. "Good morning. Welcome to The George Platform."

"Morning, Holly with a heart for an 'o'!" I said, smiling back warmly. "I'm here to see Sue George please?"

Holly quickly checked her computer screen.

"I'm sorry, do you have an appointment because Miss George doesn't usually open her diary each day until eight thirty. I'll just call..."

"It's okay," I said, shutting Holly down and having caught sight of the office at the far end of the floor. I spotted Sue George herself behind a desk in there, oblivious to my arrival. "We're old friends. I want to surprise her!"

I strode off, leaving Holly fervently trying to get a call through to Sue's extension.

I was through Sue's door at the exact moment her phone rang and her hand snatched the handset from the holster but she never got a chance to put it to her ear and speak.

"Hi Sue? We met at the lighting ceremony or whatever you are all calling what that was. Do you remember me?"

I could've gone with 'Miss George'.

I probably should've actually. It would have been more polite and respectful. But I didn't want to afford her that because my gut was 'off' on Sue George from the get-go. There was just *something* about her that I didn't like.

Sue made an instantaneous and panicked look around her office then dropped the handset back into the phone holster in shock. Clearly she had never experienced a good, old-fashioned, dramatic 'barge-in' before.

"I'm sorry. You can't just... I'm very busy... You need an appointment... Who do you think..." Sue's brain seemed to be overloading with what the automatic response should be.

"I won't take up too much of your time, Sue. I promise. The other night I told you that Paradox nightclub confirmed Stephie's commitment to attend there on the eighth of November was cancelled because of a double-booking?"

Sue continued to stutter her way up against the sudden 'attack' approach I'd taken.

Holly the receptionist with a 'heart' for an 'o' in her name appeared at the door behind me and tried to step around me and get into the room. There was a confusing clash of bodies within the door space before she got clear of me.

"Sue, I'm sorry. Do you want me to call the police or something?"

I pushed on. "You told me that I'd been misinformed and that there was no double-booking, Sue. You said that actually Stephie asked you to cancel the Paradox gig as she was feeling unwell."

Holly gave me the sort of stopped-dead-in-her-tracks look that told me there was something hidden away there in what I just said. Something didn't sit right. I mentally banked it and decided to see whether the rest of my line of questioning clunked hard with Holly as well.

"I asked you about 'Toccare' up at that ceremony thing and it was really noisy so I don't think you quite heard me, did you? Does 'Toccare' mean anything to you?" I asked.

Sue sat in her chair, staring silently at me.

"Toccare?" I reiterated. "It's Italian for 'touch'. Does that ring any bells?"

Sue shook her head definitively. I saw Holly's eyes flinch and her scrutiny of Sue's gesture did not seem to compute with her own line of thought, it seemed to me.

"No nightclub? Bar? Restaurant? Themed dance night somewhere? *Nothing*? You've never heard of it and you've never heard any of your boys and girls on your books talk about it?"

"Never!" smiled Sue, falsely. "Now, I think you should leave."

"I don't have a habit of busting in on people like this, I assure you!" I replied. "I do apologise for the intrusion. But I would really love to talk to you more about Stephie. I mean that, sincerely. Perhaps we…"

"I would love nothing more than to talk to you about Stephie and the joy she brought to people, Mr… I never caught your name?" Sue interrupted.

"It's Jake Lehman, Sue."

"Yes. Good. Jake Lehman... And you represent Stephie's parents, is that right?" she continued coldly through her fixed smile.

"Yes. That's right."

"Well, I love Margaret and Matthew very much and I've known them a great many years now. If you are a representative of theirs then I trust that you are someone of good character."

That smile didn't drop.

So I plastered the thickest, falsest smile across my face then turned my head and nodded at Holly with a 'heart' for an 'o' in her name, shooting her a purposeful wink.

"I don't hear that a lot Sue, frankly. Most people find me very disagreeable but when you get to know me…" I started down my usual, over-used attempt at rapport building.

"Maybe that's because you barge into people's offices without appointments and start bellowing questions at them about the dear, dear friend they've just lost?" Sue shot out over the top of me. "I find that sort of behaviour very disagreeable, Jake. However, I shall say again that I would love nothing more than to sit down and talk to you about Stephie and the joy she brought to people. But I am very busy and it must be scheduled in correctly. If you'd like to leave now with my assistant Holly, she can book you an appointment with me… on your way *out*!"

"That sounds great." I said. "One more thing though – Do you think I've got what it takes?"

"What it takes for what?" Sue said impatiently.

"To get on your books as a model?" I said with a genuine smile this time.

Sue looked at me like I was a piece of shit that had just been delivered to her doorstep. She looked at me for a little too long a period of time for me to believe she knew I was joking.

"That's certainly something we can talk about when we next meet, isn't it?" she said drolly.

Holly stepped forward and gently ushered me back out of the office door, closing the door behind her. I looked back long enough to catch the death glare that Sue shot at her young receptionist / assistant through the glass in the door.

We walked over to her desk and Holly slumped down in her seat and unlocked her computer screen. "Let me just check to see when Sue has some availability. It will be impossible before Christmas now as we have the big annual event at the Metrocentre coming up on Christmas Eve and then she's away over the Christmas break and…"

"Don't worry about it." I interjected. "I'd need to check my own diary anyway. But, in the meantime, I'd love to grab a coffee and a chat with you about…"

"I have a boyfriend!" Holly shot back with the immediacy of someone who was holding down vomit at the thought of a thirty-seven year old crumpled heap of a man hitting on her.

"Oh. No. That's really sweet that you'd think I had such a high an opinion of myself I'd be chasing young girls that look like you but… no. Definitely not. I'm married."

"You're married?" Holly said, just a little too incredulously for my liking.

"Yeah, crazy huh? Even us trolls occasionally meet people underneath the bridge!" I laughed.

"No. Wait. I didn't mean that like…" Holly started to blush hard.

"Don't worry about it. Listen, we're way off from where I think we need to be here. All I'm saying is you have a front row seat to everything that goes on here and who comes and goes and all that. I would love to learn about Stephie from someone like *you*, you know? Also…"

I leant in on the desk and dropped a business card on her keyboard casually and out of the line of sight of Sue – who I'd already discreetly clocked was watching us through the window in her office.

"… I would definitely like to hear anything you had to say about 'Toccare' and Paradox. Do you know what I mean?"

"I don't… don't…. know anything, really. I'm just…" Holly started to splutter.

"Listen, my office address is on there. I'm not that far from here. I've got an assistant who's a lot better looking than me if you want to be hit on by an older man who's got some smooth moves about him…"

Holly let out a little laugh.

I had her disarmed just enough to feel comfortable to bring my point safely down to land.

"Let your conscience pay me a visit, Holly with a heart for an 'o'. I'd love to hear what you have to say… Thanks for your time!"

I turned and walked off. By the time I reached the elevator and stole a glance back through the mirrored surface next to the elevator doors, I could see Holly had already pulled the card off her keyboard and was studying it hard under the desk away from Sue's line of sight, with her bottom lip bitten with trepidation.

I stepped out of the elevator and back out onto the street. The sunlight was harsh and bright, fighting a battle to cut through the biting cold that hung relentlessly in the air. I pulled my coat collar up and took a look to the sky. 'Still no snow, huh?' I thought to myself.

I pulled my phone out of my pocket as I set off down Hanover Street and saw that I had a missed call and a voicemail. I accessed it as I strode across the road, side-stepping the puddles that had formulated from the sun having at least succeeded in melting the patches of ice to water. By the time my foot hit the pavement on the other side of the road, my mind already fixatedly dreaming of the full English breakfast The Copthorne Hotel laid on, I was thrown back to reality by the sound of a voice coming out of the phone that stopped me in my tracks.

“Hi, this is a message for Jake Lehman.” The voice said surreptitiously. “This is Alia Marcus. I believe you’re trying to get a hold of me.”

## [16]

## or

## "Shocking Revelations Brought In To Kick Things Up A Gear..."

**I** called Alia Marcus straight back after ducking into the doorway of a nearby building because light rain inexplicably started to drop out of the sky after breaking through the harsh sunlight. With the coldness hanging in the air the raindrops felt like hundreds of tiny freezing flicks to the face. They weren't quite sleet and not strong enough to be snow maybe because baring down behind them was warm blasts of sun. This weather was ridiculous and confusing, especially to someone like me who judges what coat to wear each day by sticking his hand out of the window each morning and holding it in the air for ten seconds.

Because, you know? That's just basic scientific law when it comes to measuring weather, isn't it?

Anybody who thought we were heading for a White Christmas this year was stupid as far as I was concerned.

... Yes, Yes.. I know, stop talking about the weather and get back to Alia, right?

I've banged on for over a hundred and fifty pages about trying to get a hold of Stephie's best friend then she finally calls me back and I start telling you again about the weather. Sorry. Maybe I'm not cut out for this 'hard-boiled private detective narrator' shit after all?

Alia's voice was even softer on the other end of an actual telephone conversation than it was on the voicemail. She was nervous and uncertain. She explained that she'd been out of the country and had only just received all of my messages. She didn't know what she could tell me exactly that would be of help and seemed to be looking for routes away from having to meet. She wasn't cold in her tone but her voice definitely warmed when I explained that I just wanted to learn more about Stephie and I kept hearing she was her best friend.

"Who could know her better than her best friend, right?" I suggested.

"Okay. I guess I can tell you a bit about her to help you?" she said softly.

We arranged to meet in two hours at her home in Jesmond.

I had time to kill so it looked like I could sort of justify that overpriced breakfast at The Copthorne across the road after all. Now, there's many that will tell you that The Copthorne do the 'best' full English breakfast in the whole of Newcastle. That's not *technically* true. The best full English you can get is at this little café near Tynemouth, next to the school that Jane works at. It is tremendous because you get loads for very little. But, and here's a very important factor, I have exceptionally *specific* requirements when it comes to how I want my full English breakfast to be served and The Copthorne work to my specifications:

You see, for me the sausage is the goddamn godfather of the breakfast 'get together'. It's got to be juicy and the skin has to be soft. Overcooked sausage with hard, dry skin is a total affront. You mess up the sausage, you take down the whole bloody meal… Same goes for the egg - it's got to be runny enough to put your toast to work. And yes, toast! Not fried bread! Fried bread is for scumbags! Keep the tomatoes and mushrooms OFF the plate too. You're not French. And this is no farmer's field… Bacon is pure personal preference based on what you're aiming to get from the meal; Hangover cure? Cook that pig till it crunches! Standard stomach-filler? Grill it soft! If you've fried your hash browns to the point there's barely any potato left, just sack 'em off. They don't deserve a place on the final line-up… And finally, show some self-restraint. Any more than two tablespoons full of baked beans is gluttony. The beans are designed to be an 'accompagnément'. NOT a goddamn centrepiece.

You may think this is controversial. But that doesn't mean it's not *correct.*

Right, where were we?

I thought it would it be an easy post-breakfast metro ride to Jesmond, what with me heading out of the city at a time when everyone else would ostensibly be heading into it. It wasn't. The metro was still rammed to capacity. I was lucky in grabbing a seat out of Central Station and my frequent unsuccessful checks left and right were met with no boarding women or old people once we departed each station so I was able to keep my seat all the way. The downside of this was that I spent a lot of the journey recoiling from a lot of 'commuter arse-to-face' attempts and waylaid bags swinging low in my general direction.

The entire metro system and all its trains were due a complete upgrade in 2019 after decades of degradation and funding issues. Obviously that got curtailed in a heartbeat when the financial bottom dropped out of everything. The most unsafe of trains were pulled from service, forcing the metro system to go down to a heavily restricted timetable and thus pushing up the number of commuters per train each day. It never once felt like the old, clanging trains could cope. As it wheezed itself back up to motion from each stop at every station, you became generally concerned that the next corner could be the one that derailed the train so you prayed that to avoid such a thing the metro never picked up speed.

I prised myself free of my seat and forced myself through the crowd blocking my route to the door the minute the metro approached Jesmond, floundering out onto the platform and into the crisp fresh air like I'd just been birthed into the world. But birthed from a womb that was a metal carriage drenched in the smell of body odour and infuriation.

Jacket buttons done.

Collar up.

Phone checked.

On I trudged to Alia Marcus' beautiful home just off Osborne Road.

Osborne Road in Jesmond, about two and a half miles up from that little pocket on Jesmond Dene where my encounter with Mick Hetherington ended my police career, was once known as Newcastle's Notting Hill. Over the last thirty years it had transformed itself within one of Newcastle's leafiest suburban areas into a hive of up-markets bars and restaurants with some of the best hospitality the city could offer; kept thriving by its heady mix of the huge student population that surrounded it and the local residents who's general income was never lower than about sixty to seventy grand a year. It had a Waitrose on it. That should tell you everything you need to know.

A *Waitrose.*

In Newcastle.

How ridiculous is *that*? It's like hair gel in a bald man's bathroom cabinet!

That Osborne Road is just about still hanging in there in the current climate should tell you a lot about the affluence of the area its based within. A lot of the bars have shut their doors. A good few of the restaurants too. Pretty much all of the designer boutique clothes stores situated on the tiny little cove of streets off of Osborne Road itself are gone because who's buying £400 shoes and £2,000 suits nowadays with any degree of regularity when they can't even afford a £150 food shop?

But whilst the economy tanking had rubbed the shine off Osborne Road, it was still on its legs, just about, which is more than can be said for a lot of places in the North East.

I came out of the metro station and took a little sneaky cut off Eslington Terrace that I was familiar with from a cheating spouse surveillance job I did in the plush surroundings of Jesmond a few years back, then pushed on against a wind that was now picking up some steam, all the way up the illustrious Osborne Road to Grosvernor Place, where Alia Marcus lived with her professional football player fiancé, Paul Burns. Who (but of course) she name-dropped twice in the course of our one brief phone call earlier that morning.

Alia's home was behind a colossal nine-foot wrought iron gate that was dwarfed on either side by immense conifer trees. The gate was an absolute beast to move. I doubted that Alia Marcus was moving this thing on her own every time she was coming home. She had to be sneaking in round the back. I'd seen photos of her on social media. I knew what she looked like. She was a tiny slip of a woman. She did not appear to me to be one of Psychic's legendary 'ladies who lift'.

Behind the formidable gate there was the sixteen marble steps leading up to the front door. By the time I got to that and lifted the huge cast iron knocker shaped like a lion's head and positioned in the middle of two other matching ornate iron lion heads either side of it, I was coughing up a lung and feeling like I'd done two episodes of Gladiators back-to-back.

The amazing 1990s version with Ulrika Jonsson, of course.

Not that awful 2008 version Sky tried to pull off.

I seriously needed to have a hard word with myself. The leg and back ache were one thing but surely I can't be this wrecked from walking Osborne Road, pushing a gate open and climbing a flight of stairs? There was sweat in my eyes and no sooner was I about to take a second to double-over and take some time to catch my breath, the door opened and there stood my *opposite*:

Paul Burns was drenched head-to-toe in Under Armour clothing – the type that hung to ever curvature of every muscle, of course – and his face carried a perfectly etched designer stubble contoured around his action-hero shaped jaw-line. His pectoral muscles presented themselves to me as an affront to my own physicality. I'm the sort of guy who can't go shirtless in case a farmer tries to milk me. Paul's chest seemed to suggest that if you bounced a two pence piece of it, it would return back at you with the speed of a bullet.

This man's handsomeness intimidated me to my core.

"Hey? Hi. How you doing? Are you the guy here to interview Alia?" he said affably.

He seemed nice as well as handsome. I decided I was going to wait for the first chance I'd get for his back to be turned and then I was going to make a discreet reminder in my notebook to come back and egg his house later.

"I am, yes. Hi. I'm Jake. I'm an investigator from Lehman's Terms?"

Paul nodded in a sort of polite way that suggested he was pretending to give a shit. I decided that I was premature in thinking he was nice but maintained an option on egging his house regardless because his pecs continued to hurt my feelings.

"You're Paul Burns, the footballer, right?"

Paul smiled. "I am. I am, for my sins."

The 'for my sins' line annoyed me immensely. That's the sort of shit utter wankpots say to fake 'everyman' sincerity.

You've probably guessed by now by the way that I have no interest in or knowledge of football. Which considering that Newcastle is a city in which you either played football or built ships for a living but you supported the 'Toon Army' regardless, that should tell you just how much of an outlier I am in my own town. But the thing is, I'd used some of my time on the metro ride over here to do a bit of due diligence on the much name-dropped Paul Burns and I had gathered some information on him and his 'controversies'… Like the £9.8 million he cost to sign with Newcastle that swallowed up most of the club's budget that year, the non-stop injuries from pretty much day one on the team, his incendiary and tabloid-baiting tweets on social media when criticised, him being frequently accused of cheating on his fiancée (ex-model turned business-woman Alia Marcus) ruining other people's marriages in the process and, rather humorously, his appointment as a constant meme-generating platform for mockery due to his ridiculous pineapple-evoking haircut… There was a *lot* out there!

I didn't see much of that being particularly useable in getting some camaraderie going with him and, by proxy, Alia though.

"You a supporter, pal?" said Paul.

"Erm… I feel like I should say yes?" I replied. "But then I'm scared you'll start talking to me about the game and that'll reveal very quickly that I don't have a single bit of knowledge about the sport."

"That's not a barrier to being a fan of the game these days, buddy!" laughed Paul. "Come on in."

That seemed disrespectful to the fans who's support helps earn him, even in the current climate, a staggering thirty thousand pounds a week. I therefore decided I did not like Paul Burns now. And it had nothing to do with his physical appearance being by nature of its proximity a terrorisation of my doughy, broken-down, old 'dad-bod'. It was because he came across like a grade-A wanker within the first thirty seconds of meeting him.

He opened his door wide and I walked through into a living, breathing stereotype of exactly what you would expect a professional footballer's home to be like – all modern gadgets, minimalism and metal as far as your eye could see in every room. Paul led me through to the living area where, engulfed and consumed by a sofa that seemed to be the size of a small cruise liner, sat Alia Marcus.

She was older than I was expecting with about ten years or maybe less on Stephie's twenty-four years. Her jet black hair was pulled up into a purposefully messy beehive type 'do' and she had that whole appearance of 'casually-dishevelled-when-you-*know*-they'd-been-putting-the-whole-look-together-for-nearly-an hour-or-something' going on. A look Margaret Jason had down pat and excelled at. Alia? Not so much.

She jumped up from the sofa and extended her diamond encrusted hand towards me. There was probably half a million pound in jewellery on her wrist and finger alone.

"Hi, Jake?" she smiled.

"Alia, hi. It's great to finally meet with you." I replied.

Alia apologised again for not returning any of my calls or messages across social media. She explained that she had been completely broken by Stephie's death and she took some time away with Paul to get her head clear and to "support him whilst he recovered from a broken bone in his foot".

At that point I looked to Paul and smiled, but secretly the investigator in me was checking his foot out. There was no cast or strapping on either of his feet. He was walking barefoot fine. My face might have suggested friendliness towards the man but internally I was thinking "They spent £9.8 million on you, Paul lad. What sort of fraudulent long-con are you running here pal?" then I remembered I didn't give a shit about football and I went back to engaging with Alia.

But at this stage my certainty of Paul's status as a wanker was at a confident 75%.

Alia said that she'd ignored my first couple of approaches because she thought I was a tabloid reporter on a 'fishing' expedition and she had no interest in speaking to me.

"We don't have the best of relationships with the media, do we babes?" she said to Paul.

"They're fucking scum!" said Paul, now face deep in his mobile phone and not looking up.

"I got a message from Stephie's mum encouraging me to speak with you a day or so ago. She explained you were working for her. That changed my mind." Alia said.

"I can understand your reticence." I replied.

After the briefest of exchanges and offers of refreshments were swiftly ticked off, I took to listening to Alia talk about herself and what her relationship was to Stephie Jay.

Alia had been a model from the age of thirteen and "got out of it all" three years ago when she realised that the industry had no interest in what she had to offer because she'd rather rudely allowed herself to become twenty eight years old. She initially tried to go down the TV presenting route but had a serious problem following red camera lights and an even bigger problem with autocues – both of which killed any chance of a career in this field. Alia's plans to re-train and re-package herself as a 'talent agent' disappeared overnight when she met the footballer Paul Burns in a nightclub. He was there on a post-match bender. She was there supporting Stephie on another one of her 'events'. In Paul's eyes Alia was a great way to end the evening. But he seriously underestimated the fortitude of a woman who suddenly saw her 'career' now as a high-profile sportsperson's WAG ('Wife And Girlfriend').

They've been together ever since.

Stephie and Alia met whilst both modelling at The George Platform. Stephie was 'the next generation' through the door after Alia. Any possibility for an All About Eve type situation of older archetype thoroughly unravelled by the arrival of a newer variant was thrown to the wind after the first modelling gig Stephie and Alia worked together. Alia found Sue's latest recruit to be so lovely natured, caring, interesting and thoroughly irresistible that she instantly took Stephie under her wing. They quickly became the firmest of BFFs ('Best Friends Forever', I'm told). They travelled the world on assignments together. There was a period where they lived together. When Stephie's star started to brighten in direct proportion to that which Alia's faded, Stephie was quick to fight for work to keep being assigned Alia's way sometimes even at a cost to herself.

"We had holiday plans." Alia said quietly. "We were going to see New Years in down in London with a group of girls and then straight after we were going to have a fortnight detoxing at her parents' villa in Formentera."

I wrote that down.

"She was sending me texts the full week leading up to when she died telling me all the things that was going on with Max." she continued.

"Max McNae?" I clarified.

"Yeah," interrupted Paul. "He's a mate of mine. We'd been going out together as a foursome for meals and shit and they'd really hit it off!"

I nodded. I didn't mention we'd looked into Max and checked his whereabouts out around the time Stephie died. It didn't seem necessary.

"Where were you when you found out she'd..."

"Killed herself?" Alia interrupted.

"Yes." I replied.

"Tell him!" interjected Paul. "Tell him what you've been getting so bent up out of shape about. He'll tell you what I've told you – You're bloody mad!"

"What's that then?" I asked, mentally raising Paul's wanker status to 80%.

"Well, first of all…" Alia said, shooting Paul a stone-cold look of death. "I was here, at home. Nobody called me or anything in the first instance. I heard it on the radio just like everybody else. Then my phone started going crazy with the girls trying to get me to confirm that it wasn't true and that Stephie was with me, hungover and lounging around here like she does most Sundays. I just collapsed on the floor, sobbing. I couldn't get up."

I stayed silent. I didn't think she needed to be encouraged along on this.

"But you said 'killed herself' and… well… much to Paul's annoyance, I do not believe for one second that she killed herself!" Alia said.

"No, no." I smiled. "I started to ask where you were when you found out she was dead. You interrupted and said 'killed herself'. I never said those words. But, you know, let's jump off from there regardless - so you *don't* think she did?"

I quickly put the biggest broadest tick next to Alia's name in my notebook and tried to hide a smile that was wanting to break across my face at the sound of someone affirming what I'd been thinking for some time.

"Take away the fact that she wasn't the least bit troubled and if she was remotely suffering in anyway mentally, financially or otherwise she would've talked to me about it because she talked to me about *everything*… Take that away, and you're left with someone who was telling me how excited she was about all the plans we were making and what she had in store for the future. Now even if you manage to convince me that she completely lied to me and she successfully hid how depressed and troubled she was, I would still never, *ever* believe that Stephie would've killed herself the way she did."

"Why do you believe that?" I asked.

"Because she absolutely could not abide her neck being touched. She detested it. You should have seen what she was like when someone was trying to run a bloody make-up brush against it. She would never have put a rope around her neck. She just wouldn't. She would never have got herself to do that. I just don't see it and can't believe it. She would have still been building herself up to doing it and tightening it around her neck by the time someone discovered her the next morning…"

Alia suddenly burst into tears and dropped her head into her hands, muffling her sobs. Paul dropped his phone and ran over to her, dropping to his knees in front of her and taking her into his arms.

I reduced Paul's wanker status to 70%.

"Baby, you're troubling yourself over this because you don't want to accept it." Paul said softly and quietly. "But the police… and the ambulance people… and everyone who dealt with the situation? They can't all be wrong. You have to accept that!"

"I think I agree with Alia. Perhaps I should be upfront about that." I said respectfully but assertively whilst raising Paul's status as a wanker back to 80% without even flinching.

Paul shot me a hard, cold glance. "You have *got* to be shitting me?"

I shook my head just as Alia pulled hers back to look at me whilst smearing the tears away from her face.

"You don't think she killed herself either?" she asked gently.

"No. I don't."

Alia cleared her throat. "Her parents must think I'm some really cold, selfish bitch because I've not been in touch. I didn't go to the funeral. I couldn't. But I've just been avoiding them because I know they're in so much pain right now and I swore they could do without me screaming that I don't think she died the way everyone is saying she is. So I've just hid from them."

"I can sort of understand that." I said to Alia.

"The night she died she was on the phone to me. We'd been messaging all day because I was meant to go to this thing at a club in town with her but the night before she let me know that Sue had cancelled it and was sending her somewhere else. We were chatting about that and what she was going to wear to this new thing and all that sort of thing. I wasn't that pissed off I was no longer required because I didn't really want to be her chaperone anyway. But she rang me that night and left an answer phone message and she was screaming blue murder about stuff I didn't really understand. She was dead a few hours later. I don't think that the Stephie who left me that answerphone message would've just gone and hanged herself later that night. I'm sorry, I just don't believe it."

"This is where you fucking lose me, hun!" said Paul, his tone becoming more pointed and exasperated. "There isn't some grand conspiracy here. The voicemail tells you what the score is. You just don't want to accept it. She had a big falling out with her idol Sue. It broke her up. She killed herself. I'm sorry to be brutal and blunt and all that, darling. But there really isn't any more to it than that!"

Wanker status? A very restrained 90%!

Alia pushed Paul away from her. "You're unbelievable!" she gasped.

"This voicemail?" I said, leaning forward in my seat and trying to get in what I needed to ask before a full blown 'domestic' kicked off in front of me. "Can you tell me a bit more about this voicemail?"

"Stephie was due to go to this nightclub thing and she wanted me to go with her, right?" said Alia with a new found assertiveness in her voice.

"That's the Paradox club thing?"

"Correct!" said Alia. "Sue got in touch with her on the Friday – literally the night before it was due to go ahead – and said that she was having to cancel her as a very high paying personal appearance request had come in on the books, *specific* for Stephie. 'Playing eye candy at a rich exclusive party for important people up in Northumberland'. Those were Stephie's *exact* words."

"She definitely said 'Northumberland'?" I asked, writing as fast as I could in my notebook.

"She definitely said that, yes," answered Alia. "As I said, I was happy to get given the bump. I ended up crashing and having an early night but the next morning I found I had a message on my phone from Stephie from late on the Saturday night. She was driving and she said that she needed to come straight round in the morning. She said she had to talk to me urgently and she wanted me to put her in touch with one of the few reporters that Paul liked. She was right in the middle of kicking off about Sue and she said she had to go because she'd been clocked on her mobile or something and the police were pulling her over."

I kept writing as fast as I could.

"I rang the police on the Monday, I told them all this. I said she sounded freaked out and that there has to be some report on their system for having pulled her over just a few hours before she died. I begged them to look into this."

"And did they?" I asked.

"Of course they didn't!" she replied.

"Because there's nothing to look into, man!" shouted Paul. "Maybe they don't want to tell you she was pulled over, found to have drink and coke in her system or something, arrested, released and didn't want to face the shame so she topped herself!"

Ladies and Gentlemen – we have hit *100%* guaranteed wanker!

Alia sprang forward and cracked the back of her hand across his face.

He fell backwards off his knees onto his backside and grabbed his face.

"You fucking bitch!" he hissed.

"Woah! I think we need to calm down! Please… Let's not get carried away. I know this is upsetting but…" I tried to offer mediation.

Paul jumped to his feet. "You're driving yourself crazy looking for stuff that isn't there!" he shouted at Alia then turned to me. "And you need to get out of here because you're actually making her worse!"

He stormed from the room and slammed the door.

We sat in silence for a few seconds.

"You said you spoke to the police?" I said tentatively.

"Yeah. I spoke to a detective constable called Bill Tidyman. He took notes. He said that he'd pass it up the line to his detective inspector. I never heard anything back. I went to try and speak to Stephie's parents but… they were just *broken*. They were really, really wrecked by all this and Paul said it was a terrible idea and that I would be stirring stuff up. He said it wasn't going to change anything and I guess he's right overall about that because ultimately none of this is going to bring her back is it?"

Paul barged back into the room with a bang the minute her last word struck my ears. He had a laptop in his hands and he threw it aggressively onto the sofa next to where Alia was sat.

"Come on then! Why don't you just play it for him? Recruit another member to your little conspiracy club?" spat Paul. "Listen to it for yourself and you'll see you are clutching at straws here… Stephie was a lovely, lovely girl. She was. I'm not saying otherwise. But she killed herself and we're never going to know why. That's just what it is and that's just how it is."

I stared at Paul.

My eyes ricocheted to Alia.

Then back to Paul.

Then finally back to Alia where they came to a final stop.

"Wait, you still have the voicemail?" I gasped.

Alia slowly moved her head affirmatively. "I had to. It was the last sound of her voice I'd ever get. I knew it would disappear from my phone so I recorded it off there and onto an audio file."

"Ok…" I stuttered. I turned to a clean page in my notebook and gripped my pen tightly. "Could I hear it?"

Alia lifted the laptop over and opened it.

We sat in silence whilst she took to logging on and accessing the required file. Whilst she busied herself, I took to staring at my feet and steadying my breathing. Paul sat down on the arm of the sofa, not wanting to commit to a full return to the room. He cupped his hands in the pray position and raised them to his mouth.

And then with no forewarning whatsoever, Stephie's voice filled the living room.

*"... Ali? It's Steph'! Call me back as soon as you get this. I've been utterly fucked over by Sue again. I really need to talk to you but I don't want to do this on a fucking voicemail. I've seen shit tonight you wouldn't believe, honey... You definitely need to put me in touch with Paul's pal at The Guardian. I'm serious.... I just can't believe I'm going to say this but you know this party that I had...* [SILENCE] *Aww, fuck! Fuck! Fuck! I'm being pulled over....* [LONG SILENCE] *... This isn't good... Think... Think... Look, if something comes up and you can't get a hold of me check the map in my car...Yeah... Follow the map okay?"*

The recording clicked off, having ended.

I sat in silence. I caught Paul looking directly at the side of Alia's face as she slowly pushed the laptop away from her and let the tears fall down her face.

"That was all a few hours before her death?" I asked falteringly.

Alia nodded. "I played it for the police officer. I called them the minute I found out she was gone. That Tidyman guy came round, he listened to it. He made notes. He said he didn't think there was anything there but said he'd look into it with whoever the officers were that pulled her over that night."

"But he never took a recording? Or seized your phone? Or asked for you to make a copy?" I asked, genuinely confused.

Alia shook her head. "He wasn't really interested."

This was bizarre to me. It wasn't just that it seemed fairly inept and unprofessional of a police officer. I'd come to expect that from the police over the years and especially from my experience with them. It was more the fact that DC Tidyman's name kept coming up more and more. For a guy who claimed to me that he was "just the dogsbody" on Stephie's case and that he "wasn't the investigator" because there "wasn't anything really to investigate anyway", it seemed that this wasn't ringing true – he did appear to be more than just a "dogsbody", he did appear to have been doing some "investigating" and he knew there was things that really did need investigating. He just hasn't appeared to investigate them.

The guy had fed me a line it seemed. And I *really* didn't like that.

I was realistic and experienced enough to know that within the police the buck generally doesn't start and stop at the DC level though and that maybe Tidyman had been doing stuff on this case that 'up the line' was crushed before it went anywhere to cover up the fact Stephie didn't really commit suicide.

Why though?

And if it went up the line then that put me right back into the path of DI Andrews as far as I was concerned.

I realised too late that I'd got lost far enough along in my thoughts that my jaw had got tighter and tighter as I locked in the tension once again. I shook my head and blinked away the pain that was now starting to shoot into my head.

"And you've told Stephie's parents none of this? About the answer phone message? About the map in the car? Nothing?"

Alia sat silent.

"I told her not to. I actually explicitly said I did not want her to." Paul said sternly.

"Why?" I said incredulously, raising Paul's wanker status to such a platinum level now that it was reaching the level of free upgrade to utter *cunt*!

"Because it's overdramatic stuff that doesn't help them anyway. It doesn't bring Stephie back. It just gives them false leads to believe there was more to this then there actually was."

"That's not your decision to make." I said, my voice raising an octave outside of my control. "There's a possibility you've been sat on a lead here that could've…"

Paul jumped to his feet. "A lead? Are you for real pal? A lead? What are *you*? The police looked at this and said it wasn't important. But you supersede them? Who are you to look down your nose at them? Where does your authority lie? You're a gutter PI from the look of you, hanging around with degenerates and chasing deadbeats. Why should she be listening to you?"

I turned back to Alia and quickly pulled a business card from the back of my notebook.

"My email address is on the back of there! Could you please send me a copy of that recording?" I said.

Alia started to nod.

"No! No! Stuff *that*! No, Ali babe. You're not getting involved…" shouted Paul before turning directly to me and completing his upgrade from wanker in the process. "She wanted to meet with you to help her conscience. I told her it wasn't a good idea and it's turned out I'm right. I want you to go now. You're upsetting her."

I stared hard at Paul.

He matched my glare.

"You can get up out of that chair. Or I'm going to drag you…"

I stood up at a speed that surprised myself and caused him to stop speaking, slowly moving back into a position with his legs that suggested he thought an attack may be coming.

I was *done* with being looked down on, messed around and lied to.

By *anyone*.

Domineering piece-of-shit, know-it-all men like Paul get under my skin at the best of times. But the idea that he could have impacted Margaret and Matthew learning something important about Stephie's final hours tipped me completely over the edge.

"Save the machismo-soaked crap, mate…" I spat at him, my temper overcoming my reserve.

Now here's the thing: I am a self-confessed enormous dick of a person but Paul was a massive, massive cunt with a heavy element of arsehole about him too. And, to paraphrase that aforementioned Team America: World Police movie once more, the job of a dick is to fuck cunts and arseholes. Which means Paul was about to get *doubly*-fucked by me.

Watch my veneer drop in three… two… one…

"…Here's the thing: You're a fucking *talker*. I can tell that about you." I continued. "I'm good at getting the measure of people. It comes as a skill-set with doing this job as long as I have. I can tell also that you're an overpaid prat who might have all the money in the world but you still can't afford a mirror."

"What are you…" Paul sniggered.

I stepped forward. He didn't move.

"There is no way there is a mirror in this house. Because if there was you'd never have hair like that. Now, as I was saying. You're a talker. But me? I'm a fucking *doer*, son. And I'm also a bloody realist. So whilst I know that I can't beat you in a fight and you'll beat me on strength and stamina, I also feel really confident that you're so much of a talker that you won't make the first move. I'm a doer though as I said. Whilst you're talking up more threatening crap, I'm going to grab that trophy right there…"

I took a step towards the mantlepiece in the centre of Paul and Alia's living room and plucked down one of Paul's many sharp-edged footballing awards placed up there on display. Alia started to look panicked.

The panic soon spread to Paul too.

"… See? A doer *does*!" I smiled, bouncing the trophy around in my hand. "So now I'm going to go to town on stabbing you repeatedly in those legs of yours. Are they insured by the way? Do you have a rough figure on the depreciation of £9.8 million with every slashed muscle and smashed cartilage?"

The colour started to drain from Paul's face.

"You made an *assumption* about me," I said with a fake smile. "You looked down your nose at me and you thought you could push me around and intimidate me and I don't like that. In fact, I fucking detest it when people do that and I *really* detest it when I see men doing it to women too. Hopefully right now your head is educating you at rapid speed that when you make an assumption you make an ass out of you and 'umption' as the saying goes, yeah?"

"Look, hang on…" squeaked Paul.

"Shut the fuck up and sit the fuck down, Paul!" I said firmly.

He dropped down onto the sofa.

I turned to Alia. "Thank you for your time."

I started to walk out of the room, stopping and bending to go eye to eye with Paul.

"You were right about me hanging around with degenerates and chasing deadbeats," I sort-of-lied. "But you should know that most of the degenerates I hang around with are south-of-the-river dwelling, die hard Sunderland supporters. So if I was to offer them twenty quid to take a metal pipe to the legendary Paul Burns' legs, what do you think they'd say?"

Paul sat silent.

"They'd say they'd do it for half that, trust me!" I said scornfully. "So if that sound file of Stephie isn't in my inbox by the time I get back to my office, I'm going to assume *you've* blocked my investigation further. And I'm going to make a phone call to the nastiest Toon Army hating scumbag I have in my contacts."

I walked out of the room, dropping Paul's trophy on the hard wood floor behind me. I heard it snap on impact.

Now *THAT* was a goddamn chuff.

With the adrenaline pumping through my veins from my faked display of machismo, I yanked the wrought iron gate open outside of Alia's house with a new found sense of strength and strode off down the street.

My jaw was sending searing, shooting blasts of pain into my head. My back was beginning to twinge and I popped my trusty metal tin open only to find it empty of the one thing I really needed right now – some heavy duty painkillers.

I stopped for a second as I reached the corner of Grosvernor Place. Nausea was starting to build up and I could feel this awful taste coming up my bile tract. I took a second to grip a nearby lamp post and steady myself.

My mind started to race. There were so many questions… so much confusion… And Stephie's voice was fresh in my mind again. I could *hear* her. I could hear that panic in her voice. There was anger there too. Stephie wasn't "ill" that night. Stephie was on her way back from something, somewhere - that Sue George had sent her too.

I made a mental note to myself that Sue George was getting another dramatic barge-in very soon indeed. That mental note superseded the slight buckling of my legs. I needed a 'kick', man. I really, *really* needed a 'kick'.

I'd last taken some Tramadol probably about three, maybe four, hours ago. If this was what I was like after hitting my first usual part of the day without a fix then I was going to be in way more trouble than I ever initially considered.

I tried to take my mind off the *need* by firing out a quick phone call to Psychic. He didn't pick up so I garbled furiously into his answerphone as I crossed back onto Osborne Road.

"Psychic, mate! Listen, I've got some shit and a half to tell you. I don't know where you are but if you're not at the office, get back there ASAP! There was a goddamn voicemail from Stephie on the night she died. How about *that*? And I think we're getting strung along by that Tidyman prat down at Forth Street station. I think we should go back and speak to him again… Call me back!"

The next call I made was to Margaret Jason.

Again, it went straight through to her answerphone.

I left a message asking her to call me back and whether she could confirm if Stephie's vehicle was still in their possession up in Smallburn. I asked if anyone else had been up to look at it since DC Tidyman checked it out. I said I'd just come from meeting with Alia Marcus and I needed to talk to Margaret urgently about that.

I hoped she would pick up on the exhilaration in the tone of my voice.

It was the messing around with my phone and making these various calls that got me along Osborne Road and down through Eslington Terrace again, back towards the metro station, before I noticed Face – he of my personally appointed 'A-Team' from the restaurant encounter the other night – was on my tail.

It definitely wasn't the blurring of my vision and the aching nausea building up as a result of the ungodly *thirst* for some opioid drowned down with caffeine.

It definitely wasn't that at all.

I'm not convincing you, am I?

I *really* should have spotted him sooner.

## [17]

## or

## "Your Action Sequence..."

With my line of work the paranoia comes with the job as standard. You do it long enough and you start to really take notice of shop doorways and leafy suburban streets for the advantages and disadvantages they present for hiding yourself away to observe. Nearly every car park I drive into now I am constantly giving it an almost immediate scrutinising to deduce where I think the best vantage point would be if I wanted to observe the pedestrian entrance/exit way without being spotted.

The worst infliction you take away with you is mobile phones.

I'm always using a mobile phone as a back-up to sneak a photo of someone or covertly record them. I've become a master of pretending to use my smart phone innocuously enough whilst *really* recording evidence of someone being up to no good. And I always say if I can do that than anyone can. So every time I see a mobile phone in someone's hands and it feels like I'm in the line of sight of the lens, I instantaneously assume they're recording me and I start to analyse the possibilities as to why. Because in my line of work you piss a lot of people off. And pissed off people make good enemies. Maybe one of them has hired a hunter to hunt the hunter that hunted them in the first place to see how that hunter now feels being hunted? Don't tell me I sound mad... After all, it's not paranoia if they really *are* out to get you.

And as today was proving, they really were out to get me!

It was pure, golden chance that I clocked Face following me down Eslington Terrace on the other side of the road. He'd stepped too close behind me and was now starting to break even with my strides. He clearly realised this himself and decided to pull back and widen up the distance but did it in the most unnatural way possible.

As anyone who does a fair bit of surveillance for a living will tell you, everything unnatural will draw attention and the last thing you want whilst doing covert surveillance is to draw attention.

My eyes were drawn to my right by Face's sudden 'stop-and-freeze' right alongside me on the other side of the road. He clearly and incorrectly assumed that the vehicles between us would hide him from my line of sight. I noticed him and slowed my pace down straight away, in the process coming to note that there was the sound of another pair of footsteps coming up behind me on the otherwise deadly quiet street.

I sped up and ducked straight into a little kiosk newsagents on the corner of the street outside of the metro station at Jesmond and rounded straight behind a stock stand that would give me just about enough coverage to get out of sight and get my bearings.

The little old lady behind the counter give me a justified strange glance.

"Do you sell ibuprofen?" I asked quietly.

She wordlessly pointed directly behind her head.

I nodded. "One box and a box of paracetamol, please!"

I reached over to the fridge behind me and grabbed a bottle of water.

"Three-fifty with the water!" she said.

"Three-fifty? For water and painkillers? Come on, man!" I gasped.

"They're the prices!" she replied firmly.

I stepped forward and pulled a five pound note from my pocket.

"Keep the change!" I said.

"Erm… Okay? … Thank you? If you're sure?" she cautiously responded.

"I'm joking! Of course you can't keep the change. I'm not rewarding you for robbing me!" I picked up the tablets and water and stepped out of the shop.

I clocked Face straight away, standing off down to my left and thinking he was hiding out of sight on the corner with a clear line of sight of the entrance into the metro station. He'd now been joined by BA Baracus who was quick to spot me and swiftly move his wrist to his mouth and start talking.

Yes. *That* cliché.

These guys were not subtle.

And what's worse, they were leaning hard into the stereotypes. They weren't making a particularly concerted effort to blend into their surroundings. In daylight I could see these blokes for exactly what they were: all beige combat trousers and dark tactical boots done up with 'military-lacing'. There was the Barbor jackets with copious and bulging front pockets that sat atop black polo shirts and whose sleeves only just about hid the ginormous all weather/all-terrain watch.

They were private security.

Ex-military.

But more likely wide-boy, alpha male ex-military private security and not premium level covert operatives. How would I make that call, do you think? Because if these guys were top-of-the-tree covert operatives, I would not have seen them.

Face and BA Baracus took a step backwards and out of sight around the corner. I clocked them doing that whilst taking a swig of water but stealing a glance in the process. I yanked four ibuprofen and four paracetamol tablets from the packaging, stuffed them into my mouth and crunched down on them. I did not have the time to be waiting for them to dissolve.

I pushed the remaining tablets deep down into my pocket, cleared off the water and threw the empty bottle in the bin then set off straight for the entrance into Jesmond metro station. I was midway into the station when I saw a metro pulling in, perfectly timed, and heading for town. I jumped straight on it and stared back out, looking over the route I'd just walked. There was no sign of a hurried Face or BA Baracus making a dash to follow me onto the metro.

The tannoy inside the train announced "Stand clear of the doors please!" and the metro doors jiggered shut with a clunking, halting thud. As it pulled out of Jesmond, I looked up and down the carriage and noted that the metro was a lot quieter than normal… and that BA Baracus was stood at the top of the carriage, pretending to check his phone.

I turned to put my back to him and noticed that Face was stood, holding a railing at the other end of the carriage.

Okay… Okay… *Maybe* these fellas were a little bit further up the league from being just wide-boy, alpha male ex-military private security.

I grabbed my phone to send a 'red alert' text to Psychic at the exact moment we went through the last tunnel that would have afforded me a signal.

The closest metro station back to my office would be Monument and I believed these guys would be expecting me to take that. The metro was drawing to a stop at Haymarket, one stop before. I left myself no thinking time and casually rolled back on my feet to bring me closest to the door. The metro stopped. The doors opened. Neither Face nor BA Baracus so much as looked up.

The warning beeps blared.

*"Stand clear of the doors please!"*

I heard the first hiss of the doors closing and nonchalantly stepped back a little further straight out of the carriage and onto the platform at Haymarket. I allowed myself one little grin and an internal 'Fuck You' to those piece of shit, incompetent wannabe sons-of-bitches…

… And then I dropped the grin and the accompanying 'Fuck You' on sight of both Face and BA Baracus standing either side of me up and down the platform. Motherfu… Right. *Fine.* Okay. They were better than wide-boy, alpha male ex-military private security types. They can have that. I'll allow it.

I set off walking towards the large two track escalator that would take me up and out of the station. I tried to walk as naturally as possible. Well, as naturally as is actually possible when you know you're being tailed by two big, thick-necked blokes with an agenda against you.

I limped out of Haymarket metro station and turned onto Northumberland Street. This used to be a place that would be awash with a sea of people at this time of year, everyone bustling and ricocheting from shop-to-shop trying to get their Christmas shopping done whilst throngs of parents with their children queued along outside of Fenwicks department store to see their famous festive window display.

That era of Northumberland Street would have been perfect for me at this point. I would have taken two steps forward and lost these guys straight away. Instead though, Northumberland Street was like a long stretch of barely inhabited wet concrete. There was a small group of protestors starting to congregate way off in the distance down at the very bottom but for all intents and purposes there wasn't a soul to be seen.

I kept walking and used what shop-fronts were still open and didn't have boards up or barriers down to keep stealing glances directly behind me. I managed to discern that BA Baracus had fanned out and was now walking on the other side of Northumberland Street, behind me in my eight o'clock position. Face was roughly about fifty metres directly behind me, following the path I'd walked. He was still too close, I thought. He'd clearly learnt nothing from our encounter in Jesmond.

He was close but not so close that I didn't fancy taking my chances regardless. We passed the entrance point for Eldon Square shopping centre smack-bang in the middle of Northumberland Street. I ducked immediately right and ran straight out of both their lines of sight and turned into the first shop that presented itself on my right once more.

I bent over double so that my body was ducked down below the window line of the store itself. I reached out and grabbed the first piece of stock I could see – and quickly realised I was in a children's clothes discount store!

I held the ugliest pair of young girl's flower-strewn slip-on plimsoles, sized 3-5 years, and was just about to make a dash to the back of the store where their changing rooms were situated when I saw BA Baracus hurry past the front of the shop, looking pretty annoyed. He was followed eight to ten paces behind by Face who stopped, looked into the store in which I hid, surveyed it and moved on.

As soon as I thought they'd cleared past the store, I stood and started to walk towards the changing room area. An overly-eager young male stepped in front of me. His staff badge said 'Wayne' but his face screamed 'Virgin'.

"Can I help you, sir?" he smiled. "Are they for your daughter?"

Wayne started looking around me from below my waist, trying to catch sight of the child he'd wrongly assumed must be in my company.

"No, they're for me. I have small feet!" I smiled, pushing past him and heading for the changing rooms. To the left of the changing room cubicles was a staff room door that was conveniently being held ajar by a cardboard box. I threw the shoes down to my right, pulled the staff room door open and slipped off down the corridor before Wayne could say for certain where I'd gone.

The corridor was long and thin with small staff rooms and alcoves for stock on either side. It bent round to the left and one quick blast on the metal security bar of the double-doors at the very end of it led me straight out into a loading bay at the back of the old bus concourse just off Prudhoe Place.

In my head it was all very simple: I'd peg it as fast I could up and along onto Percy Street, turn left and cut past the old 'hippy green' from my youth - that had since evolved into a hipster meeting point for people who loved Nando's and Wagamama but now just stood in desolation – before sliding quickly across Greys Monument, down onto Grey Street, through the door for my office, up the stairs and straight into a screaming match with Psychic consisting of lots of 'WHY THE FUCK DON'T YOU ANSWER YOUR PHONE, YOU GORMLESS SHITE?'

The problem was 'simple' only stops being 'simple' once a minor obstacle has been introduced. And I was quite far down Percy Street when I realised that I'd picked up Murdock and he was now hurriedly crossing the road to tuck in behind me. This was more than a 'minor obstacle' so you can understand that we'd instantly moved far along from 'simple' now, right?

I'm using the term 'we' and I really don't know why exactly because if my memory is correct I don't recall seeing any of you bastards there that day, caught up in all of this and trying to help me out.

I passed the old 'hippy green' on my left and started to think how terribly unwise it felt to lead 'The A-Team' right back to my office door, if the rest of them weren't there waiting for me already of course. I decided the best thing to do was to keep the pace going until I lost them, they gave up or a confrontation was forced.

With an entrance point for Monument metro station up in front of me, I pulled the packet of ibuprofen from my jacket pocket and yanked another couple of tablets free. My heart was thumping hard from this level of accelerated exertion, my back was twinging really badly and my knee was starting to throb. I'll not even tell you how bad the veins in the sides of my head were feeling. You've pretty much got the measure of that utter agony by now, right?

I took the stairs down into the concourse of Monument metro and hit the bottom just as Murdock started making his way down after me from the top step. I decided to force Murdocks' hand and see if I could push out into sight who his 'back-up' was because I could not get eyes on Face or BA Baracus anywhere.

Despite my metro pass being safely tucked away in my pocket and perfectly fit for use, I reached the barriers and heaved my body over them with all the grace of someone taking a large, wet, bag of three week old meat and dropping it onto concrete from a two storey window. I landed, just about, on the other side and made a beeline for the escalators down onto the platform and I could see that Murdock had used a ticket to activate the barrier and let himself through lawfully. He was now no more than ten steps behind me.

Just as my foot was about to land down on the first escalator step, a hand came to rest hard on my shoulder and pulled me back from going down. I clenched my fist and turned hard ready to 'throw down', as 'real men' say, with Murdock only to find it was a tiny yet insanely wide old lady in metro security uniform.

"What do you think you're playing at?" she shouted, "Come here!"

She dragged me by the back of my coat away from the escalator, allowing the other legitimate metro travellers to get past me. This, unfortunately for him, included Murdock.

"Have you got a ticket?" asked the lady. "Show me your ticket?"

I shrugged at her whilst keeping my metro pass firmly in my pocket and fixing my eyes on Murdock as he descended down the escalator.

"No ticket?" she exclaimed.

"No ticket!" I smiled.

"Come here!" she sighed, yanking my coat some more in order to push me back through the ticket barriers I'd just jumped. I was now back out onto the concourse.

And because I learn absolutely nothing from my continued failed attempts to get ahead, I allowed myself a further little grin and an internal 'Fuck You' to another of those piece of shit, incompetent wannabe sons-of-bitches… And then I dropped the grin and the accompanying 'Fuck You' *again* on sight of both Face and BA Baracus making their way down the stairs and onto the metro concourse.

I ducked behind one ticket machine with just enough time for the two of them to pass hurriedly by. BA Baracus was once again lifting that bloody sleeve to his mouth in an extremely indiscreet manner. I couldn't have imagined he was getting the best of signals on the underground anyway but didn't feel like popping over to ask. The minute they both cleared past the corner I hid behind, I rolled my body right and off behind them to go back up the staircase from which they'd just come down.

I climbed the stairs thinking that I deserved to give myself a bit more credit. This was a team of four guys (that I knew of) with some military background judging from their attempts at 'casual clothing' and they were all clearly kitted out with some form of covert radio equipment in order to be able to sync up with one another. I was completely outsmarting them and outpacing them with…

***BAM***

… I'd just reached the top of the stairs out of the Monument metro station and veered to my left when I felt the impact of a cold, hard, compact piece of metal slam hard against my mouth. The globs of thick warm blood filling up on the inside of my lips and pouring down into my throat would be along in a few seconds.

If I'd known right there and then that I'd been hit with the butt-end of a handgun I'd probably have been a lot more panicked at that moment. Instead my legs buckled slightly causing me to fall against the wall surrounding the stairs and no sooner did I turn to find out what it was that hit me and where it had come from an arm hooked itself around my waistline and pulled me up to standing properly.

"You alright buddy? You okay? That was a nasty fall you just took there!" said the voice as my vision blurred. I turned my head to see where the voice came from and who the arm around me belonged to, only to see I was now being gripped by Hannibal.

"Keep walking!" he hissed, dragging me along on my crumbling legs. "I'll blow your spine out if you make a move on me, *prick*!"

Before I could work out whether moving against him was even an option in my current, wobbly state I'd been spun off my feet and pulled down an alleyway between the local Italian restaurant and Waterstones bookstore. I pulled against Hannibal's grip but he simply reached up without breaking his stride and back-handed me in my swollen mouth causing me to wince and my legs to give way with the pain.

I started to fall but Hannibal grabbed the back of my neck and used the momentum to throw me further forward into a pile of rubbish stacked up next to a large industrial bin at the back of the Italian restaurant. As I fell, I saw Face take a position at the bottom of the alleyway, looking outwards.

Do you want me to throw another entry in my book of *'Newcastle is a big city but a small place'* examples?

Well, just across from where I lay was the side entrance door for a really shitty, rundown church that everyone kind of forgets is there because the hubbub of retail outlets and eateries built up around it over the years dwarf it from view. It had come back into some use in the last eighteen months as it opened its doors twenty-four hours a day to provide refuge for families at night who'd been made homeless after their houses were repossessed – of which these numbers were growing at an exponential rate – and during the day it was a 'soup kitchen' of sorts, designed to provide one hot meal a day to those that were struggling in the current climate to eat… If Hannibal had timed this better for my benefit I'd have been dumped down here for a thorough life-ending kicking, only for forty to fifty hungry poor Geordies to bear witness or hopefully come to my aid.

I knew the church for an altogether different reason though. I knew it because every Tuesday afternoon and Thursday evening it hosted an Alcoholics Anonymous meeting which served some of the most aromatic and sweet tasting coffee you could possibly hope to consume in such a difficult location. I'd been a frequent visitor there for a number of years. I'd walked this alleyway many times to slip through to the entrance on my way up from my office. Sometimes when I was in the office and I felt that familiar 'thirst', I'd take a walk up here and just stand in the alleyway and say to myself "I'm Jake Lehman and I'm an alcoholic." That's all I needed, really.

Murdock arrived swiftly next to Hannibal who was now holding me down with his foot. I opened my mouth and the first proper serving of thick, dark blood poured out. My lips were so numb I didn't know it was happening until the blood itself started to soak the collar of my shirt.

"Hey Jake? How you doing? … Enough 'Kiss Chase' now, okay pal?" smiled Hannibal. "You're pissing me off."

"I do… that a lot… to… people." I stammered through the blood. "Most people… find me… quite… disagreeable becau…"

"Shut up Jake!" hissed Hannibal. "We keep missing you over at your office, buddy. We're done trying to play catch-up with you there. But, seriously, fuck you for making us get all pro-active chasing you round this shit tip of city!"

"One… of… us needs the… exercise…" I winced.

"Shush, now. You were warned, mate." he smirked. "We came to you. We asked you nicely. We gave you the benefit of the doubt. Then here you are this morning pissing around, bothering people in their place of work and going door-knocking to stir up drama. Enough is enough now."

They'd clearly been following me down on Hanover Street that morning when I was going to speak to Sue George which meant that they were a lot better than I give them credit for. Or Sue George could have contacted these guys to say I'd been down there and she didn't like it. Which would mean that Sue has the 'ear' of big, thick-necked private security types who, judging from what I could now see sticking out of Hannibal's beltline, had access to firearms.

Oh, Sue was *definitely* getting another dramatic 'barge-in' from me.

I was clearly thinking about things to add to my 'to do list' for a future I no longer had because I was far too oblivious to the fact that I was about to get shot in the head.

Hannibal pulled the gun from his beltline and rubbed the handle against the seamline of the t-shirt he was wearing under his jacket. He held the gun discreetly against his body but pointed it outwards for Murdock to take.

"Psst…" Hannibal said to his friend. "Take this!"

Murdock looked down at the gun but he seemed taciturn about taking it. Hannibal didn't spot this because he was too busy staring me out menacingly.

"I hate this city, Jake!" smirked Hannibal. "I want to go home. You've kept me here longer than I wanted to be and now I've got to piss around clearing up all your mess! I'm not happy. I'm very much not happy!"

I looked to Murdock. He still was staring at the gun being offered to him but had yet to make a reach for it.

"Hey… Hannibal?" I said.

"Who me? Who the hell is Hannibal" asked the very man I'd taken the time to affectionately nickname Hannibal only days ago.

"Yes – you! Remember? … You're the… ring-leader. This guy is… the crazy-looking… Ahhh, forget it!" I said, my voice trailing off through the pain. I spat more blood from my mouth, winced a little more from the agony and tried a different approach, whispering instead "Can… I ask… one… favour?"

"We're not really favour-doing people, I'm afraid Jake." Hannibal sneered. "Not unless the price is right. What's *your* price?"

"One… favour!" I smiled. "Come on… I'm good for it."

"What's that then?" Hannibal replied.

"I really don't… like this restaurant. Like… I hate it. I hate… it… so much! So… let me get up… and let me… make a run for it… then shoot me in the back over there!" I said, now shivering with the pain. "Because I'm okay with… dying… but I really don't want… to die behind… this restaurant!"

Hannibal seemed taken aback by the favour.

I threw in a slow, difficultly-executed wink for good measure. "They do... the most awful… awful… cannelloni… so… come on… one favour?" I said.

Hannibal smiled – then forced the handgun into Murdocks' hands.

"Switch him off!" muttered Hannibal.

Murdock stared down at the gun in his hands.

Hannibal seemed to get very agitated, staring hard into the side of his compatriot's head almost psychically urging him to fire the gun.

I thought about my sons. My throat started to swell and my eyes filled with tears.

Hannibal snatched the gun back from Murdock whilst staring furious anger into the side of his head. Murdock never turned to meet the look. He just stared straight ahead. He wasn't even looking at me. He looked lost somewhere else.

"Utter prick!" spat Hannibal. He readied the chamber on the handgun in one swift movement and raised it towards my face.

… I thought about Jack and how I knew he was going to grow up to be the best in his field at whatever he chose to do.

… I thought about Jonathan and how I imagined he would take a little longer to find his feet in whatever he chose to do in life but that he'd get there and he'd be loved because I could see already in him that he had a tremendous heart.

I saw Hannibal click the safety hammer off on the side of the handgun with his thumb and the skin whitened around his knuckles to indicate he'd tightened his grip in readiness.

I closed my eyes.

… I thought about Jane and that very first night in the pub when I stroked my index finger across that tiny scar on the corner of her forehead and kept my finger going, brushing the hair back behind her ear and letting my hand fall to the back of her neck. I remembered how she smiled, bit her bottom lip as she leant forward towards me and…

I felt so embarrassed and angry with myself for what I had put my family through in the last decade or so but in that moment I knew I was going to die fully aware of what it felt like having been *loved*.

I took a deep breath.

"BLUES!" shouted Face from the bottom of the alleyway, startling me enough to throw my eyes open and yet brace my body at the same time. It had been a long time since I'd heard gunfire but I was fairly certain it didn't sound like someone shouting "BLUES!"

I saw Hannibal immediately drop the handgun to his left hand side and I strained a glance to enough of my left to be able to see a marked police car slowly drive past the entrance way into the alley. I could just about make out from its back end remaining stationary that it had stopped.

"They're holding on a red light!" shouted Face.

Hannibal took half a step back and as he did I just thought "Nah. Nope. Today is not the day I'm going to die. And certainly *not* behind the city's worst Italian restaurant!"

I gripped my hand tight around the neck of one of the tied black bin-liners lying next to me and in one fluid motion I threw it hard and fast right at Hannibals' head. The bag of rubbish split all over him. He dropped the gun and I pulled myself to my feet, slamming my body against the industrial bin as I did so.

Murdock remained completely rooted to the spot.

By the time Face made a move up the alley towards me, I'd already mentally committed to trying to take him on knowing that if I didn't I'd be dead moments later.

My head spun, my vision was shot and my legs didn't seem to want to work in sequence with what my brain was asking of them. I staggered at speed straight at him regardless and just as he grabbed me and made an attempt to wrestle me back from where I'd came I saw there was enough people nearby for me to get a bit of a commotion going.

"Hey! HEY! Hey!" I started screaming.

People started looking.

“HEY! HELP! HELP!” I screamed some more.

Suddenly Face let go and I fell to my knees. A couple of people came running to my side and started asking me if I was okay. One kind gentlemen started helping me to my feet. I looked around the people crowding me, back up into the alleyway and found it completely empty.

In the blink of an eye my ‘A-Team’ had disappeared.

## [18]

## or

## "New Wounds..."

The offices of 'Lehman's Terms' on a good day is probably no more than a five to ten minute walk from that alleyway up by the Italian restaurant at Grey's Monument. Today was not a 'good day' though.

After saying my many thanks to the people that came to help me and after repeatedly and politely stating "I'm fine, thank you. I just fell!" to anyone and everyone in order to get free and on my way, I staggered off towards my office… cautiously looking back over my shoulder again and again, expecting Hannibal and his men to jump out on me once more at any moment. Every painful step made me curse the police some more too.

They were quick off the mark from that red light, weren't they?

Did the age-old 'mirror, signal, manoeuvre' method not offer them sight of a staggering, bleeding, old fart collapsing in the street behind them?

Then again, I asked myself, would I have really trusted them to help even if they were still stopped there when I came lurching out of that alleyway, spouting blood from what felt like a Grand Canyon sized gap inside my mouth between where the top of my gums met the inner lining of my lips.

It was barely after half three in the afternoon and already the sun was starting to set as is the way during winter. Somehow this seemed doubly-inconvenient at this particular moment – especially when you're expecting to be jumped by what you've now thoroughly convinced yourself are trained, armed, covert operatives.

… Trained, armed, covert operatives that had just been disarmed with a bin bag full of rubbish, mind you.

I got through the doors of 'Lehman's Terms' and despite having climbed these stairs in all sorts of states over the years, this time they truly felt like I was surmounting Everest.

In a blizzard.

With Vaseline smeared in my eyes.

And my legs tied together at the knees.

I pulled myself up the last of the stairs and fell through the door, hitting the floor with a thud as blackness started to descend on my vision and my body started to shake a little from the top of my skull right down to my knees. It started to feel like someone was rubbing large swathes of sandpaper across my bones.

"Holy shit!" gasped Psychic, rushing over me as I took to the floor. "Jake? Jake? Are you alright?"

The sweat was pouring off me. Psychic started to pull my jacket down and pat me down vigorously, trying to source some gunshot or knife wound that had me in such a state. I thought about getting into a detailed explanation of how the blood loss from my mouth wound mixed with the complete absence of opioid top-up in my system was not working well for me at this current time.

"Get me up!" I slurred. "Get me up!"

Psychic helped me to my feet. It still didn't register to me that there was a third person in the office sitting on the sofa expectantly right in my line of sight.

"We need… to batten down the hatches!" I stammered. "Lock everything up… There's bad shit… coming our way!"

"What?" said Psychic. "What? Who?"

"Those… blokes from outside the restaurant?" I replied through the pain. "They're out for us… and they're armed!"

"They're armed?" exhaled Psychic in shock. "Like… knives and shit or guns and shit?"

"Guns! They've got *guns*!" I said.

"How do you know? Are you sure?" he replied.

"Well… I wasn't sure when the butt-end of one smacked me in the mouth… but I became definitely sure… when the pricks' shoved one to my head and went to fire…" I grimaced.

"What the…"

"Listen, we don't have time… right now." I interrupted. "Go… lock the office door downstairs. Close off and barricade this door… Check the back route… They're coming. I know it."

"Okay… And I'll grab the first aid kit too!" said Psychic.

"Did we get an email…" I started.

"From Alia Marcus? We did. I listened to the attachment…" exclaimed Psychic. "Holy fuck, Jake! I've saved it to a memory stick and…"

I held up my hand to stop him. "That's good. That's good. But listen – you need to call her… As soon as you've locked us down… you need to… call her and tell her to… get the hell out of her house and… get somewhere safe."

Psychic nodded.

"And *please* source me some fucking painkillers? … Please?" I cried.

"Okay. I will do. And… what about her?"

"Who?" I replied.

Psychic wordlessly pointed at the sofa I had my back to now. I turned unsteadily and saw Holly, The George Platform's receptionist with a 'heart' for an 'o', sat clutching a coffee cup and looking completely shocked at the state of me.

"Are you… okay sitting there for two… more minutes?" I asked.

She nodded. Her mouth was agape.

I nodded back and mutely moved into my office space, closing the door unsteadily behind me. I crunched my body down in the chair behind my desk, took a big deep breath and grabbed the phone nearby.

The first call I made was to Jimmy Brody.

It was short and to the point.

"Jim? Remember I always.... said there... may come a day when I 'red button' you... and you're going to have to jump off the subs bench?" I said, wincing as blood dripped from my mouth into my lap. "Well I'm pressing the red button, Jim... This is a serious, serious 'drop what you're doing and get to Jane and my boys' type situation... You know what I'm talking about right?"

There was a silence.

Then Jimmy spoke.

"What do you need and where do you need me?"

I pulled my mobile phone from my pocket, swiftly pulled through the contacts and rested to a stop on one specific number – Jane's 'clean' pay-as-you-go phone from inside her 'bug-out' bag that only I had the telephone number for.

"I'm going to give you a number... and in exactly ten minutes... I want you to call it, liaise with Jane... and get to where she is... then take her where she tells you. Okay? Nowhere different... Just where she tells you... Then I want you to stay there with her until you hear otherwise... Yeah?"

"Absolutely!" Jimmy's voice said, muffled and acoustically different to what it was like when he first spoke which suggested he was already on the move. "You okay Jake?"

"I'm good, Jim. Just protect Jane and the kids, please."

I hung up.

I held my mobile phone tight in my hand. The sweat poured down into my eyes and it was at the point I reached to wipe it that I realised my free hand was completely drenched in blood, like I was wearing a bright red glove.

It was trembling so bad.

I pressed Jane's number and the line rang immediately. She answered within two rings.

"Look who's decided to finally respond to my texts!" she said far too breezily for the current situation I was about to drag her into. "I was about to call you. The kids are going stir crazy. I promised I'd go back to the house and pick up the..."

"Jane! Stop!" I said as loudly as I could without moving my mouth too much.

"What?" she said, shocked. "Please tell me things aren't even worse?"

I took a deep breath, pushed down the vomit now rising up into the back of my throat and said as gently as possible "... Hey baby? ... Remember that time we ate... clam chowder from a sour dough bowl... down by the pier in San Francisco?"

There was a painful silence.

"Aww. For *fucks sake* Jake..." Jane said.

I'd no sooner put the phone down with Jane, having clarified as subtly as possible that she was still familiar with what needed to be done next and to get the 'clean' phone switched on in order to take Jimmy's call... without ever saying any of those words too directly or overtly, when Psychic came walking into the room carrying a baseball bat in one hand and a replica of Wesley's sword from Rob Reiner's 'The Princess Bride' in the other.

The latter a very drunken purchase from The Cinema Store in London during an extremely messy alcohol-drenched weekend in the early days of Psychic's time with me and at the height of my 'fall back off the wagon' following "that Australia job we'll not get into right now".

"Which do you want?" he said, dropping both on the desk in front of me.

I stared at him incredulously.

Then picked the sword. *Obviously.*

Precipitously from behind Psychic out stepped Holly, nervously making a half-hearted knock on my office door as she wandered in.

"I did… like… a year and a bit training to be a nurse." Holly said softly. "Would you like me to look at your mouth?"

I looked at her in a way that I can only assume that the lion looked at the mouse when it offered to pull the thorn out and I slowly nodded my head.

And with that an explosion of activity took place. Before I knew what was happening Psychic had switched all of the main lights off outside of my office space, a chair had been pulled round opposite to where I sat, the lamp from the main area was brought in and positioned precariously over my head and Holly started leafing through my first aid kit. Each rummage was met with an unsatisfactory tut.

Psychic suddenly crunched down on the corner of the desk next to the both of us and plonked down a bottle of whiskey and a sewing kit.

"I can't… drink that?" I said delicately.'

"It's not for you, pal." Psychic smiled. "It's to sterilise the needle... These are for you!"

He slammed a torn-up and battered box of codeine into my hand.

"Where'd you get these?" I asked.

Psychic shrugged. "You've got no idea what's hanging around in the back of the bottom two drawers of that filing cabinet out there, buddy!"

I wasn't even six hours free of my last dose of Tramadol but my body and the subsequent blood loss was treating it like I'd been without a 'hit' for two days.

Here's the thing with being a heavy Tramadol-hitter too – there's really no conventional substitute that will do. So when some shaky-handed twenty odd year old comes at you with a white hot needle soaked in whiskey and threaded with something that resembles a bloody shoe lace, and she tells you that she is going to quote unquote "reattach the inside of your mouth to your gum", you could really do with something a LOT heavier in pain-killing capacity than a couple of hastily crunched and possibly out-of-date codeine tablets.

Psychic strapped my arms to the chair I sat in using two belts – his and mine. He held my head back and into place like he was trying to twist it off with just his brute strength. Then Holly with a 'heart' for an 'o' - but a stitching technique as delicate as Michael Myers stabs teenage girls – set to work on my mouth.

Seventeen long minutes later we were done.

Nineteen minutes later I'd changed my blood-sodden shirt into the spare that hung in the corner of my office space, swilled my mouth out and made myself a black coffee that was like acid in my mouth to taste but which my body desperately craved.

Twenty-three minutes later I sat down opposite Holly, ready to forgive her for what she did to my mouth and listen to what she had come here to talk to me about. Psychic stood outside in the pitch black of our main office area, looking down through a gap in our hastily covered window to watch Grey Street and the approach up and down towards us.

"I'm here because Sue lied to you about things that I don't think she should be lying about unless she's got something to hide." Holly began, displaying an ability to be sagacious far beyond her years.

"At this stage I'm done being lied to and if I've reached that point, you've got to wonder what Stephie's parents must be feeling like, right?" I replied.

Holly gently nodded. "Stephie was my friend. She was already a huge deal when I arrived at The George Platform on an apprenticeship. She made me feel so special every time she came down to the offices. When I got made permanent and I was not an apprentice anymore, Stephie had flowers delivered to the office for me. She said it was from all the girls on Sue's books but I kind of knew that they weren't really and that she'd arranged it all on her own."

I sat silently staring at Holly as she spoke. I wanted to interject. I wanted to say that I was done with listening to everyone's pre-amble and I just wanted the facts and for her to get to the point at which Sue lied – but I was just so tired and so sore, and truthfully speaking if I was going to finally snap and take out my irritations on someone I didn't see why it should be Holly.

"Stephie wasn't up herself or anything like that. She didn't look down on me. When Sue's girls had nights out she always made sure I was invited. She always used to tell me that the fact her schedule was so full and well organised was down to me and she appreciated it. She knew I was more than just a receptionist there."

I nodded wearily.

"Stephie said that her and all the other girls called me 'Sue's Right Arm'. I liked that because I thought it showed they appreciated that I did so much there."

"So as Sue's right arm, so to speak, you would know how and when Sue lied better than anybody, yeah?" I asked.

Holly clocked what I was hinting at straight away. She really was more astute than I had probably considered her to be.

"I booked the Paradox gig and I put all the information together to send over to Khali Matti's managers there for them to knock up leaflets to promote it. The day before it was due to go ahead Sue came into the office and told me that I had to cancel it, tell Khali there was a double-booking but then call Stephie and tell her that the arrangements had changed and there was a higher paying booking that had come in for a private engagement for her and Eva Marie."

"Who's Eva Marie?" I said.

"Eva's another model on the books but she's branched out recently into TV work. She's done a few Formula One racing events, you know pit girls and all that?" Holly replied.

I gesticulated a positive affirmation by way of a 'not really but move on' type facial expression.

"Eva Marie and Stephie were good friends. Same age, came from the same area, same TV agent down in London…" Holly continued.

"And what was the gig? What was the higher paying booking?"

"I don't know exactly. I just got told to inform Stephie and to tell her to ring in to the office to speak to Sue for more information because it was a 'HFG' event… HFG is Sue's abbreviation for 'High Flying Guests'." Holly offered without me getting a chance to ask for further clarification.

"Stephie came into the office later that same day and she was a bit pissed off to be honest. I was in Sue's office and she came straight in and she said she wanted Sue to give her more information on this change of plans because she was sick of Sue booking her on things that made her feel like a glorified escort!"

"She said that?" I asked. "That Sue was making her feel like an escort?"

Holly nodded. "Stephie's issue was that Sue got a lot of requests for private meet-and-greet type parties and she felt Sue should be a bit more choosy about who she put Stephie out in front of, not just sending her to drink champagne with some bored, rich businessman in Newcastle for the weekend and shit like that."

"Stephie said that?" I clarified again.

"Yeah. And then Sue sent me out of the office so she could talk to Stephie privately. But here's the thing – They didn't talk that quietly and I was outside of the door working on something else and I could still hear what was said. And this is why I wanted to speak to you…"

Holly leant forward in her chair.

I went to do the same and my head rung like it had just been whacked off the side of a church bell in full chime, so I thought better of it and hung back in my seat.

"… I heard you ask Sue what 'toccare' meant and she told you she had no idea and that didn't sit well with me. Because I heard her talking to Stephie towards the end of their argument, she'd talked Stephie round, she'd mentioned she'd have Eva Marie with her and then they kicked the argument back up again for a bit because Sue wanted her to accept the car service that came with the job but Stephie was insistent that she was not going to drink and she was going to drive herself there and back in her own car."

"And 'toccare'?" I pushed back.

"I explicitly heard Sue say to Stephie that she needed to be there at 9pm, she should expect to stay late and that the password to get in was 'toccare'."

I looked hard at Holly.

She silently stared back.

"Say that last bit again, please?" I asked.

"Sue told Stephie the password to get in was 'toccare'."

"But you've no idea where they were getting into with that password?"

Holly shook her head.

"For big HFG stuff, Sue will never let me see anything like that. It's highly discreet and handled very differently to the normal modelling assignments, invoicing and all that. But you could ask Eva Marie? She was there. She went there with Stephie. She would be able to give you more information, definitely."

Holly pulled out her phone and scrolled through some pages.

"I have her contact details. Do you want me to text them to him?" she said, pointing out to where Psychic stood.

"Yeah, that'd be great. I'll give you his number." I replied.

"It's cool. It's fine. We've already swapped numbers."

I looked out at where Psychic stood. I looked back at Holly. Whilst I'm getting my mouth bashed in, he's out throwing down smooth-moves on young twenty odd year old girls?

"I thought you had a boyfriend?" I asked.

"I just say that when I'm getting hit on by creeps…" Holly suddenly realised what she was saying and who she was saying to. "It's an instant self-defence mechanism. I thought *you* were a creep but then it turns out you totally *aren't* so… yeah. Shall I just text Rob then?"

It's been a long time since I'd heard him go by that name in my presence.

I nodded.

"I really want to know where this gig was that they went off to." I sighed. "You've been a massive, massive help Holly. You really have. But here's the thing, I believe whatever that assignment was that Stephie and her pal went off to is going to have had some involvement in how Stephie ended up dead. I believe that because the lies are starting to surface and the net is starting to close in around those lies, does that make sense?"

"A little." Holly replied. "You would have to speak to Eva. The only other way of finding out where this was and who booked it would be on Sue's Mac where she keeps certain files. But she never lets that out of her sight."

"And this is going to be a very uncomfortable ask but you couldn't go in really early one morning or stay really late one night and try sneaking a look?" I asked.

"Like she'd tell me her password even if she did leave it lying around like that. No, seriously. That MacBook does not go more than a metre away from her grasp, I'm not kidding. There's… No wait, there's one thing!"

I winced through the pain and sat forward.

"Sue hosts the huge Metrocentre and George Platform joint event every Christmas Eve in the red quadrant square of the mall; live music, models dancing along catwalks that go round the whole of that part of the mall, it's a big thing that she's done every…"

"And?" I interrupted.

"For the last few years I've been with her the night before, putting all the final touches together, overseeing everything, test-running the music up at the Metrocentre and all that… Right off her laptop."

I smiled.

"I could try my best to sneak a look then?"

My smile broadened.

"Holly, if it wasn't for the 'Me Too' movement or the fact that my mouth won't pucker up properly, I'd kiss you right now!"

"I'm a lucky girl then!" Holly laughed.

There was a sudden and abrupt knock at the front office door. It startled us all.

Psychic dashed into my office space and hunched down low. “I didn’t see anyone approach,” he whispered.

I pointed to the corner of my office space where there was a small wooden door that led down a spindly metal staircase and out onto an alleyway behind Grey Street.

It was a death trap masquerading as our health and safety mandated fire exit. “Get her out of here now!” I whispered back.

Psychic grabbed her and effortlessly moved Holly off to the door in the corner as I lumbered out of my seat and limped towards the front office door just as a second harsher knock landed.

I leaned against the door frame, steadied myself and peered round to look through the glass.

“Working late?” smiled DI Andrews as he stared back at me through the glass.

## [19]

## or

## "Old Wounds..."

**D**I Andrews' shit-eating grin stared at me through the glass. "Are you going to invite me in or have you got something in there you want to hide from the police?" he said.

"Have you got a search warrant?" I replied. "Or, let me think… is there a warrant out for my arrest? Have I committed an indictable offence or an offence under the Public Order Act? I'm not trespassing here so the Criminal Law Act is out as grounds for you. Or are you attempting to save life or prevent injury to someone in here?"

"Oh, are you showing off that you've got a good memory or something? No, look. This is a courtesy visit."

"How?" I asked. "There's no courtesy between us."

"I think you should let me in Jake. We need to talk." Andrews replied.

I unlocked the door, moved the chair out of the way that Psychic had rather ineffectively placed against it and opened it enough for Andrews to step through. I closed it behind him.

"I've never been here before, have I?" Andrews said, surveying the outer officer.

"I'm not interested in your small talk, Andrews. I'm really not interested in it at all. Say what you came here to say." I said sternly.

"What happened to your mouth, Jake?"

I stood silently in front of him, refusing to allow myself to wobble on my feet and show him how much pain I was in.

"What happened to your mouth, Jake?" he repeated. "Did you get punched in it by one of Newcastle United's players by any chance?"

He caught me off guard there but I stayed silent regardless.

Andrews smirked. "We received a complaint from a very irate Paul Burns saying that you'd gone round to his home today and threatened him?"

"And that complaint just happened to land on the desk of a detective inspector in CID, huh?" I said.

Andrews smiled extended across his face. "Let's just say I keep a close eye on whenever your name pops up in our hallowed halls and on our systems. You know? Like a protective older brother?"

"Go fuck yourself, prick!"

Andrews' smile dropped.

"It seems from the state of your mouth that you've been pissing off the wrong people, Jake. And from the shit that got passed down from my bosses, it seems you're pissing off a lot of people. Premiership footballers? Directors of modelling firms? The fucking mayor?"

"The mayor?" I sneered back. "You mean your best friend, Hetherington?"

"He's not my best friend. Don't even start. He was just very unhappy that you apparently made an approach to him at an event a couple of nights back. It was commented on. Look, my bosses know we have a history…"

"No. We *had* a history. You ruined that. We have nothing now. You're nothing to me. There was a fucking line and you…"

"Jake. Jake. Jake… save it, mate." Andrews shouted. "I'm not interested at all. What's done is done. I'm here to say that you're pissing a lot of people off by trying to turn this girl's suicide into something that it isn't. You're not just pissing them off, you're upsetting them. Now my bosses have asked me to come and *politely* ask that you stop. Because if you don't then…"

"Let me guess? I will be arrested for causing harassment, alarm and distress?"

"… then you will indeed be arrested for causing harassment, alarm and distress! This is the warning about your conduct so that you have a chance to course-correct it. Stay away from Sue George, stay clear of Mick Hetherington and Paul Burns would like you…"

I didn't let him finish because, well, fuck DI Andrews and the boat he sailed in on.

"You went to that Hark Roy warehouse, right?" I asked. "You saw Stephie hanging there before she was cut down."

Andrews sighed. "I'm not at liberty to disclose that but I oversaw the investigation, yes."

"You know that scene stinks, yeah? I mean you're shit and you needed a paedophile to get you your detective rank but you're not *so* shit that you don't recognise that scene for the absolute joke it was!"

Andrews let out a little laugh and took himself over to Psychic's desk, sitting himself down on the corner. "Okay. I'll ignore that staggeringly offensive jibe and I'll bite. I see you're lonely and desperate for attention so, come on then, what about that scene stank now you've clearly taken yourself out there and wandered through it one month after the fact."

"Well, you tell me this first – Are you really going with the idea that Stephanie Jason or Stephie Jay or whatever else you put down on her file crossed over the Tyne Bridge late one Saturday night and just happened upon a ready-made suicide site in an abandoned warehouse in Hebburn that had just the right amount of cord hanging and the perfect barrel to stand on? Because she sure as shit didn't get fifteen feet up in the air to hang it in the rafters herself and she definitely was unlikely to be lifting out a two hundred and forty pound steel drum from its holding and moving it into position on her own was she?"

Andrews stared at me in silence.

"I mean, you accounted for all of that, right? You're not sharing your report, obviously. But I'm presuming you're accounting for why that is an utter crock of shit, yeah?"

The silence continued.

"And then there's your boy, Tidyman. Why does he keep coming back up again and again huh?" I asked.

"Oh, here we go!" laughed Andrews, mockingly. "I was wondering how long it would be before you found a new target and general scapegoat. Have you gone off me or something?"

"Tidyman told me he was just a dogsbody on this case..."

"True!" said Andrews. "He might have run point on a lot of this but everything and I mean *everything* went up the line to me. I oversaw all of this, I seconded all of the judgements. When you say this stinks, you're saying that I tri..."

I jumped straight in over him. "I really hoped you would say that. I really did. Because that confirms everything to me. So you wrote off the voicemail? That came to you and you discarded that? And the hastily arranged catch-up search of Stephie's vehicle? That was authorised by you as a box-ticking exercise, was it?"

"What catch-up search are you talking about?" said a clearly rankled Andrews. "The vehicle was searched at the scene. There wasn't any catch-up search because there didn't need to be."

"So you didn't authorise a..." I stopped myself purposefully because I felt like I had something I didn't want to throw into the hands of a man I didn't trust.

"What? I didn't authorise what?" Andrews said.

"No, forget it. It's nothing." I lied.

"And clarify what voicemail exactly?" Andrews said.

Now, as much as I detested the man that stood in front of me, that hatred can't undo the years and years we had of studying and training together, drinking side by side and generally living out of each other's pockets. When you have *that* sort of shorthand you come to learn a lot of their non-verbal cues and expressions all the way from what they look like when they worry right the way down to what they look like when they stifle a fart.

And the look right there and then in that moment on Andrews' face suggested I'd just thrown something past his defences that had landed and made an impact. He reeled a little and then stood up, smoothing his clothes down and tightening up his tie.

"Tidyman was a dogsbody on this. That's why I pulled him out of the room with you - because knowing that over-eager puppy he'd have actually tried to help answer your questions and you aren't getting help from this police service in fleecing two grieving parents with some stupid and embarrassing conspiracy theory you're pulling out of thin air in order to fill your pockets with their money."

Andrews crossed the room back towards the door he'd come in through then stopped.

"Tidyman is off on annual leave. He had it booked long before you even started this whole stupid thing, Jake. He isn't out there as a foot solider for some bigger villain who's murdering shitty reality TV stars and making it look like they topped themselves. He's probably over in New York fucking city doing Christmas shopping with his missus."

I winced at his description of Stephie. I'd done such a deep dive on her past, learnt so much about her and looked so hard at the pain and devastation in both of her parents' eyes that I had come to develop some degree of affection for the girl. I'd most certainly come to acquire a thirst to give her parents the justice they deserved. Hearing her described so callously was like a swift stab at my gut.

"And here's the other thing," smirked Andrews. "Do you know who Tidyman's missus is? Graham bloody Hadenbury's daughter! So ask yourself this, do you really think he's going to be farting around on something like this like you seem to be trying to suggest at the risk of pissing his beloved daddy-in-law off? Get real, Jake."

Andrews opened the door. He didn't step through it. He just contemptuously looked me up and down instead. "Your biggest problem is you think everything is black and white. It isn't. You keep torturing yourself trying to take complex things that are shaded grey and fit them into a pile of one or the other and life isn't like that. You learnt the hard way Jake that life won't match your tiny little moral views because it's bigger than you. You got burnt badly by trying to force it to fit and look at the absolute state of you as a result?"

I took one strong, single step forward and pushed my head so it was forced directly into his line of sight.

"That sounds rehearsed? Was it rehearsed? Because it sounded rehearsed?" I let a fake, empty smile break across my face. "It sounded like the sort of thing that you've told yourself in the mirror over and over again every time you have to look at yourself to justify what you did to that young girl that night, what power you gave to a man that evil and the unearned rewards and benefits you took for doing so."

Andrews physically flinched and stepped back through the door to leave.

"I don't know what this Stephie Jay thing is," I continued. "But I know that I'm not going to stop until I do know. And when I'm done, there's going to be a line drawn and judgements made on the people that stand either side of it. I'm going to be very interested to see how *you're* ultimately judged."

Andrews went to speak. He had nothing. But he gobbled something together in a desperate attempt to regain control regardless. ""Listen… Jake… this is your warning... If another complaint comes in about you distressing people then… I'm sending some uniforms down to arrest you and bring you in for harassment!"

"Go fuck yourself, *Andrew* Andrews!" I smiled, enjoying him flinch once again from this final blow.

## [20]

## or

## "Reaching..."

Not even five whole minutes had passed after DI Andrews walked out of my office before I took a seat back behind my desk and called Jane on the 'clean' number.

She confirmed that she and the boys were okay, that her aunty was taken aback at the intrusion initially but she was rolling with it now and spoiling Jack and Jonathan rotten with sugary treats. She said that Jimmy had been great and that he was outside having a walk around her aunt's garden at that moment checking things out which was reassuring to hear. I asked her if she thought they'd been followed up there or whether she felt suspicious about anything at all.

"We're still alive and you've not had a ransom call yet so I guess not?" she said quietly in a tone that suggested she still held onto a sense of humour despite being very clearly and justifiably unhappy.

"This is going to be a stupid question but… are you okay?" I asked gently.

"I'm fine." She said unconvincingly.

She wasn't.

Jane has five variations on how she says the word 'fine' when responding to someone that she is 'fine' when she is in fact *not* 'fine'. There's:

1. the 'fine' that means *"I'll accept this but I think what I'm acquiescing to will be a disaster and I look forward to laughing in your face when it falls to pieces!"*
2. the 'fine' that means *"I'm not fine and you know me well enough now to know I'm not but I'm interested to see how you'll make this up to me!"*
3. the 'fine' that means *"Leave it! Just leave it! Or I'll punch your teeth out!"*
4. the 'fine' that means *"I'm too tired to argue with you so I'm using this as a placeholder but I'll get back to you at a later date when you're least expecting it to bring this back up and seize victory then!"*
5. the 'fine' that means she's… you know… actually *fine*?

I thought this was a number two type of 'fine'.

"Jake?" she said softly as I wound down the call.

"Yeah?"

"The kids are so excited about this Christmas Eve carol performance. It will break their hearts if they miss this. I can't break their hearts on Christmas Eve…"

"I promise you I will do everything possible to get this done so they can be there. And I promise you I will be right there by your side too like we agreed." I replied.

"How?"

There was a pained silence.

"I don't know…" I said with the utmost honesty.

I spent the night at a friend of Psychic's called Will. He owned a house in Blyth and that night I spent it lying on the futon pushed away in the back corner of his dining room whilst Psychic himself slept upstairs. I was exhausted and rather unrealistically hoped to catch some sleep but once again a perfect marriage of pain, worry and 'cold turkey' problems from the lack of Tramadol in my system played havoc and I ended up spending the entire night staring at the same spot of black mould on the downstairs ceiling whilst playing things over and over again in my head.

We'd decided to 'go to ground' and investigate the rest of the case 'on the fly', as all the cool covert operative type private investigator heroic types say… I *imagine*?

As soon as I'd finished my phone call to Jane and Psychic had safely got Holly free of the building, we reconvened and set about getting clear of the office and staying away from anywhere we felt Hannibal and his team could reasonably associate us with from our previous movements - Will, from Psychic's five-a-side football team that meets down at the Royal Quays every Tuesday night, was the best we could come up with under pressure.

Our journey to get there had consisted of two straight hours of anti-surveillance drills across various public transport and taxis, all of which followed on from the both of us abandoning our coats back at the office in fear of GPS 'bugs' and nipping over to the pub across from our office to use the bathroom stalls there to robustly check each other's clothing over for any possible tracking device there either. That sounds a *lot* more salacious and dirty written down then it actually was. You're all probably imagining two men in a toilet cubicle running their hands all over each other lustily or something. The reality was more like me squeezing a pocket on Psychic's pants and saying "What's that? Could that be a bug?" and him replying "That's a Trebor Mint!"

Once we were both satisfied we were 'bug-free' we set off from town and landed on this poor schmuck's doorstep right on the edge of the coast completely bedraggled just after ten at night.

Before that though, we'd arrived in Tynemouth by metro an hour or so earlier and squabbled about the best way to get from there to Will's house in Blyth. I wanted to stay on the metro a little further along. Psychic had got spooked by someone on the metro and wanted to get off and do more anti-surveillance. My body was starting to hurt so bad that I was having to fight the pain *and* find the resolve to keep being responsible and alert to the fact we were potentially being tracked and trailed alongside the fact I just wanted to stop and pass out for a bit.

We squabbled about that.

Then we argued about whether Jane was right about what she'd done in going to the GPs behind my back regarding the Tramadol thing.

Then we fought about my apparent "snobbish refusal" to accept there was no difference apparently between a 'junkie' and an 'addict', as much as I argued to the contrary.

We settled on a taxi ride from Tynemouth along the coast to Will's house and Psychic thought I'd gone in a huff with him and was giving him the silent treatment but I didn't have the energy left to explain to him that it wasn't anything of the sort. The truth was that the taxi driver had an 80s classic station on his radio and he was blasting out The Hooter's "And We Danced".

And I have a steadfast belief that you just don't talk over certain musical masterpieces.

"You might not have thought it was the best route to take, Jake. But the thing is you're a bit addled at the moment and..." said Psychic.

*"♫♫ ... She was a be-bop baby on a hard day's night. She was hangin' on Johnny, he was holdin' on tight. I could feel her coming from a mile away... ♫♫"*

"... You've got to let me help you, mate. This comedown you're on hasn't even really truly started yet." He continued.

*"♫♫ ... And we danced like a wave on the ocean, romanced. We were liars in love and we danced. Swept away for a moment by chance. And we danced and danced... ♫♫"*

They followed "And We Danced" with Boy Meets Girl's "Waiting For A Star To Fall" and I zoned out completely into a flashback straight to my childhood:

It was the autumn of 1988.

I had just turned eight years old and I was at a parish community children's disco. Our local priest had been arrested, convicted and sent to prison for raping children in the area. It had destroyed us as a small town within Newcastle itself but I wouldn't come to realise that until several years later when the full facts were afforded to me as a young adult.

A new, younger, hipper priest had been brought in to help re-establish trust and re-build our parish community. One of the ways he was going about this was to have weekly family nights in the church community centre full of games, activities and stuff like that. Every other weekend there was a kids disco - heavily chaperoned of course just in case it turned out to be one massive 'all you can fuck' trap laid by the Catholic Church – and it was at one of these very gatherings that eight year old Elaine Parkin walked up to eight year old Jake Lehman and... just as the saxophone solo kicked in on Boy Meets Girl's "Waiting For A Star To Fall"... she kissed me on the cheek and told me she liked me as "more than a friend" and that she was "going to marry" me one day.

I didn't even really know what "marry" meant at eight years of age. But I knew that I liked how my stomach felt when she kissed me and I wanted her to do it again so, like a straight up lothario, I simply nodded and said "That sounds fine!"

The first kiss I ever experienced from someone who wasn't one of my family was from Elaine that day to that song. Her round heavily freckled face blushing up a storm immediately afterwards.

Four years later Elaine Parkin had an asthma attack in the night.

She died.

Every time I hear that song it takes me straight back to that moment and that person and I get lost completely in thinking about that day when our headmaster Mr Hackman came into our classroom with eyes stained from crying and told us that Elaine had "gone to be an angel in Heaven". I hear that song and I think about what her life could've been and how none of this 'living' thing makes a whole lot of sense when it all gets split down into who gets to live a full life and who gets taken from us at so young an age.

I was deep in that trajectory of thought when I felt Psychic's arm bang on my shoulder and the words "We're here!" shake me out of my flashback.

Everything after that was a bit of a daze – a cavalcade of polite hello's to new people, blinding flashing light in my vision, tours of where the spare-room was and where the other sleeping space was, stumbles and wobbles as my legs gave out underneath me intermittently and then the next really clear memory after that was when Psychic came downstairs at six in the morning the next day to find me a pale, shivering mess with a mouth completely crusted with blood from my wound having leaked slightly without me realising.

Once he'd quietly (and with impressive sensitivity) checked that I was not dead, he helped me to sit up properly, cleaned my mouth as best he could and set us both away with the strongest run of cups of coffee that he could muster up with what Will had in his house. There was even a couple of stray ibuprofen's thrown in with the caffeine after Psychic found a box in the back of one of Will's kitchen cupboards. They did nothing to supply the 'fix' I craved but they took the chronic ache away from my mouth for a bit.

"I made a phone call last night to a pal," Psychic said whilst sipping his coffee. "I'm going to get us a clean run-around car for a couple of days just so we can leave our own well alone."

I smiled. "Smart move!"

"This is the bit where you say you've been thinking…" smirked Psychic, knowing full well that I'd done nothing but for the last eight or so hours.

"It's funny you should say that, mate." I replied. "Because I've been doing some thinking and I am wondering whether Andrews was even aware of the catch-up search Tidyman did up at Margaret's house or the voicemail. He certainly didn't look like he did when I dropped both on him last night."

"Or he's lying?" offered Psychic. "There's a strong possibility that he did what he needed to in order to convince you he wasn't aware. But come on, he told you he oversaw everything right? He said that. He said that he signed off on everything, didn't he? He admitted that."

I nodded.

"There is no way there's a voicemail as important as the one Alia tried to throw around of Stephie on her last night alive and that doesn't land on the radar of the detective frickin' inspector overseeing the so-called investigation into her death. Also there's no way the car is getting turned over by one of his team for a second time without his knowledge. I just don't see that happening."

I shrugged. "No, maybe you're right Psychic. I'd normally fully agree with you too but there was something about Andrews' reaction that has thrown me off. I don't know. Maybe there has been more than one voicemail and he was confused by not knowing which one I was referring to or…"

"Or maybe he wasn't confused at all? Maybe he wanted you to think he was but in reality it was his call to cover-up that voicemail and shut Alia down. Maybe it was him who sent the designated dogsbody Tidyman up to have a second look at Stephie's car and see if they'd overlooked this A-Z book or map or whatever it was that she was talking about in light of the voicemail resurfacing."

Psychic had a point.

"Yeah, you know you may be onto something." I said. "Based off my own experiences with him, he did destroy my career in order to advance his own and there's a clear precedent for him covering things up to protect someone who may be of benefit to him. And from what we know from talking to Holly, Stephie *was* in the company of a so-called 'High Flying Guest'.."

"Potentially someone with money and influence who Andrews could benefit from protecting?"

"Exactly!" I sighed. "He's done it before. It could well have become his preferred method of operation now. Let me run this past you then – Stephie goes to this 'HFG' party on Sue's instruction, she gets involved with someone there… Maybe not even necessarily by choice. There's an accident within the assault or it was a purposeful attack or a sex-game goes wrong or something?"

Psychic leant forward in his chair, meeting my line of sight and covering his mouth with his hands. He spoke through his hands only to say "But the voicemail?"

I nodded. "I know, I *know*. But the voicemail was after leaving the party and maybe this guy caught up with her or she'd arranged to meet him later or whatever? Maybe she leaves the party in disgust at how shady it all was or something, makes the call to Alia, hooks up with this fella, it goes wrong and whoever her sexual partner is at this time is someone big and powerful or whatever and can't be seen to get caught up in a sex scandal with a dead reality TV star so he covers it up to make it look like a suicide instead."

"So who are this 'A-Team' lot in all of this?" asked Psychic.

"Let's say they're the guy's private security detail or something, yeah? They know what he did to cover his tracks. They may have even helped him cover his tracks, perhaps? And now they're out to stop us sniffing around."

"The killer could be a powerful woman, let's not discount that." Psychic said.

"No, no. You're right. It could. But it still draws it back to who's a big, powerful, 'HFG' type with the type of influence who would have a private security detail to reinforce the clean-up they've carried out… to hide the fact they killed a gorgeous twenty-four year old minor celebrity in a sex game *and* get the police completely onside to conclude it how they want it to be concluded then make it go away no matter what?"

Psychic sat back in his chair and let out a deep sigh. He rubbed his temples and ran his fingers through his hair.

"That's what you want to throw down now?" he asked. "With everything we've got so far you want to go with the idea that she went to whatever this party is where you have to speak Italian to get in through the door, it goes south because of whatever was going on behind the closed doors there, she cuts loose, rings Alia, leaves that answerphone message then either by choice or by attack gets it on with someone affiliated to the party she's just jumped ship from, the sex goes wrong, they cover it up to make it look like suicide and then have their own private security service harass and fuck up anyone who questions this?"

I finished off the last of my black coffee and sat back. "Am I reaching? It feels like I'm reaching? I was shooting for a sort of Sherlockian type summation and then we just stand up and go back out there to go get the bad guy but…"

"We don't know who the bad guy is." Psychic interjected.

"We don't know who the bad guy is." I reiterated.

"And we don't know whether the injuries she died with would support her dying in one way and having it presented as another." Psychic pushed on.

"No, we don't know that."

"Nope. No, we don't." he doubled-down.

"The coroner of course would tell us that though, right?" I asked, already knowing the answer.

"The coroner who signed off on all of this but won't take our calls or agree to a meeting?" Psychic shot back.

"Yes, that very same one!" I smiled. "It's like she could do with a visit though, don't you think? It's very hard for me to get my charisma across in emails and by leaving messages with people at her office. I think she would benefit much better from having me go face-to-face and lay a bit of the old 'smooth moves and grooves' on her…"

Psychic laughed. "I thought we were as far behind where we needed to be with the coroner as we could get but you doing that would definitely prove there's a much further back than I realised… And Jake?"

"Yeah?"

"You're *definitely* reaching!"

Two hours later, Psychic's friend turned up with our 'cover' car.

Now, it's very hard to turn your nose up at something that is gifted to you for free and at such incredibly short-notice. And on top of that, I am no snob or discerning car enthusiast at all. However, this was a fucking pea green coloured 1987 Zastava Yugo 513.

If you have no idea what a Zastava Yugo 513 is, let me just say it is what a car looks like when a really wet, squeal of a fart makes a wish to be turned into an actual vehicle for human beings to drive around in and that wish is granted. Then someone takes it and paints it pea green. Yes, as in the same colour as the vomit in that scene from The Exorcist.

"The deal is that we return it with the same amount of petrol in it that it's got now and..."

I interrupted Psychic. "It runs on petrol? Wow. I thought we both just put our feet through the gap in the floor and pedalled the thing!"

"Funny!" Psychic shot back. "Because Flintstones references in the year 2020 are just *so* cool! Anyway, we return it with the same amount of petrol in it that it's got now and we don't touch the radio. He was really specific that we don't touch the radio. Apparently it only picks up one station, Radio 2, and if you fiddle with it looking for others you lose everything and it takes an age for him to find that one single station again. So... don't touch the radio."

"I don't even want to touch the seat with my arse, frankly. I won't be touching anything, I promise!" I smiled.

Psychic waved his hand at me dismissively and continued. "My buddy Bruce says that the gear stick is iffy and we need to get it from second to fourth as quickly as possible because it doesn't stick in third very well. We've got to hold the stick in place if we're driving in third for very..."

I waved my hand back equally dismissively. "Yes... Yes... Whatever, just promise me it's not going to randomly burst into flames if we get up to more than twelve mile an hour, please?"

I vowed I was not going to turn my nose up at the use of the vehicle but I was struggling with that vow. I *did*, however, swear to myself that I was not going to ask any questions with regards to who the hell still has a 1987 Zastava Yugo 513 in their lives because I felt that the type of person who does still have a 1987 Zastava Yugo 513 in their lives is the type of person that probably has a 'story' about it and is just itching to tell it to people as soon as the all-too-rare opportunity arises.

I was in no mood for faking my way through *that* shit.

Instead I suggested to Psychic that he puts the car to use in making some localised enquiries into Eva Marie, see if he could get a hold of her to speak to and get a clearer perspective of just what it is that both she and Stephie attended the night she died.

I said that I would, in turn, head out to the coroner's office and doorstep Alison Gregg once and for all with the questions we sought answers to. Psychic was insistent that he dropped me off there on his way.

I fought a committed fight to not step foot in that vile-looking vehicle.

A fight which I clearly lost as he sped off out of Blyth and back towards Newcastle, with me in the passenger seat of a vehicle that seemed to be barely held together and who's every single impact with the surface it drove upon shook me to my core and made my bones feel like they were shattering underneath my skin.

I could no longer tell what was shutting my body down most effectively and most painfully now – the withdrawals from the Tramadol or the indignity of being driven around in a fucking Zastava Yugo 513.

## [21]

## or

## "This Is Meant To Be A Bit Of A Jaw-Dropper..."

The thing with painkiller addiction is that it destroys your bowels. Constipation is a massive side effect but with that as well is the big, syrupy, thick piss that passes out of you. A harsh physical reminder that you're not drinking enough water, getting enough nutrients and you're filling your body with damaging levels of opioids.

I side-step the problems with my piss by simply not looking down when I stand at the toilet bowl. This state of denial works *quite* well for me. The constipation has actually been something that I've pushed myself (pardon the pun!) to believe is somewhat of a benefit: If I don't need to go to the toilet as much it means I can maximise my time better and get more done. See? Every cloud has a silver-lining and all that, huh?

The problem on this morning though was that I was technically coming up to the first twenty-four hours of being without Tramadol properly in my system with the regularity my body had become accustomed to and whilst I was just about coping with the sweating and the blurred vision… and the headaches, *oh God*, the headaches… my bowels were now starting to squeak, shoot with pain and then force my bum muscles to collapse under the strain of holding back torrid amounts of diarrhoea.

Psychic had been forced to pull this god forsaken rattling Zastava Yugo 513 over twice on our journey out of Blyth and away from the coast, finding fast food outlets for me to run inside of or discreet sides of roads with heavy foliage for me to dive into.

"You're falling to bits, Jake." Psychic said with legitimate concern as I stumbled into the car a second time, dizzied by the impromptu vomiting that had occurred alongside the diarrhea.

"I'm not feeling good at all." I replied.

"Maybe we should stop? Take a break and pick this all up again after Christmas?" he suggested.

I shook my head. "I think we've got a clock to work against now knowing those guys are out there and trying to shut this down."

"I know but you're…"

I put my hand on his shoulder and stopped him going any further. "There's some piece of evidence out there that gives us everything we need to prove Stephie didn't kill herself, that something happened to her at that party, whatever it was, and it led to her death and the cover-up. We've got to find whatever that is before those crazy 'A-Team' fuckers do. We've got to because if we don't I think this whole thing will crumble."

Psychic nodded his head.

"I think the coroner and Eva Marie will give us the evidence we need or at the very least fresh leads. But I also think that those guys have them marked for the same reason. So we've got to get…"

"Okay. *Okay.*" Psychic interrupted. "Let's go get them! Do you need to shit again before we push on?"

"If I do, I'll do it in this car. You'd never be able to tell that I did." I sneered whilst looking around the interior in disgust.

Radio 2 blasted out the legendary Tom Petty's 'I Won't Back Down' and the manner in which the lyrics resonated with our current predicament in a beautifully timed moment of happenstance seemed to hit the both of us pretty hard, causing us to both fall into silence and just appreciate the majesty of Petty's classic:

*"♫♫ ...Well, I know what's right. I got just one life. In a world that keeps on pushin' me around, but I'll stand my ground. And I won't back down... I won't back down – Hey, baby! There ain't no easy way out! I won't back down – Hey baby! I will stand my ground... ♫♫"*

We were halfway along the Coast Road leading us back into Newcastle itself with me banging away on my mobile phone trying to get anyone at all to confirm whether Alison Gregg, the coroner who signed off on Stephie's death as per the paperwork we'd copied, was in her office that day or not. We were probably no more than ten minutes or so from approaching the coroner's offices based out of Newcastle Council's headquarters and my stomach started to tie itself into knots at the prospect of stepping foot into Hethrington's 'home turf'. Then one assistant explained Alison Gregg didn't work out of the Newcastle section anymore and that as of the previous week, she'd moved across to an entirely new borough down at Wallsend in North Tyneside.

Psychic turned the car around and we headed back in the direction we had just come.

The infuriation, the withdrawals, the pain and the realisation that I was going to be staying in this goddamn Zastava Yugo 513 for a bit longer still all congregated together into a perfect storm that saw me open the passenger door as we slowed to a stop at traffic lights coming towards Jesmond – and vomit my guts onto the road.

On arrival at the Wallsend offices, I said my goodbyes to Psychic, wished him luck in pursuing Eva Marie and asked him to keep in touch whilst I pulled myself from that bloody vehicle and started trying to put myself together in a way that didn't make me look too much like I'd slept in these clothes (which I had!), not washed properly (which I hadn't!), not eaten properly in too long (which I hadn't either!) and was badly craving opioids (which I absolutely was!).

This wasted gesture simply involved me tucking my shirt in and smoothing the collar down.

I spent the next twenty minutes inside this pokey little office front, requesting repeatedly to speak with Miss Alison Gregg, taking a seat, stepping back up to the reception desk, re-explaining that I needed to speak with her and that yes it *was* urgent, sitting back down, getting back up, trying to re-approach my request but this time adding a bit of flirty charm into the mix and generally trying to wait out their continuing steadfast refusals to acquiesce to my request(s).

The good thing with these offices being some tiny little thing stuck on the side-street of a dying old town is that unlike their big city centre, local authority based counterpoints they didn't have access to some in-house security that they could put in front of me and use to escort me from the building at the press of a button on their telephone.

"Listen, Lorraine…" I smiled at the middle-aged, thoroughly-dismayed-looking ginger haired lady behind the counter with a name badge that said 'Lorraine', as I approached it for the third time. "I am really sorry to bother you again. But time is of the essence and I really need to speak to Miss Gregg. Is there any way you could…"

"I'm not even sure she's in!" drawled Lorraine.

"Is there a way you could check? Could you maybe ring up to her office?"

Lorraine sighed. "She's new. I don't know her extension."

"Could I take a walk up to her office then? Could you buzz me through?"

Lorraine looked at me like I'd just asked her to give my penis a tug.

"I can't be doing that." Lorraine said. "I don't know who you are."

"How about we make a deal?" I smiled. "I'll tell you a joke. If you laugh, you take a quick walk along to Miss Gregg's office and tell her I urgently need to speak to her. If you don't laugh, I'll just walk straight out and never bother you again."

Lorraine didn't speak. She just leant back in her chair and folded her arms in the exact manner I'd expect from a woman who's every expression thus far indicated she had never encountered in her life anything that she found remotely amusing.

"Okay," I said, smiling like I thought the warmth of my smile would heat up her funny bone. "A moth flies into a chiropractor's office. He sits down on the desk in front of the chiropractor and says 'I don't know who I am anymore, doctor. I wake up every morning. I look at myself in the mirror in disgust. I go to work every day and realise I'm just existing, not so much living. I lie in bed at night and look at the fat, flaccid, greying mass next to me that used to be my wife. My children have all grown up and as they have I've grown to hate who they've become. I think often about getting a gun and blowing my brains out.' The chiropractor replies 'I'm a chiropractor. Why have you come to tell me all this?' The moth replies 'Because your light was on?'…"

Lorraine sat stony-faced in absolute silence.

I took a step back and looked at her with a pitiful gaze and just as I was about to start explaining the punchline to her, she spoke.

"You can have a second shot."

"Excuse me?" I replied.

"That was okay. But, go on… I'll give you another chance!" she said without her face changing expression in the least.

"Right," I smiled without pausing for a second. "A man walks into a bar and asks the barman for a pint of lager and a thimble of whiskey. The barman asks him why he wants a thimble of whiskey. The man reaches into his coat and pulls out a tiny twelve inch piano and a tiny twelve inch pianist. 'It's for him' says the man. 'He gets thirsty after he plays!' Then he clicks his fingers and the twelve inch pianist plays the most beautiful music on his twelve inch piano. When he finishes the barman says that it was amazing and he asks the man where he got the twelve inch pianist from. The man reaches into his other jacket pocket and pulls out an old, battered lamp. He starts to explain that he was walking down the street one day when he saw this lamp and he picked it up and gave it a rub. Out came this decrepit old genie who granted the man a wish. The barman is entranced with the story and asks the man if he too can have a go of the lamp. The man allows this and the barman takes the lamp, gives it a rub, thinks hard and all of a sudden an ostrich bursts through the door and starts kicking tables over and biting customers. The man says 'Don't tell me, you asked for a fit bird with long legs?' The barman says 'Yeah, how did you know?' The man replies 'What the hell did you think I actually asked for? A twelve inch pianist?'..."

Lorraine looked at me. The silence resumed. The face didn't break its stone-etched expression.

Then...

"Very good!" Lorraine said, without so much as raising a smile.

She reached across, picked up her phone and in less than ten minutes Alison Gregg herself appeared in the boxy little reception area.

Alison was a thin woman with the darkest black hair down to her shoulders. She walked like she carried the weight of the world on them and the lines on her face pushed the jowls around her mouth down in a way that suggested, like Lorraine on reception, it had been some time since she'd smiled.

"Mr Lehman?" she said sternly. "I received all of your messages and my response hasn't changed from the one you were issued with from my office originally – I don't have anything further to add and I don't have the time to speak with you I'm afraid. All requests should..."

I interrupted her by thrusting the permissions letter and the document from Dreyfuss & Associates into her hands. "I understand, I understand. But as you can see I'm representing the family of Stephanie Jason and they're just wanting a couple of questions answered and they're having real difficulty achieving that. I was just wondering if you could give me ten minutes, five in fact because as you can see I talk really fast. It would be..."

"I'm afraid I can't Mr Lehman. These letters don't change that. Nothing I could say would differ from the report I submitted and which Mr and Mrs Jason now have copies of. I'm sorry. I'm really busy. I have to go."

Alison started to walk back towards the door she'd just come through.

"Hey, Alison?" I said loudly.

She turned to face me.

"Do you know who Kevin Jenkins is?"

She smiled politely. "I'm not familiar with that name, no."

"Kevin Jenkins was the coroner responsible for some of the victims in The Yorkshire Ripper case. He put his name to death reports and certificates that had been amended or changed at the request of the police to hide some of the incompetence on their behalf. Coppers were on patrol and near the victims at the time they were murdered in some cases but they never spotted anything. The theory is they just didn't give a shit about these lower class women who they'd written off as just prostitutes and stuff. So the police asked for times of death and other things to be changed so it put some distance between the murders and when the police were nearby. When this got exposed – because everything comes out in the wash in the end - do you think anyone from the police got hauled over the coals? Or do you think Kevin Jenkins was thrown into the fire alone?"

Alison stared at me. Her eyes started to slowly crunch together and I swear I saw the moisture of tears start to form. She opened the door, held it open in a manner that suggested I was welcome to walk through it after all and quietly said "You have five minutes, Mr Lehman!"

I stepped through with a smile and gently mouthed the words 'Thank You'.

Kevin Jenkins, by the way, was my old mentor when I first started out in the police. He spent thirty-one years as a uniformed police constable, was never interested in ascending the rank or anything like that. He retired six months into my probation and died five weeks into his retirement.

That Yorkshire Ripper thing was, yes you guessed it, another crackin' little bit of chuffing!

I entered Alison's office and took note of enough piled files stacked precariously along with wall space totally devoid of anything affixed there. It led me to think that, alongside Lorraine's remark at reception, this was a fresh move for Miss Gregg and she hadn't quite got herself settled in yet.

Straight through the door, I grabbed the nearest seat and dropped myself down into it. Alison shot me a glance as she made her way round to her desk. Her face suggested she'd have preferred I'd asked permission first.

"My superiors are on site today and I really don't want to have to explain why I'm giving unauthorised interview time on this so please… I must insist we stick to five minutes!" she said as she sat down.

"Five minutes isn't a lot of time so I'll just hit the ground running and I'll be happy with whatever I get through. Okay, so first up – you have no concerns about that scene at all?" I said.

"The scene of Stephanie's death?" she replied.

"Yes. Did you attend it?"

Alison nodded.

She didn't follow up with any further comment which twigged me quickly to the fact that she wasn't going to give me any more than she felt she had to and, frankly, after this long in the game it was flat-out stupid of me to be asking closed questions to a hostile interview subject.

"And you were happy with the scene? You didn't think there was anything suspicious about that? No, wait. Let me rephrase that – what did you see at the scene that led you to believe there was nothing suspicious about it?" I ventured.

"I arrived at the scene. The police indicated to me that they felt the set-up inside that particular warehouse was semi-composed as the deceased discovered it and she adapted what was there to fit her needs."

"You're referring to the cord she hung herself with? And the barrel she stood on?" I asked.

"Yes."

"And what were they basing that on?"

"Well, I'm presuming they had completed their enquiries with the warehouse owners and those familiar enough to say with certainty."

"That's your presumption? Who were the police's sources that suggested it was a semi-composed scene that Stephanie Jason came across?"

"The police informed me that they were happy with the intelligence they'd accrued that suggested the deceased used a scene that was already in one particular state rather than the deceased having set that scene to the state we found it in. I had no reason to question that assertion based off my study of the scene itself."

I twisted my face in a way that physically represented both my confusion at something that felt so unsatisfactory as she explained it and yet also something that stank of absolute bullshit.

"Moving on for time," I said. "No note. No motive. No history of depression etc. Would you normally be so quick to write off a death as suicide in those circumstances?"

There was a sharp sound of silence. I had every intention of letting the silence linger to the point of discomfort and then pushing hard on the question again but Alison's office door flew open with an assertive push and in walked a tiny little Asian man with oilier hair than the Gulf of Mexico after the BP oil crisis.

You spend enough time as a private investigator and you get an connoisseur's nose for arseholes. Keep your sinuses clean enough and you'll be able to sniff one within ten seconds of them stepping into the same room as you. I say with absolute certainty and the connoisseur's nose that comes with a fair amount of time-stamps on my card as a PI that this guy was an arsehole – a proper, tightened-up arsehole of the highest order. He didn't need to speak for me to lock that belief in. But speaking certainly did cement my opinion and reaffirm my innate radar for these types.

"Ali, hi. Sorry to trouble you. I didn't see on your calendar that you had meetings scheduled today?" said this oily bastard.

Alison smiled weakly. "Mr Lehman, this is Dr Li Wu, he is my superior within the coroner's office and..."

The man I knew now to be Dr Wu rudely stepped in front of Alison cutting my view of her off as he sat down on the edge of her desk.

"What are we here to discuss with Dr Gregg, Mr Lehman?" smiled Dr Wu.

"I'm researching a book." I said, smiling back. "I was informed that Dr Gregg was an eminent coroner in the region and worth speaking to."

"It's wonderful to hear Dr Gregg is so highly regarded." Dr Wu said, holding fast with the smile that I was now marking down a level to 'shit-eating grin'. "And what is your book about?"

Chuff… Chuff… Chuff…

"I'm writing a novel actually. It's about hanging. I wanted to talk to a coroner to make sure I got the technical stuff right, you know?"

"Yes, yes." Dr Wu replied. "I understand. And I hope that you have got everything you need because I'm going to have to conclude this meeting, I'm afraid. If you want any more help or information you can contact my office and I will be sure to help you myself. You see, I oversee all of Alison's cases now as she's very busy and needs a bit of a helping hand."

I watched Alison visibly squirm and bristle at the last few words in Dr Wu's statement. And if I have a connoisseur's nose for anything more than spotting arseholes from thirty mile out it's definitely noticing a bristling woman. I'm married to Jane and I fuck up every single day of the week that has a 'Y' in its name. So trust me, I *know* bristling women.

Before I could even formulate a response within my brain for it to be sent down to my mouth for dissemination, Dr Wu already had his hand robustly extended into my face. I took it and he rather overenthusiastically shook it at the same time that he pulled me from the seat and politely cupped my elbow with his other hand, guiding me towards Alison's office door.

That was a sterling move. I was impressed. I mean, I was also flat out infuriated that this arrogant twat had laid hands on me and cut me short of my five minutes by one minute and twelve seconds, but still, if we were considering me to be the shit on this guy's shoe then he just got me off the sole with one fluid scrape.

I had just enough time to turn as Dr Wu shut the door behind me to catch Alison lean out from behind him into my view and mouth the words "Thank you!" to me.

Why was she thanking me and why did Dr Wu start raising his voice at Alison the minute the door was closed and he thought I was gone?

I had no idea. But let me tell you something – both things intrigued me enough to go straight across the road from the coroner's office and sit in a fleapit of a greasy spoon café and wait hours for Alison to leave work that night.

I whiled away the time drinking really shitty black coffee, reading random articles I had no interest in on The Guardian app on my phone, clicking 'Like' to utter arbitrary Facebook status updates of people I used to go to school with and have not spoken to in easily twenty plus years, checking over my notes and texting back and forth with both Psychic and Jane. Neither of whom had anything monumental to hit me up with in terms of news or developments.

Then at exactly five minutes past five in the evening, I clocked Alison Gregg leaving the rear of her office building and walking across the car park towards her vehicle.

I took my chance, jumped across the street and got to the rear of her car just as she was climbing inside the freshly unlocked driver's side. I pulled the passenger seat door open and jumped inside. Alison went to scream, which is completely understandable really.

"Hey! No! Wait! Miss Gregg? Dr Gregg? It's me!" I garbed quickly, like me being *me* was a factor that would be at all calming in this situation considering we met for the first time five hours ago and for less than four minutes at that.

Alison stopped herself and stared at me intently.

"What the *fuck* are you doing, Mr Lehman? This is *completely* unacceptable!" she said loudly.

"I am so sorry. I really am. I'm so sorry. I didn't mean to startle you. Let me just ask one question? Just one question and then I'll go."

Alison sat looking at me. She eventually broke, turned away and with a sigh she said "Okay, one question."

"Why did you mouth 'thank you' to me? What were you thanking me for?" I asked gently.

Alison sank back into her seat and gripped the wheel with both hands. "You didn't say that girl's name." she said quietly. "You could've done and it would have opened up an enormous can of worms but you didn't and that ultimately kept more crap from my door, frankly."

"What crap?" I replied.

"You had one question, Mr Lehman!"

"Listen, something isn't right with this Stephanie Jason case is it? And I think you're taking all the crap that's come from it. I think that's what you're referring to, right?"

Alison sat silent, staring straight ahead.

"I think that's why the analogy about Kevin Jenkins resonated with you, isn't it?" I pushed on. "I think that's why you're thankful I didn't reopen this back up in front of your boss isn't it? Your boss who's a massive cock by the way!"

Alison smiled for the first time. She gently nodded. "He *is* a massive cock isn't he?"

"This whole case stinks and a lot of it is because of just how many unanswered questions and gaps in logic it carries." I said. "If you could help me just fill in a few of those gaps and answer a couple of the questions then maybe this thing might finally go away and give Stephanie's parents the peace they deserve."

Alison's smile dropped.

I pushed on. "The decisions that matter most in all of this when it comes to Stephanie – the how's, the why's and everything about how she died has your name on it. *Your* name. That coroner's report that I've seen doesn't have your pal Dr Wu's signature on it. It has your name. And if this thing breaks open far and wide like I suspect it could because Mr and Mrs Jason are not going to let it go, then your name and your reputation is what is going to be the one thrown to the wolves…"

"What was the name of that guy again?" she said unobtrusively.

"What guy?"

"The Yorkshire Ripper guy?" she replied.

"Kevin Jenkins?" I said, reigniting the chuff once more. "Listen Alison, all I'm asking is to buy you a coffee somewhere well away from all this bullshit and noise and just have a conversation with you, seek your expertise and what not, you know? Then I promise you'll never hear from me again and I won't make any trouble for you! One coffee, anywhere you like. And in return, I promise you this – whatever happens I will make sure that if the whole truth gets out you're not scapegoated for this."

Alison sighed. She turned and looked at me, staring at me without speaking for what felt like easily five minutes but was probably about fifteen seconds.

"Get in the back, duck down out of sight and don't speak to me while I'm driving."

I mouthed the word 'Thank you' and did exactly as she asked.

We drove in silence to what turned out to be a service station just off the A1 on Tursdale Road in Bowburn. Alison listened to the drive time show on Absolute Radio 80s as she drove along the motorway which didn't bother me in the least because it gave me the chance to re-appreciate what truly great songs 'Kyrie' by Mr Mister, 'Babe' by Styx and 'Just As I Am' by Air Supply are. Hell, I'd go so far as to argue that all three have aged into becoming outright classics actually. The car journey gave me a bit of time to close my eyes, gather my thoughts and try and quell the nausea that was welling up from the crushing pain in my temples.

On arrival, Alison asked me to walk in ahead of her and order two coffees and she would walk behind. She was adamant she didn't want to take a single chance of being seen with me. That was obvious in the seats she chose in the Costa Coffee outlet inside the service station itself. My gut was telling me that if Alison was prepared to go to these lengths after finally giving in and agreeing to talk with me, and if the made-up analogy about Kevin Jenkins was what seemed to resonate most, then there may be something useable and important in what she was going to say. I didn't want to miss a chance, so I pulled my trusty covert camera hidden inside a pretend car-key and activated it whilst ordering the drinks. When I reached the table, I put the drinks in front of each of us, casually dropped my keys down in a way where they just happened to position themselves with the covert lens pointing directly at Alison and put the empty tray down on the chair between us.

"What's your drug of choice?" she said, almost immediately.

"Excuse me?" I shot back.

Alison smiled. "If I'm going to talk openly to you I'd like proof you're willing to talk openly to me."

"What made you ask that?" I stuttered.

"I see it in your pallor and the quality of your skin at the moment. You're spasming and twitching without realising you're doing it. Your eyes definitely give it away, they're watering up like a fountain. You're coming off of something. The sweat? I've always said that 'cold turkey' sweat smells different to BO. So… yeah… I think you've got some sort of habit?"

"I… well… I was…" I couldn't find the words.

"Just spit it out. Make me trust you, Mr Lehman. I might be able to help."

"It's Jake. Call me Jake." I replied weakly.

"Ok, Jake. Make me trust you. How long are you off whatever it is?"

I let the silence linger a little too long.

"Just shy of twenty-four hours now." I said almost to myself.

Alison nearly spat her coffee out. "Off *what*? Jesus!"

I took a large gulp of the black coffee in front of me. I sighed deeply and just decided that this whole pill-popping dependency thing was going to be something else I added to the list of things that I no longer had a single fuck to give towards.

"I take Tramadol… Well, I took Tramadol. I'm kind of out of tablets now, unable to get any more from my doctors due to my wife's intervention and every stash I have of them is empty or I'm unable to get to it. My joints ache. My head rings constantly. And I've got this mouth injury that is absolute agony, frankly. Today's the first day where I realise that I've wasted so many days popping painkillers even though I was never in any physical pain, I was just masking some… I don't know, emotional pain? Mental pain? I don't know what you'd call it. But today? Today I'm in actual fucking agony. And I don't have anything that I *need.* That's some Alanis Morrisette level 'irony' right there, no?"

I smiled weakly.

"What was your dosage?" Alison asked.

"Two, sometimes three. Every two to four hours, maybe."

Alison let out a soft whistle.

"Okay. So your insides are pretty much destroyed then. But the good news is you're in the thick of it now. The first seventy-two hours are the worst. Have you ever given up smoking?"

I nodded. "And alcohol!"

"Wow! You're just bouncing through them, huh?" she said. "Well, you'll know from both of them that like anything addictive, the first three days of withdrawal are the worst. For me, I'd say the absolute worst is the first twenty-four hours. And you're through that so… you know? … Keep going!"

"Is there nothing I can take? Nothing to slow down the sweating or just take the ache off my bones a bit?" I said quietly, whilst looking around conspicuously to make sure there were no salacious eavesdroppers.

"You could get a treatment of Methadone or Suboxone but they're also opioids of another form so you're essentially feeding one evil with another evil in one regard. Counselling and CBT, as in Cognitive Behavioural Therapy, is really what you need. Because you need to tackle the weight of the need behind your action and not just the action. Does that make sense?"

I nodded.

"Drink lots and lots of water and continue to show the resilience you've got going on right now!" Alison said, smiling warmly.

I remembered at this point that my covert car key camera had just captured all of that and in any other situation I probably would have looked over to it and grimaced at its presence but I couldn't afford to be that blunt in giving its position away.

"So, we're done here now then?" Alison said with a chuckle. "Glad I could be of assistance. Thanks for coming."

I smiled. "You trust me now? Am I far enough inside your inner circle?"

"You're on the periphery, membership pending… but not necessarily being sent away!"

"Okay, that's good enough – so, let me ask you this: That wasn't a suicide was it?"

It was Alison's turn to take a deep breath. She took a huge mouthful of her drink, played a little with placing the cup back down to correctly position it and essentially did everything she could to procrastinate. I let the silence hang.

"I never had Stephanie Jason's case marked as a suicide." She began. "I went to the scene and I saw the set-up. I saw that there was congealed dust and mud on the shoe surface of every attending person there, including myself, but nothing on Stephanie's feet."

I pulled my notebook out and started writing.

"Completely clean?" I asked.

"Completely clean! I did not see how she could have got from her car, across the grass, across the warehouse floor, onto the top of that barrel and for her feet not to have got any debris or dirt on them. I noted that. I also had concerns about the size and weight of the barrel and how the fresh markings on the ground suggested it had been pulled into place but I wanted to establish how a woman of that size and weight could have done it herself. I noted that too. The police argued at the scene that they believed everything that was in place as I saw it were things that were already set up like that and Stephanie just put them to use."

"So the cord was already hanging like that and she just…"

"Fashioned the noose at the end of it? Yes!" said Alison. "And here's the thing. The knot in the cord before she was cut loose was shown to be a Jack Ketch knot which is an adaption of a Hangman's knot. A very, very old style of prepping the rope or cord from back when hanging was still legal. It's the sort of thing that isn't taught in schools and you don't generally pick it up as a day-to-day form of knot-tying. In this day and age to execute it a person of Stephanie's age would have had to go and watch a YouTube tutorial or Google it or something, you know? Which is why I wanted her internet search history to be considered. Especially in lieu of a complete absence of a suicide note and proclamations from her immediate next-of-kin that she had nothing in her life that would suggest she was 'suffering' in any way."

"And all of that went in your report?" I clarified.

"Not just in my report, I was calling it out there and then at the scene. But the officers seemed to have an answer for everything and downplayed everything that I put out there. I just kept telling them that I'd still have to raise it in my report."

"And who were the officers at the scene?"

"Well, this is where it gets funny. For stuff like this I expected the uniformed officers that first attended and discovered, you know? They only call it in for CID to attend if they think there's anything untoward or suspicious at the scene. But I arrived at the same time that DC Billy Tidyman arrived and he took charge of the scene. I presumed because it was now getting out there that this was a so-called high profile individual that CID were being brought in as a matter of precaution… Then DI Andrews turns up too. And then *he* took charge of the scene."

"And what was he like?"

"Other than the logistics of the set-up and her feet, I wasn't expressing too much concern there and then at the scene overall so they weren't stonewalling me on anything there. Tidyman seemed quick to counter everything I said and Andrews backed him and agreed. But it wasn't hugely contentious at the scene. It was *later* when it got messed up."

"How so?"

"I was able to make a proper inspection of the body down at the morgue. That's when things really started smelling off to me. I noted Stephanie's trachea was broken along with her neck, neither of which are uncommon from the act of hanging I hasten to add. But each injury registered to me as being somewhere between thirty to sixty minutes apart from each other and that would not be right."

"Wait. What?" I said, confused.

"Stephanie's trachea showed that it had catastrophic damage to it that would have undoubtedly caused asphyxiation but then her neck was snapped later. *Much* later. That generally does not happen. Also, hanging herself from whatever height that barrel was – which is what the police are stating she used as her jump leverage - would not necessarily have snapped her neck, let alone snapped her neck *and* broken her trachea. It certainly would not have resulted in one injury occurring then an hour later or so the other injury occurs whilst the body is in stasis."

"You're saying the signs indicated the wind pipe occurred first? *Then* the broken neck?"

Alison nodded her head.

"And could the second injury have occurred whilst the body was being taken down from the noose?" I asked.

Alison shook her head definitively. "The timing does not work out."

I scribbled away in my notebook then sank back in my seat and exhaled.

"This confusion… plus the absence of a note… plus the lack of motive… made me feel strongly that this was not easily and immediately definable as suicide. I updated my notes accordingly. My initial report was that this was not suicide and that further investigation was required in relation to the injuries." Alison said.

"Okay. So how did we end up where we are then?"

"Later on the following day, I was called into the office of Dr Li Wu and he told me that he had been doing spot-check case reviews on all of the staff's reports, rationales etc. and that he wanted to discuss the Stephanie Jason case with me."

"Are spot-check reviews common?" I queried.

"Not necessarily in the way he claims to have gone about them, no. And most certainly not on what I would have considered to be a 'live' case either because the information and results are changing all the time as we are receiving them. But Dr Wu came to me and said that he'd heard from the police himself that there was now a motive for suicide and that this motive was presented as Stephanie Jason being in, quote unquote, 'crippling debt'."

"We've covered her finances comprehensively. That is not the case at all." I replied.

"I would assume so. I asked Li if this had been confirmed by the parents and he said that he didn't see why they needed to question the police because if the police said it then it must be true."

Alison's eyes started to well a little bit with tears. "I tried to talk to him about the scene of death and the injuries but the meeting was interrupted by the arrival of Chief Constable Hadenbury."

My mouth dropped agape a little. "Say that again?"

"Chief Constable Hadenbury came into our meeting unannounced."

"As in Graham Hadenbury? Head of the police?"

"Yes. He walked in and joined our meeting. He started talking about the need to do independent and double-sourced forensic reviews and coroner checks now because of the number of errors and law suits etc that were being brought about from members of the public. This was the first I was hearing of such things and I really didn't understand why it was the head of the police service informing me of it. I'd been with the Newcastle office for a number of years now and I knew we had the lowest number of complaints and appeals against our decisions in the whole of the UK. I really didn't understand it."

"Or, I take it, understand what the head of the police was doing just randomly dropping in on a meeting between you and your boss at the exact moment you're discussing a case you've disagreed with the police on?"

"That became almost clear to me when Mr Hadenbury and Dr Wu said that they wanted to speak to me privately because a 'huge error' had luckily been caught in my judgement regarding the two injuries I'd recorded with regards to Stephanie Jason. Dr Wu said that it had been reinvestigated by him personally and there was no direct break to the wind pipe, just slight damage to it consistent with the neck breaking and trauma from the noose at the point of hanging. He said that there was also no time difference between the two."

"That's quite some difference between his findings and yours?"

Alison nodded as the tears fell.

"I *wasn't* wrong. I know I wasn't wrong but I was told that I was wrong over and over by my superior and the head of the police service… and I was asked directly to rewrite my report accordingly."

"Surely such a huge error on your part should have seen serious disciplinary action? They'd want to keep your report as evidence as to the massive mistake you'd made?" I asked.

"They told me that I was a great coroner and excellent at my job but Dr Wu worried that I was just overworked and that he had to take responsibility for giving me too many cases. He said that they wanted to protect me and the way they were going to do that was to get me to rewrite my report in line with what they called the 'real evidence'!"

"What did you say?"

"I tried to challenge it. I did. But Mr Hadenbury inferred that this was an order from my superior and not a question. Then Dr Wu made clear that such an unchecked and challenged error could be a career-ender if investigated further and also have glaring consequences on what he said was my imminent promotion."

"So you re-wrote the report?" I said softly.

"I did." Alison started to cry. "And by doing that I opened the gates to them getting rid of certain photographs of the scene, changing lab results and just completely reconfiguring this to fit what Dr Wu was saying it should be, not what it was!"

"Would you go on record with this?" I asked.

"I can't. I *can't*." Alison sobbed. "It would end my career once and for all if this went into the public domain. I'm just about holding on to that as it is. Please? I've told you the truth. Now will you leave me alone?"

"You've told me the truth to exorcise some of your demons. But what about Stephanie's family? What about their pain? They deserve better than this, Alison."

"I can't. I'm sorry. You can jump off of anything I've said but I can't go on the…"

"You kept the original report, didn't you?" I said sternly over the top of her.

Alison fell silent.

"You kept the original report, *didn't you*?" I doubled-down.

Alison nodded. "I have a copy. They think they've destroyed it all but I have a copy of my original findings."

"What if you leaked that? What if that just ended up in an envelope and posted out to us? What about then?"

"I can't. I can't. I'm sorry. I can't… This was a huge mistake!" Alison stood up and started gathering her things. She stepped out from behind the table.

"You're selling out Stephanie's family for a fucking promotion!" I spat.

Alison bent down and stuck her face right next to mine and in a clear but quiet whisper she said "Look at where I am now based. I never got the promotion, did I? In fact, they waited until the dust settled on this and then they *demoted* me! So… get your facts straight!"

She then walked out of the coffee shop without ever looking back.

"Can I still get a lift back now?" I shouted after her.

I don't think she heard me… Well, I *knew* she heard me. But I still wasn't getting a lift.

I flopped back into my seat and pulled out my phone.

It was completely flat and had switched itself off as a result. This was the penance paid from sitting in a fleapit café in Wallsend, killing time reading random bullshit on Facebook I didn't need to be wasting phone battery on.

I took a trip into what used to be the WH Smith kiosk next door to the coffee shop but was now some discount newsagent type variant that had sprung up since WH Smith went bust. I bought one of those little bullet-style charging docks over the counter and clipped it into my phone. Within a matter of minutes I'd got enough life to switch the phone back on.

… Only to discover that I had sixteen missed calls from Psychic along with three voicemails. I clicked on the first voicemail.

*"Well…"* I heard Psychic's voice say in what would turn out to be an inappropriate tone. *"… I've got good news and bad news. The good news is I've found Eva Marie. The bad news is she's dead too."*

## [22]

## or

## "You Didn't Think We Introduced That Character Earlier Without Good Reason, Did You?"

**P**sychic took an absolute age to get up to the service station in Bowburn to pick me up. But getting places in a timely fashion is one of the disadvantages that probably comes with driving around in a bloody Zastava Yugo 513. And I know you're all undoubtedly sat there now going *"For fucks sake, Jake. Stop going on about this stupid Zastava Yugo 513 and just get on with the proper parts of this story!"* and to each of you thinking that, I say to you "Have YOU driven or been driven around in a goddamn 1987 Zastava Yugo 513? An Exorcist-vomit coloured one, no less? *Have you*? Have <u>you</u> had a seat-spring break free of its faux leather covering and try to 'burgle' your intimate passages every time you hit a bump in the road? No? I bet you bloody haven't… So cut me some slack!'

I sat waiting for Psychic to arrive whilst overdosing on hard, strong, black-as-night coffee with an exceptionally pleasing aroma. I'd picked up a couple of boxes of Paracetamol along with the bullet-charger and I'd popped a couple just to see if it would dull the headache. I wasn't holding out any hope that it would fix the umpteen different effects I was suffering from not having pumped Tramadol into my system over the last twenty-four hours. But a bit of a relief for the headache and the pain in my mouth would be enough to make the purchase feel worthwhile.

The mixture of excessive caffeine and a couple of Paracetamol seemed to take the edge off the pain and reduce the sweats a little and by the time Psychic picked me up, I was feeling relatively jovial enough for the two of us to immediately land on each other like a couple of teenage girls who each thought they had the best gossip that they just *had* to share with the other first.

In the end, we tossed a coin and Psychic won.

"Right, so Eva Marie has been dead for the last five days. Her parents were led to believe she was on a modelling assignment in Europe when in fact she was dead in her bath-tub. Suspected overdose, sank beneath the water, was undiscovered in this form for two or so days…"

I curled my nose at the thought and winced.

"… Yeah," continued Psychic. "The smell set the neighbours off who called the parents, who went in and discovered her and it wasn't pretty at all."

"Do we know if there was a note left?" I asked.

"We do not, no. Not at this stage."

"And who's your source on this?" I said.

"It's a good one – Eva's next door neighbour is a good friend of Eva's parents. She was the one that reported the smell to them, she went inside with them when they came round to check it, she was with them when they discovered the body and she was more than happy to tell me all of this in return for a little cash and the promise she would not be named in my eventual story."

"Oh, you went with the journalist thing as your cover then?" I said, smiling.

"No. She just assumed I was the press and I didn't correct her!" Psychic replied.

"And how much cash did you give her for all this?"

"Forty quid!"

"FORTY QUID!" I shouted. "Jesus, Psychic! I wouldn't pay forty quid for information pertaining to the real trigger-men behind the JFK assassination!"

"I know you wouldn't, because you're a bloody tight-arse, pal!" he laughed. "How much would you have paid then?"

"I wouldn't have paid her shit! I would have used my charisma and charm to build a rapport with her and then learnt all of that information for free through the art of conversation."

"So you wouldn't have learnt jack-shit then, I guess?" laughed Psychic.

I lifted my arm to playfully punch Psychic and it was by attempting exactly this that made me realise how heavy and deadened my limbs felt. I couldn't even find the energy to complete the movement. Instead I just flopped my arm back down to where it was and wearily said "We know two girls went to this mysterious party. Both models, both friends with one another and both dead within a month of each, both from suicide?"

Psychic nodded. "The neighbour thinks Eva struggled to cope with the loss of her friend!"

I let out a suspicious hum whilst noticing that both of my hands were now starting to twitch. Psychic spotted it too and opted to try and distract me by way of assistance.

"Right, your turn then…" he smiled.

I proceeded to tell Psychic everything about my conversation with Alison Gregg, my encounter with her boss, the original summation she made with regards to the death of Stephie and the injuries she sustained. Psychic's jaw dropped at the mention of the time difference between the two injuries but it nearly fell off all together when I mentioned the intervention of Graham Hadenbury. I told him that there was a copy of her original report floating around but that things didn't end well between the two of us and that we needed to find a way to repair things with her in order to try and secure a copy.

"Things didn't end well, huh?" Psychic said.

"No. She walked out on me." I replied.

"Were you all out of your charisma and charm? Is that why you failed to build a rapport with her?" he said, smirking.

I flipped him my middle finger and he broke out laughing. It turns out I had just about enough energy to get my finger extended in his direction.

"So how are we going to get her back on track?"

"Well there's always blackmail I suppose?" I answered.

"Blackmail?"

I nodded and pulled the covert camera car-key from my pocket. "I recorded the whole conversation with her!"

Psychic exhaled hard, smiled and ruffled my hair. "I guess we're not fucking around or allowing ourselves to be fucked around with anymore then, huh?"

I shook my head. "We most certainly are not!"

We were seconds into arriving back into Newcastle itself and in deep discussion as to where we were next going to bed down that evening when Margaret Jason called and confirmed that Stephie's car was still stored in their garage currently and had not been touched by anyone since DC Tidyman had been up to check it in the days after Stephie's death. We arranged to head straight up there and take a look at it.

"Do you think the police may have overlooked something in my daughter's car?" asked Margaret over the phone.

"We'll soon find out!" I replied, deciding this was a better option to take than "I certainly hope so!"

Psychic and I debated the whole journey up to view Stephie's car as to whether to discuss with Margaret and Matthew the attack on me, the potential threat and the fact that I was taking it so seriously I'd put my own family in hiding. By the time we'd pulled up at the security gates of the Jason's home in Smallburn twenty-five minutes later, we'd agreed full transparency was the way to go.

We were welcomed immediately on parking by Margaret Jason coming straight out of the house to see us. I'd forgotten that this was Psychic's first time seeing Margaret.

"Holy shit, Jake! Margaret Jason is a full-on MILF!" he smiled whilst waving at her as she made her way from her front door to our car.

"Please don't try and fuck the dead girl's mum, Psychic!" I replied.

"I promise I won't… *here*!" he laughed.

We got out of the car and I made three attempts to close the piece of shit door before it finally rested shut as it was meant to. Margaret came straight over to me and we shook hands warmly whilst her eyes darted around me with concern.

"Are you… okay, Jake?" she whispered.

"I'm fine, yeah. I've just got a bit of a bug, that's all. And then I… fell over on my face, or something?" I lied before immediately pulling her away from the car so we were on our own. "I have to make you and Matthew aware of something for the sake of your own safety…"

I then took to explaining everything that had happened since we'd last spoken, the attack on me, moving Jane and the kids away and how if this was what was happening to me for digging around then it was only logical to assume the people who attacked me would like Margaret and Matthew even less for hiring me in the first place.

Margaret listened intently. When I was finished, she slowly nodded her head and said "Someone really doesn't like you pushing on, asking the questions that remain unanswered then, do they? And that tells me there's more to all this. Maybe I'm not some mad old grief-stricken mum who needs humoured after all…"

“We’re not humouring you, Margaret.” I assured her. “We actually think there’s a lot of weight to your suspicions. In fact, there’s a lot with each passing day that leads us to believe Stephanie didn’t kill herself!”

Margaret stopped in her tracks.

“I don’t want to excite you too much,” I said, “Because I’d rather not get into too much today, if that’s okay? I’d rather wait until we’ve got everything we needed concreted into place. But all I will say is that I don’t think you need to beat yourself up too much that your gut feeling is baseless. The state of my face and the existence of the guys that did it tell you that much.”

“I’m sorry you’ve suffered that, Jake.” Margaret smiled warmly. “As far as Matthew and myself go? Well, we’re behind an exceptional security system anyway and neither of us particularly have anything worth living for anymore so… let the bastards do their worst, I say. Although, I would very much prefer for you to get them before they get you. Just for the sake of your own family, you know?”

I smiled back.

Margaret said softly. “So what are you intentions here today then?”

“I think that there might be something in Stephanie’s car that may provide a clue to her movements on the night she died. The more we can zone in on her exact movements over the course of that evening, the better for us.” I replied.

I then slowly moved us back over to the car where Psychic had remained standing.

“Margaret, this is Robbie. He’s working with me on this. He’s the Watson to my Sherlock, you could say.”

I smiled as I introduced them whilst inwardly promising myself that if she offered him her hand and he kissed it I was going to kick him square in the nuts so hard it would end his days right in front of her.

Margaret smiled and offered her hand to Psychic who took it and shook it professionally whilst saying “It’s lovely to meet you. I just wish it was in less upsetting circumstances, Mrs Jason.”

She nodded and said “Please, call me Margaret!” whilst leading us away and towards the large three car garage in the corner on the right of their huge grounds. As we walked, I spotted the conservatory across the gravel driveway and caught sight of Matthew, sat alone and even more dishevelled then when I last saw him. He was slow-sipping another goblet full of what looked like whiskey whilst staring out into the garden ahead of us on the left.

Margaret caught me looking.

“How is Matthew?” I asked gently.

“He still hasn’t spoken or eaten properly since the funeral.” She replied quietly. “He hasn’t cried or showed any emotion. He just sits, staring and drinking.”

“I’m sorry to hear that.” Psychic said.

“I’m going to have to prepare for the fact that he will probably drink himself to death and there’s nothing I can do to prevent it. Although with what you’ve told me today I’d much rather those men whoever they are come and put us out of our misery so we don’t continue on in such pain.” Margaret bravely smiled as much as she could muster.

I put my hand on her shoulder in an attempt to offer some comfort and she placed her hand on top of mine, looking back up at me appreciatively as she clicked a button on the remote in her hand causing the garage door to split into two and started rolling open electronically. Once the doors rested fully open we caught sight of an immaculate garage that housed a 2018 gun-metal grey Jaguar F-Type and a new model white Audi R8 Coupe. Behind us on the gravelled driveway were two Land Rover Discovery's alongside Stephie's Range Rover Sport.

"The police found it at that horrid place in Hebburn and eventually brought it here. I don't know what we're going to do with it," Margaret said of Stephie's car. "There was just nowhere else for it to be stored really and I don't think I've quite made peace with getting rid of it just yet."

Psychic's jaw fell open at the sight of the cars lined up alongside each other.

I pointed to the Range Rover. "That's the car that was found at the scene, yeah?"

Margaret nodded.

"And it's the same car DC Tidyman came and took a look at?"

"Yes." Margaret replied. "There was a pair of Stephanie's shoes in the car when it was brought back. They were just in the passenger footwell. They're inside with us now. Other than that, nothing has been touched at all."

"Shoes?" asked Psychic.

"Yes, Stephanie loved Valentino Garavani shoes. They're a pair of high-heeled black Valentino Garavani shoes. Would you like to look at them?"

I nodded and Margaret pressed the key for the Range Rover into my hands before exiting the garage. We watched her walk away. The minute she was gone from sight Psychic turned and punched me in my arm.

"What?" I gasped.

"There's hundreds of thousands of pounds of car in this garage alone. She's bejewelled up to the bloody hilt and you settled on a two-hundred-and-fifty quid a day retainer? Are you for real? Jesus Jake, we're going to have to have a hard conversation someday about how you're running this business!"

I offered nothing in response. Instead I stepped forward and opened the driver's side door of Stephie's Range Rover whilst removing a tactical flash light from my pocket. I started to shine it around the footwell and underneath the seats. I didn't see anything particularly out of the ordinary. Psychic appeared opposite me in the passenger side footwell and started doing the same. He then opened up the glove box and had a root around in there.

"Anything?" I asked.

Psychic shook his head. "A shammy leather, anti-freeze, pink windscreen scraper, lip gloss and some mints."

"We're looking for a map!" I reiterated whilst checking the door-wells and backseats.

Psychic checked the boot thoroughly. We met back at the front of the vehicle.

"Of course we're basing this search off the idea that we've not been beaten to whatever Stephie was referring to by Tidyman who handed it off to Andrews who then in turn disposed of it." Psychic said.

"He possibly has. But we've got to check to be certain haven't we because..." I trailed off into silence.

"What?" asked Psychic. "What are you thinking?"

"We're looking for this with too old-fashioned a slant, aren't we?" I said. "We're looking for a map like we're going to find some piece of paper with an 'X' on it or something. Or an A-Z with the corner of a page folded over. No one uses maps anymore do they? Certainly not twenty-four year olds."

"They use..."

"*Sat-Navs*!" we both said in chorus with one another, allowing a sense of joy to present itself in our tone that completely negated the fact that, really, this was hugely obvious and we were both frankly utter dumb-fucks for not having been on this line of thought from the absolute outset.

I took the car key we'd been given by Margaret out of my coat pocket and dropped it in the cubby-space next to the gear stick. I then pressed the button for the ignition, only to encounter a flat battery within the engine.

"I'll move our car up and we'll charge it, no bother. There's jumper-cables in the back, I saw them before!" Psychic offered.

"You're going to charge up a top-of-the-line Range Rover Sport from a 1987 Zastava Yugo?" I asked incredulously.

Yet that's exactly what Psychic managed to miraculously pull off.

We killed some time once the two cars were hooked up and the engines were ticking over by talking about anything and everything to keep my mind occupied and away from thinking about how much my bones ached and how much my rectum now felt like it was pouring out blood when it fact it was just the last destination from which all of the cold, stinking sweat dripped down from my ever-drenched head and spine.

We talked about the best TV shows ever made. The Sopranos, Cheers, Columbo, Breaking Bad, The Larry Sanders Show, The Rockford Files, Deadwood, Magnum PI, It's Always Sunny In Philadelphia and Seinfeld were all offered by me. Psychic countered with Game of Thrones, Justified, Arrested Development and some awful-sounding thing about one of the blokes from the film Trainspotting playing a modern day American version of Sherlock Holmes with one of Charlie's Angels as his Watson. We spent at least five minutes specifically on this last programme in which I continually argued that something so stupid could not possibly exist and Psychic countered that not only did it indeed exist but that it ran for over seven seasons or something. He then tried to make me read Wikipedia pages dedicated to the show but I robustly fought against this happening.

I forcibly ran a strong enough defence against reading a single word about *Trainspotter-Sherlock* or whatever it was called, that it killed that element of conversation and we turned to inevitably discussing the bloody weather again.

"It's definitely going to snow in time for Christmas!" Psychic said.

"Nah. The air's far too cold." I replied.

Psychic twisted his face and looked at me with an expression that suggested if they lined dumb and dumber up, I'd be dumbest. "Are you saying it can be too cold to snow?"

"No, what I'm saying is heavy snow actually forms in relatively warm temperatures near the ground. Temperatures in the single digits or below zero make it too…"

"Where the hell are you getting that from? Since when were you such the weather expert? Listen to yourself!" laughed Psychic.

"I read it. I read a lot of things on a lot of subjects. I'm an educated man, you know?" I said, ignoring Psychic's mockery. "There is no theoretical point where it is too cold to snow. That's not what I'm saying, but generally the colder the air the less likely ice crystals will precipitate and form into flakes to fall to…"

Psychic started to laugh even harder now. "Jake, you big bell-end!"

"Fuck you Psychic! This is science, man!"

"Right, put your money down on this!" laughed Psychic. "How much do you want to bet we get snow on Christmas Day?"

"Well actually a 'White Christmas' is technically…"

"Don't give me that shit!" smirked Psychic. "Snow fall on the twenty-fifth! At all? At any time? I say it's a guarantee. You say it isn't, yeah? Some shite about precipitating ice crystals or something, aye?"

He started to laugh.

"Okay, dickhead!" I said, sticking out my hand. "Twenty quid says not a drop of snow on Christmas Day!"

"Deal!"

We shook hands.

Eventually there was sufficient enough charge for the engine to turn over, for me to be saved from having to hear another word on that awful sounding American Sherlock show or argue another bloody word about snow and for the dashboard to light itself up. We both dived into the driver's seat and passenger seat respectively and I tapped the sat-nav screen on the in-built monitor.

It came up with an error message and displayed nothing.

I hit it again and it said the same thing.

I went to press it again and Psychic slapped my hand.

"You're committing to the same frickin' action over and over without changing any of the variables involved and expecting a different outcome!" he said sternly.

"Jesus Christ, calm down Dr Science!" I said, stroking my hand.

"Dr Science? Really? You didn't even try there with the insulting nickname thing, did you!" Psychic laughed.

"Maybe the Sat-Nav has been affected by the battery being flat too long?" I suggested.

Psychic shot me a look that suggested I was the biggest dumb-fuck on the planet.

"That's like… not even a *thing*?" he said mockingly. "This is you to a tee with technology. You are absolutely an analogue man in a digital age and you just bang on things like an ape on a typewriter and then grunt random stuff out that shows a complete lack of understanding of even the most basic things…"

"A satellite navigation system isn't a basic thing though, is it gobshite? It's actually really complex isn't it because there's like… loads of things to it that are…" I didn't get to finish.

"That are what?" laughed Psychic. "Complex? You *think*? Come on then, what does GPS stand for?"

"Global Positioning System!" I laughed back with a scowl. "I'm thick. I'm not fucking thick though!"

Psychic leant forward and pressed the ejector button for the memory card on the slit above the in-built screen on the dashboard. "There's probably some dust on the card!"

"Oh. Dust on the card?" I mocked. "My 'flat battery broke the sat-nav' theory is ridiculous but your 'dust-molecule took down the whole system' theory is entirely plausible?"

Nothing came out when Psychic pressed the ejector button.

He pressed it again.

I slapped his hand, probably a little bit harder than when he slapped mine. "You're committing to the same action without changing any of the variables involved and expecting a different outcome!" I smirked.

"Maybe the error message is because there's no functioning card in there like there should be?" Psychic said, ignoring my pettiness whilst leaning forward and shining his torch into the slit.

I leant forward and joined him in looking into the slit. "There's something in there."

Psychic nodded. "I see it too. How we going to get that out?"

As if timed by the gods themselves, Margaret reappeared carrying the black Valentino Garavani shoes she'd spoke of. I gently took them from her hands and turned them over to look at the soles. "You haven't cleaned these or wiped them down or anything?" I asked.

Margaret shook her head. "No, why?"

"Because they were in the footwell of her car when it was recovered which means she didn't walk into the warehouse wearing them, the soles show that anyway but the fact that they can't have inanimately made their way back out to the car and placed themselves there after she died is the main factor. So that would say to me that she walked barefoot into Hark Roy and yet the photos we've seen and the information we're getting suggests her feet were completely devoid of dirt from the scene!" I replied.

Margaret clasped her hands around her mouth. "That makes absolute sense. Of course."

Her eyes began to well up with tears. Psychic gently took hold of Margaret's shoulder and asked her if she had a pair of tweezers he could borrow. Within three minutes he had led her back to the house, returned with a pair and got to work trying to pull this mysterious object from within the slit on the in-built monitor. Because, as Psychic said upon returning to the car, he's an "active problem-solver and not much of a stationary deliberator".

I made the 'wanker' sign above his head whilst he fiddled with the tweezers inside of the slit because frankly people who aren't wankers don't say things like 'stationary deliberator'.

After a minute or so Psychic miraculously achieved success and brought out a tiny micro SD card on the end of the tweezers. He dropped it into his hand and then brought his palm up close to his face.

"This isn't what these things are built with!" he said somewhat furtively.

"Where's it come from then?" I asked.

"That I can't say for certain. It's a micro card. It could have come from any bit of gadgetry nowadays, really. What I can say with certainty is that it didn't come as built-in for this sat-nav on this car. Look at the holdings on the monitor? This would need to be put into an SD adapter to fit properly in there."

"The questions now are where is the card that was in there and what does it have on it that needs hidden or taken away and what's on this, where's it come from and why has it been stashed there?" I ventured.

"Stuff it! Let's turn the interior over one more time, yeah? Lift everything out!" Psychic said, clearly fired up by wanting more answers then he'd been afforded thus far. "We can check this micro SD card out easily enough. That's not an issue. But I really want to make sure we're not overlooking the actual card for this car!"

I nodded. "I'm in total agreement. But I think Tidyman beat us to the punch."

Psychic shrugged his shoulders. "Let's not give that guy too much credit – He didn't spot this after all, did he?"

With that we took to going over the inside of the car once more, lifting out the mats, shining torchlight everywhere we could possibly think to and checking out every dark recess the car offered us. Then, on the final stretch of our final check-over of Stephie's vehicle, I ran my fingers gently along the lining of the carpet underneath her seat one last time… and my fingers caught on something small, hard and shaped like a square that my fingertip check had missed the first time round. I grabbed hold of it, brought it out and shone a light on what turned out to be a black SD card that had clearly blended with the dark of the carpet and the mass shadowing that the undercarriage of the seat afforded.

"Now THAT," smiled Psychic, "is what these things are built with!"

He took it from my hand, slid it straight into the slit above the monitor and we collectively held our breathes as we waited for the sat-nav to find its bearings and sort itself out with the new card placed back within it.

It came alive again after what felt like an eternity.

"Unless she absolutely, resolutely knew exactly where she was going in Hebburn, I would say that there's a high chance her last input destination would be the Hark Roy warehouse, wouldn't you say?" said Psychic quietly.

"Click it!" I said, finding the tension to be an unbearable additional contribution to the agony within my head right then.

Psychic did exactly that and in a haltering voice said "The last known journey inputted was from Stephie's Baltic Quays address to a postcode of NE66…"

I didn't let him finish. I simply and barely audibly said "… 2RL?"

Psychic turned and looked at me in a state of semi-shock. "How the hell would you know that?"

I took a gulp of air and supressed the building nausea as best I could before painfully yet decisively saying "… Because that's Mick Hetherington's address!"

## [23]

## or

## "Let's Start Pushing A Few Pieces Of This Jigsaw Puzzle Together And See What Picture It Makes."

I've wasted a lot of my life. I think about that a lot. In fact, I guess you could say I waste a lot of my life thinking about how much of my life I've wasted doing things that I look back on now and think "Really? Was *that* worth it?"

I once went to a local university to listen to a seminar from a criminal psychologist I greatly respected from the reading I did during my police training. However, I got lost and walked through the wrong door into the wrong room and found myself face-to-face with Germaine Greer, who was at the university as a guest giving a talk on some bloody thing about weaponising or arming the clitoris or whatever it was. The thing is she stopped speaking when I entered and I think she was daring me to turn around and excuse myself and I thought "Fuck that! I'm standing my ground for ALL men EVERYWHERE!" or some half-baked bollocks, so I stepped inside and took a seat and stayed the course… for four hours and ten minutes. Why? I don't know. Germaine Greer did not give one single shit about me sitting there. I just didn't want to admit that I was some numpty of a man who got lost and wandered into a lecture on feminism. So I stayed. And wasted four hours and ten minutes of my life.

I've watched the first four Harry Potter films and I was a grown man when I did so. Now whilst some respect should be afforded to me for realising that life is too short to be pushing on with the fifth, sixth and however goddamn many others there are, that's still a total of 612 minutes - or ten hours and twenty minutes if you will – that I'm not getting back.

When Jane was pregnant with Jack she went off for a spa day with her mother and I waited in for the cot to be delivered from Mothercare and then by seven pm that night when it hadn't arrived I finally cottoned on to the fact that I had the day wrong and I'd just wasted a day pottering for nothing.

I've jet-sprayed our back patio garden in a downpour… I've watched every episode of Manimal, possibly even twice… I've read some Stephen King books when he was first coming off the cocaine – and it showed... I once went to an Ikea on a Bank Holiday weekend just to buy a packet of their frozen meatballs and it took me two and a half hours just to get back out of the store… I went through a Toad The Wet Sprocket phase…

… And after I was first thrown out of the police service I used to sit for hours and hours outside of Mick Hetherington's home in the backends of Northumberland, up on an old dirt-track road overlooking his massive property, drinking alcohol and clutching an old wrench I'd wrapped in black tape and that I kept stashed under my driver's seat.

I'd drive up there three, maybe four, times a week and just sit there for hours and hours willing myself to find the courage to get up out of the car, go down there and beat him to death. I'd tell myself over and over again that I had to do it to protect him from ever hurting another child again. I swore to myself that my kids would be better off without me as their dad anyway but the sacrifice of not being there for them was for the greater good.

I'd drink and clutch that wrench tighter and tighter and normally at the exact moment I found what I needed inside of myself to get out of the car and go and get Hetherington once and for all, I'd pass out flat drunk behind the wheel.

Which is how I luckily escaped a drink-driving conviction and walked away with just a harassment warning on that one dark morning at four am when I was awoken on that dirt-track road by the tapping on my window of two uniformed police officers, both of whom had been called up there by none other than Mick Hetherington himself.

He'd spent weeks photographing my car and put a very persuasive argument forward to the police that he felt threatened by my being there. He didn't need to persuade them too hard obviously. They were in his pocket, so to speak, after all.

The warning was enough to light a fire underneath Jane though who pretty much pulled my access to the car, started tightening my contact with money and generally taking more control over my ability to be that stupid. Less than a month later that incident happened with Jonathan at school and Jane kicked me out.

You drive anywhere three to four times a week for months on end though and stare at it that obsessively with that much hatred, it kind of burns the address into your mind whether you want it there or not. So when Psychic asked me if I was sure that NE66 2RL was a postcode for an address belonging to Mayor Mick Hetherington, I could reply affirmatively with absolute unwavering certainty.

We hastily grabbed the memory card from the monitor on the dashboard and carefully wrapped it alongside the micro SD card in a scrap of paper I had in my pocket, before gently placing the paper inside Psychic's inside jacket pocket. We said polite goodbyes to Margaret who pushed to learn if we had found anything of note inside Stephie's car.

"We don't know quite yet," I said. "But possibly. I'll keep you posted."

"Please do!" she said, stepping back inside as we dashed to that piece of shit Zastava Yugo 513 and sped out of the driveway.

We argued all the way out of Smallburn and back to the city about where was a safe place for us to go and check the micro SD card discreetly. It would involve us firing up the laptop Psychic had stashed in the boot - which was probably smashed to pieces at the rate this rattler of a car was throwing us all around - and looking through everything that could possibly be on it. We had to have somewhere where we could sit with confidence that we were not being watched and that we could talk openly.

Somehow that led us right back to Will's house down near the beach in Blyth.

Will was a very gracious host and he kept the supply of black coffee and paracetamol coming in a steady and most useful supply. The problem was that he seemed really put out that he had to 'share' Psychic and he came across like he was extremely threatened by my friendship with him.

Second time around, Will spent a lot of time playfully punching Psychic on the shoulder as he made us refreshments when we first arrived and saying things like "Remember that absolute killer game against that team from Byker, Rob? What was it? 5-4 in the end? Close call or what!" … And then he'd stare hard at me in a way that sort of felt like "Yeah, Jake! 5-4 against Byker! How many of those did YOU score, huh? You don't *know*. You weren't *there*… Loser!!"

Which kind of forced me to sip my coffee and then say things like "Hey *Rob*, remember that time we were chasing down that utter scumbag who was stealing ten litre gas cannisters and filling them with fourteen litres of gas and inadvertently blowing up caravan parks and we tracked him down better than the police did?"

But then Will started doing all this machismo-soaked piffle where he'd wrap his arm around Psychic's shoulder and say "Dude! Dude! *Dude*! What about that stag weekend in Ibiza? Do you remember that? What could we possibly remember? We were that hammered, am I right? Oh God, do you remember them Dutch girls?"

Then Psychic would grin whilst looking bashful. And I'd be forced to have to reconfigure the displaying of my friendship medals whilst at the same time not having the energy to keep this going much longer. So I went straight in with "Hey, Robbie boy, remember when we thought we were dealing with just a straight-up investigation into the death of an innocent young girl and then covert assassin type motherfuckers started smacking me in the mouth with a gun and chasing us around the city… and what not?"

Psychic smiled broadly and gave me a wink. "I guess that's as good a reminder as any that we best get going with the work we've got to finish. Thanks again for letting us hang out here Will, mate."

Will wordlessly nodded his head whilst looking at Psychic for confirmation that what I'd just said was complete horseshit. The confirmation didn't come.

We took ourselves to Will's dining room table. Psychic pulled out the micro SD card and put it on the table. He followed swiftly by pushing open his laptop, yanking an SD card adaptor from a pocket on the accompanying laptop bag and clipping the micro SD card inside of it. He then placed the adaptor into the card port on the laptop, logged on with his password and sat back.

Within seconds the shortcut appeared on his desktop screen for the adaptor card. I reached to click it and he instantly slapped my hand, hard.

"Do not even bloody think about it, Jake!" he said.

Psychic clicked the shortcut and the folder opened and revealed six video files. I put my hands to my mouth and breathed heavily.

"Look, let's tether our expectations before we start, okay?" Psychic said as he right-clicked on the 'Get Info' tab on each file and carefully wrote down the information beneath the 'Created On' header in each box. My breathing got heavier and heavier as I realised that each and every file showed it was created on the eighth of November this year, all before midnight.

I looked at Psychic.

He looked back at me.

"This could be big, right?" he said quietly.

"This will be big!" I replied.

"Let's just take a second…"

"Shut up. Click the first one." I said sternly.

"No, listen. Hold up. We're going to, but first… Listen, we're where we are because of you Jake. You got us this far."

"Shut up, Psychic. You found this disk." I smiled.

"No, you went face-to-face with Alia Marcus. You got the information that led us to the car, you got the words about the map. We're here because of you. You need to take a second to give yourself some credit."

"I love you, man." I laughed. "But I'm in a constant state of throwing up at the moment and the anxiety is absolutely making that worse. Please… I've got to know what's on these files."

Psychic took a deep breath and clicked the first file.

The footage opened on a lit gravel path which I immediately recognised as the driveway leading up to Mick Hetherington's home. The lens on the recording camera lifted up from pointing at the ground to moving in a bobbing fashion that indicated the camera-person was walking as they filmed. We heard footsteps on gravel and Stephie say *"Smile, baby girl!"* as the lens landed on a young twentysomething fellow blonde model who we now knew to be Eva Marie.

*"You and that stupid bag contraption!"* laughed Eva Marie.

*"It's going to make me a millionaire, a billionaire and then a squillionaire. That's what this stupid bag contraption is going to do!"* we heard Stephie laugh.

Eva Marie wrinkled her nose. *"Do the password again? Go on? Make me laugh?"*

*"To-ca? Too-Ka? Too-carry?"* we heard Stephie giggle some more.

*"Do the accent!"* demanded Eva Marie.

*"Too-car-ree!"* bellowed Stephie's voice in a big, broad, comedy-style Italian accent.

Stephie swung the lens to capture the property itself as they got closer to it.

*"Why the fuck are we here, man!"* sighed Eva Marie.

*"Sue says it's a simple meet-and-greet for one of the mayor's rich pals!"* the voice of Stephie replied. *"Apparently he's a really big fan of both of our modelling work!"*

*"So he wanks off to it basically and now he wants to paw our flesh because he just happens to be in the same city at the same time as us, right?"*

*"Why do you think I insisted on driving us up here and not taking the chauffeur they offered, Eves? We're not beholden to anyone. We'll get in there, drink some clearly overpriced champagne, pose for some selfies, continually shift some dirty liver-spotted hands off the side of our tits and down to our waist and then get the fuck out of here, yeah?"* laughed Stephie.

*"Hell yeah!"* replied Eva Marie.

The door in front of them suddenly opened, bathing the lens in an unexpected stream of light and the camera dropped back down to filming what appeared to be the side of Eva Marie's waist.

*"Good evening ladies and welcome!"* came the sound of a male voice. *"May I receive the password from you both please?"*

The audio began to get muffled and then clip abruptly shut off.

I looked at Psychic. "This puts her in Mick Hetherington's home on the night she died, right?"

Psychic nodded. "But does it put Mick Hetherington there with her?"

"Play the next one!" I said as the nerves congealed with the aching pains inside my body and pushed up alongside the increasingly unbearable thirst for a fix of opioid.

The second clip sprung to life as the lens of the camera slowly surveyed an enormous open-plan living area with lots of lit candles, expensive looking soft furnishing and Italian opera playing almost inaudibly in the background. The sea of twenty or so people that the camera seems to catch are all older looking gentlemen in tuxedos talking with a lot of heavily made-up and gowned females. Even from this distance with the lens never zooming or moving in its coverage, you can tell that these females veer towards being pretty young. We see Eva Marie approach clutching two drinks and she gets close enough to then block out most of the shot.

*"This is pretty iffy, Eves!"* we hear the voice of Stephie say.

*"I'm thinking the same thing. I think we're the oldest girls here by like... twenty years!"* Eva Marie replies, laughing nervously.

*"I know some of these girls. Hell, I know a lot of these girls. They're on Sue's books. And they are not old enough to be here, on their own and drinking al..."*

A booming male voice cuts immediately across what Stephie was saying before she could finish. I recognised the voice even before the camera lens was discreetly repositioned to capture Mick Hetherington himself standing directly in front of both women.

*"I want to thank you both for coming this evening. You both look absolutely exquisite."* Hetherington smiled. *"You're going to have a wonderful time, I assure you. We're going to have a few more drinks whilst waiting for the rest of the guests to arrive and then I have a very special person I'd like to introduce you both to who's...."*

The clip came to another unforeseen standstill once again.

"That gives you your answer then, doesn't it?" Psychic said.

I started to rub my stubble hard and my breathing deepened.

"This puts her at Mick Hetherington's home and in his company at what time on the night she died?" I said, feeling my entire jaw tense as I spoke.

Psychic leant in and right-clicked on the 'Get Info' tab on that particular clip and looked to the information beneath the 'Created On' header specifically on that box.

"That clip was at forty-seven minutes past nine on the evening of the eighth!" he said.

"This information about him being part of Stephie's last night alive was distinctly absent from his tribute to her at that lighting ceremony!"

"I wonder why?" Psychic replied as he clicked on the third clip.

What followed was twenty-two seconds that played out as hurried and often unfocused footage of various sex acts being performed in pretty much every recess and spare surface as the lens scanned the room. Men were in a state of either partial or complete undress. Women, very young looking women - or *girls* if we were being entirely accurate - knelt before them performing fellatio or were bent over and being vigorously penetrated. The audio was filled with the mixed sounds of pleasurable moans, pained gasps, crying, the heavy and rapid breathing of what we believed was Stephie herself as she moved around the room… and that goddamn, obnoxious Italian opera music!

Then the clip cut to a stop.

Psychic sat staring at the screen.

I let my head drop. He turned to look at me.

"We're in agreement, right? Those are *kids* on there?" he said quietly.

I nodded as I dropped my head into my hands and stared at the ground.

"Stephie said she knew them. She identified them as kids herself. Those are bloody kids." Psychic said as his voice raised in anger. "I don't think I can click another fucking thing here, Jake… I don't know, man."

Psychic's eyes started to well up with tears.

I put my hand on his leg and squeezed his knee.

"Do you want to leave the room?" I said softly. "Because… I don't want to click another clip either, mate. But the thing is I'm going to *have* to… You don't though."

Psychic gently and slowly shook his head.

"We're in this together... To the end… Deal?" he said.

I nodded.

He clicked the next clip.

The camera now filmed from a second floor looking down from and over a balcony into the living room area. Sofas had now been pushed back creating greater space in the centre of the room. The open, flagrant and not entirely consensual-seeming sex acts were intensified in number and the lens panned its way around the floor space. The young women caught on camera engaging in such acts didn't seem to be getting any older the more clips we viewed and the longer they ran for. If anything, they seemed to be appearing younger and younger.

The lens of the camera came to concentrate on Eva Marie crying whilst held to the ground by two naked men. Her dress was both pulled down and hoisted up creating a cluster of material around her midriff that left her breasts exposed. Even amongst all the noise and from as far out as the second floor landing in which she was filmed, her sobs could be seen and heard as an elderly naked man lay on top of her, rapidly penetrating her over and over again.

The heavy breathing of the camera person continued, sounding more and more panicked with each breath. The audio was tersely taken over by the sound of a gruff, masculine voice saying *"Hey? Excuse me?"* close to the microphone of the camera and the clip peremptorily cut off.

We sat in silence.

Both of us staring at the screen, neither of us able to look at one another.

Finally, I spoke. "We just watched a rape… Well, if I'm honest I think we've just watched multiple rapes…"

Psychic sat forward and tears fell from his eyes.

"… inside Mick Hetherington's house." I continued. "And unless she suddenly appears on camera in the next couple of clips to suggest otherwise, it seems to me like Stephie Jay filmed them."

"And a couple of hours later she was dead!" Psychic said quietly.

"A couple of hours later she was dead!" I repeated back. "And if someone tries to tell me that she left this piece of shit's house, drove herself over to a random warehouse in Hebburn and killed herself because of the guilt, I'm going to kick them in the throat!"

Psychic wiped his eyes, put his head back to stare at the ceiling and took a huge gulp of air. He then leant forward and clicked the fifth of the six clips on the desktop.

The recording kicked straight into gear with a clear shot of Mick Hetherington, shot from a low angle, and in a semi-dressed state looking flush and sort of dishevelled in a manner that suggested he'd hurriedly thrown some of those clothes on in the last few minutes. Acoustically you could tell this was now filming in a completely different space and the lighting and walls behind Hetherington's profile suggested this was a much smaller room. My money was on it being a bathroom or shower-room, perhaps.

Beside him stood the man we knew as Murdock from the team of four covert operatives who'd been tailing me around the city. It was the same guy who froze in the alley behind the Italian restaurant with the gun in his hand. I'd have recognised him in a heartbeat because his face is etched in my mind. Your mind does that to you with people you think are going to be your murderer.

*"There's been a few concerns raised that you have been filming guests within my home."* Hetherington was heard to say whilst looking sternly at whoever was holding this camera by their waist. *"I'm going to ask politely for you to answer me honestly – Do you have a camera in that bag right there?"*

*"No, I don't. I was checked at the door, remember? By this guy right here in fact!"* Stephie's voice was heard to say.

The camera picked up Hetherington turning and looking directly at Murdock with an expression of anger. Murdock continued to stare blankly into the face of who we believe was Stephie.

*"Then you'll have no problem with me having a quick look then?"* Hetherington said.

*"I have many a problem with you doing that!"* Stephie was heard to say.

*"Please hand your bag over!"* he said with a tone increasing in consternation.

*"I know what is going here."* Stephie's voice shot back. *"I don't want any fucking part of this sick shit. I want to leave. Now. I want to take my friend and I want to leave now."*

Hetherington made a grab and his hand loomed towards the lens of the camera. There was a scuffle and his hand completely blocked and covered the lens itself. The screen was black but the audio remained.

*"Let go of my bag! NOW! ... This is not what I was told this was going to be. I know a lot of the girls you've got here tonight. I work with them. I know their fucking parents."* Stephie's voice said. *"Some of these lasses are only fourteen and fifteen years old. They can't even do Sue's jobs without chaperones. So how are they here tonight, buck naked and on your living room floor? What have you got going on here, Mr Hetherington? If you don't let me go now I'm going to call the police and..."*

*"You listen to me, you utter slag!"* boomed Hetherington's voice. *"You were made by this city. I own this city. So you answer to me. Do you understand? Now hand Chris here your bag then let's go downstairs and shut that mouth of yours up by putting one of my guest's dick in it!"*

The camera backs away in a manner that suggested Stephie as cameraperson was now pulling back from Hetherington to give herself space in case he went to grab her again. Instead Hetherington himself backed away too, grinning a vacuous and empty grin and reaching for the closed door that was now visible in the background. He half-turned, opened it and into the low-shot frame walked Chief Constable Graham Hadenbury, naked from the waist up.

*"What's going on Mick?"* Hadenbury said affably.

Hetherington isn't in the shot but his sigh is heard. *"A few guests have become unsettled by this young lady and the manner in which she is wielding her handbag around. Some are suggesting that she has some sort of covert camera apparatus inside which..."*

Even from this low angle the camera picked up the instant reddening of Hadenbury's face.

*"Well that just won't do!"* interjected Hadenbury.

*"I don't have a camera."* Stephie's voice is heard to say.

*"I'm afraid I can't take the chance in believing you. Let me see inside your bag."* Hadenbury replied.

*"You're not seeing inside of my bag. I want to call the police now."*

Hadenbury let out a little chuckle. *"Darling, I am the police. Quite literally, I am the brightest blue light at the top of the entire police service. I'm as high as the light will go. I am..."*

*"I don't believe you!"* Stephie interrupted defiantly. *"There's kids down there being forced to have sex with grown men. My friend is being raped. No police officer in their right mind would be in the thick of this. You're just some sick old..."*

Hadenbury struck out without warning and his hand forcibly landed out of shot but the sound most clearly indicated that he had delivered a hard slap across Stephie's face.

She gasped.

His hand loomed right over the lens again and blocked out coverage once more. There was the sound of tussling and raised male voices shouting *"Give me the bag!"* over and over.

Eventually the hand disappears and the lens comes back into focus, filming the floor of the room everyone is standing in.

*"What are you standing there like a gormless fucking ape for?"* a male voice is heard to say that I pinpointed as belonging to Hetherington.

*"What you think you are seeing is an extremely warped and skewed interpretation that is quite far from the truth. One has to believe that you are on some sort of illegal substance to think the things you are saying."* Another male says, that I believed to be Hadenbury.

The same voice continued. *"We are all extremely powerful people with huge positions of responsibility in very, very difficult times and we are entitled to de-stress from the amount of pressure our roles and responsibilities bring. Do you understand that? ... What's this young woman's name?"*

*"Stephie. Stephie Jay."* The voice I believed was Hetherington says.

*"Do you understand that Stephie?"* Hadenbury's voice said. *"Now, you have been thought of highly enough to be invited into this exclusive circle and you have abused the host's trust... As a serving police officer I am now saying to you that you are acting in a manner this evening that gives me cause to believe you are under the influence of a controlled substance, therefore under Section 23 subsection two of the Misuse of Drugs Act 1971 I am now going to search you. I should also point out that under subsection four of the same act it is an offence for you to intentionally obstruct or conceal controlled drugs from me and..."*

*"You are going to have to arrest me then because you're sure as shit not searching me."* Stephie's voice said. *"Arrest me and take me down the station. Let's talk about all this really fucking loudly down there!"*

There is a silence that is eventually broken by the sound of Hadenbury turning away from the camera and being heard to say *"You know what Mick? Fuck this! Go get Mr Grant. That's what you pay him and this absolute disgrace for!"*

Inaudible whispering follows. A door is heard to open and close – then lock!

The camera is lifted up to survey the room, catching a brief half-a-second shot of Stephie in one of the mirrors as the lens passes over the walls. She is alone.

There is a sudden whisper of the word *"Fuck!"* and the camera cut off.

"We have Mick Hetherington and Chief bloody Constable Hadenbury heading up this paedophile party? Are you shitting me?" gasped Psychic. "That's him, isn't it?"

I nodded, leaning forward and grabbing Psychic's notepad and pen. "We've also got the one I nicknamed Murdock identified as being called Chris. And we've got another one with the surname Grant, isn't that right?"

I wrote those names down as Psychic nodded.

"This girl has unequivocal balls of steel though, huh?" I said admirably as I finished writing.

"I know, right?" answered Psychic. "She's holding her own with some really powerful, despicable people there!"

"And she paid for it with her life!"

We fell into a saddened state of silence once again.

"How long is this last clip?" I asked.

"Eleven seconds!" he replied.

"Filmed at what time?"

Psychic clicked the usual round of buttons. "Ten past eleven!"

"She died at thirteen minutes past midnight according to the official death certificate. So, this is as close as we're going to get to her last moments?"

Psychic nodded then clicked the button to play the final clip.

Over the course of eleven seconds we see the camera come to life just as a pair of black high-heeled Valentino Garavani shoes land with a thud on the ground and the feet inside of them race unsteadily across the gravel driveway. Breathing is heard – gasping, heavy, *desperate* breathing. The footage cut off just as we caught a glimpse of what we believed was Stephie's right hand urgently pulling open the driver's door on her Range Rover.

Psychic sat back in his chair and put his hands behind his head.

He did it in perfectly timed sequence with my action of leaning forward and burying my head in my hands.

We sat in silence. I rubbed hard on my temples. He continually let out large, pained sighs and projected his exhaling air towards the ceiling.

Minutes passed.

"We can't even go to the police with this because it's the outright *head* of the police that is in the thick of this!" Psychic said angrily.

"Which also explains how easily this was shut down across the board!" I added.

"And why Hadenbury was turning up at coroner's offices to see that the verdict on her death matched what he needed it to." Psychic said.

"What if Hadenbury murdered her?" I asked.

"Well he's now a suspect isn't he? Because she got footage of him at a party where children were getting sexually assaulted. That's a motive."

I nodded. "And it's why he could stop the voicemail being listed as evidence too. He had the power to influence anything he wanted in terms of the fall-out from this. And I'll tell you another thing too… Andrews might well be up to his usual tricks of covering for powerful perverts but you've got another thing coming if you want me to believe that Hadenbury's son-in-law is on the original investigating team looking into Stephie's death but is *just* a so-called dogsbody!"

"Are we going with the idea that he had Eva Marie killed and made to look like a suicide too?" Psychic suggested.

"That's what my gut is telling me now." I sighed.

"Why wait just over a month to get *her* though? If this is about silencing people who went to that thing at Hetherington's house, how come Stephie gets offed that night but they wait a *month* to go after her pal?"

I shrugged.

"I don't know, mate. I don't know." I sighed. "But we can't lose sight of the fact that this is Mick Hetherington's gig, inside his home, up to his old disgusting tricks again and…"

"Who the fuck do we go to with this, Jake?" gasped Psychic, sounding completely helpless. "Who do we turn to? Do we just turn back up at Margaret Jason's house and dump this SD card in her hand and piss off home in time for Christmas? We can't go to the police. We can't inform social services. We can't even identify who half of the kids are in all of this footage!"

"We know that a lot of them are on the books at The George Platform and we know that Sue sent them up there. We know she lied about it too when I asked her about Stephie and the Paradox gig. So we go back to her, we turn the screws a bit and we start from there…"

"Where's the parents in all of this?" Psychic said, tearing up again. "How come these kids aren't running home to mummy and daddy and telling them that the latest modelling gig or whatever was actually a paedophile sex orgy and…"

"Maybe they *did*!" I said. "Maybe they did and their parents took them straight to the police – and Hadenbury had them shut straight down! Maybe they turned to the local authority and raised safeguarding concerns – and Hetherington shut them straight down too! So maybe they ran to the press – who locally are completely in bed with Hetherington and every little thing he does! THAT is what we're looking at here!"

"Shit!" exclaimed Psychic.

"We need someone we can trust who we know is completely independent of local newspapers, who hates our corrupt local authority and most importantly who'll believe us!"

"Yes!" bellowed Psychic.

"We need someone with connections outside the region and who's looking to get really loud and get this into the hands of people who…"

"No!" interrupted Psychic.

"Let me finish!" I smirked.

"No!" cried Psychic.

"We need someone who's tenacious and who hates Mick Hetherington just as much as us and…"

"Don't you say it!" he said, getting more agitated.

"We need…"

"No!" shouted Psychic.

"We need Emily!" I said with a smile.

## [24]

## or

## "Emily Ashley – Journalist-At-Large."

Emily Ashley was a legend. Well, she was a legend in her own mind but still a legend per se. She was a local journalist continually infuriated at the prefix 'local' and as a result lived and breathed for landing on that 'one' story which would put her on the national stage and get her out of Newcastle and down to Fleet Street, her own personal *Camelot.*

She'd been trying to achieve this goal for nearly eight years straight and it was starting to look increasingly less and less likely. Every time she felt that she landed 'something big' a higher power always came along and crushed her story to dust.

The story you never got to read about corrupted election results within the region and Mayor Mick Hetherington essentially 'stealing' his seat? That was hers! That exclusive you never saw about 'jobs for the boys' and how Newcastle Council offered out long-term trade contracts on a 'grace and favour' policy? That was hers as well! What about that shocker regarding police corruption and the idea that the higher-ups within the police service openly benefited from huge pay-offs from councilmen? That was hers too!

Every time that Emily landed on something that tore open and shone a spotlight inside the dirty, murky corruption that ran through this region like black oil being forcibly pumped through veins, it would be bought by the paper, buried after one swift phone call from someone in power who was named and shamed in the story and Emily was left high and dry. Of course, she'd try and take the story nationally but doors were repeatedly shut in her face because someone who knew someone would put a word in and say that Emily was "difficult" and her stories had "trust concerns".

She would openly challenge her editors in a manner many considered "unbecoming" – which goes someway to explaining why Emily Ashley has worked for pretty much every local paper in the region in one way or another and been summarily fired from all of them. And it explains why she now currently works as a runner behind the scenes on local talk radio host Liam Hitchock's late night phone-in show, Night Watch, whilst also free-lancing for The Daily Mirror on online stories with a celebrity bent.

Emily Ashley is now just *surviving* within journalism; a Bob Woodward or Carl Bernstein type crushed down into the body of a reluctant celebrity blogger and as a result she's a pint-sized pocket-rocket of perpetual indignance – with an absolute hatred of Mick Hetherington and his council who, like me, she considers to be the grand evil responsible for all of her ills.

She and I first met many, many years back when I was meeting with journalists to try and get the story of Mick Hetherington and Madeline published. Emily was the only journalist who took me remotely seriously and tried her hardest to help Jane and I. It went nowhere, obviously, but Emily stayed in touch.

We've helped each other out a little bit over the years since I set up 'Lehman's Terms'. Occasionally she'd want some deep-digging done for a story so she'd call me in and bill the paper she worked at for my time. Sometimes I'd pass a client over to Emily to get their injustices put out on a public platform to help shame the guilty parties into complying.

Things had slowed over the years with Emily having less and less outlets to get published in and my work slackening down to the state it was in pre Stephie Jay. We worked together on something a while back when the country first started to falter; a whistleblower got documents to Emily that suggested executives at Newcastle Council were creaming money off the top of certain services in order to stockpile for their own bonuses so that in the eventuality the country crashed they could take a pay-out and run.

It went nowhere. Of course.

But we always stayed in touch.

I trusted Emily a lot. She was one of the rare people alongside Jane, Psychic and Jimmy, who'd never given me a reason not to.

But the thing that I liked most about getting to hang out with Emily or finding an excuse to have her come over to our office or whatever, is that Emily and Psychic used to date for a year and a half or two.

They got together through my introduction.

And the relationship didn't end well. *At all.*

And the fall-out - beautiful as it is to indulge in from a spectator's position - continues to this day.

Dusk was setting in early on December 23rd when we brought the pea green coloured 1987 Zastava Yugo 513 rattling into Emily's little street in Gosforth. The engine was now making a noise that suggested this had been the first time in a long time that it had been put to work with such regularity across as many miles as we'd covered so far.

I was in the process of making it very clear to Psychic that if the exhaust backfired and comedically fired out smoke as we came to a stop then I was going to refuse to get back in it again, when he pulled what I felt was a purposefully aggressive stop outside of Emily's house.

"I'm not speaking to her, mind you. And you can't make me." Psychic snarled as he got out of the car.

"Fine. Fine. If you want to be a child…" I replied as I climbed out with difficulty and made my way through Emily's gate and up her path.

"I'm not the child. She's the child. And the thing is…"

Psychic stopped at the sound of me knocking on the door. Emily opened it almost instantly and broke into a smile. "Hi Jake – you got something for me!"

"Hey Em'. Mick Hetherington runs paedophile sex orgies out of his house, attended by Graham Hadenbury, head of the police no less, and not only do we have video proof but we think it ties to the death of Stephie Jay… which wasn't a suicide! Did I get all that right?" I replied, turning to face Psychic at the end.

"Eurgh!" Emily grimaced at Psychic. "Hello, you small-dicked fuck!"

"Hello Emily, you… you… erm… human form of sweat… " Psychic stuttered. "Sweat… that's erm… straight from the brow of Satan himself!"

"Right, great. With that out of the way… tell me you're not shitting me and I'll let you come in?" smiled Emily.

"We're definitely not shitting you!" I replied.

Emily immediately stepped aside and opened the door wide for us to walk through.

Once inside we got through what felt like now-obligatory "You look like shit, Jake!" type small-talk then black coffee was swiftly supplied and I set to work on telling Emily everything – who had hired us, what we'd experienced, what evidence we had and how we were out of options on who to turn to and who could help us.

Emily knew Stephie Jay... Well, she knew her as well as a journalist forced to write vacuous promo pieces for various outlets knows her subject.

But she spoke warmly enough of Stephie that I felt I needed to pre-warn her about what was next.

Then I showed her the video clips.

All of us sat in stunned silence for a long, fairly uncomfortable amount of time.

"She died that night because of what she saw and what she captured." Emily said softly.

"I don't believe she died at her own hands either!" I replied.

"No. I can see why."

Psychic had sat silent exactly as he said he would right up until this point. "We're out of options, just like Jake says. We can't go to the police because this incriminates them. We can't report this to local authority safeguarding with regards to the kids because… well, Hetherington! And press wise? I don't need to tell you do I?" he said.

Emily stared him out.

"Well, you certainly can't go to my old paper." she said. "They're heavily, heavily in bed with Mick Hetherington. The paper now is run like that man's own personal newsletter."

"I thought as much." I said. "What about Night Watch? Would Liam Hitchcock get the audio out on the air?"

Emily emphatically shook her head. "Not a chance. That man is as safe as you can get – you know half of his call-ins are actors, right? There is no way he'd touch this with a ten foot pole!"

Psychic sighed "What about just dropping it on the internet and throwing the links out to it far and wide?"

Emily rolled her eyes. "You'd be waiting and hoping for someone to bite and in the meantime Mick's people would probably find it and cease-and-desist it out of existence before anyone of any use to us has even seen it! … Now shut up, the adults are talking!"

Psychic went to retort. Emily put her hand to his face.

I was tired of these two already. This wasn't as fun to watch from the front-row when you're burning off your nipple-ends in desperate hunger for painkillers and exhausted beyond the capacity for reasonable thought too.

"We can't run the risk of this going the way of every other story you've tried to break. Whoever this goes out to has got to land it and run with it because the minute this goes out into the wind for so much as a second, Hetherington will crush it!" I said.

Emily nodded. "I have some pretty strong connections with people at The Guardian and The Independent. They would jump all over this but not immediately. They would want to do their own due diligence, obviously."

"What's to say they'd not bury it too?" I asked. "I mean, surely you've approached them in the past regarding all the stuff we know and have come across over the years? How come they didn't run with that then? Hetherington and Hadenbury have some reach, clearly."

Emily sat in silence once more and then sprung to life.

"The reason they have the reach is because they have the power, right? So let's take away the power… Do you know the story of Bao Dac Kien?"

"Here we fucking go," sighed Psychic. "She's always doing this Ronnie Corbett tangent stuff…"

"Shut up Rob, you absolutely unlikeable fool!" spat Emily.

Psychic blushed and Emily turned back to me.

"Bao Dac Kien was this legendary general type bloke in the Vietnam war. He was unstoppable. Just this mad, powerful, psycho guy and all the Vietnamese idolised him enough to want to die for him and the Americans started to generally fear the man because they came to realise that they were trying to fight someone who was truly sick in the head and had his armies fight with absolute savagery and without caring about what their lives were worth. And that's a scary thing to go up against. Especially when platoon after platoon were repeatedly telling stories to each other of this rogue Vietnamese general who kept you alive after stripping off your skin just to be able to shoot you whilst wearing your own face. How mad is *that*, right?"

Emily took a sip of her coffee and leant in closest to me with a big smile.

"… But like every powerful man, he got completely drunk on the power and started strategising battle manoeuvres that would benefit him, not the war overall. He started stockpiling armaments, riches and Lê Trọng Tấn's disciples quickly came to realise that Bao Dac Kien was becoming a demagogue and was ultimately growing to be too powerful and that he seemed to be planning to see off the Americans and take hold of Vietnam for himself. So…"

"They sent Martin Sheen upriver to kill him? I've seen this movie." Psychic laughed.

Emily did not break her eye contact with me but the curl in her mouth seemed to indicate Psychic was far closer to getting battered to death with a coffee cup than he realised. She pushed on regardless.

"In one of the greatest secrets of the Vietnam war, reported barely nowhere and left out of all of the documentaries and films and all of that shit, is the fact that a clandestine meeting was set up between Creighton Abrams' people on the US side and the heads of the Vietnamese army. The Vietnamese Generals recognised that Bao Dac Kien was making them look bad, getting too powerful and that a divided army would not survive against the enemy… so they personally provided the exact co-ordinators for Bao Dac Kien's camp of savages to their enemy – and the Americans bombed it to smithereens and wiped him out! The next day the Vietnamese and the Americans went back to fighting each other like Bao Dac Kien never existed!"

I sipped my black coffee and rubbed the temples of my head. "I think I'm lost?"

"You don't have to have a police officer of superior or equal rank to arrest a fellow officer if the officer has committed a criminal offence, right? Only when it comes to professional ethics does that apply! We don't know which officer in this force would do the right thing and step up to put the cuffs on Hadenbury. But… what Chief Constable of any neighbouring police service is realistically going to sit back and allow for a fellow high ranking Chief Constable to be involved in a paedophile sex ring and take the chance that it could get out they were aware? Let's not stress about trying to get this in the press. Let's work on getting all involved arrested so it becomes a matter of public record! And the way we'll do that is by getting the lesser of the fuckers to take out the worst of the fuckers!"

And with that Emily downed her drink, plopped the cup down with a thud, sat back in her chair and clapped her hands.

"I know Jessica Lane!" she said with a smile. "Like, know her really well. Like attended her wedding *well*!"

"Who is Jessica Lane?" said Psychic.

"Jessica Lane is the Chief Constable of Durham Police!" I said smiling.

Durham was the neighbouring police service to Newcastle's. It was highly regarded nationally because of the inventive way it continued to police its borough in the face of relentless budget cutbacks. It was also ran by a no shit-taking female Chief Constable, the first in its history, who drove corruption from its rank and file with ruthless efficiency.

"But, wait…" Psychic started.

I stopped him in his tracks. "If you ask her what I think you're going to ask her she's going to attack you where you stand because it's *you* asking it, trust me. Let me be the one to ask, okay?"

I turned to face Emily. "If you're that good friends with Jessica Lane than how come she's not stepped up before to help you when you've been working all those other stories about police corruption up here and all that stuff?"

Psychic nodded and pointed at me. "*That*!" he seconded.

"One, for the umpteenth time tonight, shut the fuck up Rob!" Emily said. "Two, she's tried many a time to help me. A lot of the contacts I've made have been because of her. But she's got a high threshold and a lot of what I had in the past didn't meet it. I wouldn't agree but I accept her opinion. *This*? Everything you've got so far? This meets her threshold. You've got to trust me on that?"

I looked at Psychic. He smiled warmly at Emily and said "I trust you, Em!"

"Shut the fuck up!" she growled before turning her attention back to me. "You guy's need to keep working this to find the connection between what went on that night and how Stephie Jay ended up dead in that warehouse. But other than that, there's enough here for me to make a call to Jessica and show her what there is so far." Emily added.

"I still think there's the possibility that Hetherington could wriggle away. Your route might publicly shame Hadenbury and what not but…"

Emily didn't give me the chance to finish. She clicked her fingers and her eyes lit up once again. "Wait! What about this: Tonight's Hetherington's odious annual end-of-year shindig at the civic centre, right?"

I nodded.

Every year, the day before Christmas Eve, Mayor Hetherington throws a lavish black-tie gala across the entire conference floor of Newcastle Council headquarters. It's all about patting each other on the back for another job well done of screwing the community out of money and services they were entitled to and celebrating their absence of ethics and integrity. When the big financial cratering started even a couple of years out people wrongly assumed the council would pull back on such excessive and unnecessary spending because of how it 'looked' to the people they represented. Hetherington and company didn't even so much as take a seconds pause. They pushed on regardless and just heightened the security at the event. Some would say they even spent more on it these last few years as an extra 'fuck you' to the critics.

"What if we cut together a compilation of all of this? The 'I own the city' is especially good alongside the images of kids being raped!" Emily said with the outright emotional detachment that comes with being a story-chaser as hardened as she is.

I winced at her words.

"We could get inside and get it blasted out in front of everyone? I reported from one of his events like this many years ago and he has giant screens on three of the main walls, projecting photo compilations of himself meeting with high fliers and politicians and stuff. It's an utter ego-wank!" she continued.

I looked at her then I looked at Psychic.

"How the hell would we pull that off?" I asked.

"It doesn't start for another few hours, does it?" she said. "More than enough time to get the worst of it cut together and get Jessica involved. Whilst she's landing Hadenbury we could be publicly exposing Hetherington!"

I looked at Psychic once more. "You think we can pull that off?"

"Get inside, you mean?" he replied.

I nodded.

"If there's security at that event then it has to be ran by one of two companies," Psychic said. "And who owns or at least has his fingers in with both of those companies?"

I smiled.

We answered in chorus with one another: "Bobby Maitland!"

"Who now hates us!" added Psychic.

"Yeah, but he hates Mick Hetherington more than us though!" I let my smile broaden.

Each of us allowed our eyes to dart around the room at one another.

Each of us let out a nervous little laugh.

"Are we going to go for this?" I said as the babble spewed forth. "Shall we go for this? … Come on, let's do this? … Let's do this, yeah?"

"This is so big it has even made me willing to work with Robbie again!" laughed Emily.

Psychic let out a big huff of a sigh and said "I don't care what you think anyway Emily because I'm dating a model now!"

"Since when are you dating a model?" I said with surprise.

"Well, she's a model agency receptionist but she's going to be a model someday." Psychic replied.

"Holly? Sue's receptionist? You're dating *her*?" I gasped.

"Can we talk about it later?" he replied bashfully.

"When have you had the chance to date her? You literally got her number and then went on the run with me. And anyway, she's a potential witness. Could you not have waited until we wrapped this up?"

"Look! I've not yet, alright? … I've just got her number and I've suggested it!" Psychic shot back.

"What did she say when you text her?" Emily said, giggling.

"She hasn't replied yet! She's busy!" Psychic said angrily.

"When did you text her?" she shot back, doubling-down.

"A few days back. Like, nearly a week. You know, just after she was at our office?" Psychic said, answering Emily but looking at me.

"Yeah – she's *not* going to be going out with you, I can guarantee that!" said Emily as she burst into fits of laughter which swiftly led to the squabbling starting.

And then squabbling continued.

And it ranged away from being about what can be read into the length of a non-reply to a text message all the way up to the fact that Psychic didn't want to "commit" to Emily after two years together apparently but also how Emily "wasn't emotionally ready for commitment" according to Psychic.

The squabbling seemed to show no signs of dying whatsoever so I eventually found the resolve to intervene and draw it to a close by suggesting that Emily contact Chief Constable Lane, even at this hour on the wind-down for Christmas, and that Psychic started copying the video clips and putting them on a memory stick for Emily to share with Chief Constable Lane.

And that's when everything went to hell in a handbasket in the blink of an eye.

"Make sure you give her a copy of Stephie's voicemail too!" I'd said.

Psychic was silent so I repeated the statement.

He responded wordlessly but nodded with panic in his eyes.

"What?" I said, nervously. "Please tell me you've not lost that fucking voicemail?"

"I haven't lost it!" Psychic replied. "I know exactly where it is – it's on a memory stick… back at our office!"

I let out a sigh of relief. "Oh. I don't know why I'm panicking anyway. Just access the work emails remotely and forward the voicemail over to Emily."

Psychic now started to blush. "I deleted the email."

I leant forward in my seat and felt my eyes narrow. "You *what*?"

"Well, I worried that they were going to hack us. We had no idea of their capabilities and what not. So I deleted everything they could take but I made sure I copied it first."

"But you've left the copies in the office? That we currently think is under surveillance?" I shouted.

"And if they were going to break in to hack your emails and shit they'd probably clear the place of all the memory sticks and external hard-drives as well anyway!" added Emily.

"Shut the fuck up!" spluttered Psychic.

"No!" I angrily interjected. "She's right! You could have utterly fucked us here! That voicemail was the perfect addition to the recorded clips we have. It times out perfectly and it incriminates Sue George and…"

"So I'll just go and pick it up!" Psychic replied. "It's cool... It's cool. It's fine…"

Fifteen minutes later, Psychic and I were barrelling along the Great North Road out of Gosforth and heading back into the city, arguing every step of the way about how I didn't need to come yet there was no way I was letting him go on his own… onto how could he be so stupid in leaving behind the only copy left of something so important… which descended into the fact that I take him for "granted"… and how if I wanted him to be "so goddamn exemplary" in his job that I should start paying him – which, as I've said, is always a stone-cold argument-ending move to victory on his part!

We parked up on a side street off Pilgrim Street and made our way over to the 'Lehman's Terms' offices through High Bridge and the backdoor of our office up the spindly emergency staircase, constantly taking turns at looking over our shoulders and checking out every inch of shadow as we moved.

As soon as the back entrance door was open, I whispered "Don't switch on the lights!"

Psychic nodded.

"You know whereabouts it is, right?" I quietly added.

Psychic nodded again.

"Okay, use your phone light if you have to but just go get it and be quick."

We stepped into the office and I quietly closed the door behind us.

The lamp in the corner of my office flicked alive almost instantly which caused the both of us to jump and the flash of it spun my vision once again, making it more than a couple of seconds before I'd pulled myself together enough to see that Murdock had pulled a seat into the corner of the room and was sat waiting for us… with a gun, rested on his leg, pointing directly at both Psychic and I.

"Hey guys! Come in!" Murdock smiled. "We've got a lot to talk about."

We were frozen to the spot.

There really was no way I could see either Psychic or I being able to make the turn back for the door without landing a bullet somewhere on our person. There was no way of us getting out past Murdock into the main office area either.

"Listen," Murdock continued. "You're floundering around Newcastle trying to break this case or whatever you private detective types call it and it's beginning to look to me like you've not landed on what you need to blow this thing up and you're not going to now that time's ran out…"

"You don't know half of what we've got… *Chris*!" I said, sneering.

Murdock didn't show any reaction whatsoever to the mention of his name. He simply adjusted himself in his chair so the barrel of his gun now had a clearer line of sight on the both of us.

"I know that half of what you've got isn't enough!" he said with a smile. "Now… Do you gentlemen have a functioning video camera to hand, please?"

## [25]

## or

## "The Death Of Stephanie Jason."

*"Is it on? Is it recording? Okay. Both of you sit back down over there. Just sit in clear sight of me, yeah? Good. My name is Chris Reiser. I was a sapper in 9 Parachute Squadron of the Royal Engineers. I've been out for just over two and a half years now… It's been hell.*

*Not what I've seen. Don't get me wrong, I'm not going to spit in the face of what the Army gave me. Not at all. I'm talking about being out. It's hell. There's no place for me, for anyone like me, out here… I mean there's sweet fuck all for anyone frankly, but for squaddies it's ridiculous.*

*I met Ernie when I was serving… Ernie is the black guy you've met, yeah? Ernie Royce. He was a good lad when we were serving together. He's gone a bit mental since coming out. He uses a lot of drugs to cope with shit in his head and it's starting to fuck him up a bit now, I reckon. Ernie was in the same unit as me and we were headed up by Jason Grant. You'll know Jason because of the scar on your mouth or as the guy that tried to end you in the alley. You know who I'm talking about, right?*

*So, yeah, Jason left and went into private security and he made a fucking boatload almost instantly. I'm serious, mate. He was creaming it in. Ernie followed him out and they started bouncing around together. They were doing the odd bit of merc'* work *as we call it. They were doing private contracts for billionaires out on the Greek islands too. They were minted.*

*Whilst they were rolling in it from keeping an eye on rich fuckers in the baking sun, we took a bad IED hit in Afghanistan and I was knocked on my arse for a bit. I had spine problems because of it and the Army pretty much kicked me to the side just as soon as the wounds had scabbed up. 'Can you still run, son? Can you still carry your kit for miles, son? Can you carry your weapon, son? Not like you used to, son? Well fuck you, son!'*

*… I was out on my arse and back in Little Hulton before I knew what hit me. Either of you boys familiar with Salford, eh? You're not missing much. I was born and bred there and I thought I'd go dead there too but…*

*... The army makes you think you matter, you know? That's what that they're good at. Actually, they're fucking great at it. They get you, they blank your slate so you are just another shaven-headed, khaki-covered sap and then they build on that slate what they want and what they need. But by the time they've finished they've got you convinced that you an important part of the grander machine... That this operation, this tour, this task, this whatever – that it can't possibly succeed without you! Now on the grand scheme of things, you know you're just one of a hundred, one of a thousand and so on. But there and then, when they need you, they'll make you feel like you're fucking imperative.*

*Then you're punted out the back door and out onto the street. They tell you there's settlement officers and training courses and all that but it's total bullshit. It's tokenistic bullshit. Before you know it you're out on your ear, walking 'civvie street'. People don't look at you like you're anything because to them you're nothing. That's how bad things have gotten now isn't it? We're all just nothing now. All of us stripped down to scratching for the same penny pieces the government have dropped from their loot bags on their way out the door, you know?*

*... People don't look at me like I'm anything. They don't know me. They don't know anything about me... They don't know the things I've done to keep those fucking rag-heads and bearded scum from sneaking away and getting on our sovereign soil and then blowing themselves up in a crowded shopping centre or stealing a van and driving it into loads of people just out enjoying themselves... They don't know the shots I've taken and the things I've done to keep these wolves from their fucking doors. They don't care to know... They don't...*

*In America at least they thank you for your service before they try and stick a knife in your back and leave you for dead in the street. Over here? They just say 'We don't care if you're not sleeping! We don't care if you're seeing your dead mates in the bastard bath with you! We only care whether you're working and keeping the cogs whirling in the machine! Now here's a pizza delivery driver job for £7.10 an hour, take it or we're cutting your benefits and taking this off you and deducting that from you and...'*

*Have you tried to hold down a doorman's job when they're standing you in shitty nightclubs in the real arse end of Salford, with flashing lights setting off your headaches that get so bad they cripple the entire right hand side of your body? And where it kicks off on a Saturday night you wade in because that's what they're paying you for... but the next thing you know you're just waking up and you've hospitalised some kid, your hands are stained with his blood and your bosses are shoeing you out the back door just like the Army did, only this time they're telling you to get out of town and keep your head down?"*

[SILENCE]

*"... I'm sorry. Just give me a minute, yeah? I'm all over the shop here. Let me just breathe a second... You know those cunts told us 'don't panic' when the pound started dropping and all that shit. They told us to trust them because they knew what they were doing and... Where are they all now eh? Where? They knew what was happening and while they were telling us to trust them, they were clearing out the millions they'd made on the side and they were fucking off out the country as it started to bob lifeless in the English Channel. And now we're just left to get on with it... We get told that all the time, don't we? Have you heard it? ... 'Get on with it!' ... Times are hard. There's no jobs to be had. It costs too much to heat your home or have the lights on or put food in the cupboards. There's no wage big enough to cover the cost of having to get out of bed and put food in you and your family's mouths. But... We just have to 'get on with it'... Get on with WHAT, exactly? There's nothing fucking left to get on with, is there?*

*... I bumped into Ernie a year out from leaving the Army. He tells me that Jason is running his own security consultancy business in Manchester and Ernie says he's working for him now. He recommended it to me and I thought I'd take a look at it and see if Jason could get me back over to Afghanistan. I'd done a couple of tours in the Achin district of Nangarhar province and everyone said it was hell on Earth. I loved it though. I'd heard rumours for a while that there were some private security details running out of there these days so I thought I'd check in with Jason and see if he had any contracts out there.*

*I met with him... He runs a company called Black Box Consultancy... We joke around saying that we can tell lasses that we work for the BBC and it would impress them and shit but it technically wouldn't be a lie... So anyway, I met with Jason and he was pretty cool but he'd gone right up his arse in some ways since getting out. I asked him about some work in the Nangarhar province but he reckoned that the game wasn't like that anymore. I asked him what he means and he says that the money's all in private close protection for rich dicks and spoilt sluts. Ernie says it's not about webbing and weapons anymore, only about looking good in black suits and ties at snobby parties. I wasn't sure but then Jason threw me a fucking grand for a night's work at some poncey party in Manchester and I was in... That's how I came to know Geoff Kelsey. Kelsey's the other lad on the team you'll have come across, you know?"*

[SILENCE]

*"So Black Box revealed itself pretty quickly to be anything else but what Jason and Ernie told me it would be: Pretty much day-to-day, we were doing surveillance to build evidence against people and blackmail them on behalf of rich corrupt bastards... Married millionaire scumbags had mistresses that needed scared off from opening their mouths when the relationship ended so we got a few grand to go flush her head down the toilet and smack her around a bit. It turned my stomach from the outset... We were roughing up and intimidating people to make them sign shit and make shady business deals go through.*

*We weren't doing good things for good people. We were just being henchmen or foot soldiers for really horrible scumbags. And every time I tried to get out the next gig paid more and more than the last. It was crazy... Absolutely crazy!*

*And here's the thing, right: You know all this shit with people saying they can't be bought or there's no price that would make them do this, that or the other? It's total and utter crap. Everyone has a price. Everyone. Every single person knows where their line is. When you don't have a penny in your pocket and your Army pay-outs don't even last you a week in the current climate... and you've got elderly parents who can't afford to eat because their pensions are for shit nowadays... and someone comes along and says 'Would you smack this fucker in the mouth for a grand?' you suddenly find you don't have a lot of follow-up questions. You can close your eyes pretty tight and block out a lot when you know you're not going to have to worry about food or rent, especially in today's society.*

*So Jason comes to the three of us a while back and he says that he's met with this mayor or MP or something up here in your city and the bloke has been enquiring about a regular, monthly, high-paying security gig at his home. The deal was that once a month we'd come up and work this party this guy was throwing, we'd do twelve hours total and get ten grand. Jason would take four and we'd split the rest straight-up and get two-thousand each for the shift... No one was going to argue with that, were they? Even when Jason started warning us that it was going to be some sort of private... kinky... closed door... thing, all of us just went 'Nope. Don't give a fuck. Pay me that two grand, baby'!*

*And it turned out to be very, very lucrative... The guy was Mick Hetherington. Your mayor. And he had money. Like lots of the stuff. He clearly knew people too, you know? He was throwing these parties and you could see by the cut of these guys' suits and cufflinks and shit that they were serious players. We did one event at his place and there was premiership footballers there. There was MPs... It was big stuff.*

*Mick trusted us, he really trusted us and he wouldn't use anyone else. And his parties took the fuck right off, man. His guests were paying thousands, I shit you not – thousands, to attend and get up to all sorts. We were told originally he was only going to have them every three months and keep them really exclusive. Then all of a sudden it's every month... Between this and all the other bits and bobs Jason was finding for us we were all taking home anywhere between five and seven thousand a month.*

*You couldn't work it out if you tried, could you? The country is going up the u-bend. Companies are tanking. There's no living wage. People are being made homeless and yet out of all of it, these high-fliers keep stepping up and throwing cash here, there and everywhere. Where is it coming from? How do they have so much of it? ... I never got an answer. I mean, your fucking mayor is one of the richest people in Newcastle and keeps getting richer while everyone else gets poorer. What's that about? Who made that deal, right?*

*I did the first couple of parties and I was always the outside perimeter guy so I never really got to know what was going on but Kelsey and Ernie talked it up a storm, man. They'd talk about just standing up on the second floor and watching a full blown roman orgy of sucking, fucking, total debauchery... But I started to see the people that were leaving at the end of the night and I was convinced they were kids, man. I was certain of it. Ernie told me they weren't and that Mick just liked to hire in young looking talent because that was the guests' kink or whatever. I was never sold. Then I got to work the inside for one party a couple of months back and I knew I wasn't wrong... The guests were all men and the 'entertainment', as Mick and Jason called it, veered very close to "young". I was looking at some of these lasses and I thought there's no way these girls are over the age of sixteen. They just can't be. There might be a couple of them, yeah. But most of them looked like they were twelve years of age and wearing twelve inches of make-up to hide the fact.*

*I challenged Jason about it and I said that this wasn't sitting right and at first he made this really snide remark, like "Yeah, but is the money sitting right?" and that got me right in the gut, you know? I pushed harder but Jason said he'd cleared it with Mick and that Mick confirmed all the 'fuckees' were above legal age and the 'fuckers' were 'well connected' and 'legit' people who wouldn't be taking chances on anything illegal.*

*Then a month or so back we're all travelling back to Newcastle for Mick's next gig and Kelsey makes a joke about the guest list being put together from a local modelling agency's kids section and the bottom rung of the care homes Mick is in charge of and I kicked off in the car... I demanded they pull over but they just kept saying they were making it up to wind me up and get under my skin.*

*That's when Jason told me Stephie Jay and Eva Marie were going to be there as one particular guest who was going to be attending had apparently paid Mick BIG money for him to have them there so he could meet them and, you know, try and fuck them or whatever. And Jason used this as a bat to hit me over the head with – How come they'd be there if it was just kids getting selected to be fucked and stuff? They're big and successful and in their twenties, you know? And I bought that... but between you and me, I didn't have a clue who Stephie and Eva were. I just liked the look of the photos Ernie got up on his phone and I thought it would be pretty cool to hang out with them.*

*I sort of knew of Eva. I'd seen a couple of her beer adverts on posters down the pub and stuff. But Stephie? I didn't know Stephie. I don't watch TV anymore. I don't have social media. The first time I knew she was 'somebody' more than just this Instagrammer or whatever was when the papers started reporting on her death. I thought it would be pretty cool to get up close with them though because they were fucking gorgeous, both of them. But you know that, right? I know you're not gay because I've done surveillance on your wife and kids, Jake... I don't know about you, pal. But you don't give off that vibe... So you're not blind and dead below – you know those women are like flat-out hot, yeah?*

*I think Jason was getting worried about me even at that point though because he put me on door duty. That's a shit house of a job... The other guys will probably say that they think the perimeter is the shit job, but I prefer that... This is just patting down and checking every rich bastard and teenage-looking tart being shipped in through the gates in chauffeur driven vehicles. Mick had a strict rule regarding no phones and no electronic devices of any kind and door duty involved searching everyone stepping through and confiscating anything for the night that I found.*

*Mick always had these stupid fucking passwords too. They were always some foreign version of the word 'touch'... Every party a different pronunciation to try and battle with. Anyone who didn't know the password or hadn't learnt how to pronounce it right, off the fuck they went back out the door!*

*Stephie arrived with this Eva girl and I was blown away. Have you seen her in the flesh? Stephie? Have you see... I mean before she, you know, died? Did you ever see her for real? Oh my God, she was magnificent. She really was. She was polite with me and all that whilst I give her a pat down and checked her bag and... Well I didn't know about this stupid compartment thing, did I? As far as I was concerned she opened her bag, I had a look in. There was nothing there to get fretting about. I didn't know she'd made this thing to be a camera bag or whatever you call it and I just..."*

[SILENCE]

*"... I apparently missed it. I didn't see she had the phone. I certainly didn't know she could film through the bag and...*

*The party that night was messy. Messy like... nasty, you know? Really nasty. Possibly one of the "nastier ones" we've done. There was some pretty fucked up things going on with sex aids, some of the girls were crying, people weren't going off into rooms any more like usual and instead just openly fucking and groping in groups.*

*I didn't like it at all. I made the decision there and then that I was done and this was my last job with Jason and the lads. I started to have a wander away from the door once the party got under way and I could see for myself that these were young girls. These weren't just young-looking lasses. They were clearly underage, right? ... And then the next thing I know, maybe an hour or two hours in, my radio piece goes buzz and I get told I'm needed upstairs - Mick's going mental because other guests reckon one of the girls has got a camera in her bag and she's been filming guests and what they're doing...*

*... I get up there and I've got Mick, half-dressed, kicking off and demanding to know who I did and did not search and I kept saying 'I searched everyone! There was no one I didn't search!' but he wasn't having it. He takes me to this room and when he opens the door he's got Stephie Jay in there and he starts asking her about whether she's got a camera in her bag and all sorts of shit about filming guests. She starts saying she doesn't have a camera and that she was searched by me at the door anyway. Mick demands she hand her bag over. She's refusing. Mick goes for the bag, she fends him off. He's now looking at me like I need to get involved and I'm thinking 'I'm not laying a fucking hand on her pal, sorry'! ... I knew we were in real trouble because my worst suspicions got confirmed there and then: This Stephie girl starts saying she knows the guests are underage because she knows their parents and she names some of them as being only <u>fourteen</u>. She starts talking about getting the police involved and Mick goes up like a rocket, screaming and shouting at her and then he brings in this bloke, Graham.*

*... You know Graham, right? Hadenbury? He's the big top dog of the police! The fucking police, yeah? They're all at it. He's right in the thick of all of this debauchery downstairs. I didn't even know who he was or how important he was or anything until much later. But he comes walking into the room and he identifies himself as a copper and starts telling her he thinks she's on coke or something so he's going to do a drug's search of her but... give the girl her due... she didn't back down and it all boots off!*

*Graham smacks her in the face, right? And then he clearly thinks better of it because the next thing you know he's saying Mick needs to call Jason and the rest of them in to deal with this. Mick's screaming at me but I'm starting to get my headaches and flashes here because I thought they were expecting me to murder her or get really hands on with her and I couldn't...*

*... I close my eyes at night and I think a lot about the expression on her face in that room. Her eyes looked terrified. She was shaking. I think about whether I assisted in making her feel that scared and it makes me feel physically sick... She was petrified but she just wasn't backing down. So Mick makes us go outside and he locks her in the room and him and Graham start totally tearing me a new arsehole, one of them is screaming for me to get Jason upstairs now and the other one is telling me that if a phone is found on Stephie then they're going to make sure I end up face down dead in a ditch or something... I do what I'm told and Jason and Kelsey come barging up the stairs. Graham starts giving them a sit-rep and Mick is shouting that it's the 'reality TV slag everyone demanded got brought along' that is behind the door and has caused all this trouble... Mick is shovelling the coke into his nose now, by the way. And he's going <u>mental</u>... Jason and Kelsey start kicking away at the door because even after its been unlocked, it still isn't opening... They kick away and every kick is pissing Mick off more and more and he's starting to tell anyone who will listen about how expensive his door is and Graham is telling him to shut the fuck up... Guests are starting to stop what they're doing and come together on the stairs to have a gawp. You know, like you do when you're passing a car crash?*

*Kelsey gets the door open, yeah? Low and behold she's not there. We all dash towards the window and the fucker has only jumped out the window and is making a run for her car... Mick is going purple now. He's telling everyone she can't get out because the security gate is locked but it very clearly wasn't, was it? Because the next thing Stephie is bloody loose, mate. She's somehow got her car straight through his gates and she's off...*

*Mick is screaming at us to go after her! The Graham guy tells us to take his car and gives Jason the keys... He says it's got a police bar on the dashboard... We're all scarpering to get downstairs and outside and Mick is now chasing after us and saying we have to get her and get her phone because if there's been a single second put out there by her anywhere from that night then he was going to have us killed... And before you know it me, Jason and Kelsey are tearing off into the night after this girl and Ernie's staying back with Graham and Mick...*

*... And all of a sudden this two grand for a shift isn't looking too fucking sweet anymore because you realise it's a paedophile's dirty money and now we're off hunting down this scared young lass and God only knows what we're going to be expected to do to her when we catch up with her.*

*I'm sick with worry and Kelsey's driving like a madman... and Jason is screaming at me, calling me a fuck-up and saying that he was going to be having serious words with me about my future with his company when this was all done... Like I give a shit by that point anyway, right? He tells me if it turns out there's a phone then he's going to hurt me bad... and we're spinning hard on proper, darkly lit, country roads now and I think we're going to have an overturn and end up on the roof or something.*

*Then Kelsey starts screaming she's up ahead. And I'm praying it's not her. I swear to God, I'm praying it's not her but Kelsey says it's her, Jason confirms it and I lean forward from the backseat and can see the closer that we gain that it is her car... They put the police bar on with the flick of a switch and the bonnet on this car lights up in blue... and... and...*

*... And the poor bitch pulls over.*

*She fucking pulls over. She's just done over the bloody top man in the whole of the police and she still pulls over. I don't know what she was thinking, really.*

*... She pulled over and... and..."*

[SILENCE]

*"Ahhh, fuck man. This isn't easy... You're going to have to bear with me, okay? ... I've never re-lived any of this out loud. It's just been in my head constantly... going round and round... I've never said it properly out loud so just... let me try and get this right...*

*... I keep saying to myself if she'd just not pulled over then she'd still be alive but I don't think that's true, really. We'd have probably ran her off the road or something. And do you want to know something? If we'd done that then none of us would be here now. We wouldn't. That's just the straight-up truth... They'd have looked at the road she was driving on at that time of night and her car upside down in the ditch and they'd have said 'Oh, it was a straight-up RTC! Poor tragic Stephie!' and no one would have asked a single question. I'm serious... We should have ran her off the road. I said that over and over but what's that worth after the fact, right? Graham told us it was far harder to cover up with the Highways Agency as he didn't have that much reach and control over them like he does his own 'boys'... I'm not convinced, you know? I mean, the guy was shutting all sorts of shit down in the end. That man has some serious power. And added alongside Mick and his influence? Fucking hell, right?*

*So we've got her pulled over on the side of this shitty country road and... we... we sat on her for ages. I don't know whether they were doing that intentionally to make it look like they were running vehicle checks or whatever like real police do but, yeah, no one pounced on her straight away... But...*

*... But... then... Jason got out the car and he walked towards her and I thought he was just going to pull the driver's door open and demand her bag or start pulling her car apart looking for a phone, but he just goes round to the passenger side and climbs inside. We heard her shock from where we were in our car. That's how messed up this was getting.*

*And... And... I'm sitting in this car with Kelsey who, I don't know that well other than the jobs we do at Black Box... we're not socialising with each outside of work, you know? And I'm begging him to tell me what's going on? He's sitting totally stone-faced and I'm repeatedly shouting 'What's the game plan here, Geoff?' but he just keeps saying that none of this would be necessary if I'd searched her properly. And I'm not going to lie to you guys, I'm starting to really get uncomfortable now... I mean, I was uncomfortable with the kids and the sex and all that... but now this was starting to really feel... feel...*

*... It started to feel dangerous, right? I can see the silhouette of Stephie and Jason sitting in the front of her car and I'm getting really scared that this isn't just going to end with him getting out of the car clutching her phone and her driving off home after a stern talking to from Jason about invading people's privacy or something... So I'm shouting back at Kelsey 'What's necessary? What is this? What are we doing here? We're snatching her phone right? That's all this is? Tell me that's all this is?'*

*Then the next thing... The next thing we see is some commotion in the front of Stephie's car, Jason's just lunged across suddenly and the car's jerked like a one thrust fuck has taken place inside of it... and Jason gets out.*

*As soon as he gets out, her body fell from view and I knew she was dead."*

[SILENCE]

*"Jason moved her body over to the passenger seat and I watched him walk round to the back of the car and make a phone call. Whilst he was on the phone he did a signal to Kelsey and Kelsey cut off the police lights... That's what kind of screwed with my head even more. Just how cold and clinical Jason was being. He was so matter of fact, you know? Like 'Yeah, we've got to get this bag of rubbish moved from A to B so let's just do this, this and that'!*

*He came over to our car and Kelsey winds the window down. Jason just coolly says 'Mr Hadenbury is arranging for us to offload the package and he says he'll meet us there. He held out his hand and there was some pen scrawled on it with a post-code and a name. Kelsey typed it into the sat-nav and Jason said to follow him but to make sure speeds were maintained all the way and to not draw suspicion...*

*... I'm starting to scream inside and it just bubbles out of me and I start shouting 'Package? What package? The fucking girl? We're calling her a package? What did you do to her? What did you do?' but Jason just walks off, gets in Stephie's car and drives away.*

*We drive in total silence... For about an hour. We go south of the river and drive at a crawl into an industrial estate. Jason's already parked her car up and he's prizing the door open on this old warehouse right up in the top corner out of sight of most things.*

*We get out and meet him and he just turns and punches me square in the face. He knocks me straight on my arse and then drops an iPhone in my lap. He tells me that this was in her bag in a compartment I should've checked and he tells me if there's a single piece of footage from that night on her phone then he was going to shoot me dead.*

*Then he tells me that Graham and Ernie are on their way down to meet with us and Graham was going to walk us through everything but we had to get ready for the set-up. Jason says I had to get up and help with the body and I just lost my shit, I started screaming 'The body? Her body? So, what? She's dead now? What the fuck?'*

*... And Jason just starts punching me, man. Like pounding. He's on top of me and he's just smashing his fists into the sides of my head and he's not screaming or shouting or anything. He's just slamming me over and over until...*

*... He just stops, right? He just got up, smoothed himself off and says that he took the necessary action to protect the team. That's the words he used... 'Necessary action'... Because that's what we do, apparently. That's the sort of people we are. Jason says it's how we're trained. It's built into how we breathe... And Jason reaches down and pulls me up onto my feet. He looks me square in the eye and he says 'There's been a problem presented. I've delivered the solution. Not one of us would've got paid if this woman had gotten loose tonight and put our clients at risk!' and I start screaming 'Paid? This isn't about being paid!' but Jason kicks me in the stomach and knocks the wind right out of me.*

*... I'm on all fours and Jason just grabs me, drags me off towards the warehouse and throws me through the door he's pulled open. I'm on my fucking face, in the dark, trying to get my bearings and then all of a sudden him and Kelsey come walking in after me... and they're... they're... they're...her in and her hair is all mushed up over her face now so I couldn't see her expression or anything... but I remember her dress was all pulled up and out of position from being dragged out of the car and there were parts of her knickers that were exposed. I didn't like that...*

*I thought about the lack of dignity and I tried... I reached out to adjust it and... Kelsey kicked out at my hand. He told me I had to shake it off and get my shit together but... they propped her up against a wall and her hair fell away and I saw her face for the first..."*

[SILENCE]

*"... for the... first... Her make-up was smeared around her eyes which is what drew my attention to them. There was no life in them at all but they also looked in pain... Does that even make sense? Her lips were blue as fuck though. I do remember* <u>*that*</u> *and...*

*... And I can't do that bit, man. You're going to have to give me a free pass there, okay? I can't do this... They told me that we were going to make it look like a suicide and Graham was going to come along and oversee it all. I just about got to my feet and I said that we didn't have to kill her... That was when Jason said that this was the instruction he was given by Mick. He said that was what they had to do to keep Mick onside because he was not someone to make an enemy of.*

*... Mick ordered her dead. I want to make that clear, okay? I was told at the scene that Jason killed her because Mick Hetherington demanded that it happen... Kelsey asked how Jason did it and he said that he'd crushed her throat with two blows. He started talking about how he was out of shape because he used to be able to do it in one and I started to retch... They both started telling me that I had to get out of the warehouse if I was going to throw up because of contamination... and they started calling me a pussy and all sorts of bullshit.*

*Graham turns up with Ernie, okay? And he took control of everything. He hands us plastic gloves. He starts ordering Ernie to go wipe down Stephie's car. He puts Kelsey to use rigging up this electrical cord that was half hanging down from the rafters. And he sends me over to bring down one of the barrels and make it look as if that's what she's stood on to jump from. Jason then gets the body prepped and works on the noose and...*

*... And then they hung Stephie's body.*

*And...*

*And...*

*Graham says that the neck markings from the ligature won't work unless there's forcible pressure so he tells Jason and Kelsey to lift her body up above their heads and let it drop so her neck gets some bruising and...*

*... And they fucking do it, man... They're fucking around with her corpse like... she's just... nothing, you know? Then when they're done Graham gets us all in a huddle and asks for the phone. Jason tells him that he's already used her fingerprint to unlock it and switch off the security settings so it's open. He says he's checked it but it's clean of anything suspicious and there's nothing from tonight stored on it...*

*I said 'So she died for nothing?'*

*They all just stared at me... Jason looked like he was going to knock me out cold, I swear to God. But then Graham says 'She died because she was just another victim of unrealistic expectations of fame. That's all. That's everything. She's one of thousands. The fear of being ordinary got to her. That's her story.' ... I remember that. I remember that word for word because I knew that he'd been practising the shit out of that all the way down to where we were and I realised that everything this poor lass had accomplished was going to be undone in a heartbeat by this total lie that was going to be landed on her... And everyone starts nodding but I wouldn't confirm shit. I would not say yes to that being this girl's story."*

[SILENCE]

*"We had a debrief back at Mick's place. He'd kicked out the guests, closed up shop and had us all back there. He was going completely mental. He kept saying how humiliated he'd been by guests leaving and demanding to know if there'd been a 'breach' and that this had never, ever happened before. He said that this could have ruined the whole 'club'... that no one would ever want to re-attend if there was no trust... He asked us over and over again if we'd checked the phone and we were sure it was clean. Even Graham was saying he'd checked it over himself and it didn't have anything on it from this evening. So Mick turns on me, yeah? He's screaming in my face and telling me that Stephie had to die because of me and because I don't know how to check a bag properly and...*

*... I don't know. Maybe he's right? The other guys seem to think that – I fucked up so she had to die. And now that's sitting on me. It sits on my chest and I can't breathe. Because if that's true, then everything that came next is on me too...*

*... Mick's shouting left, right and centre and asking for absolute assurances that this has been covered up and that the scene is believable and Graham is just cold as ice, right? He's saying it doesn't matter because he will make sure it is visited, ticked off and that it all goes away. He says it's going to be a lot easier to push reports around and control the noise for something like this then if we'd forced a crash and had her crunched into a tree or something. He then starts going off about independent crash investigators and all this shit and I can promise you that no one was giving one single fuck at that point about any of that shit.*

*Jason says that the next step is to clean up any ties that show Stephie had visited Mick's party that night but Mick says the only real tie would be her agent and the other model unless she'd told others. He said he was going to speak to the other model and that Sue would be sweet as a nut because they have an arrangement. Kelsey then spent some time going through all her messages and social media apps to see who she'd been communicating with and he said there was no mention of this party to anyone by her, she'd not live streamed anything...*

*They talked like... like... it was nothing. Like it was a bench that just needed wiped clean? Nothing added up and no one seemed to be bothered by that because they just said they'd make it go away... They paid the Eva girl a wodge of money, Sue played the game, Graham used his coppers to do what he needed them to do and the coroners jumped on board... and... and... it all just went away exactly like they said it would!*

*And then you went and took a fucked up situation and added an extra layer of fuck to it, didn't you? You and Eva! ... We were done and away and I was clear of all of this. I didn't take any more jobs with Black Box, Jason didn't want me back either so it worked out fine... and then Mick drags us all back up to Newcastle on a bloody 'clear up'. He says that if we didn't get up here and sort out what should never have happened in the first place then he was going to stitch us up... I said no to coming. Jason was fine with that but then Mick got under his skin, apparently. Mick thought it was suspicious that I wasn't seeing this through and he became convinced that I was going to break. So he demanded the whole band got back together or something. The others said they were going to hang me out to dry and throw this all on me if I didn't come so...*

*... Yeah, basically... I got in the car, came to Newcastle and found that Eva's been pushing Mick for more money to stay silent on what happened to her at his party... and then she wants more money to shut up about Stephie and...*

*... Kelsey visited her at her flat the first bloody night we were back in the city. Talk about not wasting any time, right? He took care of her and made it look like a suicide. Because that's clearly the trend now isn't it? Not a clusterfuck like the Stephie Jay thing though. He did a clean job on her. But... yeah, if you want to be keeping count on this... Mick ordered her to die too!*

*And if Mick wants to deny this, I've got recordings that say otherwise. I've got more recordings then any of these cunts realise, you know? Because I smelt this from a mile off. I could see they were going to scrape the shit off the fan and fling it back at me. So I started my phone going on everything... I've got Mick talking in the debrief, I've got Jason and the rest of the team, I've got Graham talking about what he'll do to cover it up...*

*... I've got Mick Hetherington specifically ordering the death of Eva and saying the words 'Make it look better than you did with Stephie!' ... I mean, come on, I might be a fuck-up, right? But when the fuck-up does a number on you, what does that make you Mick? For a guy so incredibly paranoid about having been recorded by Stephie Jay at one of his parties he was surprisingly bloody clueless to the fact he was being recorded by me at every other possible opportunity. Figure that one out, huh?*

*So… yeah… Kelsey did Eva and me and Ernie got put on your trail to look into you and what you were up to. And we dug up shit loads. We thought you were a total nobody, no offence. I honestly thought the quick word in the car park would be enough because you're daft but you don't seem thick, you know? … But no, you kept screwing around and asking questions so Jason said we needed to put you down. Then that went tits up, didn't it? So Mick tells us we've got to mess with your family a bit. I wanted no part in this and the more I made that clear the more they pushed me and Ernie front and centre… One minute we're photographing your wife and sons and planning to give them a scare and what not and the next they seemed to just 'disappear into the wind' and then you two started proving hard to get a hold of and none of us could get sight of you at all at one point.*

*… And that really, really pissed Mick off. He wanted Graham to start putting resources on you but Graham kept pulling back and telling Mick not to overreact. Mick then throws a whole ton of money at this and says enough's enough – He wants you two gone, he wants his ties severed with Sue and for her to be silenced and he wanted Stephie's parents put down and made to look like a murder-suicide… We thought he was fucking crazy, but the money kept going up and up and the threats started building – 'You do this or I'm going to make this look bad for you!' He didn't know that I had the recordings I did but the problem was I didn't know what the fuck to do with them, you know?*

*And here we are… The last run of it all. Jason says tonight we sort you and Sue out and on Christmas morning we go and sort out the girl's parents and…*

*… Ernie and Jason are out looking to lock Sue down now. I got put on you. Kelsey's up with Mick, finalising a couple of things, I think. But tonight it ends… You're going to shoot your pal here and then I've got to frame it so it looks like you shot yourself afterwards.*

*But…*

*But…*

*Well…*

*… Let's say it's your lucky day, right? The both of you have won the lottery, yeah?"*

[SILENCE]

*"You know in the army they train you for all sorts, you're conditioned to be able to survive when confronted with anything really. But they don't tell you about the night terrors. And they certainly don't tell you how to cope with them… They don't tell you that there's a price to pay for taking a life and that it's on you like an extra layer of skin. That you… you know… that you <u>wear</u> that bastard!*

*And it weighs a ton, you know? And it adds an ache to your body you didn't think possible. The ache doesn't go. You can lie in bed at night and be perfectly straight and still and you will still ache. It's like someone is taking a fucking hacksaw to your bones and carving off bits of it at a time… You can close your eyes, you can pump the pills down your throat but the bodies still rise up and come calling on you…*

*... They don't tell you any of this. They teach you how to kill, they condition you to wash that shit off and they desensitise you into believing that killing can become as secondary to you as breathing and walking... But it catches the fuck up with you, man. It does. And now look at me ... Look at me!*

*... If you blokes have killed anyone you'll know the 'look', right? You'll have seen that. That look a person gets in the eyes when you take their life. People don't talk enough about that 'look'... Films and shit never properly represent it... It's like this sudden snap of shock as you just 'click' them off!*

*It... It... stays with you, man... Every... Every single one of those 'looks' stays right with you. I can close my eyes now and I can see the look from every single person who's life I took. And I can see Stephie's eyes when the hair fell away from her face and... and..."*

[Chris leant forward and pulled a second gun from the back of his waistband whilst still holding the first one in his hand. He put the second gun on the table in front of him.]

*"This is for you... I'm going to keep a hold of this one, but this one is for you. You've come too far now. You've got to stop them. Time for you to step the fuck up and put an end to all of this... I've given you everything you didn't have.*

*You have my confession...*

*My phone is in my inside jacket pocket just here. Everything you need is on there. The passcode is 1948. That's one, nine, four, eight, yeah? Write that down, okay? ... You? There's a pen and paper just next to you. Write that shit down, please.*

*Okay...*

*Okay...*

*Come on, now... Come on...*

*Look, I helped murder that Stephie girl.*

*I did.*

*I might not have been the one to smash her windpipe in. I might not have hung her corpse. You can give me all the technical mumbo jumbo bullshit all you like. But I didn't do enough to save her... I froze in Mick's house and I've lied and lied and lied ever since... I did stuff I didn't want to do and I then did stuff to cover up the stuff I didn't want to do and.... I just look in the mirror now and the only thing that I see staring back at me is a demon. I mean that. I've lied and done things that are... evil... and I never wanted to be evil. I don't want to be evil, you know? But the more lies and stuff I've done, the more I guess I denied Stephie's parents the truth...*

*... And... and... I want her mum and dad to know I'm sorry. I want them to know that Geoff Kelsey and Ernie Royce are as guilty as I am in helping hunt her down for Jason Grant to kill.*

*Stephie was killed to hide what goes on at the home of Mick Hetherington.*

*Jason did it because Mick told him to.*

*I'm sorry.*

*I'm so sorry.*

*... Those... children, man... That's what they were...*

*They were...*

*They were* <u>*kids*</u> *at the end of the day. Stephie tried to do something. She died for trying to do something.*

*I'm so sorry.*

*Mum? ... I'm* <u>*so*</u> *fucking sorry..."*

## [26]

## or

## "Lehman's Terms..."

Chris – the man I'd previously nicknamed Murdock - raised the gun away from Psychic and I. He placed it inside of his mouth and, in one clear decisive action, pulled the trigger and blew the back of his head out.

Psychic rocked back off his feet in shock and landed unsteadily against the wall. The gun-burst audibly wracked the room and my head felt like it had been slammed between two bricks. I grabbed my ears and pushed hard on my temple as if I was squeezing away the pain but it didn't change anything, I staggered forward and fell to the ground.

Psychic must have thought I'd been shot. He rushed to my side and pulled me back to my feet. "Jake? Jake?" he said in shock.

"I'm okay. I'm okay. I just got a bit knocked by the gun fire, that's all."

Psychic looked over to Chris' corpse and his eyes moved up and down, surveying the spread of brain matter mushed into the wall; the thick, almost black strands of blood splatter that had been sprayed up the wall was now slowly dripping and falling back down to join the congealed pool of blood now massed on the floor beneath Chris' seat. A gentle stream of blood trailed out of the head wound and down the back onto the carpet. A steadier stream dripped from his mouth where a small funnel of gun smoke dissipated in the air, leaving a pungent aroma behind that would soon be followed by a worsening stench.

I stepped over to the tripod and camcorder that we'd been instructed at gun point to pull from the cupboard and set away to record. I pushed down on the button needed to stop the recording and let out a big pained sigh.

The headache, twitching and non-stop sweating that came from the opioid withdrawals was one thing. But the trauma of what just happened and the smell of death mixed with gun powder was tipping me over the edge considerably now. I pushed to steady myself once more and placed both hands down on the corner of the desk. I could feel the vomit rising.

Psychic suddenly placed his hand over his own mouth and steadied his breath.

"You've been around gun shots that one time, right?" he said.

I didn't answer.

Because I don't talk about that whole Australia 'thing', remember?

He carried on regardless as if I had answered affirmatively.

"Do they… you know… always smell like this because that's…"

He interrupted himself by vomiting all over his own feet. Almost immediately, he steadied himself, wiped his mouth and burst into a full recovered action.

"You know what?" he said, sternly. "Fuck this guy! No, look, I'm sorry but *fuck* him! I listened to every word of what he said and I'm really pleased that he's said it and he's given us the leads he has but that guy has been sitting on all of this and he's had all those recordings and I just don't think it's as easy as saying 'I didn't know what to do with them!' … He's done nothing whilst recounting all that to us other than say 'I knew this was wrong, I knew that was wrong and I wanted nothing more to do with it'… but he kept on keeping a hand in with it all, didn't he?"

"How many times do you have to go to a paedophile sex party before you realise you're at a paedophile sex party, right?" I replied softly whilst never taking my eyes off Chris' body.

"*Exactly*!" spat Psychic. "The guy is a fucking hypocrite! He talks on that tape about money, right? Anyone can be bought and all that? He knew from the outset that this Black Box thing was… well… He knew what their deal was and he rode it all the way to where it ended up: Murdering people for money! So fuck him. I'm sorry but fuck him!"

I nodded. "I'm not disagreeing with you, Psychic."

I took a step closer along the desk to where Chris' second gun had been placed.

I ran my fingers over my stubble and wiped the sweat from my brow whilst silently studying the gun where it lay. Psychic stared down hard into the side of my head, urging for me to turn and meet his gaze.

I didn't.

I just kept looking at the gun.

"You've got to copy the memory card in that camera, take his phone and get back to Emily as quickly as possible. We don't have a lot of time. As soon as you've left and you're clear of here, I need you to ring this in with the police. For what it'll be worth… Leave the original memory card inside the camera though, okay?" I said quietly, whilst never changing my line of sight.

"What are you going to do Jake?"

"I'm going to go get Sue before *they* get Sue and I'm going to do what I can to convince her it's better to come with me than to die with them."

"Jake…" Psychic said softly whilst taking a step towards me.

My eyes still hadn't left the gun in front of me.

I am no expert in firearms to say the least but I don't think you *need* to be in order to recognise a 'hand-around', illegal fire arm that was likely to have been bought off the Dark Web for fifty quid or something. I was close enough now to see its branding - a Browning 9mm – and that, from the wear-and-tear on it, it was a very old edition. It had clearly done the rounds and the filings beneath the ridge of the barrel and the various tapings and sanding marks on the handle backed up this assumption.

I rubbed my stubble once more and rolled my fingers all the way up to my temple where I gentle caressed the pained spots on my head.

"I've got to find a way to get her to confirm who the kids are in that video…" I said. "I've got to get to them and their parents and get them the help that they…" My voice trailed off as I realised that I had inadvertently kept stepping and moving until I was now directly stood towering over the gun itself, looking down on it.

"Jake… Jake…" Psychic said quietly, whilst stood alongside me. "Don't... If you pick up that gun you don't come back from that. I mean it. You lose the kids. You lose Jane. You become just another murderer… But those bastards will disappear into the night with Graham's help when you fail to get them. And you *will*, because… well there's three of them plus Graham's entire army who just happen to be a police force! And on top of that you're, for want of a better term, falling apart… You'll either die trying to put them down or get sent down for doing so. Let's just…"

He stopped at the sound of my breathing getting heavier. I still couldn't look away from it. "I've got to find a way to get her to confirm who the kids are in that video…" I reiterated. "I know if I can just get to her before they do and get her to come onside then she can state what she kno…"

Psychic slammed his hand down hard on the table, shocking me and forcing me to look away from the gun for the first time. "State what she knows to *who*?" he shouted. "The local authority is buggered because the head of it is the head of this whole shit show. And the pervert who heads up the police was 'doing' young girls right alongside him. So tell me, honestly. Who are we going to put Sue in the safe hands of? We don't even know if Emily has got this Chief Constable Lane onside yet!"

I nodded and sighed. "You're right… You're right, Psych'! But I'm *tired*, man."

Psychic stepped forward as my balance faltered but I held steady.

"I'm tired. I'm so *tired*. I'm tired of fighting to put a pound in my pocket to take home to Jane and the kids. I'm tired of coming up against scumbags or watching corrupt and evil people abuse power to escape justice… You know that guy said he looks in the mirror and he sees a demon staring back? Remember that?"

Psychic didn't gesture either way. He simply stared in silence.

"I *get* that. I do. I struggle to actually look in the mirror at myself these days and when I do I don't recognise the face staring back. I really don't. I'm not talking about the bags under my eyes or the wrinkles or, before you say it, all the shit the Tramadol has done to me. I'm talking about the man I am…. I'm just angry all the time; full of hate at how my life has turned out… This isn't a life. It's an existence. It's just… *enduring*!"

Psychic gently placed his hand on my shoulder and tried to lead me away from the desk. I softly and respectfully brushed it away and smiled at him instead.

"You, Jane, her parents…" I continued. "You all keep saying I'm a good investigator but I'm just a mess of a person. Well you're right about me being a mess. I replaced nicotine with alcohol and replaced that with fucking painkillers. I've spat in the face of everyone who's loved me. And how *good* an investigator can I really be because I think this guy is right…"

I pointed in the direction of Chris' corpse without ever looking over at it.

"… I don't think we would have got what's staring us in the face right now unless this bastard had walked in here and handed it to us before blowing his head open!"

"I'm sorry Jake, I don't think I agree with that." Psychic replied. "I think we were on their trail and we just hadn't tied all the pieces together quite as tightly as we needed. But we would have got there. We're only two weeks into this for Christ's sake. Look what we got in two weeks…"

I sighed and shook my head. "Mick Hetherington was at the head of this whole thing all along and we were never *once* close to landing on that fact until this guy hands it to us in one big Bond villain style exposition dump and hands us a phone full of incriminating recordings – which you need to check, by the way!"

"Bullshit! Absolute bullshit!" Psychic shot back, angrily. "This half-a-head prick right here didn't chase down Alia Marcus and hand her to us. He didn't gift us the voicemail and the clue about the map and the car, did he? We did that! We found the SD card in the sat-nav. The *police* didn't spot that. This dickhead and his women-killing pals didn't. We did though. We got all that. We didn't need bloody Goldfinger here or whichever Bond villain you were riffing on to guide us there. We got there, we got that footage, we got the sat-nav address that leads you to Mick Hetherington's address on the night she died. We got *all* that… so no, this guy didn't hand us nothing but confirmations of the route we were already walking!"

I refocused my attention fully back on the gun.

"Hetherington took away my career. He took away my pride and then didn't even skip a beat in going back to abusing youngsters." I said whilst staring at the gun again. "In fact - and this is what really, really hurts me hard - he didn't even skip a beat in turning it into a private function he held at his home for whoever was rich enough, discreet enough and fucked up enough to attend… I've got to take Hetherington down once and for all. I've *got* to, Psychic. Because if I don't I'll not be able to live with myself knowing the man is out there continuing to hold these sort of parties and do these things to kids and…"

I trailed off as Psychic slowly started to nod his head.

"*Kids*, man." I whispered. "He's got access to some of the most vulnerable, orphaned and unprotected kids in the city. He's got a modelling agent sending him her best looking minors. Come on? He's *got* to be stopped! But not only that…"

Tears welled up in my eyes and I turned away from the gun and looked at Psychic properly. "If I'm ever going to be able to look Margaret and Matthew in the eyes again… even with the existence of Chris' confession… I've got to know I've done absolute right by them for what Stephie went through… and if I don't do what we both know is the right thing here and now tonight then those three will disappear, we'll most certainly get clipped when we're least expecting it and Mick will see in the New Year for another round of child rape and… and… No one will ever see a day behind bars because Graham will never let it get to court!"

"So we murder the murderers and the paedophiles and the… is that what we've become now?" Psychic said.

I turned and perched myself on the edge of the desk.

"Do you know who Sir Norman Bettison is?" I asked.

"Aww come on now, Jake… There's a dead body in the corner of the room with its brain falling out the hole in the back of its head. The smell is horrific and you're going off on one of your stupid bloody monologues? Was Emily's jaunty fucking history of the Vietnam War not enough? I can't cope any… Ok. No… *No*, I do not know who Sir Norman Bettison is. You tell me, whilst I vomit in this bin!"

"Remember the Hillsborough disaster? Fifteenth of April 1989, Liverpool versus Nottingham Forest at Sheffield's Hillsborough Stadium, yeah? You don't have to be a football fan for that thing to be etched into you from growing up in the eighties or early nineties, do you? Ninety-six dead and nearly eight-hundred injured…" I replied.

"I know the aftermath more than I know the incident." Psychic said.

"Bettison was the chief inspector who was put in charge of finding materials for police lawyers to present to the public enquiry in the aftermath of the disaster. It was alleged that he used his position to help cover up the truth and scapegoat the ninety-six people who died that day... And whichever way you go regarding what he did or didn't do he was ultimately rewarded by being made chief fucking constable of Merseyside Police. How about that huh?"

Psychic slowly shook his head. "So he's another dirty pig of a cop. What's that got to do with what we're staring down here?"

"Decades and decades later when the truth about that day came out, it looked like Bettison would finally get what many thought was coming to him. But the charges were dropped. *Completely*. In response to getting away scott-free he said to the press *'No injustice was ever satisfactorily resolved through being unjust'*. He spat in the fucking face of every single person who lost a loved one at Hillsborough that day with that comment. That whole cover-up even decades on had become so corrupt everyone seems to have forgotten what just and unjust actually looks like! And that's what we're looking at here – this thing is so dirty that the people we need to turn to for help are the people we need to bring to justice and the victims are the…"

The words fell into silence as I slowly reached down and picked the gun up off the table. I slowly and gently wrapped my fingers around the handle and softly padded it back and forth within my loose grip.

I could feel Psychic's anxiety permeating around the room and marrying itself to the horrible, repugnant and fulsome smell of deep, coarse blood and dead flesh.

"Listen… Jake? Listen…" he said cautiously. "That was a good speech, man. It was. You used a solid analogy with the Bettison guy. That came out of nowhere, but I liked it. You really worked all the angles in terms of what you've got going on with your feelings and shit and I think there's some counselling that could work for you and maybe some anti-depressants or something like that. But you've not said *anything* here and now that justifies murder. And that's what's going to come from you walking out of here with that gun... You murdering them or them murdering you! I'm begging you, please. Don't do this?"

I shook my head. "There's no justice waiting for any of these people involved in Stephie Jay's death. They're going to kill their way clear of this. Eva Marie is evidence of that and by the end of tonight Sue George will be too. Tomorrow or the next day? Stephie's parents! And eventually me and you too! Who's to say they're not going to go after Jane and the boys as an extra measure? I'm sorry Psychic, no… If we don't do something now, like *right now*, not when the ink dries on the headlines or when the tokenistic call to order at court comes, but right *now* then justice will not come."

"Is that what you told yourself in Australia, Jake? Is that what you said to yourself in order to do what you did there? Because what you did out there nearly killed you. It fucking broke you. I talked to Jane about that period. She said it was amazing to her that you came back from that mentally at all… Tell me how this is different? Tell me, please? I'm begging you. Because right now it looks just like some really, really bad fuckers are about to get away with doing some really bad shit and you're going to step in between them and the exit and start a Gunfight At The OK Corral tribute show… *again*!"

"That's a really low blow, Psychic!" I said as the tears fell.

"No. It isn't. You just don't want to hear it. Tell me how this is different, go on."

"Because I don't have a choice now. I did then. I chose to walk into that town and do what I did. What happened there was because I chose to walk in there. This isn't a choice. It *isn't*. This is a situation where if I don't do what I know I have to do then many people are going to die. Including possibly my wife and kids. Most certainly you. I can't have that. I can't carry that on me. I carry too much and I can't carry anymore."

Psychic closed his eyes and breathed heavily, stemming the flow of his own tears.

I continued "You're saying if I walk out of here with this gun up I won't come back… I'm saying I'm okay with that as a consequence."

"I'm not." He replied.

I placed the gun in the waistband of my jeans, pulled my coat around it to cover it and turned to take hold of Psychic by the shoulders.

"We're two miles out from the finish line, Psychic. And I can't run the rest without you."

Psychic looked down at his feet and let out a heavy, guttural sigh. "Tell me how we run this all down with the most minimal chance of you taking a bullet or firing that gun?"

"Copy the card from the camcorder and the phone from his pocket, grab the memory stick with the voicemail on it, leave this place as it is and get to Emily's. Once you're there call the body in and start pulling and editing everything together with the utmost urgency. Push her to get this Jessica Lane woman on the phone or something. I'm going to go and get the both of you a guaranteed 'in' to Mick's event up at the civic centre and then I'm going to go and grab Sue. I'll get her to safety and then come meet you up there."

"That sounds so ridiculously simple." Psychic smiled.

"That's because it is." I grinned back. "We don't need to over complicate this otherwise it'll get in the way of us fulfilling our dream."

"What's our dream then?"

"We always talked about having a case where we get to do a 'Richard Kimble' on a bad dude, right? Well, they don't get any more bad than Mick Hetherington… and playing these clips in that room full of the city's movers and shakers could be an even greater achievement than what Harrison Ford did at the end of The Fugitive!"

"We're going to 'Richard Kimble' him?" Psychic's smile broadened.

"Oh yes!" I said. "You in?"

Psychic nodded. He extended his hand out to me. “Don’t get *dead*, okay?”

I concurred with a smirk whilst shaking his hand. “I always imagined the last words I ever said to you would be about me firing you for looking at porn on the work computer.”

“One – Don’t say things like that, right now! Two - There’s a thing called ‘Private Window’ on computer desktops now!” laughed Psychic.

I turned to leave and he pulled me into a deep hug.

“I’ll see you soon to see this through, *promise*?” he said.

“I’ll see you at the civic centre, I promise.” I replied.

“What time?”

“You’ll see me coming, don’t worry!” I said. “By the way, I need to borrow your pal’s Yugo!”

## [27]

## or

## "The Last Will And Testament Of Jake Lehman..."

There was a bracing and cutting coldness in the air as I stepped out of the back door of our office and made my way down the old metal fire exit stairs, each step a death trap in and of itself as ice was starting to settle over every stair. I pulled my coat tighter around me, yanked up the collar high and dug my hands deep into my pockets, pushing my elbows tight in against my ribs in a futile but overly optimistic gesture designed to keep my body heat as internalised as possible.

I passed across onto Pilgrim Street and headed back towards where Psychic had left the car in the old bus concourse behind what used to be my police station way back when. A rabbled air of chants and shouting filled up the air to my right and I turned to see a charge of a hundred or so people, clutching billboards and signs, walking up towards Northumberland Street.

They looked like they were the same campaigners that hit up Newcastle Council headquarters at Christmas last year, pointlessly attempting to shame the shameless by circling Mick Hetherington's big ego-stroking jamboree and screaming about how we can't afford to feed and house low income families yet somehow the local authority are hosting and paying for a thirty-thousand pound black-tie Christmas bash exclusively for the higher-ups and all their business contractors.

Last year the campaign led to a mini-riot outside of the council's civic centre and there were mass arrests. This year Hetherington was taking no chances and had laid on large scale private security. 'If his choice of security company in a professional capacity was anything like his choice of security company in his personal life then there'd be a lot of innocent people getting murdered tonight' I caught myself thinking.

I crossed the road quickly to avoid getting caught up in the crowds as they marched across the Tyne Bridge and headed up towards St Mary's Place. I spotted the pea green coloured 1987 Zastava Yugo 513 tucked away in the far corner of an old, abandoned car park just across from the World Headquarters nightclub on Carliol Square.

That place used to be a big nightclub of my youth. I remember going there with teenage friends at the height of the 'American college rock' wave of the late 1990s when they'd have 'rock' nights there and we'd drink watery beer, whilst hanging out in the corner – *never* dancing – and rolling our heads to the likes of The Goo Goo Dolls, Matchbox Twenty, the occasional bit of Hootie, Gin Blossoms and Toad The Wet Sprocket. We thought we were the coolest fuckers on the planet and the girls would gravitate to us.

*Spoiler Alert*: We weren't even close and they never did.

I tapered down my amazement that the pea green coloured 1987 Zastava Yugo 513 had been neither stolen or smashed to pieces by vandals by acknowledging it actually blended in with the wet, mouldy, mess of old brickwork and abandonment in which it had been parked so maybe it had camouflaged itself against attack.

The car took two attempts to turn over and then I was off shunting along like I had strapped myself into a storage trailer without any wheels and then got dragged along the central motorway at seventy miles per hour. The radio didn't seem to pick up any signal and I decided to not break the cardinal rule of attempting to change it to another, actually functioning station. Instead I drove in silence.

I'd texted Jimmy on the walk over to the car and asked him to get me a location for Bobby Maitland. I didn't lead in with that, obviously. I asked how Jane and the kids were doing and confirmed everything was okay first. I'm not an absolute *monster*, you know. I told him to let Jane know I would call her within the hour and that I needed to speak to her urgently. Jimmy let me know that Bobby would be overseeing his poker games at a bar in Byker, down by the Ouseburn.

So that's where I headed.

Time was not on my side, I was aware of that. I parked up outside of the bar, climbed out unsteadily and made my way over to the doors on legs that were getting heavier to lift, where another stereotypical bulldog of a man stood guarding the entrance. He went to step into my path and I pulled the gun from my waist and pointed it straight at him as I pushed my stride to appear as masculine as possible.

"Don't be the guy that gets killed tonight. You'll ruin every Christmas from now on for your family!" I smiled.

"I'm getting thirty quid for the night. Fuck this!" The bulldog on the door said as he put his hands up and immediately stepped aside.

I walked straight in through the entrance, sliding the gun back in my belt as I walked.

I walked up to the bar and through the jostle of all the patrons queuing for drinks I shouted "Is Bobby in?" at the staff behind the bar.

One young bar lady cupped her ear in my direction and I repeated the question. She nodded and pointed upstairs. I mouthed the word 'thanks' and headed for the door leading to the stairs.

At the top of the stairs there were two rooms, one with a card game in full flight that could be seen through a glass panel in the door and the other with no visibility through it but a familiar enough set of voices coming from the other side.

I pushed the latter open whilst pulling the gun from my waist once again and landed on Bobby sat behind a small desk and Ryan stood to his left counting money and sorting poker chips.

"Hi Bobby!" I said.

Bobby looked up. "Aw, what the fuck? What is it with you and barging in on me all the time with some… Wait. Is that a gun?"

"Don't panic, Bobby." I said with a smile, placing the gun down on the table in front of him. "I come in peace and in need of a favour."

"You brought a gun into one of my places and you talk about peace and me doing you a favour? You're stupider than you come across, lad." Bobby replied.

"And you come across really bloody stupid!" smirked Ryan.

I grabbed the gun back off the table and pointed it directly at Ryan. His smirk dropped instantly.

"I don't want *you* to say another word, is that clear?" I sneered at Ryan. "Because I'm looking for some target practise and you look like the perfect target to me!"

Ryan backed away from the table. I turned back to Bobby.

"If I was to tell you that before this night was over I could take down Mick Hetherington once and for all and I could have the Chief Constable of the police arrested and pulled from power, what would you say?" I said.

"I'd say you're making the sort of claim that's so silly a Christmas wish even Santa would laugh his beard off that you've suggested it!" Bobby replied with a furious expression.

"I have recordings… audio recordings, video recordings… and a dead body in my office that all back up the fact that Mick Hetherington runs a paedophile sex ring, Chief Constable Hadenbury was part of it and that Stephie Jay was witness to it and tried to expose it and was killed as a result."

Bobby started to laugh.

I turned the gun to point at him.

His laughter stopped.

"Knock Knock?" I said.

Bobby was not playing. Not at all.

"Knock Knock?" I repeated, tightening my grip on the gun.

"Who's there?" he replied cautiously.

"Europe!"

"Europe who?"

"No," I replied. "*You're* a poo!"

Bobby looked at me in confusion. Silence filled the air.

"If I wanted you to laugh, that's the joke I'd tell." I said. "This is *not* a joke. I am deadly serious. I have the evidence that there's a paedophile sex ring being ran and…"

"And how does this involve me exactly?" Bobby spat out at me.

"A few weeks back you told me that because of your clemency towards the Willis kid I owed you a favour. I'm returning that favour now…"

"You came in here telling me *you* needed the favour so how does this work exactly?"

"Well actually I need two favours from you to be able to return the favour I owe you. If that makes sense?" I smiled.

"Just about." Bobby snarled. "Go on…"

"If Mick Hetherington gets pulled from his position, his reign ends and that opens things up for you and your boys to do a bit better in this city without having to bow down to him or make the extortionate pay-offs he demands for you lot to get anywhere, right?"

Bobby murmured half a nod at best.

"I can guarantee that outcome for you tonight… and I can throw in the added bonus of destabilising the police hierarchy in the city too – which I can only imagine would shine a big spotlight on the boys in blue and take it off whatever things you like to get done without scrutiny."

"And what's these two things I've got to do in return?" Bobby said, suddenly leaning forward in his chair as his expression softened into one of partial interest.

"One," I said with a smile. "You've got to confirm if you have any contacts with whoever is running the security at Mick's little shindig up at the civic centre tonight and you've got to help my colleague get inside within the next couple of hours."

Bobby smiled back. "I could get that done, aye. Next?"

I span the gun in my hand so the handle now faced out towards Bobby and the barrel pointed back at myself. I opened my fingers up from around the grip so the gun was free to take.

"Two, I want you to show me how to use this properly please…"

I sat back down behind the driver's seat comfortable in the knowledge that Bobby would make the calls he promised and connect Psychic and Emily to the right people at the right time. I then grabbed a pen from my pocket and quickly wrote the words '1 in the chamber, 12 in the mag' on the back of my right hand so that I could clearly remember the advice Bobby had given me around the use of the gun and the number of bullets I had available with no ability to reload.

The first number I dialled was the one Psychic had given me for Holly, Sue George's receptionist and personal assistant. She answered within two rings.

"Hello?"

"Hi Holly? It's Jake Lehman…"

"Oh, hi." She said, suddenly quietening her voice down. "I can't really talk right now."

"Listen, I need your help. I urgently need to get a hold of Sue…"

"She's with me now." Holly whispered.

"What?" I said.

"We're up at the Metrocentre!"

I glanced quickly at my watch. It was after eight at night. The days of the Metrocentre having extended festive opening hours were long gone. They died out as the Metrocentre itself perished from the might of what it once was in the region into becoming just an enormous smorgasbord of pound shops, outlet stores and boarded up retail premises all under one roof. The big entertainment complex with the cinema and the restaurants was the first casualty of this economic collapse, the rest of the place followed at a slow drip.

"I thought the Metrocentre was closed?" I asked.

"It is, it's all locked up and everything but we're here setting up for the big annual charity thing tomorrow." Holly replied.

"Ok, listen…"

"No, wait. I have something to tell you…" Holly said.

"Hang on. Save it, I'm coming to you, tell me then. Sue is in danger. I can't get into it now but..."

"What do you mean 'danger'?" Holly interrupted.

"Holly, you've got to listen to me. You and Sue need to..."

"She's nearby, should I tell her? Do I need to call the police?"

"No, wait." I blurted. "Don't do anything. Don't call the police. The police can't be trusted right now. There's security there with you, I presume?"

"There's some guy... Like one guy? Bobbing around somewhere waiting for us to finish up but I don't know where he is or... Look, the signal is really terrible here. I can't really hear very well."

"Don't say anything to Sue, just keep her there. I'm on my way to you. Where are..."

You're breaking up..." Holly cut in.

"Where are you in the Metrocentre?"

"Did you ask where we are? We're in the Red Quadrant!" she replied, her voice breaking into static.

"Stay there. Keep Sue there. But stay there." I said.

"Are you saying stay here?" the static seemingly said.

"Stay there! I'm coming."

"How will you get in?" Holly said through the poor reception as I hung up too prematurely.

I immediately called her back because she raised a valid question that I hoped she could provide the answer to but the call did not connect through!

"Fuck!" I muttered.

I then scrolled down in the contacts list and let the list stop on Margaret Jason's number. I took a deep breath and kept the conversation going with myself.

"Don't pick up, Margaret!" I whispered. "Don't pick up!"

The phone rang once but then connected straight through to her voicemail. I breathed a sigh of relief and then drew a deep breath in just as the beep hit.

"Hi Margaret, it's Jake at Lehman's Terms." I said falteringly as I exhaled. "I want you to know your daughter didn't commit suicide... I know this with certainty now and you need to know this too. I want you to know you're not mad... You were right... Stephanie tried to do something good in a bad situation and she was murdered for it. And... I guess I was ringing to sort of get your permission to make them pay for what they did but..."

I took a pause, gathering the right words.

"... But the minute I pressed your number I realised that it's a given that these men need to pay for what they did to Stephanie... and... I promise you I'm going to do that. Tonight will bring about the closure you and Matthew need, I give you my word... We'll speak soon, yeah? Okay?... Okay!"

I killed the call and stared at the phone.

I don't know, maybe I should have wrote that down and worked a second or third draft through before making that call.

The car windows were starting to steam up at the same time that a frost cover was starting to form on the chassis and glass outside. I turned the engine on and put what passed for a heater on too. In doing so I caught a glimpse of me in the rear view mirror. I paused and held eye contact with myself for the first time in quite some time.

My eyes twitched with the pain and I let the cold sweat fall unwiped into my eyes. I blinked through the saltiness inside of the sweat drops but remained locked in a staring contest with my own reflection.

"Ok, Jake…" I said out loud to myself. "What are we doing?"

I flashbacked to a childhood where I was borderline neglected by my parents and raised essentially by my grandmother and grandfather instead. I remembered August 1991 and desperately wanting to see Joe Johnston's The Rocketeer when it was released. I remembered my grandparents telling me they didn't have the money to take me whilst it was still so expensive and that if I wanted to see it I had to wait until it moved out of the city centre cinemas and started showing at the old Playhouse cinema down by the coast, where tickets were only £2.50 each back then. I remembered stealing a ten pound note from my grandmother's purse and taking a metro ride to Manors to see it on the sly when my grandparents thought I was at the local weekend youth club I attended whenever I stayed with them, which was often. I remembered getting caught when the cinema ticket dropped out of my coat when I got back to their house. I remembered my grandfather apologising to my grandmother about "the missing tenner" and her looking at me with tears in my eyes and to this day I still remember the exact way in which she said *"Oh, Jakey!"* with such absolute sadness. I remembered my grandfather sending me to the room they had set up for me and telling me he'd talk to me later when he'd "calmed down". I remembered sitting alone up in that back bedroom for what felt like hours but was probably only twenty or thirty minutes, crying at the thought that I'd upset the people I loved so very much and willing myself to believe that it was 'worth it' because The Rocketeer *was* frickin' awesome but knowing deep down that it wasn't because *nothing* was worth hurting my grandparents. I remembered my grandfather coming to my room and talking to me for a long time in a very calm and measured way about honesty and integrity and being someone that a person can trust. I remembered him telling me about things he did when he was a boy that were dishonest and naughty and what he learnt from doing them. And I remembered him pushing a folded up piece of paper into my hand and telling me that this was what he was taught to learn and abide by from his father and he said it wouldn't do me any harm to do the same…

I have carried that piece of paper with me every day of my life since then. My wallets have changed. The contents have changed. But the one constant has been this one curled, yellowing, folded piece of paper with a minor piece of sellotaping in the middle where the fold has worn a slight tear in the consistency of the paper.

I reached into my pocket, took out my wallet and removed that piece of paper from its little fold at the back, behind the card slits. I slowly mouthed the words written in my dead grandfather's handwriting silently to myself despite knowing them off by heart anyway:

*'Do the right thing. And if you can't do the right thing, do the decent thing. Because normally the two are tied together anyway.'*

With the piece of paper held in one hand, I dialled Jane's 'clean' number with my other.

She answered immediately.

"Jake?"

"Yeah, it's me."

"Please tell me you're okay?"

"I'm okay. I'm good. Are you and the kids okay?"

"We're as good as we can be. How is this thing looking, Jake? Tell me honestly because the boys are starting to get really wound up at the thought of not doing their carol concert tomorrow morning and I just can't bring…"

"They can go!" I said as convincingly as possible.

"Really? What? Is this thing all done? Are you serious? Are you coming for us tonight?" Jane said as her voice picked up.

"Listen, no. There's still a fair bit more for me to do here to wrap things up but in terms of you and the boys, you just go to the carol concert okay? Make sure Jimmy drives you down and…"

"Do you really think that's wise if you've still got things to tie up?" she asked.

"Well, no. If I absolutely had my way I would say stay where you are. But I'm thinking of the best I can offer for the sake of the kids… How about this then, I'll text you in a couple of hours with absolute confirmation it's cool? If you don't hear from me in a couple of hours, don't go – Fair?"

"Yeah, okay! You're going to be there though, right? You're going to meet us there if we do go… Because you promised?" Jane replied.

I fell silent.

"Jake?" she said, filling the quiet. "Jake? I need you to be honest with me here?"

"Jane, look… There's a situation here that could get worse unless I take drastic action. I don't see anyone else out there that's going to step up. I don't see…"

"No, no, no." Jane shouted straight over the top of me. "No. I've heard this shit *before*. I picked you up off the floor every night when you came back from Australia, remember? I listened to you say shit like that every night in the darkness of our bedroom while towelling off your sweat. You haven't forgotten that, right?"

"You've got to listen to me now, Jane. I'm serious. Please, just listen." I said as I felt my throat lump up and my eyes well with tears. "These people have done really bad things… They've done bad things to children, for fucks sake… *Kids!* Some of them only a couple of years older than Jack. And Stephanie Jason died trying to expose this. Tonight, these people are going to do away with everyone else who is involved in some capacity or another. And I have to stop them."

"Jesus Jake, listen to yourself. Please. You're a father of two with a limp and a painkiller addiction…"

"I'm a full day *clean* actually!"

"Bloody hell, you must be jonesing off your tits right now?" gasped Jane. "So you're a father of two with a limp, withdrawal symptoms and a chip on your shoulder. And if you're the only one that can save the so-called fucking day then this must be a pretty dire situation that I don't want you anywhere near."

"Wow. Cheers baby!" I said, forcing a smile that she would never see.

"Jake, I'm not being cruel here for the fun of it. I'm trying to do the most urgent form of 'tough love' possible. Whatever this situation is, I don't want you in the thick of it. Any situation that has us having to abandon our home and flee into the night because…"

"Jane?"

She stopped and went silent at the sound of her name.

I took a second. "I bit the bullet all those years back on trying to live with the fact that 'you know who' was out there having done what he did to that girl back in the day. Remember?"

There was silence.

"Jane, you know who I'm talking about right?" I said gently.

"Yes." she replied, the sound of her voice breaking was noticeable even on that one word.

"I told you at the worst points of trying to get myself back up on my feet that the hardest thing was always wondering if he carried on doing it to other kids… younger kids… kids whose parents we know… And that I could have stopped him… and should have stopped him, you know?"

"Jake, you've…"

"Please," I said as the tears fell harder. "Please, let me finish. It's worse than you can possibly imagine, Jane. I'm talking actual sex parties where people pay to attend and do all sorts to young girls. Him and… high ranking police officers and business men and… Stephanie was murdered for trying to expose that this was happening."

"Jesus!" Jane whispered.

"This is the worst possible outcome for looking into Stephanie's death for her parents. To find that she died because of her dealings with a man I could have and should have stopped years ago…"

"What more could you possibly have done?"

"Oh come on," I said in shock. "I did *nothing*. I accepted my fate far too easily and then dropped myself head first into the first bottle of spirits I could get my hands on. I did nothing in comparison to everything I could've done. And I have to make up for that now... I *have* to."

I fell silent once more and sat back to wipe the tears away from my eyes. Eventually Jane spoke. "Jake?"

"Yeah?" I said quietly.

“Twelve years ago, I chose *you*. Of all the blowhards, dipshits, nice guys and preening model wannabes that walked through the doors of that pub, I chose you. And that choice gifted me a marriage and two beautiful, wonderful little boys. And when that bottom dropped out of your world and you fell to pieces, I chose to stay and hold you together because I knew you would’ve done the same for me and I also knew you were a man who had the strength to come through the other side. I chose to stay when you came back from Australia, broken and screaming in the night, failing with your sobriety and… and… I chose to stay because I love you and if I’m honest I didn’t know how to give up on you. I chose to support you in setting up the business. I chose to stay with you and get you help again in the face of this Tramadol thing which… trust me, feels like a fucking betrayal in a lot of ways, frankly… and do you want to hear something that will shock you? I’ve never regretted my choice. So, I’m choosing right now to believe you when you tell me that you have *got* to do this but it is absolutely on one condition and one condition only!”

“What’s that?” I said.

“You come back to me and the boys and we’re together on Christmas morning. No matter what. You don’t do anything that gets in the way of that. You do what you have to do but not at the risk of not fulfilling this obligation.”

I smiled once more and sat silent, the tears falling freely now.

“Do you hear me, Jake?” Jane’s voice said, filling out the darkness of the car.

“I hear you and I agree to the condition, baby!” I laughed gently.

“And Jake – one other thing? And this is non-negotiable and sits at the very head of these conditions!”

“Yeah?”

“This is *it*, this is your one and only shot at shutting that sick fuck down once and for all. There won’t be another chance and I’m not going to support you through pushing yourself to breaking point to get one. This is it…”

I nodded whilst sitting silently watching the condensation clouds dissipate on the windscreen.

“Jake?”

“Yeah?”

“Are you nodding your head right now or shaking it or something?”

“I was nodding!” I smiled.

“You know you’re on the phone, right?” she laughed.

The glass in the car cleared and I moved off up out of the Ouseburn Valley and crossed the Byker Bridge as this piece of shit 1987 Zastava Yugo 513 clattered along into Manors and I took the slip road to head on over the Tyne Bridge on route to the Metrocentre. In a last desperate act to keep some faith in the lowest possible expectations I had of the car, I banged the car radio’s ‘on’ switch one more time in the hope it would pick up even just a few minutes of radio signal to break the silence in the car and separate me from my anxiety as I headed into Gateshead.

The radio sprang to life and I was instantly met with the sounds of Big Country's "You Dreamer". The chords within this minor classic from one of the most underappreciated bands in my lifetime instilled in me a bit of respect in good ol' Radio 2 for throwing out a tune like this the night before Christmas Eve when every other station across the land was most likely playing Wham's "Last Christmas" or Band Aid or shite like that.

The song's intro guided me right through all the new-fangled, hate-inducing slip roads off the Tyne Bridge and on the B-roads to the Metrocentre itself. I found myself no longer sweating from detoxification but sweating a much warmer type that came from the adrenaline starting to build inside of me.

As the first verse was drawing to a close I flashed back to the first time I remember hearing that song in the summer of 1995, underage drinking in the one pub in Newcastle that me and my mates knew didn't give two shits about serving alcohol to kids. Rachel Hepburn came up to me whilst I was getting the round of drinks in and told me that her best friend Debbie Briggs liked me – and then she said it again but emphasised the word 'like' in that way we all kind of did in the 90s because we apparently didn't trust each other to read between the lines and pick up subtlety or something.

Rachel and Debbie came over and sat with me and my friends and we talked and laughed and it was all good because Debbie kept softly touching my leg under the table and a couple of my friends kept clocking that she was doing it and giving me that 'eye' that boys did to one another as a secret gesture held within a perverted squint with a wink on the end that said "Go on son! Slip her one for me too!"

I was the only lad in my group of friends that hadn't properly kissed a girl at that age… and *fuck you all*, you judgemental bastards before you even start… but I had done a pretty good job of hiding that fact from my peers by simply a) bullshitting with wild abandon about the amount of girls I'd pulled and b) peppering the events surrounding these romantic incidents with details stolen from movies I'd watched (*"She swam by me and got a cramp. I saved her life, she nearly drowned. I took her bowling in the arcade, we made out under the dock!"* You know, that sort of thing?). I didn't want my first kiss to be round a pub table in front of all of my mates jeering so I made an excuse to go and put some music on the jukebox.

Debbie came with me.

We chose this song.

Just as the first verse kicked in, she pushed me up against the wall next to the jukebox and started kissing me. She put her tongue in my mouth. No one had ever put their tongue in my mouth before. I had no clue what to do with it. So I just started gently batting it with my tongue, trying to pin it down and stop it from waggling because it seemed reasonable to me in that moment to make the assumption that a person's tongue in your mouth should be treated like an opponent's thumb when playing 'Thumb Wars'… and Debbie pulled away, said "Yeah, don't do that!" then went straight back to kissing me again.

I was thinking about all of that as the song broke into its chorus and a smile had formed surprisingly across my face at the memory without me realising. There was a little heat to my face that suggested I was blushing a bit too.

And then twenty-five years' worth of additional history, incident and pain got re-contextualised by the lyrics contained within the chorus…

*"♫♫ …Oh you dreamer. Is this the way that you believed your life was gonna turn out… Oh you dreamer. Is this the better world that you were making all those plans for… ♫♫"*

… and just like with the smile that had appeared on my face a second earlier without me ever seeing it coming, the tears suddenly fell and my mouth curled into an expression of pain. The second verse was already well underway before I came to the realisation that I was screaming out loud in animalistic fury.

## [28]

## or

## "A Brief Unnecessary History Of The North East's Premier Shopping Destination..."

**B**ased in Dunston, near the River Tyne, the Metrocentre has been a landmark feature in the North East since it opened in 1986. It was borderline legendary in my youth because it was a giant – and I mean *giant* – shopping mall that didn't just have shops, it also had a bowling alley *and* a cinema and… get this… it had a goddamn theme park stuck in the corner of it so, if your parents were anything like mine were, back in the late 80s they'd drive you up there, drop you at the entrance with a pocketful of tokens and then piss off to have some time to themselves going around the three hundred plus shops, pubs and restaurants all under one roof.

The theme park thing died in 2008. Not because of some kid getting decapitated on the rickety little rollercoaster like some people like to allege. It died because it cost a fortune to keep maintained and folk had stopped giving a shit about it long before it shuttered its doors, giving way to even more shops and fast food places under the 2,200,000 square foot of space it housed.

The whole of the Metrocentre is split up into a series of coloured quadrants. They're not themed or anything. It's not like if you want clothes you go to one coloured area, household goods one coloured area, entertainment another or anything like that. They don't want to make it *that* easy for you, obviously. There's blue, yellow, green and, what many consider to be the main centrepiece, red. Each night when the Metrocentre closes, huge steel shutters come up from a grate in the floor that close off each quadrant from one another.

The red quadrant is also where all of the entertainment events and shows get put on in the huge open floor space outside of what used to be House of Fraser. It's where Sue George has hosted her annual Christmas Eve charity fashion show 'thing' every year with a catwalk that spans out around the entire space with seating and stalls and little kiosks contained within its centre. Each year, underneath this apparently decadent four-walled tent of fairy lights, music blasts out as the best looking people on The George Platform's books strut their stuff around the walkway, wearing all the clobber and kit clothing stores in the Metrocentre are trying to actively flog to *you*, the discerning shopper who's got caught up in the 'party atmosphere' on Christmas Eve because you were stupid enough to leave your gift buying until the last possible moment and came to a huge retail complex to get it done.

Now, let me be clear, all of that is the Metrocentre of yesteryear, really. It's just kind of a bit of preface to give you an idea of the size of it. I wasn't trying to do that Dan Brown thing where you're reading The Da Vinci Code and he just goes *"Robert Langdon walked into The Louvre..."* and then he just copies and pastes the whole of the Wikipedia page about The Louvre and you're sat reading page after page of boring descriptive shit about it.

Ah, man. Who am I kidding, huh?

We're nearly done here aren't we and I've hardly shaped up to be some successor to Dashiell Hammett, Raymond Chandler, Walter Mosley or Mickey Spillane, have I?

Anyway, the Metrocentre of today is a decidedly different beast to the one most of us grew up with and very different to what it became famous for. With the cratering of the country, a lot of huge big retail companies either went under or got the fuck out of dodge. Their presence in the Metrocentre in the massive retail space they took up disappeared in weeks around the same time that the cinema and restaurants all shut up shop and left. Rent went up to cover their disappearance, a lot of shops couldn't cope and they went too. Now it's just mostly boarded up shop fronts or quickly thrown-up outlet or bargain-basket type stores. What used to be a prolifically utilised tourist destination is now just miles of tiled floors riddled with cracks and dents, flickering overhead lights and echoing emptiness.

The idea that Sue George was maintaining her association with this venue suggested to me she was more loyal than I gave her credit for. The notion that she actually expected anyone to give a single shit about her modelling 'show' and to drive out to the Metrocentre to watch it on Christmas Eve indicated she was just as stupid as I believed.

I was so deep in thinking exactly that... Well, look, I've been nothing but honest with you folk so far there's no point starting to lie now we're on the homeward stretch, so let me start again:

... I was so distracted by Radio 2 playing "Crazy Crazy Nights" by Kiss back-to-back with Boston's "More Than A Feeling" on a cold December evening that I had not picked up at all on the fact I'd be tailed into the completely vacant Red Quadrant car park by a black Ford Escort with its headlights off. I pulled to a stop just as the signal started to go on the radio. The dying sound as the radio appeared to give out was:

*"♫♫ ... The Rangers had a homecoming. In Harlem late last night... And the Magic Rat drove his sleek machine over the Jersey state line. Barefoot girl sitting on the hood of a Dodge... ♫♫"*

"Holy Shit!" I exclaimed to no one but myself. "They're playing 'Jungleland' now!"

And with that the radio fell silent and the car engine dropped out quickly afterwards.

"Oh, come the fuck *on*!" I muttered.

I climbed out of the car and slammed the door behind me, stepping out into the cold night air. I pulled my phone from my pocket and clicked on Holly's number once again. The call didn't connect.

"Mother-Fu…" I mumbled as I thrust my phone back in my pocket, placed my hands on my hips and started to survey my surroundings. It had been a long time since I'd been up at the Metrocentre but it had most certainly been during opening hours when the doors were open and barriers weren't down at every conceivable entrance or exit.

I eyed the outside of the multi-storey car park in front of me, staring hard at it like there was one single remote chance that I was capable of scaling the side of it and getting in through one randomly unlocked access door inside that just *happened* to have been left open…

Suddenly car headlights lit me up and a vehicle slow-crawled towards me. I got as much of a shock as you'd expect when you're waiting for armed ex-soldiers carrying out kill-orders for your mortal enemy to jump out of the shadows and murder you. I placed my hand to my waistband, took a cautious hold of the firearm tucked down by my hip and pulled my coat closely around myself to hide what I was holding.

The vehicle stopped directly behind mine and out got DC Billy Tidyman.

He grinned from ear to ear. "You're a hard bloody man to track down, Jake Lehman!"

I eyed him suspiciously. "Why are you trying to track me down?"

"Because I think you and I need to talk and because I think we're shooting for the same goal here?" he replied.

"What makes you think that, Detective Constable?"

Tidyman stopped in his steps as he got closer to me and he squinted his eyes at my general being. "Bloody hell, Jake. You look like you're about to drop dead!"

"I'm hearing that a lot lately, I'm not going to lie. Now, you said something about the same goal, yeah?"

"Yeah." Tidyman said, switching his concerned face back to a fixed grin. "You're trying to get to the bottom of this Stephie Jay thing, right? And I'm starting to realise now that I'm getting hung out to dry on it and I want to help you."

My eyes narrowed. "Hung out to dry how?"

"There's something deeply wrong going on with this whole thing. Since we talked I looked back over the stuff that I know was meant to be in that file and there's no mention of it."

"Like what?"

"Well, like the voicemail recording and its accompanying transcript for one. I got that from the Alia Marcus girl. I passed that straight up the line to act on. It disappeared. I was told a search of Stephie's vehicle had been authorised off the back of it. It hadn't. I had to sneak out myself to look for clues."

"Are you serious?"

"Serious like a heart attack, pal." Tidyman said as his smile dropped and he took a step forward. "And here's the thing: The guy I was reporting everything to and who controlled everything and finalised that whole file was my DI!"

"Andrews?"

"Andrews!" he said quietly. "Exactly! Andrews is working directly for the people responsible for whatever the fuck it is that's going on here. He's covering tracks to suit their demands and I think he's shaping this for me to take the fall."

"But you're Hadenbury's son-in-law, aren't you?" I said. "They're not going to go after you, surely?"

Tidyman leant against the Zastava Yugo and I waved my hand at him.

"What?" he said cautiously.

"I wouldn't lean against that. It'll fall apart beneath you!"

"Oh, okay!" he laughed then stood back up straight. "Don't take any heed from me being related to Hadenbury, even through marriage. Hadenbury is an absolute prick, mate. He will throw anyone under the bus. That man has huge political aspirations outside of his Chief Constable tenure and he's not going to let anyone get in the way of that. Not even his daughter's husband."

Tidyman let out a pained sigh and looked away from me for a second before turning back and taking another step closer to me.

"I want to help you." He said. "I want to help you get whatever you need to lock this down and get justice for Stephie's parents."

"Where do you think I'm at on this then? Because I've been working my nuts off on this for two weeks and from what I've been told you were off on annual leave, so…"

"I wasn't off on annual leave. That's just what I've made DI Andrews and my team think. I've actually been working my nuts off on this too. I've got more than what you realise and I want to bring it together with what you've got."

"Listen, Tidyman mate. You're saying all the right things here but… I've just got to be honest; I don't trust you because I don't know you. What I do know of you is that you're a member of a really corrupt police service, you're the son-in-law of the head of that police service and that…"

"I get you. I get you. Okay, what if I was to say that for the last two weeks I've traced a registration number of a vehicle that led me to a company called Black Box Consultancy?" Tidyman smiled. "What would that get me?"

"Go on…" I whispered, semi-shocked.

"What if I told you that I had located direct ties between Black Box Consultancy and Mayor Hetherington? Ties that showed he hired them, paid them and that something I found in Stephie's vehicle when I searched it connected it specifically back to the man that runs Black Box?"

"What's his name? No, wait. What did you find?" I gabbled. "No, no. Wait. What's his name and what did you find?"

"Slow down," smiled Tidyman. "Slow down. I'm not handing you my virginity without a kiss first, you know what I mean? Trust me a little in return – tell me what you're doing parked up here? How about we start there?"

"I came looking for someone." I replied.

"Okay, cool. We're getting somewhere." He laughed. "How about you tell me who you came looking for and we'll see if it is someone I'm looking for too?"

"You tell me the name at Black Box first?" I said.

"Would it mean anything to you anyway? Do you have anything on Black Box?"

"I do, yeah. I have a *lot* on them and none of it is good. Let's just say I have the names of every single one of them involved in this and who did what to who. If you've found what you say you have your name should be one of my names."

"Ok. What about the name Jason Grant?" Tidyman said, broadening his smile back to an enormous grin. "How's that?"

"That's very good!" I replied. "And who have you shared your findings with so far?"

"Absolutely no one!" laughed Tidyman weakly. "I'm out on my own here, pal. Who do I turn to? My direct line manager is the one destroying evidence. My father-in-law is the head of the police service and he's best mates with Mayor Hetherington…"

"So what's your plan with all of this?" I asked.

"Exactly what any other good officer would do in my situation. I'm going to build an airtight case and then I'm going to go to the IOPC!"

For you non-acronym obsessives out there, that's the Independent Office for Police Conduct. They used to be the Independent Police Complaints Commission.

They're essentially the British version of Internal Affairs.

Okay? We're good? Cool, so…

I took a step closer to Tidyman like he had with me and hoped that my gesture would be seen as me meeting him in the middle, so to speak. "You're serious?"

"You keep asking me that," he smirked. "Yes, I'm serious. I wouldn't have lied to my wife about where I'm nipping out to and then spent the best part of the night driving around looking for you after two weeks of working alone on the side-lines trying to get to the bottom of this if I wasn't. So please, trust me, and tell me who you're here to see?"

I was warming to Tidyman but my gut was still just that little bit off. And let me tell you something friends – because, by this point, I'd hope we *are* friends – a private investigator's gut is NEVER off. If it is, he or she shouldn't be in this game. Simple as.

I was just about to throw down a final all-important litmus marker on what could possibly be our new burgeoning friendship when he spoke first.

"Are you here looking for Sue George?" he said.

"Why would I be looking for Sue George?"

"Because she might have important information on Stephie and if she does then that puts her at risk of Black Box, doesn't it? It's not complicated!"

I eyed him suspiciously.

"I've worked backwards on the booking thing," Tidyman continued. "I know that Sue changed Stephie's booking. I just don't know why. And I want to know. So I have questions for her. And if you're here tonight looking for her, that would suggest you have questions for her too."

Tidyman was further behind my own investigation than I originally thought. I decided to throw the litmus test back out there before I dug too deep down in revealing anything.

"If I *was* here looking for her, would you be able to flash your warrant card with security and get us let in to speak to her?"

"What security?" laughed Tidyman. "Mate, this place is dead on its arse nowadays. But yeah, I think I could get us in alright, don't worry about that."

"Cool." I smiled.

"So is that a confirmation? We're here for Sue?"

"I didn't say that. Now you're asking me to trust you, right?" I winked.

"Right!"

"So let me ask you this, and your reaction will tell me whether you're the type of guy that I want to be doing business with or not."

"Okay," Tidyman smiled nervously.

"If you met with Alia and got the voicemail and passed it up to Andrews, and you reckon he destroyed it rather than log it as evidence, than surely she must have passed you the copy of the sex tape too?" I said salaciously.

Tidyman paused. The pause was just long enough to tell me *something*.

"Yeah, yeah. The sex tape." He finally replied.

"And answer this honestly – did you watch it?" I said, smiling a purposefully dirty smile.

Now, let me interject very quickly here and confess that I have this 'thing' that Jane is always taking the piss out of me for. She calls it my 'forced machismo'. It's this thing where I'm in the company of other men and I question my own level of masculinity so I accentuate and over-exaggerated my Northern accent and get properly crude and… worst of all, according to Jane… I start referring to her as "the missus" and tell made-up stories about her nagging and all that.

This was one of those 'forced machismo' moments.

The minute Tidyman took a step forward, leaned in and said "Of course I did mate!" with a leer and an accentuation on the word 'mate' I realised I'd need to 'bring' it if I was to 'sell' it, so to speak.

"With that big-dicked footballer?" I smirked.

"Yeah!" laughed Tidyman.

"She fucked like a rabbit on ecstasy didn't she?" I giggled.

"Oh yeah!"

"And those tits, right? My god, I looked at my wife's tits after watching Stephie Jay and I thought 'What the hell am I coming home to them for every night?' you know?"

See? Do you see how proper *manly* I come across now, eh? It's 'locker room talk' so brilliantly mastered you wouldn't know it was faked, would you?

"I know that feeling all too well mate." Tidyman laughed.

By this point, you're all remembering the most important lesson of all, right?

And *what* is the most important lesson?

That's right, chuffing is one thing but what do you do when you think you've reached your maximum capacity for the chuff?

**Chuff, chuff, chuff**!

And then **chuff** some more.

"You know the footballer in the tape is a secret business partner of Mick Hetherington's right?" I said conspiratorially.

"*No*," gasped Tidyman. "I did not know that."

"We're pretty convinced that it's the sex tape that got Stephie killed. She tried to blackmail the footballer fella… What's his name again?" I queried.

Tidyman's panic lasted a matter of seconds before he replied. But it was enough to give me the read on him I needed definitively. "Oh, I can't remember. I'm terrible with footballer's names. Remind me?"

"Max, I think. I think he's called Max. But anyway, we're leading with the idea that she was blackmailing him and it was affecting him doing his secret deal with Mayor Hetherington so the Mayor helped him out of a hole and got rid of Stephie."

"Woah!" whispered Tidyman.

"There's just one problem though." I said.

"What's that?"

I took a step back and smiled. "There's *no* sex tape!"

Tidyman looked at me, his eyes narrowed and his smile dropped. He stood in silence.

"And I think you knew from the outset there wasn't and I think if you were to be trusted you wouldn't have lied at the first available opportunity about that. Here's the thing, my grandfather always said to me that you measure a man's integrity by how quickly he lies when he doesn't have to and…"

Within a split second Tidyman had dropped a leg back to pull himself into a defensive position and drew his police asp from the back of his belt line, extending it out into full locked striking capacity in one fluid movement.

"Shut the fuck up!" he snarled.

I raised my hands slowly.

"Put your hands down, you stupid idiot. You have no idea what you're bumbling around in do you? All you had to do was just take the warning you were given and… and… you know what? Forget it. Get down on the ground, face down and put your hands on the back of your head!"

I slowly started to take a knee. As soon as the first knee hit the ground, I stopped and smiled.

"What can you possibly be smiling about right now?" Tidyman said whilst pulling a mobile phone from his pocket. He unlocked it and dialled a number one handed whilst holding the asp still in a strike position with his other hand. "Keep getting your face to the ground, dickhead!"

I slowly dropped the other knee.

"It's me." Tidyman said into the phone. "I've got Lehman. He's at the Metrocentre… I think the George woman is here too, that's why he's here. I think he's trying to get ahead of you… Where's Chris? I've got no idea… Listen, I'm going to lock Lehman down until you get here! … Red Quadrant car park! Get here, a-sap!"

Tidyman clicked the phone off as he put it back in his pocket.

"You just don't get it do you?" he said, staring down at me. "We don't live in a world of hard-work paying off anymore. That's ridiculous. It's about your face fitting with the people that hold all the sway. Do you honestly think in this day and age the graduate scheme within the police is all about your two-one grade and how you excel in the interview? Absolute bullshit, pal! It's about who's repping you behind the scenes. And you're not going to get repped by anyone if you don't serve their agenda. Hadenbury has his men who represent him who in turn require people on the ground to serve his agenda. I'm out here on the ground doing exactly that because you know what, Jake? I went from completing my probation to a Detective Constable in less than half a year because I repped the agenda I was presented with. Do I agree with the agenda? Do I fucking have to? Does the agenda serve me well in the long run? Yes it absolutely does. You never really worked that out did you? You know, adapting to suit the requirements of the people who hold the power?"

I started to laugh.

"That's what Andrews always used to say about you whenever we'd see you bumbling around town, acting like you've still got a foot in the game…" Tidyman continued. "He said you never really could see that this world doesn't match your ideals and it won't ever change to fit them but you're too thick to see that. He's right – you're a fucking fly charging at a speeding car with the insane belief that you're going to smash against it and turn it into a crumpled heap. And what happens to a fly when he hits a car windscreen at seventy miles an hour, Jake?"

I continued laughing.

"What can you possibly be finding funny at this very moment?" he spat. "Do you even realise you're going to die tonight and die for what? Some blonde bimbo who thought she was the goddamn Kim Kardashian of the North East or something? You're a joke!"

I laughed even harder.

"What's so funny?" Tidyman asked.

"You know how just a second ago I said there was one problem and it was that there was no sex tape?"

Tidyman looked at me confused but didn't speak.

"Well, there's actually two problems. That was one of them. The other is that you brought a police asp to a gun fight!"

"What?" Tidyman said, taking another step back in alarm.

Before his second step had landed on the tarmac, I'd pulled the gun from my waistband and fired it twice aiming as low as possible in the process. I'd slid the safety hammer off at the exact moment my fingers gripped the handle and I pulled it from my jeans, just like Bobby Maitland had showed me. And being careful not to blow my penis off in the process, just like Ryan hoped I would.

Both shots slammed into each of Tidyman's ankles, knocking him straight off his feet and sending the asp slamming to the ground alongside him as he let out an unsettlingly high-pitched scream.

I instantly jumped up and rushed over to him as best I could whilst my ears rang so hard they messed with my balance. I got down alongside him, pressing the gun against his temple.

"Tell me this, please, I have to know…" I said. "Did I look cool as fuck just then or what?"

Tidyman howled in pain.

"Hey, Billy? Please, it's my first time. I was aiming for a Bruce Willis in The Last Boy Scout vibe, how did I do?"

Tidyman's howl turned to screams.

I furiously patted him down and pulled his mobile phone, car keys and a set of handcuffs from his pocket. Just as I did a text message flashed up on the screen of the phone from an unstored number:

*'ETA – 30 Minutes'.*

I quickly slammed the handcuffs onto Tidyman and clicked his car unlocked.

"How much do you weigh?" I said. "And don't lie?"

"Fuck you!" screamed Tidyman.

"Okay, it's probably best I don't know anyway." I said. "By the way, *this* is going to hurt."

With that I grabbed the cuff of Tidyman's jacket and started dragging him to the back of the car where I opened the boot.

"No… No…" Tidyman started to gasp amidst his screams.

I pushed my arms as deep down underneath the sockets of his own arms and lifted as best I could… then dropped him to the floor. I just couldn't find the energy needed to complete the lift. Tidyman screamed some more when he hit the ground.

"I'm going to try again, Billy!" I said, gasping for breath. "And on the next one if you don't help me to help you get in this boot I'm going to stand you up on your ankles."

And with that I tried again.

And this time Tidyman seemed to accommodate my struggle and be much more helpful in using the top half of his body, handcuffed and all, to pull himself into the boot. I positioned the gun at Tidyman as he started to cry.

"You got into bed with Hetherington, Hadenbury and their little foot soldiers," I sneered. "And they didn't even give you a gun? What's *that* about? Look at me, one of those foot soldiers gave me a gun and they don't even fucking like me! What does that say about *you*?"

Tidyman went to speak but I immediately cut him off by slamming the boot shut on the first syllable of the first word of his first attempt at saying something to me.

I then promptly vomited on the ground in front of me.

I stumbled around to the front of the car, reached into the driver's seat and unclicked the handbrake. The car wobbled for the briefest of seconds and then rolled back across the car park and disappeared from sight into the darkness.

A loud crunch filled out against the silence as the car come to an abrupt stop in the hedgerow that lined the car park.

I turned and my eyes immediately fell back upon the pea-green 1987 Zastava Yugo 513 before me. I looked back over my shoulder at where the Ford Escort had just disappeared to and let out a pained huff of breath.

"Aww, bugger!" I said out loud to myself like I was a hero in an 80s or 90s action movie where the character had to say shit out loud that he never normally would because otherwise the audience would never get to hear the witticism in any other context. "I should've traded up!"

## [29]

## or

## "Run It All Down..."

Psychic's update via text message landed as I circled the exterior of this side of the Metrocentre for the second time. I was six minutes and two bullets of thirteen down from the thirty minute 'estimated time of arrival' deadline for what I presumed was Hannibal, aka Jason Grant, and the rest of his team.

I drove up to shutters and considered shooting at the locks but stupidly could not see in the dark of my surroundings where the right or best place to fire would be, especially without a ricochet that knowing my luck would spring back and hit me in the face. I'd banged on what I thought were security doors. I'd driven up, got out and yanked on every huge metal shutter pulled down over every entrance and every window then pushed against it just to see if it had any give whatsoever if I was to ram it. The only one with any sort of flimsiness whatsoever was the grate pulled down over the red quadrant multi-storey car park entrance.

I tried calling Holly's phone twice over.

"You've got to think faster here!" I said out loud, trying my hardest to cheer myself on.

I re-read Psychic's message once again and allowed myself the slightest of positive nods in affirmation that Emily had gotten a hold of Jessica Lane, who had apparently dropped everything to FaceTime with them both and was now making her way to Emily's home to look over the evidence. They'd been doubly busy because on top of that they had even completed a hastily prepared compilation of Hetherington's most damning and guilty statements and acts made up of the videos we'd found and the audio recordings Chris left us before blowing his brains out. Psychic had even liaised with Bobby Maitland via telephone with regards to the next move.

Meanwhile, I couldn't even get inside *one* bastard building.

I stuffed the phone back in my pocket and let my eyes dart around what was in front of me… Large brick building ensigned with the words 'Red Quadrant'. Which was in turn attached to a colossal glass building belonging to Debenhams, the last major department store still hanging on in business at the Metrocentre and spread across four massive floors on the furthest corner of this side of the complex. And running up the side of that was a four storey car park. Five if you included the roof.

Red quadrant building… attached to a giant department store… with its own multi-storey car park… I needed to get into the red quadrant still stuck in the belief that Holly had took heed of the last words I said to her - stay there until I got to her and keep Sue with her!

I couldn't find any other way to get in and knew that going in via other sides would be met with not just more of the same but also big steel grids up from the floor blocking me from even getting anywhere close to the quadrant I actually wanted to be in.

Think!

*Think!*

My eyes kept drawing back to that multi-storey car park with its rickety metal shutter pulled down over its entrance.

My mind started flashing back to the occasions we'd visited the Metrocentre as a family and how Jane always preferred using that car park in particular because it was always easier to manoeuvre around, plus the kids loved getting out and going over the glass walkway into Debenhams and riding the zigzag of escalators in the centre of the store down into the Metrocentre itself.

My brain started pushing itself to try and remember just how thick in width that glass walkway was and whether it could fit a shitty pea-green coloured 1987 Zastava Yugo 513 across it and…

Jane's voice suddenly appeared in my head.

It does that, you see.

Everyone has that little voice in their head.

You know? Their conscience forming itself as a little sweet angelic thing or a red devilled miscreant. Mine is formed in the sound of Jane. It first appeared that way out in Australia whilst I lay bleeding out in the desert. *"I know you don't want to kill anyone,"* it said to me. *"But if you don't, you won't get home. We need you home. You have to do this."*

Only now it was trying to slow my brain down just a fraction and help with the processing of options. *"This is crazy,"* it said to me. *"Are you sure you've explored every option? It seems to me you've settled on the stupidest one available to you pretty fucking rapidly here."*

I slowly started nodding and that silly action hero monologue started up with myself once again, clearly for no one's ears but my own. "We're going to get this piece of shit car going again then we're going to ram the car park gate, drive this thing up onto the fourth floor, jump over the glass walkway and punt straight through the Debenhams doors, take the escalators down to ground floor, shoot our way through a display window, get out onto the red quadrant, grab Sue and Holly, get the fuck out of there, get back to Emily's, stop for a KFC on the way, make them safe there so that Sue will hand over accounts information showing monetary connections to Mick Hetherington then head off to confront the devil himself and take him down once and for all!"

*"That is the most ridiculous fucking thing I've ever heard!"* said Jane's voice inside my head. *"I'm serious. That is insane. That will never work and…"*

I turned the engine over and was met with the sound of complete silence.

I tried again.

Nothing.

*"You're trying to ignore me."* The inner voice said. *"It's not going to work. I mean, I don't even want to touch on the fact that you rolled away a perfectly good, far superior vehicle with Tidyman in the boot and left yourself with this. Now you're going to have to go fetch that car to use and time is running out because that 'A-Team' is getting closer and..."*

"PLEASE!" I screamed. "Give me this, PLEASE!"

I placed one hand tight around the wheel and gripped the ignition key tightly with one hand. I took the deepest breath and exhaled.

"I just need a win. Please. Just one. I'm so tired. I hurt so bad. I've pushed on with this through the worst ache and thirst for... for..." I said, staring at my eyes in the rear view mirror in front of me. "... I've come so far. So fucking *far*. Don't knock me back down now, *please*?"

I took another deep breath.

"Okay..."

I turned the key and the car weakly kicked the engine into life.

"Thank you!" I mouthed to no one at all in particular.

I pulled on the seatbelt, pushed the car into gear, removed the handbrake and took off at speed, pulling the wheel in full lock round so the car veered off towards the multi-storey car park... I pushed it into second gear as the car picked up even more speed and I braced for impact at the exact moment the bonnet slammed straight into the metal grate over the entrance. The grate gave maybe an inch before bouncing the car backwards as if the grate itself were a rhinoceros on a hot day effortlessly flicking away an irritating mosquito.

I recoiled back over in my seat which was not the direction I had prepared myself physically for at all. The engine cut out at the exact moment the radio choose to spring to life, filling the interior of the car with the opening seconds of funk at the start of KC and The Sunshine Band's "Give It Up" as I stared down at the metal grate still standing within its original position.

"Mother-fuc..." I started to mutter as the glovebox door dropped open and out fell a mangled pack of Marlborough Light cigarettes. I shakily reached over and picked the pack up off the passenger side footwell and found there were two twisted up cigarettes left inside. I pulled one out and give it a long, forlorn sniff then stared it at it for just a few seconds.

"Maybe in another life?" I whispered whilst tucking the cigarette behind my ear at the very moment that an almighty creaking sound was heard and the grate gave way, flopping to the concrete floor with an even more deafening clang that shook my jaw.

A smile broke out across my face.

*"That one was free,"* Jane's voice inside my head said. *"I just hope to God you know what you're doing!"*

"Got to go, got to go, got to go!" I said loudly to myself as "Give It Up" continued to kick in its intro… Now, if I was to say to you that KC and The Sunshine Band were an American disco and funk band formed in the 1970s and just about hanging on in there in there in 1982 when this track was released, what immediate assumption would you make? No, look, don't judge me on this okay? Based on how the best disco and funk of that decade was all coming from black bands and black artists, it would not be offensive to assume KC and The Sunshine Band were one such black band, no? So you could probably understand my shock when I found out that 'KC' from KC and The Sunshine Band was actually called Harry Wayne Casey and he was, well *is*, the whitest guy you'd ever poss…

Okay.

Okay.

Fine, I apologise. Let's get back to this:

I got the engine turned back over on the first attempt and sped through the open entrance of the multi-storey car park just as the funk intro gave way to the first verse:

*"♫♫ ... Everybody wants you. Everybody wants your love. I'd just like to make you mine all night. Na, na, na, na, na, na, na, na, na, na, now - Baby give it up ... ♫♫"*

"Got to go, got to go, got to go!" I kept repeating to myself as the car zipped along the first stretch and I locked the wheel round the curve of the first bend up onto Level 1.

*"♫♫ ... Everybody sees you. Everybody looks and stares. I'd just like to make you mine, all mine. Na, na, na, na, na, na, na, na, na, na, now ... ♫♫"*

The front bonnet of the car hit the slope up from Level 1 onto Level 2 and the whole of the 1987 Zastava Yugo 513 shuddered as I pushed down on the accelerator and tightly gripped the gear stick. The engine started to vibrate as I built up further speed whilst holding it in second gear.

*"♫♫ ... Baby give it up. Give it up. Baby give it up. Give it up. Na, na, na, na, na, na, na, na, na, na, now - Baby give it up. Give it up. Baby give it up… ♫♫"*

"Don't you quit on me now, you beautiful little bitch!" I said to the Zastava Yugo as it now started to react to the ground beneath its tyres like it was a hovercraft in full motion against the surface of an enormous lake. I rounded out off the slope, up onto Level 3 and lost control of the back end of the car. If there'd been a single other parked car or pillar in sight I'd have smashed into it at speed. Instead I managed to just about get the car back on the straight whilst furiously floundering with the steering wheel as if I knew exactly what the fuck I was doing.

You steer *into* the skid, right?

Or is it *out* of it?

I can never remember that.

I *do* remember being in the car with Jane one time when she was driving and she hit an ice patch, the car started to skid and she simply took her hands off the wheel, covered her eyes and screamed. I know it's definitely not *that* method.

I rounded the corner onto Level 4 and knew from familiarity that coming up on the right would be the glass walkway leading off the car park level and through a large glass lit entrance front into Debenhams. It'd be a tight turn onto…

*"What happens when you find this entrance has a massive steel barrier down over it too? You think the car is going to cope with hitting that?"* Jane's voice inside my head sprung up.

"Now's not the time," I said out loud, playing the one-liner spouting action hero role for no one but myself once again. "Got to go, got to go, got to go!"

*"♫♫… Can you give it, can you give it, give it up? Come on baby I need your love... Give it up, some of your love. Come on and play the game of love... Everybody is on me, give it up… ♫♫"*

The glass walkway loomed up in front of me and I saw a metal extendable gate pulled over the doors of the Debenhams entrance.

"We can take that, right?" I said to the Zastava Yugo. "Come on, let's do this – be the little engine that could, yeah?"

I pushed harder down on the pedal and the entire car vibrated in a way that almost begged me to push the gear up to third but I daren't because of what Psychic had said about that when we were first gifted this car. I'd read The Little Engine That Could enough times over the years to both of my boys to know that story almost off by heart.

"I think I can, I think I can, I think I can…" I started saying loudly like I was reading the book to them there and then. "I thought I could, I thought I could…"

I needed to maintain some semblance of control at speed to make a hard corner turn onto this glass walkway zooming up ahead so that I still carried enough force to break through that security barrier on the other side. I started racking my brains to recall what we'd been taught in advanced driving school in the police service for carrying out a handbrake turn with an immediate execution of speed at the end.

Funny how the brain works, isn't it?

I can tell you word for word what Harrison Ford said to Jeroen Krabbé at the end of The Fugitive. I can tell you what the track number is for "Lift Me Up" by Jeff Lynne and on which album (three and Armchair Theatre – you're *welcome*!). I can even tell you what clothes I was wearing as a young boy and where I hid in my grandparents' house when I eavesdropped on them the first time they suggested to my parents that they gave up care of me and allow my grandmother and grandfather to take guardianship. I can remember police legislation and by-laws like I'm Dustin Hoffman in Rain Man too.

But the *technical* stuff?

I'm always struggling with that…

"Stuff it!" I shouted as the back end of the car slid past the glass walkway itself and I pulled down hard on the steering wheel, clipping the handbrake on at the same time that I slammed my foot down on the clutch.

The back end spun out just as the front managed to find its way between the bannisters either side of the walkway. I released the clutch and handbrake at the same time as I steered straight one-handed and crunched the accelerator down.

The Zastava Yugo lifted up at the front as the back wheels followed over the walkway and we crashed aggressively and awkwardly through the security gate across the doors, it snapping under the force with which I hit it.

"♫♫... *Come on baby, I need your love. Can I touch you, can I love you... Come on baby, baby, I love you. Can you give ...* ♫♫"

The radio died on impact along with the engine as the car hit the tiled floor of the department store and proceeded to carry on skidding along at speed. There wasn't a display stand or mannequin forceful or weighted down enough to stop the Zastava Yugo as it crunched and slid against me pointlessly pulling at the wheel to right our path.

The only sound now was the increasing scream coming from myself as immaculately dressed mannequins bounced off the bonnet and metal clothing rails snapped, coiled and smashed through the windscreen.

The car came to a thundering stop with an enormous bang as it drifted sideways into a huge metal railing that circled the entire bank of escalators in the middle of the floor.

I took a second to gather myself and then pulled myself from the wreckage, noticing that the cigarette was now missing from behind my ear and wherever its 'brother' was inside that pack, it was now flung somewhere far away too. Not that I would've lit it anyway. Well, I'm saying that to you, dear loyal reader who's stuck with me this far, because I can get away with saying it seeing as there was no lighter to ignite it even if I wanted to and pressing down on the cigarette lighter inside this Zastava Yugo 513 at that point would've surely been like pressing the trigger switch on a bomb.

Had a lighter or matches been kindly provided alongside those stray cigarettes though? Man, who *knows* if I'd have taken now of all occasions as the time to get back on the nicotine train. After all, if you've picked up anything about me by this point that you'd throw all your casino chips down on it's that I have addiction issues and I show little in the way of consistency in my battle against them. But, hey, what's *your* major malfunction, huh? Let's talk about *you*, yeah?

No.

Please, show some decorum here.

This is not about *you*! Go write your own book.

Sue and Holly are in danger. Maintain some semblance of focus, okay?

The car was all but destroyed from the middle of its chassis right the way back out to the front of its bumper. I stumbled away and vomited just a tiny bit then used my sleeve to wipe off the bits of vomit attached to my stubble, my drenched forehead and the little bit of blood coming from my mouth.

If you've come this far in my telling of this story than you'll know by now that I have the deepest possible affection and the highest regard for the 1987 version of the Zastava Yugo 513, which as we are all aware is the *greatest car ever made* in the history of automobile production! Anything you feel I may have said to the contrary up until this point would be an error on your part, I assure you. Go back over and read this thing more carefully, please.

My body now carried a whole new degree of pain throughout it and the only good thing that came with it was that it was a type that wholly distracted from the searing ache and thirst my bones and muscles craved for some goddamn Tramadol.

I passed a broken mannequin half covered in really quite a nice lace strapped negligee. I stopped and checked the label. 'Reger by Janet Reger'. Ivory lace, no less. *Very* nice. It'd been a long time since I'd seen Jane wear anything like that. Certainly pre-children, I have to say. She could still carry that off. I turned the label over and checked out the price.

*£46.00?*

For a baby-doll sexy nightie type deal? That's crazy talk!

*However…*

I'd put Jane through so much lately. You know, there's the Tramadol thing she's trying to process and the fact that she's had to flee her home because her husband uncovered a paedophile sex ring within the highest echelons of local authority power and then got a hit squad put on his tail. She deserved a little bit of the expensive stuff in life. It'd certainly been a long time since we'd been able to afford shopping at somewhere like Debenhams. We still technically *couldn't* afford to shop there – which is why I quickly yanked the negligee from the mannequin, rolled it up into a tight ball and stuffed it into my jacket pocket.

There was no alarm ringing.

That was the first thing that hit me as I staggered away from the wreckage. Well, the first thing AFTER the impromptu 'no-more-fucks-to-give' act of petty shoplifting. But, yeah, no alarm? That's kind of unusual when you drive a *car* through a locked and secured department store built within the biggest shopping mall in the whole of the North of England, don't you think?

The second thing that caught my attention was the enormous glass-fronted side that ran down Debenhams facing out into the Metrocentre's red quadrant and which gave a clear line of sight halfway down the red mall before the lifts and second floor balconies started to obstruct the view.

This line of sight afforded me view of the ultimate 'fuck you' to me:

A giant steel security barrier that ran up from the floor outside of Debenhams all the way to the ceiling and blocking entry into the red quadrant from this point. We were not going to be ramming *that* thing down, soundtracked to KC and The Sunshine Band, I can guarantee you that much.

"You have *got* to be shitting me, man!" I whispered.

And here comes the inner voice again:

*"You really fucked it didn't you? You're two bullets and eight minutes down. That Jason Grant fella and his mates are probably down there already. They likely used a door that they found propped open with a brick or something. But you? You had to go drive a goddamn 1987 Zastava Yugo 513 through the top floor of a department store and get yourself trapped."*

I stared out of the big glass front, four floors up with the steel security grate directly outside my window. My eyes darted back and forth, up and down, looking for any angle and sure enough there it was – a small window pane behind a 'staff only' board on the far corner of Debenhams that actually faced out onto the Metrocentre *behind* the security grate that ran floor to ceiling. I moved as quickly as possible over to it, passing through a bedroom furnishings section on the far side and grabbing a broken metal clothing rail as I walked.

This was a security flaw designed purely to be taken advantage of, surely? You know like the state-of-the-art alarm systems in any of Steven Soderbergh's Ocean's movies where they are completely impenetrable… except for just that one little thing that only an expert in the field of blah blah blah can take advantage of. Here though, no expert was required. My thinking was if I could get through that 'staff only' access board and out onto that window line than I would end up behind the security grate and where I needed to be.

One quick body weight slam against the board opened it off its moorings and I was on the other side and, sure enough, on arrival at this small window I could now technically stand behind the security grate. Two storeys below me was a set of escalators leading both down and up from the ground floor of the red quadrant.

You could jump down to that, *right*?

I mean, I was yet to be born with the knowledge you know me to have acquired from the prologue. In this *particular* moment, however, I was fired up only with the images of Stallone in Cliffhanger, Schwarzeneggar and the waterfall in Predator, Willis and that fire hose on the roof of the Nakatomi Plaza in Die Hard and Jackie Chan in… well, pretty much everything, but especially the final shopping mall blow-out in Police Story.

I looked across and down at the escalators then quickly ran to grab a small mattress from the bedroom display that I dragged back to the small window pane. With one swift strike of the metal clothes rail against the glass, the window shattered cleanly and the glass fell to the ground far below.

I was immediately met with the sound of music pumping out from down on my left where Sue's set-up for the charity event must be. I strained my ear a little. That sounded like that kitschy novelty Christmas song from The Darkness. No wonder they couldn't hear me crashing my way in to get to them when they had that blasting away.

I slowly started stepping out towards the edge, dragging the mattress out with me. The ledge gave me about a quarter of a metre of space to stand on as I peered over at the escalators.

*"What the hell are you thinking, Jake?"* Jane's voice whispered in my head.

"What the hell are you thinking, Jake?" I said quietly to myself.

*"You're insane!"* the voice said. *"You're never going to make that!"*

"I must be insane!" I said to myself.

I took a deep breath, grabbed both sides of the mattress and held it out in front of me. I then started striding backwards a couple of steps and took a pause. Maybe the blurred vision from the opioid withdrawals wasn't a bad thing after all, really? If I can't see exactly what I'm about to do than maybe that's a good thing, right?

I pushed the gun deep down into my waistband, hoping it would stay in position and with the heaviest of exhales I ran towards the gap… and *jumped*!

Now, just imagine me freezeframed in mid-air right now in order to give us all time to talk about this:

Have you ever been in a situation where you committed yourself to something and then within seconds of passing the "Are you sure about this, because there's no going back from this point on?" stage you instantaneously regretted it and wanted to go back but you couldn't? I got frosted tips in my hair in 2002, so trust me when I say I know what I'm talking about.

One time, when I was thirteen, I was trying to impress this girl when me and my friends were hanging out in Wallsend Park on our rollerblades (In-Lines, *first editions*, show some respect, yo!) and I just casually threw out some bullshit about this mythical occasion when I took a full rolling run from the band-stand all the way up to the tennis courts and then used the embankment to slide down and make a jump over the THIRTY something concrete stairs that led to what used to be the old sewer point (but is now a lovely duck pond, shit ye not!). Now, obviously that was a complete lie from the ground up and obviously it did not need to be fact-checked. It just needed to be used for the sole purpose for which it was spouted, which was to impress a girl into kissing me, and that was that! We would then have all sat around and listened to me re-enact this great achievement *verbally* - that just happened to have occurred without any witnesses around and all parties would interject occasionally with oooohs and aaaaahs etc. and the girl in question would swoon and what not.

But no. Oh no.

Barry fuckin Chaytor had to start giving the "big 'uns" about how my act of Airborne glory "just wasn't possible" and that it "wasn't even physically logical" and shit like that. Then dissent grew in the ranks and others started to doubt it and before you knew it, I was standing up and putting my hands on my hips and shouting "I'll prove it to you all!" like Superman arriving at the scene of a crime in costume having just been Clark Kent two seconds earlier.

The pre-Jane voice in my head just went "I'm sorry, what the *fuck* did you just say?"

And off I went to win the hand of a 'fair maiden' who was so important to me back then, desperate as I was just to receive even a modicum of female attention, that I can't even remember a single thing about her today other than the fact she wore a peach coloured Jason Donovan t-shirt that day.

Now, the first push along from the band-stand I started immediately building quite the level of speed, let me tell you. So much so that by the time I dropped my knees and slid down the embankment towards the huge stairwell I actually found myself thinking "You're going so fast that you just might pull this off… Holy SHIT, you're going to do this! Man, you're going to fly like a…"

And you know what? The actual millisecond that my rollerblade-clad feet left the top of those stairs and I launched myself into the air the first thing I thought was "Well, this just is not going to work out *at all* like you have it going on in your head, is it? Let's just stop this silliness and go home. It's Saturday teatime, Baywatch is on and…"

I woke up in hospital.

I'd broken a lot of bones.

A *lot* of bones.

And I broke them clearing nine of thirty-odd steps on that run of stairs.

That girl that I was trying to impress? She wasn't allowed to hang-out with me anymore after that day because her dad said that I must have had, quote unquote, "mental problems to be doing stuff like that".

So flash forward to the twenty-third of December, twenty-four years later, with me trying to boogie-board a single mattress off the fourth floor of a department store onto an escalator two storeys below and down into the shopping mall on the ground floor.

There I am, four or five metres out in mid-air and completely blind to how I'm doing in terms of the distance to go because of the fact I chose to hold a mattress in front of my face like a ready-made crash-mat and all of a sudden the voice in my head kicks into play. But it's not the voice of Jane, like I've come to hear since that day in Australia. It was my own voice, aged thirteen years of age, and I heard it very clearly say "Well, this just is not going to work out *at all* like you have it going on in your head, is it? Let's just stop this silliness and go home. You've got two cans of Sprite in the fridge and seven episodes of The Rockford Files re-runs stored up in the Sky+ box!"

Unfreeze the freeze frame:

The top half of my body made it past the escalator's handrail. The bottom half? Not so much? And if you're pushing for exact detail here than I'll go with less "not so much" and more "not at all". My ribs and diaphragm slammed into the handrail. The mattress made it over safely you'll be pleased to learn and swiftly fucked off down the escalator without me. My body tipped and my head smashed onto the metallic sharp edges of the step. I actually felt the hard edge of the escalator stair go inside my forehead just above my eye and blood sprayed from my head as the rest of my body crumbled over the rail after me, throwing me into a discombobulated heap that then proceeded to fall backwards down the rest of the stairs.

I landed in a bloodied and broken heap at the bottom, clear of the steel security grate that had closed off the red quadrant mall, but ready to vomit.

I couldn't move properly because of the pain so I titled my head slightly to my left, opened my mouth and just let it pour out of me onto the cold tiled and dirty floor beneath me. My body seared with pain around the torso as muscles worked to exorcise the vomit but did so in tandem with what felt like a couple of very broken bones.

"Got… to… go… Got to… go…. Got to… go!" I painfully muttered to myself as I carefully turned on my side then gently started easing myself to my feet.

I took a second to look back up at from where I'd just jumped.

*"No one will ever believe you did that, you know?"* Jane's voice said inside my head.

I threw half a little salute back up at the broken window pane four storeys up then staggered myself onwards.

I put my hand down to my waistband to make sure the gun was still there. It wasn't. It was miraculously waiting for me two or three feet away at the base of the escalator. I painfully bent down, picked it up and stuck it in the back of my jeans so my coat would hide it well.

The blood pumped from my head wound. The speed at which it fled from my body was now accentuated from my bending over. I pushed myself on as best I could, wobbling and occasionally banging into standees and benches along the mall itself. You know what would've worked great with me right there and then at that moment? Two tramadol, a strong black coffee and a Lucky Strike Light. You know what I had to comfort me instead? Mariah fucking Carey because the music had now changed up ahead to her 1994 beloved-by-everyone-but-me "All I Want For Christmas".

I could see a half built catwalk, a sea of unopened fold-out chairs and a couple of gas cannisters used for the inflating of balloons. They were all scattered underneath a sea of fairy lights and stood beneath them, amidst the somewhat organised chaos was Sue and Holly. Sue had her back to me.

I limped on.

Holly saw me first at the exact moment that the music died off enough for me to catch Sue in full flight with her tirade.

"… This is beyond unacceptable!" she ranted. "We are ridiculously behind. People talk about being desperate for work and needing money. Where are all the agency staff we were promised to get this finished? Who's going to clear away the cannisters and finish the catwalk? I mean, the fucking catwalk isn't even built! We go live tomorrow at one and we don't even have a catwalk! This is the worst it's ever been! Tell me this, Holly – what is the point in us wasting our evening putting out chairs and finalising playlists if there's no catwalk for people to sit and observe or for our boys and girls to walk on?"

Holly pulled the large iPad she was holding close to her chest and stuttered "Erm… Sue?"

"What?" snapped Sue.

Holly apprehensively pointed out toward me and Sue slowly turned.

"What the…" gasped Sue.

"Hi Sue," I slurred as the pain started to borderline cripple my ability to function. "Boy, do *we* really need to talk!"

## [30]

## or

## "Run It All Down: Part II – Shit? Meet Fan!"

**"W**hat the hell are you doing here?" screamed Sue. "How did you get in?"

"Well, I did ring the bell but you had your music on too loud so you left me no choice," I smiled weakly. "I had to drive a car through the top of Debenhams, but thanks for asking!"

"Holly! Call the security guard NOW!" shouted Sue.

"Sue! Sue! Listen," I said slowly. "We need to talk as quickly as possible and we need to get out of here even quicker because you're in danger!"

"From YOU!" sneered Sue as she tried to turn and walk away.

"Sue, can we please just listen to him for a couple of minutes?" Holly said softly.

"No!" spat Sue. "Call the police!"

"Yeah," I replied. "Let's call the police – Let's talk to them about the child models on your books that you farm out to Mayor Mick Hetherington for him and his cronies to abuse at private parties he hosts at his home. Let's talk to them about the fact that you changed Stephie's bookings to suit the perverted demands of some private client of Mick's who wanted to letch on her and you put her in the pathway of all the abuse going on at Mick's place when you sent her up there. Let's…"

"Sue?" Holly interrupted, her face twisting in pain and shock.

I pushed on regardless of how much this next bit was going to push the knife in deeper towards Holly's heart. "… Let's talk to them about the fact that Stephie was killed on Mick's orders because she recorded evidence of what he was doing. Let's talk about the fact that another of your models, Eva Marie, was brutally raped at the same party that you sent her to as well and then she was murdered by the same people that killed Stephie… Let's tell the police all of this but, here's the thing, let's not tell *this* police service though? Because you and I know that the head of this police service is forehead deep in all of this too. Let's go national instead, yeah? Let's talk to *truly* independent police officers. Let's talk to the press. Let's talk and talk and…"

"This is absolutely ridiculous!" Sue laughed emptily. "I'm not going to stand here and let you say the most outlandish things without…"

"I have video recordings. I have audio recordings. So, without what? Go on? Without what? *Evidence*? I'm drowning in fucking evidence, Sue." I shouted, causing my ribs to send shockwaves up my body and make my neck feel like it was being throttled. "Those parents put their trust in you! And you farmed their kids out, for what? For a few hundred quid? A thousand? What? How much were you getting for each of them? Tell me? Did the sick fuck throw you a bonus if they kept quiet afterwards?"

"You… You have no idea what you're saying…" stuttered Sue.

I noticed Holly look down at the iPad in her hands then back up at Sue with a look of fully formed disgust in her eyes.

"What did you say to them? All those kids, Sue? What did you tell them? How did you keep circulating them back up there every month and get them to embrace what was done to them? What did you promise them?" I growled. "You promised them all the fame and all the baubles and you held Stephie out as the idol they could one day emulate, I bet."

"No…" Sue said, the stern defensive tone disappearing from her voice.

"The only thing I don't have right now," I bluffed a little. "is the stone-cold figures on just what you were paid to do something so ruthless as to coldly supply such innocent and vulnerable prey to the predators!"

"Stop it!" Sue whimpered. "You have no idea what you're talking about… I built this business up from thin air into what it is now!"

"A supply chain for sick beasts?" I sneered.

"Fuck you!" Sue spat back. "This entire region was the first to go to shit and Mick Hetherington has single-handedly helped to hold as many head's above water as he possible could. He has found revenue streams that no one else would have thought of!"

"Yeah, too right. But I still don't see him going on Dragon's Den to pitch this idea about leasing child models out for businessmen to fuck…"

"You just don't get it. It's not about that. That's not what's happening…" Sue screamed.

"Bullshit!" I said.

"It's not! You're fucking naïve. Listen, my business was going to go completely tits up when the UK economy flatlined. I was in serious trouble. London stopped taking my calls. Most of Europe wouldn't do business with me and I was in serious trouble. Then Mayor Hetherington comes to me and explains that he has a social group with international reach and that if I can supply models to be additional guests then he would make sure that I'm paid well and when no one else is paying you a penny and your business is your life you stop and you listen to something like that… Yes, you're making digs about the bookings being more for kids than for our adult models but that's because Mick said the younger models brought more of a fun and less jaded vibe than the older ones. But they *weren't* being sent up there for sex. All their parents signed off on them going. All of the events had at least one of my over eighteen year old models there as an agreed chaperone. Not a single complaint was ever made by anyone that something untoward went on up there. That's a fact."

"I don't believe you." I said.

"I don't care," she sneered back. "If sex went on up there it was not part of the agreement and it was not to my knowledge. That's not the business I'm running. But, and it's a big but, if some of the younger girls were having sex up there that's up to them. It's nothing to do with me. What fifteen year old girl isn't losing their virginity ahead of the so-called 'time' anyway? Come on, get real?"

"Are you fucking listening to yourself? What fifteen year old girl is commonly losing her virginity to grown men at tuxedo-clad sex parties ran by their Mayor?" I looked at Holly as I finished what I was saying. I could see the look of revulsion in her face but I continued. "How did Stephanie Jason end up there? I've said what I think. You tell me in your own words."

"Stephie?" Sue replied.

I nodded.

"Mick contacted me at short notice. I already had Stephie's friend Eva going up there by request but he came back to me and said that he had a friend he'd met at a conference who was a huge fan of Stephie's work too. He said that he would pay a large sum of money for a personal meet-and-greet with her and…"

"Define that!" I said sternly.

"Define what?"

"A personal meet-and-greet?"

"They pay to hang out with her. Not have to worry about sharing her with a crowd of people. They drink expensive champagne, take selfies together, talk…" Sue said calmly.

"And you expect her to set her own terms at the end of the night, right?" I said contemptuously. "Like all the escorts?"

"Fuck off, she wasn't an escort and I didn't treat her like one!"

"But she didn't want to go, did she?"

"Of course she didn't. But then she didn't want to go to the Paradox thing I had originally booked her in for either." Sue said. "Stephie was pretty much *done* with all of this modelling and… and… If it wasn't for me explaining just how important she was to the survival of my business I think she would have walked away from all this a year earlier. Stephie wanted to do charity work and be a WAG or something."

"But you needed her to stay where she was?"

"I did. I'm not ashamed to say that." Sue said. "Stephie wasn't aging out of the game at twenty four like a lot of girls. She was still in high demand. But in high demand for what you're insinuating, you're completely wrong!"

"How much? How much did you make for sending Stephie up there?" I asked.

"I'm not going to discuss that with you." Sue shouted back. "That's none of your business!"

"Sue, I have recordings. I have the fucking narrative now. I know what's been going on. And you're in danger. I can't emphasise that enough. But I want you to share with me what you were paid, how you were paid and how it ties indirectly or directly to Mick Hetherington because I need to bring you in and I need you to help me. Everyone involved in this is dying…"

"You are absolutely off your head!" screamed Sue. "Have you listened to yourself? You're every bit the mad man that Mick said you were! There is no grand conspiracy here. You're talking about a local Mayor helping a local businesswoman to keep her business afloat and help young people in the region who want to build their network professionally and… and… and… what happened to Stephie was a heart-breaking tragedy and I'm lost without her but it had nothing to do with Mick or myself or…"

"You are so loyal to Mick fucking Hetherington." I grimaced. "Even right up until this point! And for what? Tell me? Two hundred? Three hundred quid per kid? What was it?"

"Don't be so ridiculous!" laughed Sue falsely.

"I want to see your books, Sue!" I said stepping forward. "I want you to open up your books, I want you to show me which accounts the money for those kids came from and I want you to show me your correspondence with Mick or whoever the intermediary was that he used to keep himself clean."

"I will have nothing to do with…"

Before Sue could finish, Holly stepped forward and held out the iPad.

"This is synced to her MacBook," Holly said. "I don't know how far you'll get but she did everything on that and she does all her emails through this when she's not on it so maybe you could start here?"

Sue span on her feet, shooting the look of death. She reached out to grab the iPad but Holly pulled it back and stepped out of her reach.

"You little shit! You have no idea what you're talking about!" screamed Sue.

"They were my *friends*!" said Holly, through tears. "Bethany has never been the same since she went to one of those events… Stephie is dead and she was lovely and… and… now Eva too!"

"Eva committed suicide, for crying out loud!" shouted Sue.

"Why? WHY did she though?" Holly bellowed back. "What did she see that…"

"Eva *didn't* commit suicide!" I interrupted whilst staggering closer to the two of them. "Eva was murdered and it was made to look like a suicide. Just like Stephie. I have the facts relating to that on tape too."

Tears fell harder from Holly's eyes.

Sue's face dropped into a semi-state of shock.

"I wasn't joking when I said to you that Mick Hetherington is in the process of using a group of four ex-soldiers to clean house on what he sees as the whole sorry incident of what went on the night Stephie died. And do you want to know how loyal that prick is to you, Sue? He's sending those same men up here tonight to kill you too!"

"You're lying!" Sue started to cry.

"I'm not," I replied. "They're on their way now. They're probably looking for their own department store roof to drive in through as we speak. So I'm going to help you get out of here Sue, I give you my word. But it's on one condition…"

Sue looked at me, her eyes were breaking with pain.

“You sit down with me and your laptop or your iPad or whatever and you lead me through everything you know about the arrangement you have with Mick and…”

Before I could finish, the sound of a loud *“HEY!”* echoed around the main red quadrant floor space we stood within. I turned in shock and saw a young kid in a security uniform striding towards us.

“Stay there!” He shouted. “Are you the one that broke into Debenhams? I’ve called the police so don’t even think about running!”

I turned quickly to Holly and whispered “How were you two planning on getting out of here anyway?”

“The security exit down the corridor near Debenhams!” she replied.

“Back the way I came in?” I whispered.

“Yeah, but at ground level!”

I sighed.

*“Did you REALLY check every door and possible point of entry before you opted for the crazy car stuff? Really? Did you? REALLY?”* said Jane’s voice inside my head.

“Let’s start walking…” I said, putting my arm around Holly’s shoulder and my hand on the base of Sue’s back in an attempt to push them on. Sue bristled against my touch at the very same moment that a shot rang out.

We were all so busy looking around to see where it came from and whether the sound was actually gunfire or just a piece of furniture falling over that none of us realised that the front of the security guard’s forehead was missing and blood was spraying out as his body slumped face first lifelessly to the floor.

Sue started to scream. Holly was quick to follow. I kept my hands where they were on both of them and pushed them both quickly.

“RUN!” I shouted.

Two more shots followed.

We ran through the chairs as three more shots swiftly rang out, pinging off nearby display stands and shop fronts as we moved. The second and third of these bursts of gunfire gave me enough bearing to realise that they were coming from the direction of the one walkway up the mall back towards Debenhams that I had just staggered from moments earlier – the same walkway that was our only exit out seeing as all other routes had the same floor to ceiling grate in our paths that had pushed me to jump out of a fourth storey window to get past.

I pushed Sue and Holly in the direction of an escalator in the furthest corner of the red quadrant that would lead us up onto the second floor. As I did, I pulled the gun from my waistband and wildly fired back in the direction the bullets were coming from.

I volleyed two shots back. Plus the two in Tidyman’s feet? That’s four gone!

Sue fell before Holly pulled her back up.

There was a momentary pause in gunfire being returned our way so I took a second to congratulate myself on the fact that of the two shots I’d fired back over my shoulder whilst looking ahead and running up the escalator, *all* of them had clearly taken out their intended targets. I was very obviously some sort of ‘Chow Yun-Fat in Hard Boiled’ level of awesomeness who…

… Nope. Scratch that.

The gunfire quickly started up again, shattering the glass railings either side of us as we got to the top and slid out of view together behind a small information stand that was fixed in the centre of the second floor.

"Believe me now?" I smiled at Sue.

Her eyes fell down on the gun in my hand.

"Oh yeah," I said. "I forgot to mention. I have a gun too. It's not mine. But… look, it's a long story. I'll tell you all later… Anyway, I should also tell you both that I'm currently going through withdrawal from very heavy pain medication that I had developed an addiction towards and it's not going well and…"

Another shot rang out.

I stuck my hand back out around the side of the information stand and aimlessly fired another shot.

That's another one to add to the two as we struggled up the escalator *and* the two in Tidyman's feet?

That's five gone! … Five minus thirteen? *Eight* shots left!

"Sorry," I said. "Where was I? Yeah, so pain medication withdrawals with all the blurry vision that comes with that and then this headwound here…"

I gently tapped on the gaping wound on my forehead.

"… I just, you know, I'm going to do the best I can here okay? I need you both to know that but… they're ex-soldiers who know what they're doing and I'm… well… I'm the best you've got!"

I snuck a look round the side of the information stand and a plan started to formulate. Well, it wasn't exactly a plan per se. More a rapid-fire montage spin through my mind's eye of every action film I'd ever seen in order to desperately steal any bit of inspiration I could. I stopped on the final scene of Butch Cassidy And The Sundance Kid.

*"They ran out from behind cover and were shot to pieces by the Bolivarian Army, weren't they?"* Jane's voice said.

'That was never technically shown!' I felt compelled to think back in reply to my own thoughts.

"Jake…" murmured Sue.

I turned back to look at her. Her hands were now covered in blood and she was staring down at a large swatch of red that was starting to emerge on the trouser material around her thigh.

Holly gasped.

I immediately took Sue's hands and pushed them both down on the thigh area. Dark blood merged up through the spaces between her fingers.

Holly looked to me.

"Put your hands on hers and push down hard!" I said to Holly.

Holly nodded.

"Sue?" I smiled. "I'm just going to tell it to you straight – I need to get you out of here to save you because if we stay here you're going to die. And if you die? You're going to hell for what you did to those kids!"

Sue started to nod her head. “I know… I’m… scared…”

Another shot rang out, echoing around the mall.

“Is there information on there that can prove what Mick has been doing? Payments to you? The list of every kid he’s hired? Who paid you? When? Where from?”

Sue nodded. “All of that.”

“Are you going to help me?”

Sue never stopped nodding.

“Okay. Stay here…”

I pushed myself up onto all fours and did the best semi-crawl I could muster considering my ribs were broken, my vision was blurred and my entire body didn’t move the way I wanted it to. I pulled myself into cover near to the edge of the elevator, looking down across the whole of the mall and across to the red quadrant walkway leading back towards Debenhams. That’s when I finally lay my eyes on them.

There was three of them.

They all wore paramilitary-style black face coverings but were otherwise dressed in ‘civilian’ attire. All three ducked down in a line behind a piece of the assembled catwalk and directly in front of a huge forty foot electronic billboard.

My eyes scanned the area, looking for the cleanest shot I could take. I mean, frankly the ideal would be some sort of metal beam that I could fire at which would then ricochet a bullet off of it, across the mall floor, ping off a metal shutter, fly back towards those cannisters with all the balloons tied to them, recoil off *them*, bounce off the billboard and then fly straight into one of their heads before continuing straight through the brains of the other two. Then I would stand up and do a little Riverdance on the spot whilst lightening came down out of nowhere and struck me, pushing power through my entire body causing all of my wounds to repair themselves and give me…

… Wait. Rewind.

The *cannisters*!

Whilst each of the three members of the ‘A-Team’ took it turns to fire bursts out in every direction apart from the one little pocketed area I hid behind, I wiped the sweat and blood from my eyes and squinted as hard as I could.

‘You can do this!’ I said to myself out loud.

*“I want to say there’s no fucking way whatsoever you can do this!”* Jane’s voice inside my head said. *“But, frankly, I thought there was no way you were going to survive that entire Debenhams debacle so… stuff it, crack on and let’s see how far you get!”*

I started to slow my breathing down.

Thirteen bullet magazine – Thirteen rounds initially available… Five rounds down… Eight rounds left. That’s eight chances to do what needs to be…

… I fired a shot.

I’d no idea where it went but it didn’t seem to land anywhere near where I wanted it to. I fired two more. There was the sound of bullet hitting metal in response.

Four shots sprang quickly back in my direction and I rolled deeper behind the corner of the elevator for cover.

I steadied my breathing once again.

"They're going to kill you, Jake! … And they're going to finish Sue off too… But they'll *have* to kill the kid as well!" I said to myself, referring to Holly. "They can't kill the kid!"

I fired another shot. Bullet on metal rang out once more.

I exhaled deeply and at the exact moment I had emptied my lungs, I saw one of the three stand up and point his firearm towards me. I didn't hesitate and pulled hard and decisively on the trigger.

There was the sound of small pop followed instantaneously by an enormous bang as the cannister blew out, with the force of it firing the standing male backwards and through the screen of the electronic billboard behind him. The screen smashed and a burst of flame fired out from inside of it the minute the male's body made impact with landing there, the cannister itself following him in and whizzing around within the billboard's frame.

The flames started to build a little and work their way up the billboard almost instantly.

Other than the crackling sound of fire, there was complete silence.

I started to laugh and pull myself to my feet – one desperate shot had blew a billboard out and killed all three of them? What were the *chances* of that happening, huh? Well, the chances were ridiculously low weren't they? Which is why it was all the stupider of me to steady myself against the side of the elevator once I was stood up and then shout "Which one of you did I just blow the fuck up? Was that Jason? … Jason Grant? Was that *you*? Or was it Ernie Royce or Geoff Kelsey? … I know your names now! Not that it matters because you are dead as…"

A shot pinged out on the metal of the elevator just above my head causing me to drop to the ground and return a shot, leaving me now with just two left. I got one clear look at the black man I now knew to be Ernie Royce as he made his way forward away from the fire that was now building all the way up the electronic billboard and heading in the direction of the second floor we were all stood on.

"Fuck!" I muttered as I pulled myself away.

I'd just gotten back to my feet when out of nowhere Ernie, now minus his face mask, came running across the second floor from completely the wrong direction since I'd last saw him. Eight or nine feet out from me he threw himself up at the exact moment I raised the gun and his legs span around in mid-air.

His feet kicked the gun clear from my hand and sent it barrelling across the tiled floor away from me. Almost half a second later his other foot slammed into my jaw and tipped me to the ground, head first with my legs feeling like they landed on top of me two weeks later.

My eyes flashed with white and my head now hurt with so much pain a piercing sensation pulsated into my ears and down my jaw line. I couldn't see and I was struck momentarily deaf as Ernie knelt down, pushing his knee into my throat and cutting off the air supply to my head.

"Where… the… … did… you… come…" I spluttered.

"It's called Parkour, bitch!" Ernie grinned.

Ah, yes. *Parkour*! Outside of the opening scene of Casino Royale – the great Martin Campbell one, not the shitty David Niven one – and that underrated French movie, District 13, it is most definitely the pass-time of death-wish carrying wankers. Wikipedia will tell you that its aim is *"…to get from one point to another in a complex environment, without assistive equipment and in the fastest and most efficient way possible. [It] includes running, climbing, swinging, vaulting, jumping, rolling, quadrupedal movement (crawling) and other movements as deemed most suitable for the situation."*

Meanwhile Jake Lehman will tell you that it is totally and utterly stupid and should be outlawed because one) he nearly missed the birth of Jonathan when he got stuck on the Tyne Bridge after they had to close it down due to a couple of ginger Parkour loving fucks deciding to climb it and jump around on the very top of it like a couple of monkeys and two) he can't do it and resents the fact he can't do it seeing as Daniel Craig's stunt double made it look *awesome* in Casino Royale.

"I really don't like you!" sneered Ernie, pressing harder with his knee.

I tapped his leg and gasped "Let me… tell… you… something…"

Ernie eased off ever so slightly and I gasped for air.

I got enough oxygen into my lungs to be able to say "I get that… a lot. Most… people tend to… find… me very… disagreeable!"

Ernie reapplied pressure to my neck.

Suddenly a gun shot rang out close to us. Ernie jumped back off me. I looked back over myself and saw Holly standing there, holding my gun in one hand and the iPad in the other.

"Let him go!" she shouted.

I started to pull myself to my feet as best I could, really now starting to struggle to find not just the strength to do so but the resolve to stay actually standing once I was up.

"Shoot… him!" I whimpered, now drawing a blank as to how many bullets were left whilst slowly coming to the realisation there was a strong likelihood zero bullets were actually left.

Ernie's hands went to his waist, reaching for his own gun - that was no longer there. He put his hands up and started to smile, slowly stepping forward towards Holly as he did. The minute he did I laid eyes on his gun that was now three metres away from where he'd kicked me to the ground.

I started stepping towards the waylaid gun.

"It takes a special sort of resolve to fire a gun at someone, darling!" smiled Ernie.

"Shoot him!" I shouted, striking away the uncertainty as to what was left in the gun's chamber.

Holly started to look uncertain but her grip on the gun tightened nonetheless.

I slowly and carefully reached down and picked Ernie's gun up.

"I know the resolve it takes." Ernie continued. "I know it because I have it and I can see it in other people and you don't have it, girl! I don't see it!"

Holly fired the gun.

Which was awesome, right?

*What a girl*!

Especially in those circumstances with that level of pressure and…

… No. No. Stop. You know what? *FUCK* Holly!

Because there *was* one shot left in that gun and it bypassed Ernie completely and slammed straight into my right shoulder, knocking me back and setting off Ernie's gun in my hand. I crumpled to the ground and let out a scream.

It's at this point that you can take my comments regarding gunshots in the prologue as sacrosanct. Action heroes in movies *are* always taking a hit and they never flinch. In fact, you know the only person who's ever taken a gunshot to their person in a film and reacted actually realistically?

The president in Oliver Stone's JFK!

You know what no one tells you or shows you?

That the pain is so immediate, harsh and absolutely intense that it causes you to shit your pants. Not a lot… Well, I guess it's determined by how much you had in your bowels at that point but, still… It's totally irresponsible of TV and filmmakers to show you all that gunfire and the occasional 'flesh wound' or whatever with the hero just pushing on. They never have a true-to-life moment where Bruce Willis or whoever the action hero is picks himself up and shouts "Fuck that *hurt*! Now, let me just go change my boxer shorts and wet-wipe the back of my legs then let's go get these bastards!"

I withered on the ground as blood flowed out the back of my shoulder, indicating both that the bullet had passed straight through and also that I still had blood left to lose which, judging from the wooziness in my head, was rather surprising to me.

"JESUS CHRIST!" I screamed.

"I'm so, so sorry!" Holly yelped whilst walking towards me. "I'm sorry. Are you okay?"

"NO, I'M NOT OKAY! YOU SHOT ME! AND IT REALLY…"

I stopped and caught sight of Ernie lying motionless on the floor. His jaw was two foot to his right and blood cascaded away from his face, filling out all over the tiles around him.

"… Wait. Who shot him?" I grimaced through the pain.

Holly now took note of Ernie's corpse and retched.

"You shot me… That was with one bullet left, right? So who…" I slowly looked down at Ernie's gun, now on the ground at my feet where I'd dropped it when Holly shot me.

I was about to speak again but a small explosion ripped out of the top of the nearby electronic billboard near to us, setting alight to the fairy lights that hung all along the ceiling around us. Each bulb in nearby vicinity to the billboard started to pop and the cabling on which the lights hung started to give way and drop loose.

"We better get Sue and get out of here!" I gasped.

"Sue's dead!" Holly said as tears reformed in her eyes.

"What?" I replied. "She's…"

"Dead!" Holly said. "She's dead!"

I exhaled hard and let the pain I'd been fighting against just take over my entire body; the head wound, the broken ribs, the foot imprint embedded into my jaw, the goddamn bullet wound in my shoulder. I used the news as a release and screamed "FUCK!" as loud as my body could muster up.

More fairy lights popped and wiring lit up in flames. There was an explosive burst that came out of the electronic billboard intense enough despite being so far away that it knocked me off my feet.

I painfully pulled myself straight back up. "Holy fu… Listen, we better get out of here!"

Holly stepped forward. "Six… Seven… Eight… Zero."

I looked at her quizzically.

"Six, seven, eight, zero!" she repeated. "That's the pin number for her iPad! She told me before she died… Hetherington's email communications are from a Google mail account under the name 'Paul Forbes'… She told me that too!"

I started to smile. Just a little bit though. Because we didn't know what we had on the iPad to get excited about yet.

"She said she has account information on the Quick Books app on her iPad. I have the password for that too. She's told me the accounts to look for that can be linked back to Hetherington… so how about you let me get you the hell out of here and I help you get Stephie and Eva the justice they deserve!"

I started to nod. For a second I forgot about the fact Holly had shot me just moments earlier and I decided that I was now beginning to really, really like this girl.

"You know something Holly?" I smiled. "This almost, almost, almost makes me forgive you for shooting me!"

Holly took a step forward and let a smile form through her tears. "Get stuffed. I'd never fired a gun before and you were all like 'Shoot him! Shoot him!' and there's fire and stuff going on and minutes earlier Sue had died on me and…"

I never saw him coming.

I couldn't even tell you from which direction he came.

But I can tell you from the state of him that there was very little chance he pulled off the same Parkour stuff Ernie did to get on top of us. Either way, Jason Grant sprang out of nowhere and punched Holly mid-sentence clean off her feet, knocking her unconscious and sending the iPad scattering across the floor and towards the edge of the second tier we were stood on.

He turned to face me and I could now see that the left side of his face and ear were all burnt red raw and starting to blister. The hair on the same side was burnt off too and the blistering had started to run down his neck towards what looked like charring on the collar of his shirt.

I think my 'wonder shot' which burst the cannister and made the billboard explode caused that so you can imagine as a result Jason probably had some 'strong words' that he was wanting to impart to me.

He strode towards me. I quickly bent down to pick up the gun at my feet but my body seemed to work at a considerably slower rate than my brain was commanding it to. No sooner did I get my hand to the gun than Jason's knee slammed into my face and knocked me straight onto my backside. My arse hadn't touched the ground for more than a second before he followed through with a swift kick to the side of my head, sprawling me down to my left.

"Hi Jake!" he shouted as he reached down, picked me up and pulled me to my feet before hooking me straight in my gut and sending blindingly intense convulsions straight up to my brain. Blood sprayed from my mouth as my ribs now started to feel like they were exposed through my skin and being twanged like strings on a guitar.

I saw the blood from my mouth hit the tiled floor and I knew I was in serious trouble. Jason grabbed my throat and pulled me back into a standing position.

"You know, I hate this fucking city!" he sneered into my face. "I really, *really* hate it! It's all 'why-eyes' and 'beer-can sandwiches' and 'man' at the end of every bastard sentence. It makes my skin crawl… so I very much begrudge you pissing around and making me get dragged back up to this utter shithole again!"

He squeezed harder on my throat. I had no fight left in me to even raise my hands and even attempt to try prizing at his fingers.

I could feel myself starting to fade.

Jason pushed me backwards at the same time that he let go of my throat and I fell instantly to the floor without any means to hold myself up.

"The stupid thing is I actually admired your tenacity at first, you know?" Jason grinned. "But then your resilience really started to piss me off, I'm not going to lie. You need to understand what your place is and the problem is you don't. You still think one man can make a difference and in this day and age that's just dumb. Even if it *were* true, you're absolutely not that man. Look at you, just… *look* at you! Who the fuck do you think you are? Who do you think you're dealing with?"

"I am… definitely… no big deal…" I stuttered through the pain. "But I… blew your face off… dickhead! … So how shit… does… that make you?"

Jason smiled.

The fire was now spreading out across the ceiling and dropping enough bits of flaming tile down onto the ground to now cause the unfolded chairs to catch fire too and create sporadic enflamed puddles around the bottom floor of the red quadrant mall. The fairy lights continued to pop and the cabling continued to snap and drop. One piece of the light display dropped right down across the bannister between where I'd been thrown and where Holly lay unconscious.

In the middle of the two of us lay Ernie's gun. Jason started to walk backwards towards it whilst maintaining eye contact with me.

"You're right!" he said. "You're absolutely right. You struck lucky and did this to me, I'll give you that! But, here's the thing…"

He kept on moving towards the gun.

"… I was just going to kill you, pick up my pay cheque and head back down the motorway in time to open Christmas presents with my girlfriend! She's a model, by the way. How about the irony in all of *that*? But you've done this to me so now…"

He slowed his steps down but kept moving.

"... Now? In the grand scheme of there being a reaction to every action, I have to respond. So here's what I'm going to do – I'm going to kill you. That's a given. That's what we call a forgone conclusion, son! Then I'm going to throw this tight little piece of arse over the balcony... what a waste, by the way... and then after all that I'm going to nip back to my hotel and put a cold compress and some Sudocrem on this thing..."

He pointed at his face.

"That's not a... minor burn," I gurgled through the blood coming up out of my mouth. "That's a... Two-Face from Batman job... right there!"

"Keep the quips coming, boy!" smirked Jason. "Because once the Sudocrem has dried in I'm going to go find your wife and I'm going to rape her in front of your fucking kids... then make her watch as I blow their brains out in front of her. Then I'm going to leave her to work out how to live with that..."

Jason turned on his heels and bent down to pick up the gun as he shouted "That bitch was a two-bit social media whore. You put us all through *this* and cost all these people, including your family, their lives for what? A goddamn Facebook model or something!"

*"Okay. You chose to put yourself here."* Jane's voice said, appearing inside my head at that exact moment. *"And you're here – So what are you going to do? You need to come home to us, Jake. You need to get up and you need to come home to us. Because if you stay where you are you're dead. Holly? She's dead too. Your wife? Your children? Stephie's parents? All of them die as well! You have come this far and if you stay on the floor embracing the pain and waiting for the bullet you're going to..."*

I shook the voice away and placed both palms flat, either side of my legs.

I thought about everything that had been taken from me... I thought about the career I loved, the passion I had and the dreams I held... I thought about the pain I had put Jane and her family through... I thought about Madeline... I thought about all the laughing that'd gone on behind my back, the jokes that had been made at my expense as I slumped and limped my way around the city on 'The Beg' for anything that paid so much as a pound... I thought about Stephie and the fear she must have felt when the police lights gave way to Jason getting into that passenger seat alongside her and the pain and panic she would have experienced as her trachea was broken and she slowly choked to death in that car out on that road... I thought about Eva and how her parents deserved to know the truth just as much as Stephie's... I thought about all the grainy frames in those video clips that made up the faces of young girls being raped by men who'd paid Mick Hetherington thousands for the 'privilege' of attending his home to do so... I thought about Mick Hetherington and that odious smile of his and how he'd most likely arrange another party the next month with girls supplied from another source, most likely the care homes and foster units his own local authority ran, unless he was stopped once and for all... I thought about my boys and their smiles and the cute way in which Jonathan says certain words and how Jack likes to wake me up on the weekends I'm actually at home by kissing me on the nose, like he's done since he was two years of age...

… and I pushed myself up onto my feet and thrust the pain as deep down inside myself as I could manage, surging forward unsteadily but at enough speed to pick up enough momentum to get to Jason before he'd had a chance to stand up properly. I grabbed him and swung him off-balance and into the glass rail next to us that circled the whole of the second floor, the gun dropping from his hand and clattering to the ground below. Before he had a chance to push himself back from the rail I landed on top of him, throwing my weight against him.

Agony coursed through my entire body. My vision started to blur out. My legs started to buckle. I saw Jane's face smiling at me.

*"I chose you!"* her voice said.

I grabbed Jason's throat, pinning him where he stood and I slammed my fist down into his face. He recoiled and blood spread across his face at the same speed the look of furious anger and hatred did too. We began to tussle along the rail and straight into the path of a load of cabling and fairy light wires that hung loose from the ceiling.

"You fuc…"

I didn't let him finish.

I grabbed the nearest piece of cabling and started to furiously wrap it tight around his neck, pulling tight as I went and causing shards of broken fairy light glass to embed into his skin and small lines of blood start to emerge.

"This?" I spat as Jason's eyes bulged. "*This* is how you hang someone, you sick fuck!"

And with that I pushed myself over the railing and took Jason with me. I landed with an immediate thud on the small, half a metre alcove on the other side of the railing and the bottom end of my body started to slide out over the edge pulling me down to the ground below.

I grabbed out at the bottom end of the railing to take a hold as Jason's body swung out into the open space alongside me. Some of the cabling gave way which dropped him lower - but not so low that it prevented his feet from hitting the ground. Or stop his neck from snapping. The sound of it doing so echoed around the mall, even above the sound of the growing flames.

I held on with one hand as best as someone could when their ribs are shot and the other arm has a bullet wound in it. The pain now shot up my body like electric shocks and I had nothing left. My hands were slippy with blood and sweat and I could feel the cold metal of the rail slide out of my grip.

I had nothing left.

… I thought again about Jack and how I knew he was going to grow up to be the best in his field at whatever he chose to do.

… I thought again about Jonathan and how I imagined he would take a little longer to find his feet in whatever he chose to do in life but that he'd get there and he'd be loved because I could see already in him that he had a tremendous heart.

… I thought again about Jane and that very first night in the pub when I stroked my index finger across that tiny scar on the corner of her forehead and kept my finger going, brushing the hair back behind her ear and letting my hand fall to the back of her neck. I remembered how she smiled, bit her bottom lip as she leant forward towards me and… I closed my eyes as my vision started to blacken completely and my hand around the railing started to open.

Force was applied against me that shook my eyes open only to see Holly's bloodied face right in front of mine on the ledge as she started to agonisingly pull at my shirt and underneath my arms.

I screamed.

"Use your legs… Help me out here!" she gasped.

She lay back as she pulled and yanked at my body, breathlessly getting me fully up onto the ledge with my head rather ungentlemanly landing between her legs. She quickly stood and cautiously helped me to my feet.

"There's no easy way of doing this." She said as she pushed me over the railings back onto the safe side of the second floor.

I hollered in pain as I landed then lay on my back, starting to feel myself slip into unconsciousness. Then Holly's hand blasted off the side of my face and slapped me into a semi-awakened state once again.

"You're only halfway done, remember?" she said, clutching the iPad and dragging me to my feet.

## [31]

## or

## "And... Breathe..."

Holly and I hung off each other as we managed to limp ourselves along the second floor away from the fire, down a set of stairs onto the ground floor and then out along the red quadrant mall towards the security corridor exit by Debenhams. We'd never get to take that route though because up ahead of us police and fire officers worked to unsecure the security grate in front of us.

It dropped down, opening up the mall and providing a pathway for meathead firearms officers to come circling towards us.

Holly had her arm wrapped around and underneath the top of my torso and was hoisting me as best she could considering she was a tiny little slip of a thing and I was a bloated six foot plus mess of a man.

"You're not going to pass out are you?" she asks nervously.

"You mean from the blood loss? The blood loss from the bullet hole?" I replied.

"I said I was sorry – but in fairness I also saved your life too!" she offered before being interrupted by DI Andrews pushing through everyone and coming to an abrupt halt in front of us which in turn caused Holly and I to stagger to a stop too.

"Jesus Christ! Are you…" he stopped himself from finishing his sentence whilst looking me up and down and realising that saying the word 'okay' as I bled to death in front of him would probably lead to me grabbing one of these firearms officer's guns and shooting him dead there and then.

"We found the body back at your office!" he says.

"The recording? Did you…" I started to speak but the pain in my face bristled and then sent sharp shocks to my brain so intense they weakened my legs. I leant in hard against Holly, forcing her to stumble and DI Andrews to step forward and take hold of us both.

"I watched it…" he replied before faltering and holding his hand to his head and freezing. "… Jesus, Jake! This is bad. This is bad, right?"

"You tell me Andrew?" I said.

I saw him wince at my dig but he seemed to let it pass so I took a step forward and lifted his chin so he met my eyes. I took a deep breath as best I could through my swollen face. "Remember I told you a long time ago that a line was drawn and that we both needed to make a choice about what side of that line we stand on? Remember that?"

"You've never let me forget it, have you?" he answered.

"It's not too late to step back over. It's not." I said. "It should have been put out there for everyone to see and stopped a long time ago. You know that deep down, don't you? But it's going out there now for everyone to see. *Tonight*. Everyone is going to know the truth finally. And you have to decide right now where you want to stand… You can be the one who takes people down or one of many that are taken down?"

A burning Christmas tree on the second floor gave way and fell to the ground directly behind us, creating an almighty crash that unsettled everyone. DI Andrews and a couple of waiting paramedics jumped forward and started to lead us out.

"What are you asking me for?" DI Andrews finally whispered in my ear as we walked. "I don't understand where it is you're asking me to stand right now."

Paramedics helped Holly and I into the back of the ambulance.

"You don't know?" I started to say as they lay me down on the wheeled stretcher.

"Jake?" Andrews said. "The confession on the recording is one thing but…"

"If I thought you could be trusted I'd show you the recordings of the child rapes too. And the recordings of your Chief Constable assaulting Stephie the night she died. Maybe you might want to go check out the boot of the Ford Escort parked in the bushes over there too!"

Andrews looked at me with confusion.

"You'll find Tidyman – who tried to stitch this whole cover-up at the police end on you by the way!"

Andrews' face twisted with immediate anger.

"What have *I* done in all of this?"

"It's probably… more… like… what *haven't* you done? He's going to claim… that…" I winced with the pain. "… He was submitting important evidence… up the line… and you were disposing of it."

"That didn't happen!" gasped Andrews. "I know you won't believe me but…"

"There's no loyalty among the corrupt, huh?" I smiled.

Outside of the ambulance was the sound of commotion and arguing, with a fifty-something, strikingly good looking red-headed woman appearing with two uniformed officers either side of her at the back of the ambulance's open doors.

"Jake Lehman?" she bellowed with commanding authority.

I weakly raised my hand and made a little wave, noting the Durham Police insignia on the officers uniforms in the process.

"I'm sorry, who are you?" Andrews asked.

"Who are you?" the woman barked back.

"I'm Detective Inspector Andrews, who are…"

"GET HIM OUT OF HERE!" the woman shouted as the uniformed officers reached inside to take hold of Andrews.

Andrews pulled back and screamed "Who the fuck do you think…"

He couldn't get to finish his sentence because a tussle broke out that started to shake the ambulance from side to side. The woman confidently stepped in between the Durham officers and Andrews.

"Listen," she said calmly now. "Listen to me. I'm Chief Constable Lane of Durham Police and I'm politely asking you to step *down* out of the ambulance, immediately stand *down* from your position or I'm going to have you dragged *down* to the ground and arrested in front of your colleagues. If you don't, I'm going to have your career flushed *down* the pan in an instant. Are you *down* with that?"

"You had that… rehearsed… before you got… here… didn't you?" I smirked through the pain.

Chief Constable Lane shot me a look that suggested now was not the time nor was she a fan of what we shall refer to at this moment as 'quippery'.

Andrews looked at me.

"Don't look at him!" Lane shouted. "He has no power of arrest! *I* do. I'm the one with my hand on the flusher here, Andrews. I'm the one that's got a feeling a 'suspicion of perverting the course of justice' arrest is the right way to go with you. So look at me…"

"Jake?" Andrews said to me quietly. "I understand where it is you're asking me to stand now. Let me help you."

"GET HIM OUT OF HERE!" shouted Lane.

The uniformed officers successfully secured hold of Andrews and pulled him from the ambulance as Lane herself squeezed past him and sat down alongside Holly, opposite me on the stretcher.

She held out her hand. "Jake Lehman, I'm Jessica Lane."

I weakly took her hand.

"You smell like shit!" she said.

"I shit my pants!" I said softly.

"You shit your pants?" Lane said loudly.

"Shush, man!" I gasped. "*Jesus*!"

"You shit your pants?" she repeated more quietly this time.

"I got shot and… it made me do… a poo in my pants! … I don't really want to… get into this any further if I'm honest… The 'shame train' is not something… I want to ride with you because I have only just met you but… yeah… I smell like shit… because I shit my pants… I shit my pants because this crazy bitch right here… shot me!"

Holly smiled and extended her hand. "Hi, I'm Holly!"

"Jesus, that wasn't a springboard for you to introduce yourself, man!" I griped in agony.

Lane smiled.

"Okay, this is a, pardon the pun, shit-show but first things first I need you to know that you can trust me. We're two days out from Christmas and I've dropped everything to jump boroughs without explicit authority and dig my hands in the shit on this. Again, no pun intended. That should tell you everything you need to know in terms of trust, okay? I don't have to be here right now… but I am!"

Lane turned her head to Holly.

"Can you give us a minute?" she said softly.

"She *stays*!" I said. "She risked her life to get more evidence on Hetherington. They were her friends that have been murdered. And she saved my life too… I mean, she also shot me so, you know, fuck her but… yeah… she stays!"

Holly smiled warmly.

Lane nodded reluctantly. "I got here, I watched the footage, I listened to the audio recordings and I've alerted *my* Police & Crime Commissioner, not yours. Yours is partying right now alongside Hetherington and Hadenbury up at the civic centre if my information is correct so… we're not risking disclosures we can't control there. Word has gone straight up the line to the Home Office, the IOPC and the HMIC. They've all told me to hold back…. But I'm here regardless and not only am I here but I've got a team of some of my best and most trusted officers cannonballing up the A1 to get here too and we're going to go raid Hetherington's party tonight!"

I nodded and smiled at the confirmation.

"But I need you to do something for me," Lane said quietly. "I need you to call your friends now and ask them to stand down."

I looked at her quizzically as she continued.

"They're on their way up to council headquarters which I've urged them not to do and they've chosen to ignore what I felt was a command that should be heeded. The public display and the humiliation they're intending is *not* the way to go."

"I won't do that." I said. "I'm going there now to…"

"Dude, you're going *nowhere*!" interjected the paramedic. "You've lost a lot of blood and we suspect you've got quite a bit of internal bleeding. We need to get you to hospital."

I shook my head and painfully waved my hand at him.

"I've seen the footage, Jake. I'm here because I'm prepared to act." Lane said. "But I need to act with haste and I need to do this right. This entire region is on the cusp of going up like a nuclear blast. What do you think is going to happen if all of these people marching in the streets tonight find out that the local authority have been screwing the system, screwing its people AND screwing their kids in the sickest possible sense? They'll tear them apart and leave the body parts strewn all over the Civic Centre car park! That's not the way this can go!"

I shook my head.

"Time is running out, Jake." Lane said as she leant forward and gently took hold of my hand. "I promised your friends I'd come and make sure you're safe which I've as good as done so I now need to see you on your way to hospital. All of *this* that happened here tonight? All of this we can take a look at later down the line. What you did tonight? That takes some serious…"

"No, no." I interrupted, sitting myself up painfully on the stretcher. "Stop. Just stop…I don't think you understand. This is my party. You're my guest…"

"Listen to me, Mr Lehman…" Lane attempted.

"Oh, it's Mr Lehman now? Ok. No, listen to me. I'm getting to council headquarters and I'm going all in alongside Emily and Psychic. That's just what's happening. There's no other variation. Now, whether you want to drive me, whether I have to hijack this ambulance, I don't really care."

"No *other* variation? I can have you arrested and handcuffed to this stretcher and then go and do what needs to be done. This isn't a performance. This is not the final stretch of the action film, Jake. This is serious. I cannot and will not..."

I pulled my hand away.

"I really, really need you to understand something, Chief Constable Lane..." I took a deep breath against the pain and steadied myself as I pointed around at the complete cavalcade of injuries I now carried. "... I didn't go through all of this, I didn't put my family at risk... I didn't do this to just go sit on the substitutes bench, okay? Hetherington destroyed my life. I have to see this through."

"This isn't about revenge!" Lane replied.

"This is about *justice*!" I shot back, causing the pain to intensify.

"I don't know what you want me to say here. But I cannot let your plan in its current form go ahead. This is about swift, clean and most importantly discreet arrests that don't pour petrol on the fire. We are not dragging these people out the front door tonight. We're tagging, bagging and pulling them out through the back, driving them back down to our borough and awaiting further instruction from well above even me – *that's* how big this is!"

My eyes started to well with tears. "I need this... *please*."

Lane looked at me. She took back hold of my hand.

"They're at the civic centre in town, waiting for my call to put things in motion..." I stammered. "I've come so far... so far... Hetherington took everything from me. *Everything*. There's not a part of my life... that... doesn't carry some stain or damage from him... I can't close my eyes without... thinking about the things... he has done and... how I should have done more to stop him. I need this... I need to stare this evil in the eyes tonight and... I need him to know that through it all, he... never completely broke me... That I *endured* everything!"

Her eyes narrowed as her stare burrowed into me.

"For fucks sake, you're one of *them* types huh?" she sighed. "Are you going to die on me? Because I'm in so much shit on the whole for potential overreach already, I can't have you prick my conscience ever so slightly by dying on me too!"

The paramedic stepped forward once again. "I really, really don't think we should waste any more time in getting this man to hospital."

Lane twisted her mouth and took a seconds pause. "I hear you. But what could you do to buy him another hour?"

I smiled and tipped my head towards the paramedic stood above me.

"Can you stitch this, wrap this and bandage this?" I said as I pointed to the most significant injuries about my person. "And, this is going to sound really cheeky but could someone nip back to Debenhams and pick me up a clean pair of underpants?"

# [32]

# or

# "The 'Richard Kimble'…"

The ambulance barrelled along the Scotswood Road with full sirens wailing and lights flashing having crossed over onto the north side of the Tyne. I lay on the stretcher having bandages applied and temporary glue pushed across certain wounds. Lane sat on the floor at the back of the ambulance making her own calls, shouting to be heard over the sound of the ambulance sirens. Holly sat alongside me, holding my phone to my ear as I talked to Psychic.

I could've told the paramedic about my opioid dependency and my twenty-four hours plus withdrawal from it but I didn't. No, actually I *couldn't*. I was in such a state of sheer agony the likes of which I'd never experienced before that I knew for the first time ever I actually *needed* the strongest possible pain-dispensing opioid to dilute some of the hurt if I was going to survive the next couple of hours the way I needed to. So whilst I snatched a brief conversation with Psychic, a paramedic shot a small syringe of morphine into my system through my already bruised and bloodied left arm. I started to feel for the first time like my body was not on fire from the inside out.

"Bobby got us in. We're tucked tight inside, no one knows we're here… Are you okay?" Psychic said quietly down the phone.

"I'm not, no. But I'm hanging in there and I'll see you soon." I said.

"You let me know when you're here and ready and I'll cue you in. I've got full control of the music, the lighting, everything…"

"How? How will I know…"

"Emily is going to get you a mic. The minute you start speaking I'll start throwing out everything you need, don't worry. Psychic replied.

"And you're sure you're all set with the clips?" I asked.

"Like you wouldn't believe!" he laughed down the phone. "This is going to be monumental!"

I thanked Psychic and said I'd see him soon.

Then, just as I went to hang up he spoke. "Jake?"

"Yeah?"

"Emily is still an unbearable bitch!"

"Emily's our lifeline, lord and saviour. Show her the respect she deserves!" I smiled.

I hung up and Holly went to hand me my phone back. I asked her to text my wife and tell her that she was good to take the boys to their carol concert tomorrow morning after all. Jane's reply came back instantaneously:

*"Yeah, but will YOU be there? xxx"*

The minute the ambulance pulled to a stop around the back of Newcastle Council's civic centre, the true enormity of what we were facing started to really hit home. I could hear the crowds of protestors around the front entrance echoing out in unison into the night air. The flashing blue lights of a police presence out at that end of the building bounced off the surface of walls and bus stops across the road. The chants suggested a crowd of some enormity.

I slowly stepped down from the ambulance with a paramedic's assistance and Lane removed her high-visibility police coat and placed it around my shoulders. I noted that marked Durham police vehicles had pulled into the rear car park alongside us. I looked nervously to Lane.

"Are you sure about this?" she said gently.

I shook my head but said yes regardless.

Holly stepped forward and kissed me softly on the cheek. "I'll see you in there!"

Lane signalled to her officers who started to form around us as we walked. She put her phone to her ear and said "Hi Emily, we're here and coming in through the back!"

As I was helped towards the back door of the civic centre, I stumbled slightly and the paramedic held me on my feet. I saw some dark-suit clad private security guards up in front. One of them stepped forward.

"Are we going to have a problem, gentlemen?" asked Lane.

The security guard looked to me. "Mr Lehman? Mr Maitland sends his regards and says he'll see you soon. I've been told to inform you that your colleague is safely inside?"

He winked and stepped out of the way.

I looked confused and Lane picked up on it. I shrugged at her and we walked on.

We passed through the ground floor foyer of the building and could hear the sounds of East 17's "Stay Another Day" come to an end and blend straight into "Do They Know It's Christmas" by Band Aid up ahead in the conference suite / ballroom across the way. If they're going off even the sturdiest of Christmas Compilation albums as their playlist for the evening then they must be scraping the barrel with the shit ones at the end of the track listing by now, surely?

The pain medication had well and truly kicked in and whilst it wasn't making all of the agony subside it had certainly taken away the throbbing in my head well enough to clear up my vision and not make every single movement I made feel like razor blades were grinding at my joints.

We didn't get within four feet of the door leading into the ballroom area where we knew Hetherington and company would be when Chief Constable Hadenbury himself appeared from a side corridor with none other than Janet McKinley, our borough's Police and Crime Commissioner, by his side. They were just about to re-enter the conference suite again when Hadenbury clocked Lane and did a slight double-take. He was dressed in a perfectly cut tuxedo and wearing a garish Santa hat of which the bobble end bounced when his head did the two-move glance at Lane.

Janet was bedecked in the sort of gown that looked like the mutton had hired a lamb costume for the evening.

"Jessica?" Hadenbury shouted, stopping at the doors. "What a surprise? What is going…"

He stopped himself on sight of uniformed officers from her borough coming up directly behind us. His facial expression turned to abject horror on squinting at me through all my blood and swelling, realising there and then who I was. Janet looked to Jessica and her officers then back to Lane.

"May I ask what's going on?" Janet said. "We would have expected some sort of notification if you were needing to…"

Lane stepped past Janet and shut her down before her sentence concluded.

She held out her hand towards Hadenbury's torso. "Graham, I need you to step back away from the door here and listen to me very carefully indeed…"

"You don't direct me, *girl…*" sneered Hadenbury.

"Oh," smiled Lane knowingly. "We're doing it *this* way? Okay… Mr Graham Hadenbury I am hereby arresting you for perverting the course of justice contrary to Common Law, on suspicion of arranging and facilitating the commission of a child sex offence contrary to Section 14 of the Sexual Offences Act 2003, on suspicion of misconduct in a public office, complicity in a criminal offence, namely aiding and abetting the murder of…"

"WHAT THE FUCK ARE YOU TALKING ABOUT?" screamed Hadenbury.

"Graham?" gasped Janet.

"You do not have to say anything. But, it may harm your defence if…"

"JANET! GO GET MICK AND HIS TEAM, NOW!" shouted Hadenbury.

Between his shouting and the rising sound of the crowd outside, some of whom were starting to see past the police line outside and through the glass doors into the foyer, my head was starting to ring again.

*"♫♫…it's hard but while you're having fun. There's a world outside your window, and it's a world of dread and fear… Where a kiss of love can kill you, and there's death in every tear. And the Christmas bells that ring there are… ♫♫"*

Band Aid continued to reverberate through the doors in front of us. Local police officers emerged in the foyer to our left, seeing Hadenbury lit up screaming and shouting and Durham officers trying to get their hands on him.

"Sir?" said one of the Hadenbury's uniformed men as he walked towards us in a group of six. "Sir, are you okay?"

"OFFICERS! ARREST THESE PEOPLE NOW!" Hadenbury hollered.

"Stand your men down, *NOW*!" Lane shot back. "Don't do this, Graham!"

Lane's officers got between her and the approaching local uniformed officers.

"OFFICERS, THIS IS A…"

Lane never let him finish. She re-positioned her body so she had both Hadenbury and his officers in her line of sight.

"Gentlemen," she shouted. "Chief Constable Hadenbury is being arrested on suspicion of the following offences; perverting the course of justice, arranging and facilitating the commission of a child sex offence, misconduct in a public office and complicity in a criminal offence in relation to the aiding and abetting of the murder of Stephanie Jason. How do you guys want to play this out? You want to get named as witnesses to the arrest or you want to see yourselves listed on a charge sheet printed out and hung alongside his?"

The officers slowed their steps to a halt. They started to look at each other with confusion before one of them stepped into the line of sight of a shocked and appalled Janet McKinley.

"M'am?" The officer said barely audibly to Janet. "What do we do here?"

"Stand down!" whispered Janet. "Stand down!"

"JANET?" screeched Hadenbury.

Janet turned her back on him and looked to Lane. "I hope and pray that you have all your facts and evidence in order because these are incredibly serious charges that could end either his career or yours!"

Lane pointed her hand to me. "You might want to follow this gentleman inside through those doors!"

I smiled. "Hi Miss McKinley. I think we're going to be having a lot of conversations over the coming months… If you'd like to come with me?"

Janet simply looked me up and down. Her face screamed confusion, revulsion and contempt all stirred up and left to manifest itself as one singular expression. Suddenly Emily appeared out of nowhere and thrust a cordless mic into my hand. She gasped as she did so.

"Jesus, Jake. You look…"

"Shit? Yeah, I'm hearing that a lot lately!" I smirked.

"Are you okay?"

I nodded. "Let's do this!"

I side-stepped Hadenbury as he lunged at Lane but was quickly thrown back against the wall by uniformed Durham officers who promptly spun him on his feet and started to handcuff him in the rear position. The Santa hat atop his head flopped gormlessly over his face as they did. The last words I heard as Emily pulled upon the conference suite doors and led me through them were Lane's as Hadenbury was escorted away.

"Let me try that again… You do not have to say anything. But, it may harm your defence if you do not mention when questioned something which you later rely on in court. Anything you do say may be given in evidence. Do you understand, Mr Hadenbury?"

I walked into the suite to find a sea of tuxedos, gowns and tawdry Christmas decorations. Band Aid had thankfully finished and been replaced with speeches coming from a very tinny microphone. There at the front of this 'ocean' was Mick Hetherington himself, tuxedo-clad with his tie undone and holding court with the mic in his hand. He was seemingly midway through another ego-stroking speech to his disciples.

"… Anyone who knows me knows that my core belief at the heart of everything is that it is *all* about the work. If you put in the work, if you're prepared to work, if you believe in the work you do then you *will* succeed. That's why whilst the people of this city continue to flounder and fail and blame everyone but themselves, the city *itself* prevails. That's because of the people in the room here tonight. The people who care about Newcastle Upon Tyne and put in the work here within these hallowed halls to keep it functioning. We've faced great resistance from its residents this year yet we've never let it affect the work we do. I'm proud to head up a team that has you people on it. I'm serious. You all make my job so much easier and you deserve tonight. Tonight is all about *you*!"

The amassed crowd started to applaud.

Hetherington held up his hand to quieten them down so he could continue with the next part of his speech. I kept applauding.

I kept applauding until it became the only, uncomfortably noticeable sound in the room and people started to turn to see where the sound was coming from. On sight of me some people became to audibly gasp and wince, moving off to the side to make room for me as I staggered forward as best I could with Emily walking nearby alongside me for support.

As I did so I noticed suited private security staff span out around the room and scattered up against each wall inside the conference suite. My eyes suddenly fell on Bobby Maitland tucked away as discreetly as possible in the corner of the room. Ryan stood to his right as always. Bobby covertly lifted a champagne glass in my direction as the briefest of salutations.

I clicked the microphone on, let a little bit of the feedback play out from its head and then lifted it to my mouth to let out a shattering fake "WOOOOO!!" in order to secure the last lot of attention in the room.

"No, No, Mayor Hetherington I cannot allow you to be so humble!" I said loudly and clearly. "Tonight most definitely is about *you*. It's always about you, isn't it? Because you <u>own</u> this city don't you?"

Hetherington lifted his own microphone, looking decidedly panicked as he did. "Ladies and Gentlemen, please don't be alarmed. This is Jake Lehman. Mr Lehman has a little bit of a dangerous obsession with me and police have spoken to him in the past about that, haven't they Jake? … You *really* shouldn't be here. This is an exclusive and by invite-only event for staff and associates of this great council."

He smiled odiously at me whilst his eyes filled with venomous hate.

"I'm going to ask our security team to come forward," he continued, "and assist in removing Mr Lehman from the building so we can get on with enjoying…"

I lifted the mic back to my mouth. "You *don't* own this city? No? My mistake. I guess this isn't you then?"

I dramatically clicked my finger on the hand that wasn't now numbing from the bullet wound in my shoulder. The screen up behind Hetherington, at that point flowing with a photograph slideshow of various Newcastle landmarks and different events that had taken place within the city that year, suddenly clicked to black and then instantly played a video clip:

There was Hetherington on camera staring at the man we now knew as Chris Reiser. He turned back to face whoever held the camera but that you and I know was Stephie Jay on the last night she was alive.

*"Then you'll have no problem with me having a quick look then?"* Hetherington was heard to say.

*"I have many a problem with you doing that!"* Stephie replied off camera.

*"Please hand your bag over!"* he said.

*"I know what is going here. I don't want any fucking part of this sick shit. I want to leave. Now. I want to take my friend and I want to leave now."*

Hetherington's hand grabbed out and covered the lens. The screen was black but the audio remained.

*"This is not what I was told this was going to be. I know a lot of the girls you've got here tonight. I work with them. I know their fucking parents."* Stephie's voice was heard to say. *"Some of these lasses are only fourteen and fifteen years old. They can't even do Sue's jobs without chaperones. So how are they here tonight, buck naked and on your living room floor? What have you got going on here, Mr Hetherington? If you don't let me go now I'm going to call the police and..."*

*"You listen to me, you utter slag!"* Hetherington's voice shouted. *"You were made by this city. I own this city. So you answer to me. Do you understand? Now hand Chris here your bag then let's go downstairs and shut that mouth of yours up by putting one of my guest's dick in it!"*

The clip cut out and left the sound of disgusted murmuring and gasps filling out around the room in place of the footage itself. The occasional camera flash went off too.

"That's definitely *you*, right?" I smiled. "That's you saying you own the city isn't it? Someone has literally just accused you of having fourteen and fifteen year old girls naked on your living room floor amongst the guests you have in your own home and your only response was to call your accuser a slag and tell her that you own this city? What's that about Mick?"

Hetherington was incandescent now. He grabbed at my microphone in the first instance, failed and used his own, shouting "SECURITY!" to the team scattered around the room.

The security officers employed for the evening all looked off in the direction in which Bobby Maitland stood, who in turn simply placed his champagne glass down on the table and walked out of the room. The security staff followed on mass.

"This is NOT what it looks like at all." Hetherington screamed. "I assure you that recording is doctored. Can someone PLEASE call the police?"

The crowd continued to audibly gasp and talk amongst themselves.

"The police?" I shot back into the microphone. "Maybe we could call your good friend Chief Constable Hadenbury?"

"CLIP THREE, NOT CLIP FOUR!!" shouted Emily suddenly, causing me to jump back a little bit from where I stood and become destabilised, almost falling over.

"I KNOW, I KNOW! SHUT UP, MAN!" came Psychic's voice out of the darkness somewhere.

The screen lit up once again with a new clip:

The first shot showed Hadenbury, naked from the waist up, walking into the frame and saying *"What's going on Mick?"*

Off camera Hetherington is heard to say *"A few guests have become unsettled by this young lady and the manner in which she is wielding her handbag around. Some are suggesting that she has some sort of covert camera apparatus inside which..."*

*"Well that just won't do!"* replied Hadenbury.

*"I don't have a camera."* Stephie's voice says.

*"I'm afraid I can't take the chance in believing you. Let me see inside your bag."* Hadenbury said.

*"You're not seeing inside of my bag. I want to call the police now."*

*"Darling, I* <u>*am*</u> *the police. Quite literally, I am the brightest blue light at the top of the entire police service. I'm as high as the light will go. I am..."* Hadenbury laughed.

*"I don't believe you!"* Stephie interrupted. *"There's kids down there being forced to have sex with grown men. My friend is being raped. No police officer in their right mind would be in the thick of this. You're just some sick old..."*

Hadenbury struck out and slapped Stephie off camera.

The clip cut out once again and the crowd were now starting to ignite. There were screams of shock, boos, someone shouted "What the fuck, Mick?" and other people started to storm out.

Emily leaned in close to me. "They're probably worried they're going to appear on the next one!" she whispered. "Are you okay?"

I nodded slowly although the dizziness was now starting to intensify and I could feel the agonising pain start to rebuild itself inside of me at a rate of knots.

"Move on to Stephie's death being ordered by him – trust me!" she whispered with a smile.

I looked back with an air of perplexity, unsure as to what we had directly other that Chris' confession but knew enough about Emily to trust her.

"That, ladies and gentlemen..." I said into the microphone. "... *That* was Stephanie Jason. Or as many people around the region will know her, Stephie Jay – the 'Queen of Newcastle' as Mick Hetherington here was eulogising her as only a week or so ago. Eulogising her, of course, because Stephanie died on the eighth of November this year. A month or so later her friend Eva also died. Both apparently committed suicide. Both attended that party at Mick Hetherington's house that you've just seen a couple of snippets of there!"

Hetherington started to back away from the spot in which he stood. Chief Constable Lane appeared behind him with another Durham officer. He caught sight of them. She smiled and nodded. He froze on the spot.

"Neither Stephanie Jason or her friend Eva Marie committed suicide. They were *murdered* on the instruction of Mayor Mick Hetherington because of what they saw and what they were intending to speak out about at the party that night!"

"HOW DARE YOU?" screeched Hetherington as he made a move towards me that was halted by the extended hand of the Durham officer.

Before I could continue, the screen lit up once again and another clip played:

There, on the screen behind our heads, was Chris Reiser sat in that chair in my office in which he would go on to take his own life. He stared directly into the camera lens and the clip kicked in as he was midway through saying something.

*"... They told me that we were going to make it look like a suicide and Graham was going to come along and oversee it all. I just about got to my feet and I said that we didn't have to kill her... That was when Jason said that this was the instruction he was given by Mick. He said that was what they had to do to keep Mick onside because he was not someone to make an enemy of. Mick ordered her dead. I want to make that clear, okay? I was told at the scene that Jason killed her because Mick Hetherington demanded that it happen... Kelsey asked how Jason did it and he said that he'd crushed her wind-pipe with two blows..."*

The footage flash cut to a different part of Chris speaking.

*"... We had a debrief back at Mick's place. He'd kicked out the guests, closed up shop and had us all back there. He was going completely mental. He asked us over and over again if we'd checked the phone and we were sure it was clean. Even Graham was saying he'd checked it over himself and it didn't have anything on it from this evening. So Mick turns on me, yeah? He's screaming in my face and telling me that Stephie had to die because of me and because I don't know how to check a bag properly and..."*

The footage flash cut once again. In that split second between when one clip of Chris cut out and another began, it became very noticeable that the room had fallen completely silent.

*"... Mick's shouting left, right and centre and asking for absolute assurances that this has been covered up and that the scene is believable and Graham is just cold as ice, right? He's saying it doesn't matter because he will make sure it is visited, ticked off and that it all goes away."*

Another flash cut in the edit occurred.

*"...Jason says that the next step is to clean up any ties that show Stephie had visited Mick's party that night but Mick says the only real tie would be her agent and the other model unless she'd told others."*

Flash cut…

*"... Mick drags us all back up to Newcastle on a bloody 'clear up'. He says that if we didn't get up here and sort out what should never have happened in the first place then he was going to stitch us up..."*

Flash cut…

*"...Kelsey visited her at her flat the first bloody night we were back in the city. Talk about not wasting any time, right? He took care of her and made it look like a suicide. Because that's clearly the trend now isn't it? Not a cluster fuck like the Stephie Jay thing though. He did a clean job on her. But... yeah, if you want to be keeping count on this... Mick ordered her to die too! And if Mick wants to deny this, I've got recordings that say otherwise. I've got more recordings then any of these cunts realise, you know?"*

Flash cut…

*"... I've got Mick Hetherington specifically ordering the death of Eva and saying the words 'Make it look better than you did with Stephie!' ... I mean, come on..."*

That last piece of footage faded out and suddenly out of the speakers came an audio recording of Hetherington's own voice: *"You're going to have to do Eva in. She's costing me a fucking fortune. And for Christ's sake make it look better than you did with Stephie!"*

The screen faded back up as the recording ended and melded into footage of Chris Reiser still sat in the chair, talking away to the camera:

*"... Mick then throws a whole ton of money at this and says enough's enough – He wants you two gone, he wants his ties severed with Sue and for her to be silenced and he wanted Stephie's parents put down and made to look like a murder-suicide..."*

The clip cut to an abrupt stop.

Tears rolled down Hetherington's face. Someone from within the crowd threw a champagne flute and it smashed off his chest. He flinched dramatically and went to run from the room. The uniformed police officer grabbed him and Lane stepped up to the crowd.

"STOP NOW!" she shouted authoratively.

I pulled the microphone back up to my mouth. "Ladies and gentlemen, Sue George of The George Platform died tonight. She was murdered by a group of ex-soldiers hired by Mick Hetherington to silence anyone who could expose his paedophilic tendencies and the parties he throws for people who hold the same perversions as him. I was hired by Stephanie Jason's parents to look into her death because they knew there had been a cover-up. They just had no idea for one second it related to something this horrifying. I look like I do because of the attack I suffered at the hands of these ex-soldiers, one of whom you saw making a full confession in that video just now… Well, I look like this not just because of *that*. I also drove a 1987 Zastava Yugo 513 through the top floor of Debenhams and…"

"WHAT?" shrieked Psychic out of the darkness.

"GODDAMNIT, NOT NOW!" Emily yelled back on my behalf.

Lane stepped forward and took the microphone from my hand whilst shooting me a look that rather deservedly said 'Where were you going with that exactly?' She raised her hands to the crowd in the room and spoke decisively as camera flashes lit up her face and the faces of those of us stood near her. My head began to ring and shudder. My vision blurred.

Just as Lane was about to speak, Psychic's voice rang out once more. "THAT WAS THE GREATEST 'RICHARD KIMBLE' EVER, JAKEY! … I LOVE YOU, MAN!"

The Chief Constable scowled then pushed on. "Ladies and gentlemen, we're going to be affecting an arrest of Mr Hetherington, I'm sure you'll understand why now. I'm going to need you all to start dispersing. The party is over, as I think is abundantly clear. I ask that you please don't dawdle as the protests outside are getting quite inflamed."

The crowd started to jeer. People screamed "Hang the bastard!" and there was a surge forward towards Hetherington at the exact same moment that everyone in the room heard the severe smashing of glass in the foyer and the stampeding sound of chants and shouts coming from outside the civic centre. It seemed word had started to spread to the campaigners and protestors from the people who had left in revulsion that Mayor Hetherington had been exposed as a paedophile and was in the process of being arrested.

Lane turned to her officer and ordered him to handcuff Hetherington and get him out to the van at the back. She turned to both Emily and I, pushing us in the same direction. We just reached the relevant fire exit door and heard it clang heavily shut behind us when the conference suite broke open and became overrun with irate protestors out for blood.

Emily dragged me as best she could but my legs were now starting to falter pretty badly as the agony overtook the adrenaline and the white blurring of my vision came back into effect with a vengeance. Psychic and Holly appeared rather magically by my side and took to helping Emily hoist me along in the direction of the paramedics who were rushing towards us.

Officers slammed a handcuffed Hetherington into the back of a police van, marked with Durham insignia, and were just about to shut the doors when I cried for them to stop. Everyone looked round.

"We've got to get out of here NOW!" shouted Lane. "*You've* got to get out of here!"

"Wait!" I gasped, lurching forward and taking hold of the police van doors to steady myself. "Hey, Mick? Remember what you told me? … Remember what you told me about your so-called 'shit-list', yeah?"

Hetherington looked at me with eyes now completely overflowing with revulsion and his mouth totally twisted with loathing.

"Well, I never cross a name off *my* 'Shit List'! Never forget that!" I said. "Once you're on it, you're in it. The only way *you* get off it is to die!"

Hetherington leant forward and went to speak.

I slammed the inner cage door in his face. A police officer swiftly followed with the thump of the outer van door too.

I was unconscious before my body hit the floor.

## [33]

## or

## "This Is The Big Emotional Pay-Off Bit..."

**I** woke at two am in a hospital bed in a private room, three hours after passing out in Newcastle Council's staff car park. I had what turned out to be twenty-three stitches to the forehead wound above my eye with the eye itself now completely swollen shut. My lips were bruised and bloodied. The cuts on my hands were clean and bandaged. The bullet wound in my shoulder was dressed properly and there was an ice wrap around my broken ribs. There was also an intravenous drip sticking out the inside of my arm and I presumed blood was being pumped *in* as I didn't really think I had any left to pull *out* of me.

I slowly squinted my one good eye and got it to focus well enough for me to look around the room I'd been placed in. There in the corner, fast asleep, was Psychic stretched out in a hard plastic chair. I coughed and he immediately stirred.

"Hey?" he said sleepily.

I smiled.

"They're trying to get a hold of Jane but she's not answering her phone!" Psychic whispered whilst moving his chair closer to the side of my bed.

"It'll be abandoned at ours. She'll only be using the 'clean' one!" I replied.

"Oh, of course!"

"How long until I can get out of here?" I susurrated.

"Jesus, Jake." Psychic smiled. "You've only been here five minutes. Get some rest, man!"

"Maybe just an hour or so." I groggily said as my good eye closed.

"Hey Jake?"

I opened my eye once again.

"Where's my mate's car – *really*?" Psychic asked.

"It's at Debenhams!" I replied.

"Debenhams *car park*? Like… what floor?"

"Not so much the car park – more like the ladies nighties and bedroom furnishings section!"

Psychic dropped his head into his hands and groaned. "He's going to kill me, dude! That was a full-on collector's edition!"

"It's a hell of a car!" I retorted. "You can tell him that from me too!"

Psychic pushed his head back up and propped it into his hands, his elbows on the bed itself and eyes fixed squarely on me.

"Jake?"

"Yeah?" I grimaced.

"Can you believe we fucking did it, man?" he said smiling.

I tried to shake my head but it hurt so I stopped instantly.

"We did it!" Psychic gripped hold of my hand and squeezed.

I winced.

"I'm sorry. I'm sorry. But… Holy shitballs, Jake. I can't believe what we've done! Now, you promised me you'd tell me the truth about how you beat out those bastards that were chasing us?"

I swallowed a little. "Accidentally shot one in the face, blew one through an electronic billboard and threw the other one off a ledge with a cable round his neck!"

Psychic gasped and then fell silent.

"Please tell me you said 'Hang around!' when you threw one of them off the ledge?" Psychic finally said in a conspiratorial whisper.

I shook my head.

"Aww man." Psychic said. "I bet you're kicking yourself a little bit now?"

I nodded.

There was a knock on the door of my hospital room. Whoever was out there didn't wait for an answer and it gently opened to reveal DI Andrews standing cautiously in the doorway.

"Hi?" he said tentatively. "Can I come in?"

Psychic looked to me. I winked my good eye at him and he nodded.

"I'm going to go try and nail a nurse! I'll be back in ten minutes!" he said standing up.

"Three!" I said, smiling.

Psychic flipped me his middle finger then turned it so that it brushed right past Andrews' face as he walked out of the room. The door closed behind him and I was alone with my once best friend and now great enemy.

"How you doing?" Andrews began. "No, wait. That's stupid. Let me go again… So, Hetherington and Hadenbury are in custody. Tidyman is in hospital currently two wards down from here. He's under police guard and as long as I still carry some modicum of power he'll remain in custody until Janet McKinley decides what the next move is. There's a special outside team combing the footage to identify other potential predators…"

I nodded as Andrews flopped down in the seat Psychic had just vacated.

"… We're trying to work at a rate fast enough to beat whatever your journalist pal has got planned but that's not looking likely. This will be breaking out on the twenty-four news networks at dawn."

I stared at Andrews. He continued to talk obliviously.

"I'm expecting a suspension any hour now. Jessica Lane is liaising with Janet, Home Office representatives and the HMIC are apparently circling already. They're going to be asking hard questions as to how I ran a division of CID and didn't spot this whole thing being twisted and corrupted from beneath me as well as above me."

"That's because you're corrupted too!" I said slowly.

"I don't thin…" Andrews stopped himself and course corrected. "I'm so sorry, Jake. I'm so fucking sorry. All those years… There was a line, you're right. There was and I chose to go and stand on the wrong side. I kept staring down at that stupid detective's exam paper way back when and coming up short every time and… and… then I get that nailed away and the interviews… I kept falling short at the…"

"Hey Andy?" I said, calling him by his actual name for the first time in a long time.

"Yeah?"

"I don't want to hear it, okay?" I quietly affirmed. "I've had pretty much a twenty-four hour run of trauma-soaked squaddies trying to justify their murderous acts, a modelling agent try and explain away why the economic crisis gave her the right to sell the children on her books to the nearest bank of paedophiles she could find and now you… Sorry, pal. I'm just not in the fucking mood."

Andrews nodded.

"Oh, for added clarification, I'm not really sorry and you're not my pal!" I smiled.

Andrews added a couple more nods to that too.

"You ever think about Madeline?" I asked.

"Who?"

"That tells me everything!" I sighed.

"No, no. Wait. You mean the girl from that night on Jesmond Dene back in the day, right?"

"*There* we go!" I said.

"What do you mean do I ever think about her?"

"Exactly that. Do you ever think about her? Do you wonder what became of her? Whether she's okay? Whether she came to further harm?" I asked.

Andrews sighed. "You wouldn't believe my answer regardless but I'll still give it to you – yeah, I *do* actually. I wonder what became of her. Mick got her moved out of the city pretty quickly and…"

"At the rate I've seen people die over these last two weeks on his command, I wonder now whether she was *ever* moved and whether she's actually in a deep grave in the woods somewhere."

"Well, that would be on me wouldn't it?" Andrews said staring down at his own hands, becoming lost in his own thoughts.

"If you want a free-pass away from that, it won't come from me." I replied. "Because yeah, it *would* be on you. And I'm done carrying the guilt alone for all the other young girls that he's preyed on over the years when he could and should have been stopped. You can pick some of that up now as well."

Andrews continued staring down at his hands. A silence fell over the room until eventually he spoke.

"You're owed a whole other life, Jake. I know that. I helped take that from you and I will never truly understand why I did that when I loved you like a brother so fucking much. I can't give that back to you. But…"

Andrews took a second and composed himself a little.

"… Look, I grew up with my dad constantly accusing my mum of sleeping around, yeah? Year after year he'd accuse her of going with her colleagues or her friend's husbands. And then one day she shagged his brother, rubbed it in my dad's face and booted him out of the house! She told us years later that she got so sick of getting accused of it and suffering like she had done it that she thought if she was going to get the punishment regardless then she may as well have done the crime anyway!"

"Why the hell are you telling me this exactly?" I asked.

"Because if they're going to be accusing me of scurrying away evidence in order to protect people and I'm going to get shafted for it regardless than… stuff it! So, all I'll say is that no gun coming out of the Metrocentre is going to have your prints on it and all of the CCTV from last night is shown as not having recorded anything. Corrupted disk drives or something. And the last I heard was that they're struggling to find a reliable witness as to what exactly went on in there. The young girl you were with claims to have been unconscious throughout the whole encounter and…"

The door to my room opened and Psychic came back in carrying a takeout coffee and a bottle of water. He looked sternly across at Andrews.

"Visiting hours are between 'Not Now' and 'Why haven't you fucked off yet'!" Psychic said as he walked in the room. "And get your dirty arse out of the friendship chair!"

I smiled.

Man, I love that guy.

Andrews reluctantly stood up and put his hand out towards mine, leaving it there for me to take hold of and shake.

"Maybe in another life time, who knows?" Andrews smiled.

I left my hand where it was and forced him to retract his own, make a little embarrassed nod with his head and leave the room, quietly shutting the door behind him.

At seven am the next morning I walked out of the hospital against the doctor's orders. Well, more accurately, I hobbled and staggered my way out, shuddering with every step. Psychic had rather graciously helped me wash up a little and put on some clean trousers that he'd bought from a shop down in the foyer – tan coloured corduroy 'grandad-style' pants that he bought to try and be a prank-playing prick I suspect but which backfired on him because I thought they looked *rather nice*, actually.

He pulled his car around and I uneasily climbed inside and winced from the pain in my ribs and shoulders as I got into the passenger seat and he helped me with my belt.

"There's a couple of things that I need to get off my chest before we set off!" he said rather dramatically. "The first is that I think we should use the getting-that-dead-guy's-brains-off-the-office-wall task as an excuse to finally decorate because you're always out on the adventures and I'm always the one in the office anyway and I really fucking hate that magnolia shit we've got going on!"

"Okay!" I said.

“And secondly, I think after this whole saga I deserve a raise.”

“But I barely pay you as it is?” I smiled.

“Well then, after this whole saga I deserve a raise from barely getting paid to getting paid something?”

“I think that’s incredibly fair!” I nodded.

“Oh and one more thing – you may or you may not hear a rumour that might possibly circulate regarding Emily and I fucking in a hospital supply cupboard in the early hours whilst you were out of it… That rumour is decidedly…”

“True?”

“Yeah, that’s *absolutely* true! … Oh, she’s such an awful human being Jake! She truly is. I think she’s despicable and I really wish we could just cut her dead and not have anything more to do with her because she’s horrible… But I think I’m in love with her, you know?”

I smiled and sank back into the seat as Psychic pulled away from the hospital car park and out of the city, towards the coast.

I limped up the gravel path of the local church on the outskirts of Tynemouth and could hear an ungodly cacophony of young voices attempting an ‘interpretation’ of “Little Drummer Boy”. Forty percent of them appeared to be singing three hours later than the other sixty percent. My own children were somewhere in the mix of this sound, singing up a storm.

A dark, nasty, black cloud strewn storm.

The air was crisp and condensation clouds barrelled out of my mouth as I slugged my way along. I reached out to steady myself on a cast iron fence that ran the full length of the path only for the bitter ice that had coated it to send a shock to my skin. I approached the door to the church at the exact moment that it opened, intensifying the noise for the briefest of seconds, as Jimmy stepped out doing his coat up.

“I saw you coming!” he said. “Man, you look like shit!”

I smiled and he embraced me into a hug that caused me to nearly buckle with the pain it inflicted around my body.

“Sorry!” he gasped.

“It’s okay.” I grinned. “Are they in there?”

He nodded.

“This is the bit where you say ‘You should see the other guy’!” Jimmy laughed.

“There’s not a scratch on him!” I said. “This is actually the bit where I tell you from the bottom of my heart how thankful I am for what you’ve done!”

Jimmy shook his head. “Don’t worry about it. I know you’d do the same for me… if I was stupid enough to put myself in the situations you do!”

“I’m going to get your money sorted as soon as I’ve got Christmas out the way, I promise.”

“There’s no rush, mate.” Jimmy said. “The money was second to the friendship. It always is, you know?”

I nodded and held out my hand. He took it and we shook.

“Anyway, I’ve got some news for you, Jakey boy! Guess what?” Jimmy grinned.

"What's that?"

"I'm getting back out on the circuit!" he said.

A huge smile broke across my face and then dropped instantly. "But you're old as fuck, Jim? Who's going to box you? The Grim Reaper?"

Jimmy playfully threw a couple of jabs wide of me and then started to move off back down the gravel path. "Listen, kidda!" he laughed. "If I can survive two songs worth of your kids singing than I can survive twelve rounds in the ring with anyone!"

And with that Jimmy was gone.

I awkwardly pulled open the church door with my good arm and stepped inside.

It sounded like the children had moved on to "O Come, All Ye Faithful" as I stepped around the back of the church and awkwardly made my way down the aisle, staggering side to side to try and get sight of where Jane would be sat.

*"♫♫... ... O come ye, O come ye to Bethlehem! ... Come and behold Him... Born the King of Angels! ... O come let us adore Him... ♫♫"*

Eventually my eyes landed on her. I saw her face from the side and could see that her smile beamed with pride as our sons sang their hearts out terribly up on the altar in front of me but her eyes scrunched occasionally at the abrasiveness of the sound.

Man, she was as beautiful right then and there as she was the first day I walked into that pub and saw her across the room.

A few shocked parents' heads turned as I walked and I managed to slide into the pew quite nicely next to her before she even noticed. When she did, Jane let out a gasp that drew way more attention to us than I felt was needed.

Her eyes darted up and down at my swollen, bruised face and the umpteen different bandages and dressings that seemed to poke out of the clothes I'd had Psychic pull together for me.

"What the..." Jane whispered.

"Shush!" I whispered back.

"What the fuck happened?"

"Don't say 'fuck' in God's house, he doesn't like it!" I smiled.

"Are you serious right now? Look at you, and you're telling me off?"

I leant in and kissed her softly on the mouth.

"How are you even *here*? You look like you should be in hospital!" Jane gasped. "You are so pale, Jake. I've never seen you look so..."

A loud hush echoed up from behind us.

Jane span instantly round in her seat. "Don't you shush me, Amy! I swear to God I'll bite your lips off!"

"Woah!" I whispered. "*Jane*!"

"And don't you start!" Jane said quietly as tears start to form. "Look at what they did to you..."

I nodded.

"You got them though, right? And Hetherington?"

I nodded again. "I got them *all*, baby! It's over. You'll see when we get out of here. Let's just talk later and…"

"I've got to get you to hospital!" she spoke softly.

"I've been. I didn't like it. Don't worry about it. The important thing is I'm here. I promised you I'd be here and I'm here… And I promise you I'm going to make you more promises and keep *them* too."

Jane gently took hold of my face and kissed me.

With her lips still pushed up against mine she softly mouthed "You look like shit, Jake Lehman!"

Applause rang out and around the church.

For just a split second I legitimately thought I was having a romantic comedy type moment and the applause was for Jane and I reconciling in a crowded environment like in those films where one of two characters has made a public declaration of love to the other with everyone else cocking an ear to the big speech. Then they kiss and the camera would then pull up and out whilst Pete Townsend's "Let My Love Open The Door" kicked in over the soundtrack.

Then I remembered that this was real life, not a film.

And that the applause was just a tokenistic and fairly obligatory gesture from the parents for their children, up their singing their hearts out on the altar.

My childhood was pretty much a never-ending smorgasbord of films and soft rock. I wasn't so much raised by my parents as I was by The Hendersons from Bigfoot & The Hendersons or any of the dysfunctional families featured in many a Steven Spielberg movie. I didn't have close friends per se but I did have The Goonies and The Monster Squad. All of the friendships and socialisation I had in my teenage years, I realise now was born from a pity or an obligation on someone else's part. Looking back I realised that all my dreams of being a police officer were birthed out of the fact that this was the most commonly heroic character routinely seen in the movies I watched. Maybe if I'd been born a generation earlier I'd have dreamt of being a cowboy, who knows?

And here's the thing that comes from exposing yourself to an inordinate and obsessive amount of cinema. It bleeds into your life in weird ways where you do things that are pretty cool and then you wonder to yourself why there's no sudden rise of Hans Zimmer style electronic guitar and keyboards coming up in the air around you – then you remember that this is reality, and not a film!

You go shopping with your wife and children and you suddenly drift off into your own thoughts and start looking around the supermarket, thinking to yourself what John McClane type shit you'd pull off if terrorists suddenly seized control of this local branch of Tesco and you were the only man inside who could thwart their devilish plans.

You do actually come to think that maybe one man can make a difference because you've seen Serpico and To Kill A Mockingbird and what not and your grandparents push the reminder into your head that those films were based on real people who did those things or inspired those stories so there's no reason why you can't be like them too and do those things. And then someone like Mike Hetherington comes along and shows you the truth… the real stark reality:

One man *can't* make a difference.

The house always wins because the house owns and runs the house you're playing the game in. They set the rules.

That's what I *used* to think, anyway.

That's what used to eat away at me as I searched at the bottom of a Jim Beam bottle for something to prove this line of thought wrong. That's what I hoped the Tramadol would dampen down the pain of every time I popped a pill. That's what I'd say to myself over and over again when crunched up in the back of a hire car with tinted windows on a measly eleven pound an hour for some insurance company, taking photos of some schmuck who's claimed an injury at work that's left them unable to walk but is now over there playing five-a-side football with his mates.

Then Stephanie Jason died.

And the fallout from proving she did not kill herself seemed to indicate that one man can make a difference against the 'mighty machine'.

You've just got to make sure you're doing it for the right reasons.

My reasons? I knew all the way back in the offices of Dreyfuss & Associates that it was never about the money even though I so desperately needed it. I think if I'm honest it wasn't even all *just* about the look in Margaret Jason's eyes. I think it was about the fact that I'd lost any faith that the truth existed anymore and I needed an excuse to go seek it out, in whatever its form.

I'd had my career stolen from me on a lie. I lied to my body every day because of my addiction. I lied to my wife both advertently and inadvertently. The Jasons' were being forcefully fed a lie they should never have been exposed to. Powerful careers were being built on nothing but lies… I had to know if the truth even *existed* in what was left of our society anymore and I had to know what it looked like for the sake of my children.

So… yeah… movies might be inherently deceitful in hiding the fact that a side effect of getting shot is that you crap your pants *or* that you can't jump from a fourth storey window to surf a mattress down an escalator without really screwing yourself up... *OR*, and this is a big one, that any of us are actually the 'lead' character in this life on any sort of special journey, you know?

Movies have this innate ability with susceptible mugs like me to make us think that we're *special* or something. Like we're on a 'journey' and we're going to experience a 'great moment'. Or worse than that, that we're all owed this 'great journey' and that we're all meant to be extraordinary and lauded for something?

Hell, every sporting event I ever took part in as a kid I went into thinking I was the underdog in search of his third act chance to show he's got the heart of a champion or some nonsense. It took me until I was seventeen to realise that there was no 'third act'… I was just shit at sports.

Even when I joined the police, I still inwardly believed that it was fated that I would end up as a detective who would crack a huge case and end up all over the papers as this heroic figure who took down a serial killer or something.

Maybe that's why when Hetherington did what he did to me I reacted like I had some guaranteed 'storyline' *stolen* from me, you know? Like he'd got in the way of my divine right to be the next Popeye Doyle or John McClane. But maybe the 'storyline' wasn't ever about me being a hero cop who saves the city from a tyrannous villain. Maybe my 'storyline' was to be Jack and Jonathan's dad and nothing more significant than that? Or maybe it was that I had to age into being looked on so poorly and insignificantly around this city that I could slip through the cracks and achieve what I did for Stephanie Jason?

I guess to some of you you'll think that I *did* get my great 'hero moment' in the end, just like in a movie… I mean, I did drive a fucking 1987 Zastava Yugo 513 through the top floor of a department store at sixty plus miles per hour and then jump out of its fourth storey window. AND I did get to pull off a 'Richard Kimble' too so…

… Okay, maybe movies do carry *some* truth every now and again.

The biggest truth, I guess, is that one man *can* make a difference… and, to quote Jane, "pull off some pretty cool, deep blue hero shit" in the process too…

You've just got to set the right *terms* for how you're going to go about making that difference.

… Was that too wanky?

I feel that was too pretentious to end on.

What do you think?

You folk deserve better than that, I reckon.

Thank God, we've got the Epilogue(s), right?

## [Epilogue 1]

## or

## "Here's The Freeze-Frame End Title Cards…"

We're coming up - at the time of telling this whole sorry saga to you - on the one year anniversary of Stephanie Jason's death. Her parents have moved away from Newcastle but there was something in the local paper a few days ago that said they're coming back to the city to lead a candle-lit walk along the Quayside on the anniversary of her death. I plan to drop them a line in a day or so to see if it's true and suggest meeting up. You know, as you do when your singular bond is investigating and avenging the murder of their daughter and the subsequent conspiratorial cover-up. *("How you guys doing? You look well. That's some tan? Have you been away? Hey – remember that time I flushed out your daughter's murderer and hung him from the second floor of the red quadrant in the Metrocentre?")*

We're just over a month away from me being one year clean on all fronts too.

That's right, motherfuckers, I'm off those 'magic' pills that were doing sweet eff' all anyway… Jane and I discussed pain management with the doctors whilst in recovery from my injuries and thereafter I began treatment for my addictions.

There was that short stay in a rehab unit, just as Jane had said there would be. Then I started up some Cognitive Behavioural Therapy (CBT) stuff that I keep a hand in with once a month now. I also attend Narcotics Anonymous twice weekly too. And yes, it's in the same church where Alcoholics Anonymous is and I make a point of not avoiding that spot where Jason Grant stuck that gun in my face.

I don't hide away from the demons anymore.

That's the *old* me.

Psychic and Emily spent Christmas morning together and then pretty much every other day together thereafter. They still hate each other, apparently. Yet from this hate was forged "the important realisation that [they] love each other and want to be together." That's Psychic's explanation anyway. You and I will hopefully be going on other adventures together in the near future and when we next meet up, I'll eat my own foot in front of you all if those two are still in a relationship… or one of them hasn't been murdered at the other's hands.

Holly?

The fierce little warrior girl who wrote a heart for an 'o' in her name? Well, would you believe that she's now Jane's teaching assistant at the school she works at?

The George Platform shuttered its doors, obviously. There was no one who could run it the way it had been exhaustively built to run quite like Sue George and she was dead. She'd assembled no one in her image, so to speak, to be able to take it over. Not that there was anything to take over anyway. Even if Sue had lived she would have seen her business almost instantaneously die when all the facts relating to Hetherington's sex parties came out in the press. Who would want to go near a company that had done the heinous things Sue George did with the children on her books?

Out of a job, Holly retrained as a teaching assistant on an apprenticeship programme and Jane mentored her all the way through it. Sometimes when the work flow is prolific enough we chuck her a few quid and she comes and runs the reception desk at 'Lehman's Terms' as well – just so she doesn't have to go take a dodgy bar job in the city and have creepy coppers come in and letch all over her. She's a family friend now too. Our son's love her. I think Jack's burgeoning puberty indicates he actually *loves* her though.

Psychic would go over to our office the day after Boxing Day to let in cleaners we'd hired (in order to re-do the work the crime-scene cleaners were *meant* to have done) to get every inch of Chris Reiser scraped and scrubbed off our walls.

It was on this day that he found a large manila envelope pushed through the 'Lehman's Terms' letterbox without any postage. Inside was Alison Gregg's original report, results and photographs pertaining to her initial assessment of Stephanie Jason's body. Of course we made copies before handing it over to the newly appointed investigatory body that was overseeing the downfall of Hetherington, Hadenbury and the corruption that ran rampant through the city because of them… we also made sure Emily got a copy too!

Emily, with Chief Constable Lane's covert assistance, broke the story wide open nationally and a team of investigative journalists at The Guardian worked with her to identify everyone they possibly could who featured as a guest in every inch of the footage taken from within Hetherington's home. Other newspapers, spotting the more salacious elements that came from such a scandal, started jumping in on the act and before you knew what was happening the television news between Christmas and New Year in the UK was flooded with ostensible formal denials and explanations from some of the country's most prominent MPs, local councillors, professional footballers and businessmen as to why they were shown as having appeared at or taken part in illicit parties involving underage girls.

Emily's stellar reporting would ultimately lead to the official cause of Eva Marie's death being stricken from the record and a fresh investigation launched. Eventually her suicide would be reclassified, as with Stephanie's of course, for what it actually was: *murder*.

Chief Constable Graham Hadenbury was charged with a plethora of criminal offences but managed to negotiate himself a lesser sentence in court by turning on his own 'team'. He didn't just name names, he backed up every statement with evidence of their acts, payments they'd received and so on. Hadenbury had kept file after file on every dirty officer who'd been on his books. He theorised that one day they might grow a conscience and he would need to help 'reconfigure' their moral alignment for them should this happen. Instead he used the information to bring them all down with him.

The 'Hadenbury Files' would go on to expose one of the largest rogue units of police officers in the Independent Office for Police Conduct's history and see upwards of thirty officers across the borough - varying in rank, service history and department – sacked, arrested and ultimately jailed.

The mass exodus of dirty coppers from a police service that was already all but crippled by a funding and staffing crisis anyway couldn't have come at a worst time. The riots at the city's civic centre the night of Hetherington's arrest were just the start and most of Newcastle city centre was in turmoil right the way into the next year in one way or another, Christmas be damned. There wasn't a police presence strong enough to contain or control it and eventually the city broke. In February the army was put out on North East streets to take back control… We're not quite clear of the turmoil just yet as a region but things have calmed down now mainly because the masses have run out of things to burn.

I bet you're thinking DI Andy Andrews was one of the 'rogue coppers' to go too, right? Surprisingly *not*. It turns out Andrews was telling the truth when he said he never buried evidence relating to Stephanie's murder. It was felt he was however guided a little *too* strongly by his superiors to conclude the investigation in the manner they wanted him to – they themselves being members of Hadenbury's rogue unit within the police service.

Andrews' problem was that his moral 'flexibility' in return for repeated and undeserved promotions was far too easily exploited by the more heavily corrupt and corruptive police officers above and below him. He was initially suspended just as he thought he would be. He'd then go on to try and help the IOPC with their investigation, trying desperately to pull enough credibility and respect back that he could step back over that line we'd talked about together.

It was all too little too late.

Before the Spring had arrived, Andrews had resigned from the police service and disappeared. No one has any idea where he is. For real. His home and his car were left to go to wrack and ruin, eventually both getting repossessed further on down the road. His parents initially made an appeal for his whereabouts then quickly fell silent which indicated to Jane and I that he'd contacted them in some capacity and alleviated their worries.

Psychic thinks he's gone and killed himself and his body lies undiscovered to this day. Some days he and I argue over the ways in which Andrews could have offed himself. Because, you know, we can't always wind each other up about films every time there's a slow day – which is refreshingly rare these days. And to be honest, joking around about the paedophilic subtext of The Karate Kid doesn't sit well nowadays.

Andrews must have stuck to his word about one thing for the first time in his life, though: Whatever CCTV footage existed up at the Metrocentre *did* disappear and whatever guns were pulled from the scene never got traced back to me. No police officers ever came knocking at my door and my anxiety that they were going to soon subsided. I know, I know. You're all thinking that this all sounds very neat and trite or whatever. But the truth is the truth – I've got this far in telling you my story without lying to you, I don't know why I would start now in the goddamn Epilogue.

What went on there that night and any intended ramifications in the legal sense seemed to just miraculously and neatly go away because no charges were brought and no one out there seemed to want to speak up for the hired hit squad of a couple of powerful paedophiles. The killings of Jason Grant, Ernie Royce and Geoff Kelsey forced me to take stock of Australia and the trauma that had clung to me over the years since. Counselling helped a lot.

Let's just say I worked through some shit and leave it there, huh?

I can see you all are getting antsy, wanting to fuck off now that you're in the Epilogue and I *know* at least one of you has already pre-flicked to the back already, noticed that there's an 'Epilogue 2' and started brewing your Lord of the Rings: Return of the King comparison jokes… Fuckers!

'Lehman's Terms', as a business, pulled up from the freefall it was heading into before Margaret Jason came into my life. Emily made sure we got a lot of press attention and Psychic and I, after considerable deliberation, took to milking it for every drop we could get. I'm not sure all those TV and newspaper appearances will have done me a whole lot of good in the long run when it comes to covert surveillance and undercover work *("Hey? You! In the bushes? Aren't you that guy who was on BBC Question Time?")* but it did the business wonders seeing as nearly every law firm in the region wanted to ride our coat-tails and be partnered with 'Lehman's Terms' for their litigation support.

One such law firm? Dreyfuss & Associates, of course.

Katherine Banks calmed down considerably, helped along by the fact that she secured all of Hetherington's victims as D&A clients for civil suits against the local authority and the police. On Margaret and Matthew Jason's recommendation, she brought Psychic and I in as "consultants" at a very generous rate of pay, helping them to put the evidence together for the civil cases.

Suing a local authority, that had but not a pot to piss in and had been moved into 'protective measures' by the government, for vast sums of compensation proved as successful as lock-picking with a piece of spaghetti for Katherine Banks and her team in the long run. In the end, some victims and their families chose to seek justice through alternative avenues…

The name Murray Reitman won't mean anything to you at this stage in the story.

Murray lost his wife in childbirth when she gave birth to their only child, Katie. He never remarried and raised Katie singlehandedly. She was his *everything* and he was so proud when she was headhunted at the age of twelve by Sue George to feature in a local advertising campaign.

It would go on to destroy him completely when the police knocked at his door two years on from that to explain Katie Reitman was one of the victims featured in the videos Stephanie had recorded up at Hetherington's house that night. Katie had lied when she had said she was staying with friends. She had lied afterwards about the mental anguish and physical pain she was in as a result of her virginity being violently taken from her. She had lied to protect her father from the pain she knew he would experience upon learning what happened to her as a result of joining "Sue's Secret Team" like the other 'cooler' girls at The George Platform.

Murray Reitman fell apart and took to drinking heavily. He felt a failure as a father and could not make peace with not having protected his only child from what he considered to be the ultimate evil. He also felt in his heart of hearts that the court system was as corrupted as the system that allowed Hetherington to thrive in the first place. He convinced himself *completely* that some technicality would mean that this malevolent man would never do a day in prison for his crimes.

Reitman's 'salvation' came in the most bizarre of forms, namely Bobby Maitland.

Because, if you'll recall, Newcastle is a big city but a small place.

Hearing through his network of staff, friends and people who owe him favours about the specifics of Katie Reitman, Maitland worked to make sure that the father and daughter got justice that was equal to the pain they had experienced but also representative of the anguish all of Hetherington's victims had encountered.

Which is why when Mick Hetherington was released on bail, warned not to return to his home in Northumberland as it was now unsafe following a large fire and instead opted to hire a remote cottage in the back ends of Cumbria to hide out in until his court date, it was Maitland's men who followed him down there.

It was Bobby Maitland's men who also picked the locks of said cottage and dragged Hetherington, bound and gagged, to an awaiting car where he was driven back to the North East.

There, in the deepest woodland within the Rising Sun Country Park, he was dumped on his knees in front of a freshly dug shallow grave that Murray Reitman himself stood alongside of. Hetherington was doused with petrol, pushed into the grave and set alight by Katie's agonised father. The paedophile's screams echoed around the park and some say they were heard miles down wind onto the other side of the Coast Road.

Less than an hour later, Murray and Katie were on a plane out of the city. They were never seen or heard of again... But Bobby Maitland tells me that they're doing okay.

Bobby Maitland and I are good friends now by the way. And *that's* weird.

Jane had very mixed feelings on seeing the news footage of Hetherington's corpse being carried in a black bag out of the Rising Sun Country Park.

I had mixed feelings myself. I'd wanted him dead for so long. I'd dreamt sometimes obsessively about doing it myself. Now he was gone, by someone else's hands. It wasn't for me *of all people* to comment on vigilante justice either. The only actual clear thought that emerged from the news of his death was that I was wrong to tell him the only way he'd get off my 'Shit List' was to die!

… Because even with the announcement of his death, I realised that whilst I was able to move on even more from the infamous night of December 23rd I'd still never cross that name of his off my list as long as Madeline's whereabouts from nine years earlier haunted my conscience.

## [Epilogue 2]

## or

## "I Am Everything Because Of You..."

Now, flashback to that freezing cold Christmas Eve morning up in Tynemouth:

The minute Jack and Jonathan's carol concert was finished, Jane forcibly returned me to the hospital; medications and treatment were continued, I was assessed for internal bleeding and – like a goddamn Christmas miracle – I was able to get back out of there with enough of my wife's concerns abated that I was home in time for Christmas morning in our own house, under our own tree… handing out unwrapped Christmas presents because Jane had been too busy hiding at her aunt's and I'd been too busy getting shot to get them sorted for the kids.

The boys were delighted with their presents regardless, Jane was happy to be back at home and I was truly joyful to be in their company and drawing huge swathes of comfort from the smiles on their faces. We were going to her parents for Christmas lunch after all because it's hard to get a festive meal for four with all the trimmings prepped when you've been faced with all that we had those last couple of days.

Jane was in the kitchen warming up some croissants for us to have as a Christmas breakfast when Psychic let himself in through the back door and instantly caused quite the commotion with Jack and Jonathan.

"This is quite the surprise!" said Jane, giving him a kiss as he wiped his feet on our backdoor mat.

"Well, me and your husband have some unfinished business on this Stephie Jay case!" he smiled as I lugged my bruised up carcass into the kitchen where they stood, leaning hard against the crutch that the hospital had sent me away with.

"We do?" I replied quizzically.

"I think we do, don't we?" Psychic said as he smiled, reached into his coat pocket and pulled out the box containing the Rolex watch that Stephie had bought and had engraved for her father, and which had been in our office safe until now.

"Fuck!" I muttered. "We *do*."

To the resounding shouts from Jane that I had to be wrapped up sufficiently as I was still recovering, etc. etc. and the demand that I was dropped off at her parents within the next couple of hours, Psychic and I set off in his car up to Smallburn.

We argued all the way there about how he owed me twenty pound for the distinct lack of snowfall and he squabbled back that the bet was for the whole of Christmas Day so he still had everything to play for. We kept that entire disagreement going all the way up to the gates of the Jason's home where we were let through almost immediately upon pressing the intercom at the security gate.

"You know, I think I'm going to wait here if that's okay with you?" Psychic said as he brought the car to a stop right outside the concrete steps leading up to the front door.

"You sure?" I asked.

Psychic nodded. "Unless you want me in there with you, I think it'll be better if we kept the numbers low in the room."

I patted him on the shoulder just as Margaret opened the front door. Psychic looked past me and gave her a polite wave. He smiled at her then under his teeth muttered "If her husband doesn't get his shit together, I'm going to get all up and over that wife of his, I swear to God!"

I turned the pat to a punch and started to get out the car.

"You're a disgrace, man!" I laughed but at the same time could see where the lust sprang up from – Margaret Jason looked like she'd aged in a fortnight from the stress and the grief, yet she still looked absolutely amazing.

She looked at me as I struggled to my feet with my arm in a sling, half my forehead plastered and my face pretty much swollen over with bruising and cuts.

"Jesus Christ!" she gasped. "What happened?"

I smiled. "Thanks for not making your first words something about how I look like shit! That's all I've been hearing lately."

"I mean, you *do* actually look like shit don't get me wrong!" she attempted to smile. "But I thought it would be rude to lead with that."

"Would now be a bad time to conclude your case?" I asked softly, taking her by her hand. "I know it's Christmas morning but for reasons that will become apparent when I speak to you and Matthew, I hope you'll understand why it was important to come today."

"Oh we're sick with waiting anyway and we're not celebrating Christmas as it is so this works out fine with us!" she replied.

I nodded. "And how is Matthew?"

"He's not doing good at all." Margaret said, tears immediately falling down both sides of her face without her expression or voice ever changing. "I had to get the doctor out the other day. The drinking and lack of food is starting to really take its toll."

She pulled on my hand so that I was led behind her as she stepped back into her home.

"I really hope you don't have something today that will tip him over the edge." She said.

"Have you both been watching the news since yesterday? Have you seen what's been going on in the city?" I asked.

"Matthew isn't watching or reading anything. He's just staring at that rose bush, day in and day out. I have though." Margaret said. "Awful, shameful stuff isn't it? You know, we moved in the same circles of some of these people that are getting arrested. We've actually dined in the company of Mayor Hetherington himself occasionally. It just goes to show, you never can tell with these people can you?"

I nodded as we made our way out to the conservatory. As Margaret opened the door for us to step into the area in which Matthew sat, I quickly turned to her and whispered "Here on out, varnished truth or unvarnished truth?"

Margaret gulped down some air and quietly said "Unvarnished! Absolutely… I need everything!"

I gripped her hand then let it go and moved across the room towards Matthew.

"Hi Matthew!" I said, decisively lifting his decanter of bourbon and half-drank glass off the small table in front of him and putting them on a nearby ledge. With my one good arm I awkwardly pulled a nearby chair so that it was directly placed in front of where he sat. I plopped myself down, used my sleeve to wipe the surface of the table in front of me then removed the Rolex box from my pocket and plonked it dramatically on the table in front of the both of us.

Margaret's eyes squinted to catch what it was that was on the table then delicately moved herself from the door we'd just came through to the sofa near to the both of us. She perched herself on the edge of one of the arms and started to breathe heavily.

"Matthew?" I began. "I'm going to make something very clear before I get going with what I need to say to you both. What you are about to hear is the one of the most awful things parents could hear about their child, but I firmly believe there is peace to be found for both of you in the real, unvarnished truth. And when I'm done, your wife is going to need you. She is, Matthew. I swear by almighty God, you've got to draw some strength from inside yourself and you've got to go to her and you've got to take hold of her because you can't let her face down the real, unvarnished truth on her own. Okay?"

Matthew's eyes flickered down to the box on the table and then immediately sprang back to that locked gaze with the rose bush out in the garden. I could hear the gentle sniffles and contained sobs coming from Margaret to my left but I never broke eye contact with Matthew.

I took a deep breath, tapped twice on the Rolex box in front of me as a sort of flash reminder to push on and to distract myself from the thought of not going ahead with this.

I exhaled, nodded almost to myself and then began:

"Your daughter did *not* commit suicide. She was murdered… She was murdered by a man called Jason Grant who worked with three accomplices. They were Geoff Kelsey, Ernie Royce and Chris Reiser. They worked under the instruction of one man, Mayor Mick Hetherington, and with the guidance of another, Chief Constable Graham Hadenbury…"

Margaret exhaled hard in shock.

"… Stephanie was pushed to attend an event at Mayor Hetherington's house on the night of the eighth of November alongside her friend Eva Marie, by her agent Sue George. She was told that a very rich friend of Mayor Hetherington wanted to meet Stephanie, have his picture taken and essentially have her as his companion at this event.

Sue George did not let on to Stephanie or Eva Marie that this was actually an orgy of sorts involving very young underage models that were on her books and young people from care homes that were under Newcastle Council's control. Stephanie and Eva went up there thinking it was just another paid public appearance that they'd done many a time and they essentially walked into a trap. Eva was sexually assaulted that night and Stephanie captured footage that would expose Mayor Hetherington and Chief Constable Hadenbury for their sexual acts against young women. She escaped with that footage on her phone… I'm telling you all of this because of the news that has broken in the last twenty-four hours so you can understand the context. I'm also telling you so you are aware in advance because as the story develops Stephanie's involvement to it and her murder is going to come out too…"

Margaret now started to sob heavily. I resisted every urge possible to go and comfort her. I needed to do this a very specific way and I needed to do it clean and quickly.

"… Mayor Hetherington ordered Stephanie to be stopped before whatever she'd recorded got out. Jason Grant, Chris Reiser and Geoff Kelsey caught her vehicle up in Northumberland and Jason murdered her inside of it by striking her on the throat. Her body was then driven to Hebburn where Chief Constable Hadenbury and Ernie Royce met them at a site Chief Constable Hadenbury knew to be abandoned and accessible. They then framed the scene that you are now familiar with. In the weeks that followed both Chief Constable Hadenbury and Mayor Hetherington used their power and connections to have post-mortem and coroner reports falsified. I have had this confirmed by the original reporting coroner…"

Margaret's broken voice sobbed from across the room. "Matt…"

Matthew's eyes flickered and tears started to stream down his face. His expression didn't change though and he never moved his gaze away from out there in the garden where tiny slivers of frost were forming on every surface as far as the eye could see.

"You'll see on the news that Hadenbury and Hetherington have been arrested. In the coming days you'll hear of the death of Sue George too. I wanted to come here today Matthew for two reasons. The first is that I wanted to look you in the eyes and I wanted to tell you that I killed the man who murdered Stephanie. I killed two of his accomplices too. The fourth killed himself in my office, on tape, after making a full confession. I need you to know that I did that and… I need you to tell me that this was okay? I needed you to know that they didn't get away with what they did. They murdered your daughter and I made sure that they were held to account because I think that is what you and Margaret deserve…"

Margaret's sobs built up in volume.

My eyes and throat started to well up too.

I coughed, cleared my throat and wiped my eyes. "The second reason I wanted to come today is to make sure you got this on Christmas morning because I think that's what your daughter would have wanted."

I gently pushed the Rolex box across the table so it was now completely in front of Matthew, easily within reach. He didn't move. I extended my hand across the table and flipped the box lid open myself and softly pulled the watch from its cushion.

It was a gorgeous, reconditioned vintage Rolex Submariner. Black in colour with an oyster face dial. Collector's price? Probably around the £8,500 mark. This was a beautiful piece, completely free of ostentatiousness, that a true collector of fine watch pieces would *love*.

I turned it carefully in my hand and lifted it to his eye-line so that the inscription on the back of the watch could not be avoided.

"She had a watch as rare and valuable as this inscribed with this particular message, Matthew. So it must be really important, you know?" I smiled.

Matthew's eyes wavered down and froze on the watch.

His jaw unlocked for the first time since I'd been in his company. The tears started to pour from his eyes and his breathing deepened.

*'I am everything because of you, Daddy! SJ xx'*!

Suddenly and falteringly Matthew started to stagger himself up into a standing position. Margaret rushed to his side and he gripped her desperately and pulled her close to him. He then drunkenly grabbed out at my coat collar and the strap on my sling, pulling me up onto my feet. He moved towards the conservatory door and pulled at it as Margaret pushed hard to hold onto him.

A wall of cold air hit us all in the face as Matthew stepped out into the garden at the exact moment pained and unsettling wails started to emit from out of him. He swayed forward onto the frozen grass, falling to his knees. Margaret rushed to his side. I cautiously walked over to join them.

He looked up at me, sobbing and pointing at the rose bush in front of me.

At that exact moment large soft snowflakes began to fall from the heavens. Huge clumps of the stuff like someone up there had just found a box of it and turned it upside down over the whole city.

Matthew kept sobbing and trying to find the words.

They didn't come initially. But then…

"I planted this here… the first weekend we moved in! … Fourteen years ago…" he cried. "Stephie helped me… This was hers. She…"

The sobs became uncontrollable. Matthew fell into Margaret's arms and they remained locked together, crying as the snow blanketed them and the garden around them. Margaret pulled her head away and silently mouthed the words "Thank you!"

I gently nodded my head and slowly backed away, closing each door as I made my exit out of the house and back out onto the front drive.

There in front of me was Psychic, leant against his own car bonnet; collar pulled up and coat buttoned thoroughly. He laughed and stuck out his arms on sight of me as I carefully made my way down the steps towards me.

"Well!" he giggled, looking up to the sky.

"What are you doing standing there in this, man?" I smiled.

"Accentuating my moment, sir!" he laughed. "Pay up!"

I stuck my arm inside my jean pocket and pulled out my middle finger which I then thrust in his general direction before climbing delicately into the passenger seat.

The radio was blasting one of the greatest Christmas songs ever recorded.

That's right: Darlene Love's "Christmas (Baby Please Come Home).

You know Darlene Love, the singer, was Mrs Murtaugh in the Lethal Weapon movies, right? *Did* you know that? … Seriously? I love this song but I didn't know that connection until like a year ago or something. How crazy?

*"♫♫...The snow's coming down. I'm watching it fall. Lots of people around... Baby please come home. The church bells in town. All singing in song. Full of happy sounds... Baby please come home. They're singing "Deck The Halls". But it's not like Christmas at all. 'Cause I remember... ♫♫"*

The song abruptly disappeared from the speakers in the car at the flick of one of Psychic's fingers and he grimaced. "I'm sick of Christmas songs!"

"What do you mean? It's Christmas *Day*!" I replied.

"I know but I'm sick of them! Put another station on!"

"They'll all be Christmas songs, dickhead – because it's *Christmas Day*! Stick Jungleland on. Have you got Bruce Springsteen's Jungleland?"

"Do I look like Spotify to you? What are you barking song requests at me for?" laughed Psychic as he started to slowly pull the car around on the Jason's drive.

"What is Spotify and why don't you have any Springsteen CDs in the car?" I said.

"It wouldn't matter if I did, the car doesn't have a CD player!"

"What do you MEAN the car doesn't have a CD player?" I gasped.

Psychic started to drive off towards the gates. "How old is your frickin' car, Jake? Most cars don't have CD players these days!"

I huffed and banged a button on the car stereo to switch it back on and flicked to another station. The interior was immediately filled with the electric guitar and synthesiser sounds of one of the greatest songs ever recorded.

"If you try to switch this off, I'll snap your wrist!" I shouted, turning the volume up as John Parr's voice went to work. "Oh, and Psychic?"

Psychic nodded his head in acknowledgement as he turned out of the estate and sped off down the road.

"Merry Christmas, mate!" I smiled.

*"♫♫... Play the game you know you can't quit until it's won. Soldier on, only you can do what must be done... You know, in some ways you're a lot like me. You're just a prisoner, and you're tryin' to break free... I can see a new horizon underneath the blazing sky. I'll be where the eagle's flying higher and higher. Gonna be your man in motion. All I need is a pair of wheels. Take me where the future's lying... ♫♫"*

**The End**

## [Acknowledgements]

This book was initially written and completed in late 2017 before 'real world' events involving reality TV stars committing suicide started occurring around the UK. The book in its original form was then delayed from being published out of a fear of appearing crass in the face of these tragedies.

A heavily recalibrated version of the book was then redrafted one year on in which I incorporated what was initially two very separate 'Jake Lehman' adventures into one narrative. I then had a fear that I'd bastardised both novels to the point of impenetrability which is where I found the use of 'constructive readers' to be immensely, incredibly helpful:

Helen Grover, Emily John, Rob Leatt, Paul Bagnall, James Grant, Thomas Ludlow and Mark Flaherty read the book you now have in your possession in a variety of different states and offered invaluable and beneficial feedback on plot, characters and spelling / grammar. I thank all of them so very much because without them Lehman's Terms would not have got across the finish line.

Mark Flaherty also took time out of his very successful graphic design company to not only design the front cover for this book but to work on helping with the social media campaign required to promote it. From a very simple brief ("I want the cover to sort of emulate those old 70s and 80s hard boiled, pulpy private detective novels!") he quickly delivered a cover I adore and which I think suggests you very much should judge a book by its cover in this instance.

Lehman's Terms carries a very specific and hopefully well realised 'vibe' about the world of private investigation in the modern age – only with a big, broad fantastical flourish generated from this author's adoration of glossy 1980s action comedies and buddy movies. That aforementioned 'vibe' came from my own personal experience in working in the field of private investigation and running a very successful and highly regarded investigation agency around the North East of England for a number of years. This could not have been achieved without the training and long-standing mentorship I received from Peter Jenkins and Kevin Hall at ISS Training and if you come away from reading this with a sudden itch to qualify as a professional investigator and become a real life 'Jake Lehman' then those gentlemen and that company are the market-leaders in the field to go with.

A massive thank you also goes out to Steven Dyer – the real life inspiration for 'Psychic' – who has whiled away many a boring hour in a surveillance vehicle with this author and who's sense of humour and lovable personality made many a surveillance operation so much more tolerable. Every element of the character of Psychic that my constructive readers found most likeable and enjoyable was stolen directly from Steven and I'm lucky to have him as both a colleague and a friend.

Finally, since childhood I have always had a passion for writing but an abject fear of rejection when it comes to how my writing would be received.

A fear so powerful and palpable that I have never, ever been able to get past it to make that all important and courageous leap to put my work out there for public consumption, much to my Grandmother's chagrin as she relentlessly urged me to be a writer. I'm sorry I waited too long to make this a reality for her.

This is a huge first for me and it could not have been achieve without the enormous support from Jennie Howie who worked to get this book out for others to (hopefully) enjoy by being its author's proof reader, personal counsellor, editor, supplier of well-timed parcels of encouragement and kindness. Thank you, Jennie.

Thank you for taking the time to read this book. It means so much to me. So much in fact that I can't find the right words to express it. Hopefully if enough people read it and enjoy it then 'Jake Lehman' may head out on another adventure sometime…

**Leonard McClane**

Printed in Great Britain
by Amazon

37887541R00199